Saints of the Syndicate

Natalie Nicole

SCARLET LANTERN
Publishing

Scarlet Lantern Publishing

Author's Note

Trigger warning! There are scenes/topics within the following pages that may be triggering or uncomfortable for some readers. Assault, murder, stalking are a few to name. If you so choose to continue...you have been warned. If you choose not to continue, you will not be judged.

Prologue

I do not belong here.

It's been two weeks since I came to this campus and to say I don't belong here would be the understatement of the century. I'm currently sitting under one of the massive oak trees here in the quad, glancing over some of the reading I have to do for class tomorrow and people watching. It's a fascinating thing to see how all these kids just frolic around campus without a care in the world. They are constantly flashing around keys to the newest vehicles their parents got them or talking about what luxurious vacation they will be going on next.

They all wear the newest designer tags and brag about the almost daily shopping trips they take. Glancing down at my thrift store purchases brings a flush to my face even though no one is paying attention to me. I worked my ass off for six weeks before I came here to have enough money to go to the nicer thrift store where I lived in LA and splurge on some newer clothes. The rest I put away in my meager checking account until I could find a job here.

Thankfully, I found a coffee shop right near campus and I have an interview there next week. The hours won't be much, but they will be just enough to cover my phone bill and any necessities. Even if I don't get it, I've found some other options too. I may not fit in at this private university, but it won't deter me. I *need* this education more than anything in the world. If for no other reason than to prove to everyone who has doubted me that I will not be another waste of tax dollars like my mother.

No matter what challenges I face here being a complete underdog, I will prevail.

Glancing around the quad area one more time, my eyes stop on three bodies. It's fascinating how everyone around me goes quiet when they show up. It's almost like they're afraid to speak around them and it's even more interesting when students rush to get out of their way.

I've only caught sight of them a few times, but their dominating presence always intrigues me. I've heard whispers in class about how they are campus royalty and to stay out of their way unless you want trouble.

I've thought about asking others in class who they are until I'm caught staring at them. The ugly knowing sneers always have me retreating back into my shell and just burying my face back into a book. Only one person so far has attempted to make friends with me, but I've been extremely cautious when I talk to her. I don't know if she thinks I'm some sort of circus act or is actually genuine about her interest in me.

Regardless, I'm going to hold off with her a little longer until I figure out if there's a motive behind her friendly attempts or not. Maybe if she is actually true with her intentions, I'll ask her what the deal is with these three god-like entities I'm currently creeping on beneath the bill of my ball cap.

Almost like a knowing sixth sense, their eyes all glance my way. My breath catches in my throat before I rush to look back down at my textbook. My body flushes in embarrassment and my heart rate speeds up to an unnatural pace that has me wanting to puke.

I don't dare break my textbook concentration until the quad slowly resumes back into its usual buzz of activity. As I will my body to return to normal, a few dominating questions filter through my brain.

Who are they? Why did just a quick glance from them ignite my body on fire? Why does my body always seem drawn to them even when I've never been in close proximity to them?

Shaking my head to clear the questions, I have to internally laugh at myself. I'll never know the answers to those questions.

Or will I?

Chapter 1

Sinclair - End of September- Senior year

Fucking hell. How much longer is he going to keep *talking*?
Jesus Christ.

Sitting here at the deliberation table with Declan on my right and
Giovanni on my left, we listen to our bastard fathers ramble on to
some of The Trident's recruits before their official initiation
ceremony. He's going on and on about *"the importance of our
secrecy"*, *"how lucky they were to be selected as a member of our
prestigious organization"*, and our absolute favorite one *"how enriched
and powerful their lives would become with us as their family"*. It took
everything out of me not to start laughing my ass off.

Bull. Fucking. Shit.

Sure, I guess you could say our lives were above par compared to
most.

Our three families ran the school we were currently attending.
Fuck, my last name is the name of our school.

Blackwell University, established in 1862, when our great-
whatever-grandfathers had made it rich off the California gold rush.
They were some tough old bastards who decided the west needed a
school for the wealthy to go to, and to help pull other loaded fuckers
like themselves out west.

But they were also suspicious as fuck and created The Trident
Syndicate, otherwise known as the super-secret society of Blackwell
University.

We are the wealthiest of society. A male-only organization where
your membership is usually passed down from father to son, blood
oath kill to blood oath kill.

You keep your social status by being a ruthless bastard. Most of us have killed at least once, if not multiple times. We hold the power of a mafia or cartel family, but with the shadows as our protectors. They only wish they could accomplish half the shit we have while never entering the spotlight, unlike them.

As I sit here listening to our fathers drone on and on, I really wish they'd just shut the fuck up and fuck off back to their tower in the city, aka their offices, and get off our campus already.

I spin the Trident ring on my left middle finger. Some call it a nervous tick. I call it keeping my big mouth shut so I don't end up dead at my father's hand for "embarrassing" him in front of the fresh meat.

"Anything to add to the discussion, Mr. Blackwell?" my father asks me, pulling me out of my fucking boredom trance.

"Yeah. Do what the fuck we tell you to do, don't fuck up my drink request, and *don't* fucking piss me off," I reply to my father's idiotic question directed to the newbies while pissing good old Arthur off simultaneously.

Win. Fucking. Win.

With a short death glare toward me before resuming his stoic bullshit face of authority along with Declan's and Giovanni's fathers, they finally end the meeting with some other nonsense that we three are surely not listening to at all.

"Mr. Blackwell, Mr. Carter, and Mr. Martinelli, you three stay behind for a few," Robert Carter, Declan's father, says to us with a look that would scare most, but not us.

We were raised on those vicious glares, among other various punishments. If they think we are going to cower, they're wrong.

I turn to Deck first, then Gio, my eyebrow quirked as if to ask, *'Any idea what this is about?'* I get slight responses in return saying 'no clue' but not to alert the bastards we are communicating.

Once everyone else is gone, we all turn our chairs to face our sperm donors, square our shoulders, keep our faces neutral, and prepare for whatever these psychos have ready to throw our way.

Simply sitting in his chair of royalty, acting like a king, my father glances at us, then at Robert Carter and Lorenzo Martinelli, Giovanni's father, before delivering the biggest 'we fucking hate you three' news of our lives.

"Unless you boys find suitable options that we approve of by the time you graduate, which we doubt will happen, we have found you each a suitable woman to marry next fall. You can then start producing the next generation of men for our society."

Silence.

We are all just staring blank-faced at our fathers as they smugly stare back at us like they just made a few more billions to wipe their asses with.

Declan breaks the silence first, standing up so fucking quick his chair smashes into the stone floor.

"Hold the *fuck* up?! Are you grimy bastards saying if we don't bend to your dumb fucking rules, you're setting us up with arranged marriages?"

"Declan...Watch. Your. Tongue," Robert says through gritted teeth.

"Oh, go snort some more coke off another stripper's ass. You can go fuck them while you're at it if you think I'm agreeing to that horse shit."

Yup. Deck's beyond pissed, but he is the mouthpiece of the three of us. So Robert's power-play toward him is about as useful as a gun without the firing pin. His words aren't even registering in Deck's head currently.

Robert stands, clearly not enjoying his son calling him out on the shit he's seen him do, all while his wife and Declan's mom, Cindy, is sitting at home battling cancer. Worthless fool.

"Declan Ryan Carter! Sit the fuck down! You will agree to this along with Giovanni and Sinclair. Do you want to take over our positions in the company once you graduate? Well, this is how you do it. None of you move into the company unless you're married."

And there goes my stoic resolve. I snicker, finally drawing their eyes my way.

"And what's so funny Sinclair?" Lorenzo asks with a flat tone.

"That you think we are that fucking stupid."

"Excuse me?"

"Hmm...Didn't realize you were all going deaf already. Guess I'll say it again. It's funny you think we're all that fucking stupid."

Silence from them, but I see the tells that say each of their tempers are flaring. So I continue, standing alongside Declan.

"Do you think we're so unbelievably stupid that we'll agree to marry these 'daddy dearest' princesses, take your positions in the company—which are our goddamn birthrights—and you all get to 'retire'? *Bullshit.* We all already know none of you have zero motivation to leave your spots at the top of each company or here at the Syndicate. You just want us to marry whoever the fuck you choose because they're nothing more than business deals to make you more money, and not to mention our lives even more of a living hell. Am I wrong?"

More silence from our fathers. Yeah, that's what we thought. They're greedy pricks who would rather die than lose their standings either here or at the companies.

"Well...Since you aren't going to reply because we are correct, you can take your offer and shove it up your deranged ass, Arthur."

And on that note, I turn around and walk toward the door, knowing Gio and Deck are right behind me.

Fuck this.

Fuck them.

I need a fucking drink ASAP.

As I storm out of the cathedral room where our assemblies are held and into the catacombs under the university toward the lounge area, I hear Declan grunt next to me.

"I'll grab our phones from the lockers. Pour me one also."

I step into the lounge area and pour a couple of shots of vodka for the both of us, wondering where the fuck Giovanni is. "G come out yet?" I ask as Deck comes up to the bar.

He slides my phone over and tosses back his shot. "Not yet. Knowing him, he's trying to save our asses with his superstar IQ or some Houdini shit like that. I sure as fuck wasn't about to stick around to find out. I would've probably reached over and slit one of our fathers' throats if I did."

"Fuck it. Send him a text and tell him to meet us at the club. I can't stand being here for another moment."

I toss back my shot, loosen my tie, and head toward the private parking area where all members of the Syndicate park when we're summoned for council. I hop into my SUV as Declan gets into his, and we both drive to Club Luxe. Once we arrive, we flash our custom-fitted organization rings at the security guard to open the iron gates and then speed toward the alcohol, terrible decisions, and willing pussy.

Chapter 2

Giovanni

I sat there as Sinclair and Declan stormed out of the council room, staring at our fathers for a second before I spoke.

"You cannot possibly be serious about this."

"We are," they all replied in unison.

I spent a second gathering my thoughts before I spoke again.

"And what exactly were our grandfathers' thoughts on your rather bold order? Seeing as how they are all still living, they hold the true power here in the Trident, regardless if they are actively involved or not."

My father's jaw clicked, Sinclair's dad's hands clenched into fists as his knuckles turned white, and Declan's father gripped his tumbler of whiskey so hard it was ready to break.

They knew I had them.

They all hated their fathers, our grandfathers. While they were still criminals the same as us, our grandparents were the old-school criminals with actual hearts of gold, unlike the men before me.

Don't get me wrong, I saw my grandpa Gianluca break a man's hand with a baseball bat for whatever crime he committed at the age of six. Even back then it was like just another day because in our world it was. That also meant they upheld the rules and rights of being a Trident member.

By The Trident Syndicate's laws, if there was an older and basically "retired" member of the three families still living, they held authority over all active members. Their word was the law, and you didn't argue with it. By looking at the reactions to my statement, our fathers must have forgotten about that little bylaw. Not surprising in the least.

"Right...Well, seeing as how they do not have any knowledge about your decree here, should I make a call and see what they have to say about it?" I boldly asked while keeping a poker face.

I know this is going to royally bite me in the ass later, but I will not see any of us into a forced marriage that only benefits these fools.

Lorenzo stays quiet, probably planning his revenge against me already. Too bad I can out hack anything he tries. Robert still hasn't moved and is staring daggers at me. He's death gripping his drink while wishing it were one, or all of, our necks. Finally, Sinclair's dad stands and buttons his 7,500-dollar custom Armani suit jacket before speaking.

"Now let's not get carried away there, Giovanni. We don't need to bring *them* into this. I'm sure we can come to some type of...understanding of sorts."

"The understanding is simple. We refuse. While everyone else may be your puppets waiting to be told to dance, we are not. You should have realized that by now. If not, then I'm sorry to say...You're all fucking morons."

And that breaks their calm demeanor.

Robert sneers at me. "Disrespectful little shit!"

"Giovanni Lorenzo Martinelli! What in the ever-loving fuck is wrong with you? I did not raise you to be such an insolent, rude child!"

"You do realize the punishment for disrespecting one of the elders, correct?" Arthur calmly says through the midst of the others' rages.

I sit back in the chair and cross my arms over my chest, letting them know they don't scare me. They haven't for years. Just because I'm the quietest of us three, doesn't mean I'm going to instantly cower to them.

"Lorenzo, you didn't raise me. The hired help raised me while you were fuck knows where stepping out on Mom while she drank herself to death. And yes, Arthur, I do know the punishments. Unlike you, I have our code of conduct memorized. This means you are all directly violating one of the biggest codes. By not conferring with the true authoritarians of the Trident on such a big decision, especially our fucking futures, you could all have your memberships to the syndicate stripped and all of your positions outside these walls gone too. Just one call and everything could be gone for all of you," I finish while standing.

They are shell-shocked by my declaration.

Good.

"Now if you'll excuse me, gentlemen, I have better places to be than here."

And out I walk to go find the others and fill them in on the potential that is World War 3.

"What fucking bastards! They seriously thought they could get away with that shit without talking to our grandfathers?" Declan damn near fucking screams inside the club.

Thank fucking God we have a private suite for occasions like this. Otherwise shit would hit the fan.

Club Luxe is one of our business ventures outside of our fathers' knowledge. It's our private playground where we go to get away from all these shit storms that are our lives.

"Shut the fuck up about it already, Deck. Jesus Christ. We'll handle it like we always do," Sin demands, trying to contain his rage at the same time.

"What we need to do is—" Declan rages on, ignorant to our speaking.

"Declan!" we both yell, which startles him, but at least he shuts up and focuses on us.

"Enough already. Also, someone is gonna have to cover my tab tonight until we get back home." I grumble as I take a swig of the drink in my hand.

"Why?" Sinclair asks with a quirked eyebrow.

"I may or may not have said a few choice things after you both stormed out like pissed-off gorillas. So I have a feeling all my shit is locked out again," I reply with a smirk on my lips before downing my shot.

Declan finally sits down with one leg over the chair. He takes two shots back to back before a shit-eating grin splays across his face.

"You pissed off the devils reincarnated? How the fuck did you accomplish that there, Gio boy?"

With a roll of my eyes and a middle finger to his face, I relay the conversation to them. Through the retelling, their faces go through a few emotions. Rage is a constant, though.

"Stupid fucks," Sinclair mutters. "Thank fuck you have that shit memorized. I sure as shit don't."

"Me neither. Nor do I care to either. But that's why we have you, genius boy," Deck says with a tip of his glass in my direction.

Declan laying on compliments means he is on his way to getting royally trashed tonight. Although I don't blame him. Tonight was one of the shittiest meetings in the history of us all being Trident members, and that's including our initiation and hazing weeks. Those left us all with the same scars along our left palms, brands on our right thighs, and all three of us getting our dicks pierced by losing a bet to Declan during a drunken hazing.

That shit hurt like hell, but it has paid off quite well since then with our countless female endeavors. We've even earned ourselves the god-awful nickname "The Three Orgasm-teers". It's utterly ridiculous, but it somehow brings women out of the woodwork to try and take a ride on one or all of our 'sinful swords'.

"Taking it we are gonna be dragging his ass out of here in an hour, what's your bet?" I say to Sinclair while still looking at Declan. He hates when we bet on his drinking habits.

"A hundred bucks. Forty-five minutes. Tops."

"Deal."

"Cock suckers," Deck mutters while grabbing one of our bottles before standing up to gaze out at the club below.

He doesn't even bother arguing anymore about us betting against him.

"You fuckers are both gonna owe me in the morning. Holy fucking Tuesday."

"Care to elaborate on how we are both gonna lose there, bud?" Sinclair asks him.

"Yeah...My future ex-wife is down there on the dance floor walking toward the bar to sit down. That's why."

Sin and I glance at each other before getting up ourselves to look down into the club along with him. It doesn't take us long to see who has stolen Declan's attention.

"Holy shit," I mutter while feeling my cock spring to life in my suit pants.

Sin whistles. "Fucking hell."

"Yeah," is all Declan can say in reply.

And after that...we are all speechless.

She is absolute pure perfection.

Chapter 3

Declan

In all these years, I never once thought it was possible for my frigid dead heart to spur to life. From the day I was born, I've been held to impossible expectations and beat within an inch of my life when I didn't appease my father and his tyrannical ways of life. At least until I was able to fight back against the beatings. I've since let myself go beyond the limits of feelings. I fight, fuck, and party with zero thought as to the consequences.

I simply...Do. Not. Care.

No one has ever given a fuck about me other than Sinclair and Giovanni. We all bear similar scars of mental and physical abuse from our tormentors. We just wear our wounds differently.

Sinclair is a control freak from hell. He's calculated as fuck in everything he does. Whether it's slitting someone's throat, his daily routine, or barking demands. He rarely loses control of any situation he is in. The only people who break us are our fathers. But fuck, they bring out the worst in all of us.

Giovanni retreats to the confines of his computers. He is a self-taught genius with them, which has saved our asses more times than any of us care to admit. He also has a photographic memory of even the most mundane information, like the utter ridiculous Trident codes of conduct that have ruled our lives since before we were born.

Myself, I live for the thrill. Be it the adrenaline rush of racing my customized Bugatti Chiron Sport down the California freeways, the toxic mix of pills and alcohol that fuel me, or the rush of dirty, raunchy sex whenever and wherever I can get it. If it can numb the utter hell that floods my subconscious on a daily basis, the monsters lurking just beyond the depths of my mind that are just lusting for the chance to fully pull me into their depths of zero return, I'll do it.

The demons we all carry on our backs would be enough to send a sane person, fuck, a *normal* person on a fiery path of destruction that could level Los Angeles in an hour tops. The absolution of our sins we perform on an hourly basis is enough to send God himself on a spiral toward the pits of hell that are our lives.

But here I am, standing beside the only two people I would lay down my life for and not think twice about it. We're looking down at the crowd of people, and she has already brought an increase to my pulse. There's an unknown warmness spreading through my body from just from looking at her, and it almost drops me to my fucking knees.

What the hell?

I find myself gripping the railing overlooking the club to keep my balance. I'm not quite sure if it's the alcohol and pills coursing through my veins or the shift in my soul from this chick. I steal a quick glance at Giovanni and Sinclair to see them as completely enthralled as myself.

"You guys are looking at the same person I am, correct?"

Sinclair doesn't move his gaze from her. "Short silver sequin halter dress with the low back that allows us to see the dimples above that voluptuous ass. Five-inch black stiletto heels. Simple makeup to accentuate her natural beauty. Long brown hair that fades to blond. Also, she looks absolutely out of her element, like she cannot wait to escape her situation? Yeah. I fucking see her."

I snort at his statement. "Observant bastard. But yes, *her*. Giovanni, how quick can you pull information?"

"Already on it. I'm going through the CCTV footage from the front door for the last half hour, since she doesn't seem like she has been here that long." He goes silent for a moment. "And got it."

I don't know why I'm even surprised he found her that fast, but I am. Apparently, Sin is also as he finally glances away to look at Gio. "Well? Are you going to fill us in, or do we have to beat it out of you, asshole?"

"Insolent crybabies," Giovanni mutters. "If you must know, I started with our school to see if she goes there, and lucky for us, she does. Bethani Larie Reece. Twenty-one. A sophomore scholarship student at Blackwell University. Double majoring in journalism and photography with a minor in Russian. Her birthday is November fifteenth. Originally from Seattle, Washington, but the last known address before moving here two years ago is in the slums of LA. The reasons are unknown. Doesn't say anything about family or any more personal information either. No social media, nothing else. Almost like a little ghost trying to hide something or just that private of a person."

We both gape at him momentarily before Sinclair speaks for us. "Jesus Christ, G. You just got all that off your phone in under thirty seconds?"

With a shrug and a smirk, because he is a cocky shit like that sometimes, he replies, "You would know how to do this shit too if you actually listened to what I've attempted *to explain—multiple* times—with you pricks. But *nooo*, you'd rather rely on me for the information, since you're both lazy shits like that. But to answer your question, yes, I got that off my phone in under thirty seconds. I was already pulling it up before either of you said anything," he finishes with another smug grin.

Right pompous asshat he is somedays.

I finally glance back down to find Bethani seated at the bar with what looks like a couple of friends near her. What happens next sends my blood boiling, and by the stiffening shoulder of my friends, they are also seeing it.

There is some douchebag, beady-eyed looking fuck walking up behind her chair and putting his hands on her shoulders. She stiffens quickly but then loses it just as fast as her face turns stoic. She almost looks pissed off. *Good.* Even from up here, I can see the fear that temporarily washes across her face, and it makes me want to storm down the stairs and knock the satisfied smirk off that fuck stick's face. "Giovanni..."

While not looking up from his phone, he grits through clenched teeth, "Fucking on it."

I take a quick glance over at Sin. He is white-knuckling the railing to our private suite the same as me.

"Motherfucker!" Gio yells while damn near breaking his phone.

We both look over at the pulsing fury that is evident on his face, and I know Sinclair is wondering the same as me. *What the fuck is going on?* G storms over to the security line phone we have up in the suite and starts yelling as the person answers, "Karl! Get your ass up here NOW!"

I look back over at Sinclair, whose eyes are on Bethani. I finally turn back toward Gio as Karl, our head of security, comes barreling through the door. But he doesn't make it too far into the room before Gio has his hand around Karl's neck and is slamming him back into the hallway.

"Do we not pay you and the rest of security well enough?" he demands as Karl's face is shell-shocked. Fuck, though I'm pretty sure my face looks the same. Giovanni is the most docile of us. It takes a lot to rile him up like this, but when he's pissed, watch the fuck out.

"Y-yes, sir. You pay us all ex-extremely well," Karl mutters.

"Then why in the ever-loving *FUCK* did some pompous asshole make it through our fucking doors with a fake ID? Ex-fucking-plain. *Now!*"

"S-sir?"

"Fucking hell, Gio. Will you fill us in before you have a fucking coronary or kill our head of security already?" Sin demands.

Giovanni turns his murderous rage toward us and through gritted teeth says, "That fuck stick down there with his hands on Bethani has some shit bag fake ID that Roman let through. The picture is him, but the info shows a sixty-seven-year-old man who died seven months ago. Whoever that prick down there is, he took the guy's license, carefully pulled it apart, put his face in it, and then fixed the license back together. All the fucking training we give these guys and they let dumb shit like that pass? Fuck. That!" He turns his anger back to Karl. "I want that son of a bitch out of the bar in the next minute or every single one of you will be fired at the end of the night! Make sure you confiscate his license and do *not* leave fingerprints. You're down to forty-five seconds. GO!"

Karl hauls ass downstairs while we all return to the balcony to watch the show. We stay silent while we watch the crew take whoever this guy is out of the club rather unwillingly. He's saying all sorts of shit we can't hear because of the music, but something he says has Bethani's face paling for a moment, and I can't help but wonder what the bastard said.

Finally, Sinclair speaks, "So you gonna elaborate on your...outburst there, G?'

After stewing for a few, he finally says, "Yeah...Like I said, our security let a bullshit fake ID through the door. It makes me wonder if Roman got paid off somehow to let the bastard through. Or is he that damn stupid? I'm already cross-referencing him with the area, but nothing is coming up since all his information is trash. Either this guy doesn't want to be known because he does illegal shit, or he has the right people to keep his shit hidden because they know they are against us. To top it all off, as soon as I saw Bethani's fear, I instantly wanted to rage against the guy to protect her. Fuck, I haven't even talked to her yet and I'm already drawn to her like no fucking other and just want to protect her. Fucking hell."

Sinclair rolls his shoulders and cracks his neck. "Not sure why either, but I already feel the same way, dude. Let's just keep an eye on her from up here until she leaves. Then we'll come up with a game plan later on how to grab her attention. We've shared chicks before on occasion. This doesn't seem to be that different than any other day of the fucking week."

"Fine," Gio relents, but it doesn't seem like he's in the same mindset as Sin. Yeah, we've all fucked the same girl at the same time, but Bethani seems different than our normal MO already, and I haven't even talked to her yet.

Glancing back down at her, she finally turns toward the balcony. I swear my fucking heart stops as her eyes meet mine, even though she can't see me as anything more than a shadow. Her fucking perfect aqua eyes meet mine, and she gives us the most dazzling smile ever behind gorgeous full lips. With a quick wave and a mouthed 'thank you' toward us, she turns back toward her friends, and I feel like I can finally breathe again.

"Fuck," Sin mutters.

Gio mumbles something in Italian. I'm assuming he is agreeing.

"We're completely fucked already, aren't we?" I question.

Neither of them answers, but I already know they agree.

This girl. That ray of utter fucking sunshine sitting at the bar...

Is going to be our fucking kryptonite.

Chapter 4

Bethani

S itting here in my tiny, musky as hell dorm room for the 'scholarship students', I glance around at the sad excuse of what my life is.

God...how is it that I miss the streets of LA?

This is my second year at Blackwell University, and I am honestly still regretting it. When I first received the letter from the university, I thought this was my chance to make something of myself. To finally prove to all those assholes at the Washington State Children Services that I wouldn't turn out like my mother. That I wouldn't be just another product of a drug addict whore who turns tricks to get her next fix.

Thank God her one client noticed me and had an actual heart.

I'd probably be dead by now if it wasn't for Jim. Which reminds me, I need to reply to his email from last week. Even if it is just a bunch of fluff lies. He is one of the few people who has ever given a damn about me. The only others I can think of are Ramona who ran the homeless shelter and Stella, the only person on this campus who isn't a complete stuck-up snob. We met last year in the Intro to Journalism class. She wants to be a fancy fluff journalist for the rich and famous. As pretty as she is, she can do it in a heartbeat.

Me, on the other hand? I want to photograph and report the terrible aspects that most of society doesn't understand or completely ignores. I have a passion to bring to life the shitty things of my past and put them on full display. I want to make people realize there are real problems going on in this world. Hunger, abuse, homelessness, pain, suffering, sickness (mental, physical, emotional), and so many other wicked, terrible things.

That's the only thing keeping me here at this absolute high society hell hole playground for the rich and clueless university. The credibility I can get from making it through here will give me the needed notoriety at a media firm to continue with my goal: saving those who don't think they can be saved because their life has been the same for generations and no one knows how to break it.

Top university of the west coast? Eye-fucking-roll.

More like a top university of how to become the next high-class Stepford wife or the next Mr. Whatever the 17th of asshole-ism and playboy status.

My phone chimes, which brings me out of my hateful thoughts.

Shit. My head wandered off for fifteen minutes when I should have been reading my Journalism 2 book.

Stella: Hiii lovey! Want to come over for cheesecake?!

Me: Hey Stella. What do you want?

Stella: Why would I want anything? I just miss you!

Me: You saw me yesterday in class. I miss you too. But you only bring out the cheesecake when you want me to do something. So, what is it?

Stella: I bought your favorite...A whole Tiramisu cheesecake and your fave drink supplies!!! :)

Damn her. She *knows* she has me. Shit.

Me: You are a viper sometimes, you know that?

Stella: Ehh? So, how long until you get here?

Me: Be there in 20.

Stella: Yay!!!!! Also, bring that adorable silver dress too.

Me: WHAT? Stella...What do you have planned? Tell. Me. Now!

Stella: Ugh. Buzzkill. Fine. WE are going to a club, Miss Boring. And if you don't want a video of me dumping your fave cheesecake in the trash then you will buck up and get your butt over here so we can get ready! :)

Me: ......

Me: Fine! You win devil woman! ONLY because I will hurt you if you throw that cheesecake away and you know it.

Stella: Loveeeee youuuu :) :) :)

Me: Yup. Blackmail is love.

Damn. Double damn her. God, I love Stella, but some days she is too much.

Stella flings the door open as soon as I knock on her apartment door, bouncing up and down like a cat on crack. "Took you long enough!" she says, then bounces on me and crushes me with a hug. "I'm so totally excited for tonight! We're going to have a blast, girl."

"Crushing. Me. Stell," I wheeze out.

She quickly lets me go, grabs my hand, and drags me behind her like a lost puppy. "Sorry, boo! I'm just excited!"

"I can see that. Now, where are the cheesecake and alcohol? You are not touching me until I have at least a piece and a drink."

"Kitchen island, already waiting for you, sexy lady." She winks.

"Yes. Broke college chic is all the rage there, devil woman. How people think you are a total sweetheart is beyond me." But as we reach the kitchen, and I see my bribe gift waiting on me, I stop and give her a hug. "You are lucky I love you. You do realize that, right?"

Her megawatt smile lights the room. "I know! Now hurry up and drink your bourbon and eat your cake! We have to get ready!"

"You do realize I drink whiskey, not bourbon, right?"

"Sure, sure! I just showed the person a picture of whatever is your all-time favorite, paid, and walked out the door."

"Wait...you got me."

"Yup! Johnny Walker Blue! I know this semester has been rough for you, plus I had to bust out the big guns to get you to agree to go out tonight!" Yet again, another blinding sweet smile plasters her face.

"For one, that is an almost four-hundred-dollar bottle. Way too damn much, Stella. For two, damn you! You're about to make me cry!" She knows this semester sucks for me. Most of the teachers are fucks because they know my status here. The turnover rate for scholarship students is ridiculous. If you make it past freshman year, you are lucky. But all the others who got here and left either flat out weren't cut out for college or did it as a screw you to the college they wanted to get into. Even one semester at Blackwell will get them insane perks at their real dream schools. Something about the image of how a Blackwell University student loved them more. Insert eye roll here.

"Awwww...I didn't mean to make you cry, love! But you desperately need this, Bethani. I know this is a huge change from the shelter in LA, and I can't imagine the way people treat you, but you have to know there are other good people here. This will be a good stepping stone for it. I'm inviting a few others to meet us there. I promise that if you give them a chance, you'll like them. I mean, it took me half of our first semester last year to finally get you to say more than two words to me."

I snort. "Girl, you were a walking, talking, sugared-up Malibu Barbie. I'm honestly surprised you don't bounce off walls with as much Red Bull as you ingest." I pause, taking a deep breath and exhaling before finishing, "And I will attempt to give them a chance. Just don't expect sunshine and rainbows to fall out of my ass. You know I'm not comfortable with how everyone here just throws money and last names around like they are all walking Greek gods and goddesses."

With the eye roll she throws my way, I'm surprised her eyes don't stay back in her head. "Okay. I'll give you that one. Yes, some of them are completely pretentious and stroll around like they are walking the red carpet daily, but not all of them are that way. Hell, even I try to stay away from them. Which I can't, since my papa owns the biggest modeling agency in the United States."

"Shit. How do I constantly forget about that?"

Her dad, Chad Monterey, is the CEO and founder of Monterey Modeling Agency. But regardless of how much money they have, Stella, her parents, and six other siblings are all super down to earth. Granted, they still live in a mansion, but it's not ostentatious. That's actually where I stayed for all the breaks and in between summer classes. Her family took me in and treated me like a daughter. While the whole thing was still super weird, and I mostly clung to Stella, I did open up a little bit to her family. Not much, just enough so they didn't think I was going to rob them blind like some trash hood rat.

"Easy, and you know that. But anyway...finish your shit, then grab another drink and meet me in my room so we can get ready!" And with that, she turns and leaves me to my thoughts, homemade cheesecake, and in my opinion, the best fucking whiskey known to man.

"What is this place?" I mutter to myself.

"Club Luxe, boo. Only the best place to party here in Sonoma," Stella quips. "Oh my gosh! Hiiii, Roman! I'm *so* glad you are the doorman tonight! That other guy is a dickhead."

Roman grunts, but his lips turn up slightly in enjoyment at a tipsy Stella. I may have drunk a third of my bottle of Johnny Walker Blue, and Stella had about four skinny cocktails while getting ready, so we are both a little more giggly than normal.

"Licenses, ladies?" Roman, the absolute hulking man of a doorman in a three-piece suit, says while shoving his hand our way.

Stella hands hers over and he quickly studies it, then hands it back and sticks his hand my way.

"Uhh...here ya go...Roman?" I say while he snatches mine away to study it before handing it back.

He quickly opens the door and grunts a "have fun" our way before we walk inside to what I can only describe as the most top-notch place I've ever stepped foot into.

While Blackwell University is old-school money, gothic architecture, and dripping with condensation, Club Luxe has super clean lines and a new money look. Dark matte black and silver walls, modern/slightly industrial bar area, a similar style of couches, high-top tables, and chairs throughout. Purple lights from the floors shining to the ceilings give everything a super classy air around the place. Surprisingly enough, for how expensive everything clearly is, I don't feel totally out of place. At least not like I do every day on campus. Here I actually feel like a normal college student who isn't living a dumpster fire life.

"Come on! Let's grab those open chairs and order drinks while I'm texting Benny to see where they are!" Stella yells while grabbing my hand and dragging me to the bar.

We grab our seats, order two drinks each since this place is so damn packed, and I just look around while Stella texts whoever she said she was texting. Huh, this place even has a second level with what looks like private suites. Guess the name really suits the place. *Shocker.*

The next thing I know, I'm being introduced to Benny, Jeremy, Rhett, and the catty bitches with them when a set of hands touch my shoulders, making me jump.

"Hey! Watch it, ass—"

"I told you I'd find you, sweet cheeks," he says into my ear, making me freeze for a second.

You have got to be fucking kidding me.

I school myself quickly and turn his way.

"Peter."

"Bethani."

"What do you want?"

"To talk of course. I've missed you."

"Yeah? Well, I haven't missed you. So just fuck off to your *boys*."

"Bethani...We are going to talk," he grinds out while digging his thumbs into my back, which I know are going to leave marks. But I won't let him know it hurts.

"Actually...I'm here with friends. So no, we aren't going to talk. Not here. Not now. Not any other time either. I thought I made it clear I didn't want to see or talk to you *ever again*?" I sneer.

"And I told you our conversation wasn't—" his sentence is cut off when a pair of guards walk up and interrupt. *Thank God.*

"Excuse us, sir, we need to see your ID. Now," one of two giant-ass security guys says to Peter as they stand close to him.

Lord. Do these guys drink Miracle-Grow or something? Wow.

"Oh, fucking Christ! I showed it to you when I came through—"

"Either give us your ID or we can escort you out," the other human hulk says.

"Fucking fine." Peter quickly hands them his ID while scowling at them like his usual spoiled brat self.

Gag. What did I see in him again?

"Awfully young looking to be sixty-seven years old. Don't you think, Z?" Hulk number 1 says to Hulk number 2, now named Z.

Peter's face pales, and he attempts to stammer out a response, but they snatch him up and turn him toward the door to escort him out. They don't get far before he looks back at me and mouths 'I'm watching you, Bethani' before spewing all sorts of shit to them. It makes my heart stop temporarily.

"Bethani? Is he still a problem?" Stella asks nervously while the others just stand there, unsure of the whole situation they witnessed.

I quickly grab the glass closest to me and take a big swig, allowing the liquor to burn its way down before answering. "That's the first time I've seen him since the end of last school year. He doesn't know my dorm room, and I changed my number, so how he found me is beyond me."

"Are you going to be okay? I can call my dad, and he can help."

"NO! God, no. Thank you for the offer, but I'll be fine. If I see him again, I'll just go to the campus security and let them know," I say while finishing off the last of my first glass before setting it down to pick up the other we ordered. I need something to keep myself from losing my shit.

"If you say so, girl."

I gave her a small smile, then turned to everyone to make small talk to help keep me distracted. As I begin conversing, a watchful presence washes over me. My gaze flits toward the VIP area where three towering figures stand there and look like they are watching the crowd. I can only assume it's the owners, so I quickly flash a smile and mouth 'thank you' before returning to the conversations in front of me.

30 minutes later

"Hey...I think I'm gonna head out. I'm starting to get a headache," I say to Stella as my vision slowly starts to blur and the pounding behind my eyes gets progressively worse.

I see the look of concern on Stella's face but quickly shut her down before she tries to intervene. "It's nothing. I promise. It's only a ten-min walk back to my dorm. I'll text you when I get there."

"Pinky swear, Bethani?" she says with a glare, while I roll my eyes at her juvenile request. I go to stand up but quickly sit back down as a head rush hits me. I act like I'm just adjusting my stilettos and staying bent over until I can gather enough composure to pull off my ruse that I'm not completely obliterated. *Holy shit, what did they put in those whiskeys?*

This is a bad idea thinking I can walk. Like one of the top dumb ideas. But I've already said I'm going to walk, and I'm not about to back down to the challenge. Maybe I'll just take these stupid heels off once I get outside. That should help.

Standing up slowly so I don't give anything away, I give her the pinky promise she asked for along with a hug. Then I say my goodbyes to everyone else and start the slow and determined walk out of the club, praying like hell the fresh air will help.

Walking past a seriously pissed-off-looking Roman, I say goodbye to him, and as I turn to start walking, I trip over a giant crack in the concrete sidewalk, falling to my knees like a ditz.

Way to go, Bethani, you freaking klutz, I think to myself.

"There was a crack there you missed, doll face. Easy enough to miss. Don't worry, your knight in shining armor has you." A deep voice breaks through my head while his arms pull me up.

"Wait...What? W-wh-what's going on?" I slur.

A dark chuckle from the guy beside me finally breaks through my drunken stupor a bit. He finally starts speaking again as he rounds the corner of the building, forcing me along with him. "Oh, sweet, stupid Bethani. I *told you* I was watching you. Now I have you exactly how I want," Peter says darkly as he turns me to face him and slams me back into the block wall.

My head connects first and bounces off as the rest of me finally hits it. I hiss in pain through the black spots clouding my vision as I feel the wall digging into various spots of my upper body, slicing mini lacerations into my back and arms while a trickle from my head slowly soaks into my hair.

"The. Fuck. P-Peter? W-why?" I grit through my teeth while trying to stay awake. Alive? Whatever I was doing.

As his hand grips my neck to force my face to look at him, he tightens it more and more as he speaks, "I fucking told you. I told you you'd be fucking sorry to leave me. I was willing to look past your bullshit sob story of a life and make you the perfect little wife for me. All you had to do was *listen* and do what I said. But no—" he stops abruptly as something in the background catches his attention.

"Fuck," he mutters. "We are not finished here."

My head hits the wall again and my world goes effortlessly black.

Chapter 5

Sinclair

"Something's not right," comes from Declan as he is staring out over the railing.

Standing up to walk up next to him with Gio following suit, I ask, "What do you mean?"

His expression gives nothing away, except the slight murderous edge to him. "Gio, check the bar cameras. I think he drugged her," he says, his voice showing no emotion. I know Declan's rage is just at the surface, ready to boil over. "She is almost at the door now."

I finally glance toward her and see she is desperately trying to hide. My hands grip the metal railing, and I feel my own temper being pushed to its limits.

"Let's go," Gio grits out. Which means Declan was right. That sick fuck drugged her.

Fuck. Fuck. *Motherfucker.*

Looks like someone may die tonight, I think to myself. My adrenaline skyrockets as we all barrel down the stairs.

When we reach where the crowd starts, I push the button on the wall to kill the music and turn all the lights on. "Bar's fucking closed. Cash-out your shit and fucking leave," I belt out as I look toward Karl, giving him a signal that means we are not fucking around. He knows that he is on our shit list now, along with the bartenders for not noticing someone *fucking drugging* another person at their bar. Like Giovanni already said, we pay the morons for the fucking excessive training. And it's expensive as hell to make sure we have the best.

Obviously fucking not.

But of course, Declan speaks what I'm thinking. "Glad all that money spent on training paid off."

I grunt in agreement as we reach the door and look for Bethani. We then turn to Roman, willing a little of the rage his way. "I'm only going to ask this once, Roman. Which way did she go, and was there a guy with her?"

As he falters back a half step, most likely because we all look like we are one step away from breaking every bone in his body, he stammers out, "S-she turned left just past me, tripped on that spot there. I went to help and some guy nodded at me and picked her up. They went down to the corner and turned..." Roman doesn't get to finish as we all blow right past him to race toward the side street between our building and Ralph's Music Emporium.

"I fucking hope one of you has a weapon on you. All I've got is brass knuckles," I say while slipping on my custom-made matte black titanium knuckles.

"All I have is the hidden knife in my belt." Deck grimaces.

With a huff from Gio, as he slows us all down with tactical hand signals, he whispers, "I've got the Glock with me. Thank fuck one of us was smart enough to remember. Now fucking stop so we can hear what's going on. I think I hear them."

We all stop right by the corner, staying dead silent as we listen to what is hopefully Bethani. We are screwed if it's not them.

"I fucking told you. I told you you'd be fucking sorry to leave me. I was willing to look past your bullshit sob story of a life and make you the perfect little wife for me. All you had to do was listen and do what I said. But no—" was all he got out as we rounded the corner, finding Bethani pinned to the wall by a death grip around her neck.

Fuck. No.

Red clouded my vision as I stormed toward them with Gio and Deck right on my heels. The prick's face wasn't super visible, but we all knew who he was. The same dick face who had his hand on her in the club.

In quick succession, as he realized we were on the verge of raining complete hellfire his way, he slammed Bethani back into the wall and turned to run.

I quickly dive for Bethani and just barely catch her as her unconscious body crumples from the blow. My shoulder slams into the pavement in the process.

"Fuck!"

"Declan! GO!" Gio shouts. I assume he tossed the gun his way and let our favorite psycho off his leash to play. "You all right, man?"

"Not worried about me, G. She is knocked out cold. Go get the SUV so we can lay her flat and get her back to our place."

"Keys?"

"Shit...hold on to her so I can get them."

As Gio palms his hand under her head to cradle it, a violent string of curses falls from his lips. "Her head is bleeding. Get out from under her and give me your coat, Sin, then grab the car and call Deck. Need all three of us to get her back."

I hurry up, shrug my coat off, and call D while hauling ass toward my matte black murdered-out Mercedes G-Wagon AMG G63. "Get back to Gio NOW."

"Heading that way now. Fucker got into a vehicle without plates, and I lost him. Shitbag."

"Head's bleeding. Almost to my vehicle—"

"FUCK!" he yells, cutting me off, then ending the call as I reach my G-Wagon. Quick as hell, I unlock the doors, open the back door, and press the button to lay the seats flat so it's all a giant trunk. I shut the door, hop in the driver's seat, and turn it on as I hightail it the two blocks to the alleyway.

As I whip my vehicle into the alleyway, I press the button to open the back hatch door. Thank fuck it opens like a normal door. I see Declan is already back. His face is absent of emotion, but his eyes are blazing in fear for Bethani, disappointed of himself, and a flame toward the vengeance we are going to rain down on this sick bastard for what he did.

While we may all dabble in criminal activity of different levels—from hacking into random shit for the fun of it, to the blood we've all had to spill as a requirement, no, demand from our fathers if we wanted to stay alive ourselves—there is one thing we have all been blatantly clear on. Women and children are *off. Fucking. Limits.*

The back hatch closes, bringing me out of my daze, and I punch the gas to get back to our penthouse on campus.

Gio starts bitching at me, "Jesus Christ, Sin! Are you trying to fucking give her a worse concussion than she already has? The hell!"

I ignore his attitude. I know it'll only make everything worse. "One of you call the doc?"

"Yeah. Just texted me that he's waiting at the elevator for us. Don't fucking kill us before we get there," Deck retorts.

Smart-ass.

"Still can't believe I let that bitch get away," he mutters to himself, obviously still pissed. For being the tallest of us, he has trained himself ruthlessly to be the fastest. It's one of the things he is super proud about, and I know in this situation, especially with these chaotic feelings coursing through our bodies toward Bethani, his ego is taking a massive hit.

"Pretty sure we all were shocked by the scene we walked into, not including the fact that he bashed her head against that wall. We all tried to keep her from any further injury than God only knows what he did before we got there. Not your fault, man."

"Whatever," he grumbles.

As my hands grip the steering wheel in a white-knuckled rage, I'm completely unaware of the world around me as I attempt to gather some control over my temper. Hearing Giovanni's precise voice as he speaks to our private doctor that we hired breaks me out of my ruthless trance.

"Yeah. Two minutes out, tops." He pauses. "Mini lacerations all over her back and arms. Severe strangulation abrasion around her neck from his hand and"—pause again—"two gashes in the back of her head. Both between one-three inches long. Plus whatever he drugged her alcohol with. Eyes blown, can't stop the bleeding. Pulling in now. Be. Ready."

Holy hell. How I didn't kill us driving back here is beyond me. It's a small grace I'm thankful for as I quickly pull into the parking garage under our campus penthouse.

I slam the SUV into park, earning threatening glares from the guys and an eye roll from Doc Coves. I get out of the vehicle and slam the door as Doc opens the back for Declan and Giovanni. Declan is out first as I reach the back, and we both tug on G's legs while he has a precious hold on Bethani. When we finally get him out into the light of the underground parking lot, we all gasp at the state of her.

Pretty sure my heart stops too in the process. *Holy shit.*

Her long hair is wrecked and matted all over the place. From the hits to the wall, being moved around, and what looks like an insane amount of blood flowing freely all into her hair and Giovanni's clothes. Her body looks like a limp noodle, and her face is so sickly pale that I could almost throw up from it. But the giant handprint around her neck, which is already turning black, purple, and blue, brings my focus and my temper back into the forefront of my head.

This sick and demonic individual is going to pay.

"Sinclair, I need you and Declan to open the elevator and help grab my bags over there. I'll help Giovanni get her into the elevator as carefully as possible," Doc says, kicking us all quickly into gear.

As we make our way up the elevator, the doc gives us strict orders once we get her into the mini sterile room we have for ourselves. (Sick, I know, yes, but we are not going to a hospital for some damn stitches we can do ourselves. Sue us.) We are to go get showers and keep ourselves busy while he gets her taken care of. He doesn't need us to tell him how to do his job and hover like little shits. He gets resounding grunts and glares from all of us.

Like the seasoned hardass he is when dealing with our attitudes, he pins us right back with glares. "Not kidding, guys. You do as I say, or I'll go back down that elevator and you can find another doctor in this area who's not under your daddies' payrolls."

"Fucking fine," I mutter.

"I'm sitting outside the door after I'm done," G mocks back.

Deck's staring at the ground while mumbling, "I'll be in the gym, G."

"Same. I need to punch shit before I explode."

Without looking at us, G says, "Just answer the damn phone if I text you."

The elevator door dings open to our penthouse, abruptly ending our conversation. We head to the sterile room, lay Bethani down on the small twin bed we have with a protector on it, then probably all say a prayer of some sort. With nothing more that we can do, we all head to our personal showers to attempt to decompress.

As I'm standing under my rainfall shower with the water turned up just past boiling my skin off, I work to temper all the feelings coursing their way through my body. I drop to my knees and do something I haven't done in years. Not since my father made it clear that there was never going to be a God to save my worthless fucked up soul.

With my elbows on my knees, face in my palms, I send God a prayer that Bethani pulls through all this.

Please, whoever is up there. I haven't even heard what I can only assume is her melodic voice yet. Haven't got to see how her eyes shine when she is happy and laughing. Haven't got to experience anything yet with her. Please let her be okay. Fuck, let her be okay.

I can already feel it settling through my body as I stand back up to wash off before going to our gym.

She is going to be the heaven to our hells. Our complete and absolute hopeless destruction.

Chapter 6

Declan

As the doctor closes the door so we don't 'disturb' him, *whatever*, I turn and head to my room to quickly change into some basketball shorts and Nikes. I don't even bother washing off yet. What's the point when I'm going to be sweating my balls off for the next few hours? Seeing the few drops of B's blood on my arms just fuels my anger and aggression, and I desperately feel the urge to numb the chaos running through my veins.

Also, B? When the fuck did I come up with that?

Stopping and thinking about it for a second, it makes a small smirk break on my face as I imagine her cute little ass all pissed off about it. Yup, gonna call her that once she gets better.

I can already picture the eye rolls coming my way.

Fuck. She better recover.

Focusing back on the hate I have toward the sack-less cunt bag who put his hands on her, I finish changing. Quickly, I grab one of the few Percs I have left for my knee pain, grab the bottle of water, and chug both down before grabbing my headphones, phone, a joint, and lighter. Everything in hand, I head toward our custom gym on the lower level of our penthouse.

Note to self...go get more Percs from one of the doctors so you can walk normally, dumbass.

As I'm heading down the stairs, I glance toward the hallway and already see Gio sitting there on the floor opposite the hallway with his laptop on his lap. "Are you combing through footage from the club?"

Without moving his eyes off the screen, he snorts. "Fucking trying. The guy is smart."

"Huh? How so?"

"Only found him on two cameras out of the countless we have throughout the place. The guy is either sneaky or somehow knows where a bunch of our shit is. Don't like either option. Just answered Bethani's phone also and got a little info from her friend who was with her. Not that it's helping either, which pisses me off more."

That sours my mood even more and I scowl. "And the friend said what exactly?"

"*Apparently* he goes to school with us and is a senior, but all she knows is his first name because she only met him a couple of times. Peter. Bethani told her she broke it off with him when he tried pushing for more between them. Guess he wanted her to become his 'yes sir trophy wife' and wanted her to quit school. Only dated spring semester for maybe six weeks..." he trails off.

"But?" Sin says as he steps up behind me, obviously waiting for the wrench we know is about to be thrown our way. Because shit can never be fucking simple.

G sighs. "But...I can't find the guy in the school system. Anywhere."

Pretty sure Sinclair's face looks eerily similar to the slack jaw expression I have. Since when can Giovanni not find something on our school server system?

"What do you mean exactly by that statement, Giovanni?" demands Sin.

With a pissed as fuck look as I've ever seen directed our way, he grits out, "I mean *exactly* what I fucking said, *Sinclair*. Facial recognition, *nothing*. The senior roster of students, *no one* by the name of Peter. I even checked the underclassmen. The guy is fucking attending our school somehow as a ghost or under some false identity. So don't get all shitty with me about it. If you think without your dick for a second, you might be able to guess how the guy is here, which is the only goddamn theory I have currently. And if it's right, finding the twat is gonna be hell."

I mull over his words for a second when realization flashes across my face and I groan a response. "Fuckkkk...Arthur Blackwell, Robert Carter, and Lorenzo Martinelli. Do you really think there is Syndicate business going on that we don't know about? And why in the fuck would something like that be going on here where we have control?"

"Think you just proved the point to your questions, Deck. If our trash-ass sperm donors are involved, we are royally fucked ten ways. By the time they were seniors here, our granddads had basically stepped down toward retirement. What control do we have other than the school?" Sin states, which I can't disagree with.

Our fathers would rather be dead than let any of us have any power.

Giovanni nods in agreement. "Exactly. We are nothing but circus acts to them, and they are the ringmasters trying to keep their control. It's been that way for years, and we all know it. They hate us solely for the fact we don't ask them 'how high, master?' when they demand we jump." He stops, clearly something breaking through his mind as he furiously types on his computer. "If anything, I bet this 'Peter' bitch actually goes here under a false identity as a way to watch us. He then reports back to our fathers somehow. It all makes sense with the stuff from earlier and the arranged marriage bullshit they tried throwing our way. If they can make us completely miserable and break us that way, then they can turn us into their little drones that don't ask questions, just do what they say." Another pause as he types more. "If that is the case, I'm gonna need my full setup in my room to find out what I can. We may need to play along slightly to throw them off if I find out this shit is true." He finally stops, clearly done talking to us as he flips his hand in the air to dismiss us.

Sinclair and I finally head toward the gym, and I light my temporarily forgotten joint on the way down, needing the calm it brings me so I don't trash the gym like the last time I was this all over the place emotionally. After taking a big hit, I pass the joint over to Sin, but he grunts a 'no, thanks' as he puts his headphones on his head and cranks the music while wrapping his hands for one of the bags. I make my way over to the treadmill, needing the added burn to my lungs on top of the weed to really purge the adrenaline flowing through me.

I throw my headphones on, hit one of my playlists, and set the treadmill to about a nine point five. I love the excitement that flows through me as I can finally zone out and let everything fade away in my mind. There is only the music and the feeling of my muscles burning as I push my body for the next hour, never stopping or changing my pace.

An hour later, my mind is clear, and I am absolutely fucking exhausted from running ten miles at whatever bullshit hour of the night it is. But as I stop the treadmill and step off to grab a bottle of water and towel to dry off the tsunami of sweat running down my body, I remember to finally look at my phone and curse. There are six messages from Giovanni.

"Fucking helllll."

I groan because I know what is coming my way. I sit down on the bench to check the shit storm coming.

G: Update from Doc, you coming up?

G: Declan?

G: ......

G: You rat bastard. I fucking TOLD you to answer your phone. Let me guess. Treadmill? Never mind. Don't fucking answer that.

G: Idiots. You are both idiots. Anyways, Doc said the gashes on her head weren't as bad as we thought. The alcohol and drug in her system thinned her blood too much, which is why it looked worse than it actually was. Glued them up. Took blood to figure out the mystery drug in her system. Obvious concussion. She is gonna feel like shit for a week but will make a full recovery.

Thank fuck!

G: Also, she is sleeping in my room since neither of you morons can answer a goddamn text message. Sucks to suck fuck sticks!

That motherfucker.

Me: Fucking hell man. Let me grab a shower and I'll be there.

G: Huh? You DO know how to use a phone? Interesting.

I send him seven middle finger emojis.

Me: See you in 15 cocksucker.

G: You wish I was sucking your cock right now. Door's unlocked. Just be quiet.

I don't even bother responding as I pocket my phone and speed past Sinclair. He was still as zoned out as I was, until he catches me hightailing it out of the gym toward my room.

As I dash into my room and strip out of my clothes while turning on the shower, I glance down and see my dick is hard as fuck. Mostly from G's text, but now that the water is running down my body, I think of Bethani here with me.

Fuck it. Gio isn't in here to make this go away, so I might as well fantasize about B's pussy taking my thick, long, pierced dick.

Giovanni and I are both bisexual. But once we both realized our sexual orientation, we agreed to keep it between us, and we only fuck around on occasion. Condoms only with each other or any of the bitches we fuck until we commit. Don't need any of that nasty STD shit.

As I grab my dick and slowly start stroking from base to tip, I flick the Prince Albert piercing and let out a groan. My head falls back into the shower wall that I apparently backed into to stabilize myself. My mind fully goes into the fantasy as I add pressure to my dick and start stroking faster.

Bethani thinks she is being quiet and sneaky as she tries to slip out of her clothes before getting in here with me.

"Baby B, I know you're out there. So get out of your clothes and get your sweet ass in here."

"Dammit, Declan, how do you always know?"

I smirk. "Always know when you are close by, sunshine."

As she opens the door, steam billows out, and before she can react, I reach out to grab her hand and pull her into my arms. "You always smell so good, baby."

She giggles. "Ew. I just got done working out. I'm gross."

That only makes my cock grow harder between us and pulse, making her breath catch in her throat. I tilt my head down to her ear and whisper, "You are never gross, sunshine. Knowing you were just all hot, sweaty, and sexy turns me the fuck on. It makes me want to bury my dick in that sweet tight little pussy of yours and pound into you until you are screaming my name over and over, baby." Then I nip at her earlobe and slowly work my way down her neck, nipping and sucking and kissing until I hit that sweet spot where her shoulder and neck meet.

She moans long and loud as she pushes her body closer to me.

"Already desperate and needy for me, baby B?" I ask as one of my hands slowly skates down her body, cupping one of her full beautiful ass cheeks. Then giving her a firm smack, which only makes her yelp and moan more.

"Greedy girl. What do you want, baby?"

She slowly looks up at me, eyes flaring with heat, lust, and a carnal desire for me that makes me moan. Fuck, she is so damn sexy like this.

"I just want you, Declan. Please. Fuck me, baby," she whispers.

I can't fucking take it anymore. Bringing my hand behind her head, I slam my lips into hers for a punishing kiss. As I push my tongue past her lips, a deep growl escapes me, and her sweet taste envelops me. It only serves to ramp up my desire for her.

I suck and nibble her lips, most likely bruising them a bit, but she loves when I mark her like that. Forcing myself to pull away, I cradle her face in my hands. "You are so unbelievably beautiful, sunshine. You know that, right?"

As her eyes finally open a bit, she answers under hooded lashes, "Like you three would let me forget it, even if I tried." Then she rolls her eyes.

Hmm...wants to be a sassy little shit, does she? Well, that can be rectified.

I smirk. "Turn around. Hands on the wall. Legs together. Now. Little Miss Smart-ass."

Little shit just stands there. Well, we can play that way if that's how she wants to be.

I quickly spin her around and place her hands against the wall, trapping them there with my left hand while my right lines my dick against her dripping pussy. I thrust up into her, burrowing my dick completely to the hilt and moaning at the added pressure to her already tight pussy from keeping her legs together.

"Hang on tight, sweetheart," I whisper in her ear as I pull almost all the way out, then slam back into her as hard as possible.

"Declannn," she pleads. "Don't. Stop. Please."

I laugh. "Not a fucking chance in hell."

I let go of her hands, and I grab her hips and resume with our hard and fast fucking. I'm loving the sensations rolling through both of us, and I pound into her over and over and over, never losing the power behind my thrusts.

As our moans and groans pick up the pace, I know we are both close, so I quickly move my hand to the front of her and find her clit. I press on it, hard, and circle it at the same time; all while keeping pace.

Not even thirty seconds later, her body starts to shake as she screams my name out. Her pussy clamps down on my fucking dick like a goddamn vice grip, instantly sucking my balls up into my body as my orgasm blindsides me. My body is locked up tight as my dick pulses deep inside her.

"Fuck fuck fuck fuck. FUCK!" I shout as black spots distort my vision.

"Unghhhhh! Mother of shit!" I pant as I see my now semi-hard dick still in my hand and the remnants of my cum washing down the drain.

That was the most powerful orgasm of my damn life, and I haven't even been with B yet.

As I slowly gather myself, I finish taking a shower, then dry off so I can throw on some sweats and a cutoff. Running the towel through my hair to get rid of most of the water, I glance at my bed before walking over and grabbing a few pillows and my comforter. I already know I'm not leaving her side tonight, so I might as well accept the fact I'm going to be shoving my tall ass on one of Gio's tiny fucking couches. Unless I beat Sinclair to the futon.

Dashing down with all my shit, I slowly step into G's room and glance around. G is on the bed next to Bethani, still working on the laptop. I look toward the futon and see Sin isn't there yet.

Score!

I quickly pull it flat and toss my shit on there and make my ass comfortable as Sinclair walks in. He's scowling at me while giving me the middle finger. I give him a big, cocky-ass smile and a loving middle finger back. "Guess we both had the same idea, huh?"

"No shit, Sherlock. I'm not sleeping in my room knowing she is in here with Dr. Know-it-all up there."

"Bitch, whatever. Neither of you paid attention in our anatomy classes in high school. The only reason you two passed is because you both cheated off my work, and you both fucked the teacher. Jackasses," Gio retorts, glaring at us while closing his laptop and then rubbing his hands over his face. "Fuck it. I'm tired and can't think straight with that thing anymore. If any of you hear any weird noises from her in the middle of the night, there are trash cans on both sides of the bed. She starts throwing up, we need to rush her into the ER because the concussion is worse than we thought. Doc gave her meds and antibiotics for all the scrapes. Can't give anything else until she wakes up and we can assess her, though," he finishes while closing his eyes and lying back against the headboard.

Sinclair and I both glance over at Bethani's sleeping figure, the mood quickly turning somber as we take her in.

Her hair a complete mess, and her skin shiny from whatever the doc rubbed on her arms. The bruising around her neck is getting more pronounced. The whole scene makes my stomach churn, and acid works its way up my throat. I quickly look away before I have to use one of those buckets myself.

"Shit," I mutter. I take deep breaths, willing my stomach not to betray me.

"We will find this slimy bastard. We will make him pay, and we will keep her fucking safe from here on out. Regardless if she wants it or not."

I glance over at Sin, taking in his clenched fists and dark expression. This whole thing has all of us completely fucked up. Over a chick we don't even really know but are obviously all pulled toward like moths to a flame.

"Yeah, man. Pretty sure from the sorry-ass state we all look right now, that's pretty damn obvious we all agree." I smirk, attempting to lighten the mood.

With an eye flick and smirk my way, he responds, "Doesn't fucking matter how sorry we all look right now with this." He waves his hands around our sorry asses in our grown-up slumber party state. "Still needed to be said. If someone else touches her without her permission or even looks at her wrong, I'll burn this fucking campus to the ground with no fucks given."

"Agreed," Gio says before rolling over to B and gently giving her a kiss on the forehead. He then mutters something in her ear before lying back down, which prompts Sinclair to do the exact same thing before he grabs his shit and damn near shoves me off the futon.

"Move over, fucker. Not sleeping on that tiny-ass love seat shit fancy boy there likes."

With a middle finger and 'fuck off', I jump up to go give B a kiss on the forehead but wrap my giant-ass bear paw around her little hand. It's so fucking soft and delicate.

After I kiss her forehead, I lean down and whisper, "*We got you, baby B. You'll never feel alone again, sunshine. Wake up soon, baby. Can't wait to officially meet you.*"

Chapter 7

Bethani

H oly. Shit.

Why do I feel like I got hit by a semi-truck, dropped down fifteen flights of stairs, and rolled around in a dumpster fire? *Good gracious, my head is killing me.* Damn it.

"Uhhhhhh," I groan. "Why did I drink so much last night?"

"Being assaulted is more so the reason you feel so terrible right now, Tesoro," a deep, sexy as fuck voice says beside me, violently bringing me out of my hangover haze.

I quickly sit up and instantly regret that dumb-ass decision. "Owwwww! What the fuck?" I moan as my hands cover my face, and I burrow myself into my knees.

The next thing I hear is pounding footsteps coming from somewhere, and the door to whatever fresh hell I'm in slams open, making my headache flare even worse.

"She's awake?" another sexy voice asks.

"Obviously," voice one beside me says, dripping with sarcasm. "And your caveman antics of slamming my door open didn't make it any better."

"Fuck off, G," voice three says. He's way too damn loud.

I stay burrowed in my knees as I demand, "Can you kidnappers please shut up...Or at least talk quieter? My God, am I in hell? Ugh. Even my own voice is too loud."

"Sorry, Tesoro."

"Yeah, sorry, baby B."

"What? No apology from peanut gallery member number three?"

"Hmph. Just wondering when these pricks came up with nicknames for you already." A deep sigh comes from him. "Sorry, kitten."

As I slowly come to my senses, I tentatively raise my head, praying the slow movements will keep the drum line rolling through my head at bay.

When I first open my eyes, I blink several times to get the fuzzy haze out of them. When they finally focus on what's in front of me, my mouth falls open and my eyes go wide in shock at the three gorgeous as sin men. Which earns me small smirks from each.

"W-who in the hell are you three? Where the fuck are my clothes, and where am I?"

The one sitting next to me is the first to speak. "I'm Giovanni Martinelli, everyone's favorite." He smirks. "Nipple piercings over there is Declan Carter, and brooding stick up his ass beside him is Sinclair Blackwell. We are the owners of Club Luxe, the same ones who had fuck face removed from the place and chased him away when he was attacking you after drugging one of your drinks."

Oh. My. God.

I'm sitting in the place where the gods of the campus, the children of the families that rule this school and town live. *The* motherfucking kings of Blackwell University.

No no no no no. NO.

Slowly, I edge off the bed, not taking my eyes off them as I back away. I pray I can find something to protect myself from these assholes. Sinclair takes a step toward me, and I stop him in his tracks with a hard glare. "Don't. Fucking. Move. Asshole." All their eyes go wide, and their mouths fall open.

Good. Rich bastards.

Glancing over at the one named Giovanni, I ask, "Where are my things, and how in the hell do I get out of this bullshit playboy palace?"

"Uhh...Tesoro..."

"Do NOT call me that. Just give me my things and tell me how to get out of here. NOW."

Quickly, he gets up and grabs my phone and clutch, showing them to me.

"And my clothes?"

"Ruined from the blood. The doctor changed you into some of my old junior high clothes. Didn't think you wanted to wake up naked."

I stop to think for a moment, which only makes my head hurt worse. I scowl at them more. "Fine. Whatever. Just set my shit at the end of the bed, tell me how to get out of here, and back the hell up away from me."

They all stand there like stunned statues for a few moments before Declan clears his throat to speak. "You really shouldn't be alone. You've got a pretty good concussion, sweetheart, and need someone around you to make sure you don't get sick or whatever."

"Yeah...I'll take my chances. I am not spending any more time in this place with any of you."

"And why the hell not?" Sinclair throws at me. He has his arms crossed, legs spread wide, obviously ready for battle. Ha! Two can play that game.

I square my shoulders, cock a hand on my hip, and point while throwing as much queen bitch attitude as I can back at him. "Why the hell not, you ask? Are you fucking kidding me?" I screech, ignoring the pain pulsing through my body. Gonna pay for that later, but oh well. "Why in the ever-loving fresh hell would I want to be around any of you? All you are is stuck-up rich fucking playboy snobs who think only with your dicks and use your pretentious last names to walk this earth like some sort of high-class royalty that can do no fucking wrong. Ever. You plow through women quicker than I can change underwear and walk this stupid-ass campus with god complex blinders on. You're oblivious to anything else other than yourselves. Now why would I want to associate my 'scholarship sob story' self with the likes of any of you, you ask? Yeah...think that's pretty fucking obvious. This place is hell enough. I really don't need any more pity looks thrown my way because I'm some charity case. Fuck. That."

And with that, I quickly grab my shit off the bed and storm past them all, slamming the door behind me. Thankfully I find their private elevator, of fucking course, and get the hell away from them before I make the twenty-minute trek to my shithole underground room.

When I finally reach my room, I grab some Tylenol, take a couple, and crash on the bed. I think for a second that everything is okay until I look toward the mirror and gasp. My hair is all over the place, I see mini cuts all over my arms, and know there are more on my back from the dress. But seeing Peter's hand mark around my neck, the sick black and blue bruising, is my undoing.

"Oh my God," I whisper as those traitorous tears start cascading down my face before turning into a full-blown snot-nosed sobbing and gasps for air.

I'm so unbelievably sick of everything that's happened in my life. I've fought like hell through living with a crack whore for a mom who couldn't tell me who my own father was. At the cusp of teenager-dom, I was taken and thrown into the foster system until I proved them wrong and became a legal adult at seventeen. Then I had to make my way through the streets of LA as a homeless person, busting my ass to get this god-forsaken scholarship to better my life. Only to then meet a "nice" guy who assaults me because he is a petulant child who doesn't like being told no. And to top it off, the Kings of Blackwell University saved me...I acted like a damn psycho and lost my shit on them when they saved my life.

Guess I may or may not owe them an apology. Eh, let's go with maybe not for right now and put a pin in that. They are still snob-ass playboys. Sexy as fuck, god-like chiseled out of stone with tattoos, piercings, and eyes ranging from a pale steel gray, emerald green to an ocean blue. But still, snob-ass rich playboys. So yeah...

As all these thoughts, fears, and chaos run through my head, I finally succumb to sleep. I pray that when I wake up, life won't be quite as shitty.

Righttttt.

Chapter 8

Giovanni

S tunned silence is all you can hear in my room, other than the occasional whirl of one of my computers that's running a program. Declan, Sinclair, and I are all standing or sitting with slack jaw expressions at Bethani's outburst.

Scholarship sob story? Why would she think that about herself when almost a third of the campus is here on a scholarship, full or partial, for sports or specific academic majors that are more on a unique side and not offered in most state schools?

I finally gather my thoughts enough to formulate words. "By chance do any of you have an idea what she is talking about with the scholarship stuff?"

Declan shakes his head, running his hands through his hair and letting out a deep breath. "Not at all. Aren't most of the sports players on a scholarship of some sort? So why would she be any different?"

"I'm...honestly not sure. But something doesn't add up." I jump up from the bed quickly and head toward my computer rig. "Go sit over on the chairs and look toward the flat screen."

"The fuck did you do, G?" Sinclair asks, finally finding his voice.

I sigh, knowing for sure one of the three people will be for sure pissed off at me when they find out. "May or may not have slipped one of those tape GPS sticks on her phone under her case last night," I mutter while launching the app and mirroring everything to the flat screen for us all to see.

"Dude...creepy much?" Declan says.

"I can see why he did it. So should you, D."

That surprises me. Turning to head toward my own chair with the remote, computer mouse, and keyboard, I quirk a surprised brow Sinclair's way. "Honestly figured you'd be the upset one." He shrugs, looking toward Declan as I flop down on my 'fancy love seat'. "I wasn't sure how she would take waking up to all of us. It was a precaution for a worst-case scenario, which obviously happened. But when I was trying to find her dorm to let a roommate know she wouldn't be home, I found nothing."

"All students have dorm rooms. What are you talking about?"

"She doesn't. She and one other student have a P.O Box in the student center near the back library entrance that no one really uses anymore." Then I click on the TV, watching the little dot moving quickly through the campus, nowhere near any dorms. "This was the other reason I stuck it on there, and I figured that I'd deal with the repercussions later. I mean, she isn't even heading toward any of the dorms. Where the fuck is she living if she is a registered student here?"

And from there we stayed silent, watching Bethani's GPS tracker move through campus at a pretty swift pace, given the trauma she faced last night. Finally about ten minutes later, she reaches a building.

"Why the fuck is she going all the way to the back of the campus? That's like a twenty-minute walk, right?"

"Hold on...does that area seem familiar to either of you?" Sin asks.

"To answer your question, Deck, yes. Given her schedule, she walks twenty to thirty-five minutes one way depending on which class she has." I stop as I pull up campus blueprints. "And it should seem familiar. That building is mostly storage for different things departments don't have room for twenty-four seven. And it's the original catacomb entrance for the Trident members, now the emergency exit if by chance someone infiltrates the main underground entrance. It's also where every member walks through for their commencement ceremony."

Realization dawns on Declan's face as he remembers. "Oh yeah! The long creepy-ass hallway lit by torches! Pretty sure I was drunk and stoned. Pissed our fathers off something fierce that day." He starts laughing, which makes us start cracking up right along with him. "Wait, I did something stupid, didn't I?"

That only makes us laugh even more as Sinclair tries to remind him. "Dude...you went"—he laughs—"to the bathroom"—more laughing—"then fucking ran back in with only your robes on. You were buck naked"—Sinclair struggles through the hysterical laughing—"screaming I'M SUPERMAN, BITCH, WATCH ME FLY, and jumped up on the table and ran down it trying to fly." That does us in as we all double over in laughter. We're barely able to breathe because we are all laughing so damn hard, and we soon have tears running down our faces.

After a few minutes of hysterical hyena laughing, we are able to bring ourselves somewhat back to normal. Only somewhat, because let's face it, we are all fucking cynical.

"You pissed our dads off so fucking bad that night that our grandfathers took us to Vegas to celebrate, which only pissed them off more. We got stuck dusting the damn school library for it. That took us a month and I wanted to murder you by the end of it." I snicker as I'm wiping my face off. "Pretty sure I still have the PDF file saved on how I was gonna do it in full detail. Asshole."

Declan shrugs at my declaration. "Can't really blame you. I wanted to end my shit after that month of hell. I know king fuck face beside me here threatened to chop my dick off if I ever did something that stupid again down there. And I like my dick way too much to tempt the fates because I'm pretty sure that threat still stands."

"Fucking right it does, bastard. You make me have to dust a fucking library again, and I'll start with ripping your dick piercing off before moving on," Sin threatens.

That makes me cringe in pain. "Grumpy ruthless bastard you are."

"Buzzkill," Deck retorts while crossing his arms and pouting.

"Anyways, you guys got any ideas for why she is still there?" I say while pointing at the TV. "The dot went inside the building and hasn't moved for almost fifteen minutes now."

I sure as fuck hope one of them has an idea as to why she would be on that side of campus where no one ever goes, except for the occasional outdoor party since campus security is too lazy to patrol out there. Or where we go on occasion to bring any and all sorts of torture, usually death to a person who crosses the Trident. We have a well-constructed, underground bunker just past the open field in the woods that's hidden exceptionally well. I know I've personally been there three times since I was inducted into the Trident, twice to assist an elder member with 'worthless scum' who have tried to fuck them over for one reason or another.

But the last time I was there was actually for a personal vendetta against one of the servants at my father's house who admitted to supplying my mother with a constant supply of alcohol at the height of her depression. He told her he loved her and would do anything for her. She believed it. She got all the alcohol her body could handle and he got a comatose fuck buddy who was too drunk to function but wanted to feel loved. Not even the love from her only child, me, at nine years old could fill the void enough to make a difference. Then she died a year and a half later from passing out drunk in the bathtub. I was eleven and I was the one who found her lifeless body floating in the tub. That day a big part of my soul died, and I vowed to find the fucker supplying her and end their worthless fucking existence.

I finally found him two years ago and ended his life seven months ago after slowly and methodically destroying his life to nothing. Watching the life drain from his eyes was the day I finally found a semblance of peace over my mother's tragic death.

"GIO!" they both yell, pulling me from my thoughts.

"Christ, where the fuck did you zone out to?"

I shrug as a response to Sinclair's bossy attitude. "Nowhere. What were you guys saying?"

Sin just keeps his hardened gaze on me, clearly unimpressed and no longer speaking while Declan starts talking, "We were saying how she called herself a sob story. Is there any way to hack the admissions and see if there is a program or something like that going on for the underprivileged that isn't talked about normally? Because nothing else makes sense. None of the other scholarship students live that way. They are either in dorms or the off-campus houses."

"Yeah. I can do that. Give me a little bit. But what are we going to do about it if she actually lives"—I wave my hand to the TV screen —"in the storage area for the school?"

Sinclair shrugs. "Probably just an area she wants to chill at until her roommate is asleep or at a party. Fewer questions to deal with until she can shower and hide everything."

Jesus. He really is dense sometimes.

"Whatever. Both of you get the hell out so I can work. Maybe one of you can cook some food or something since, you know, you two are pretty much useless when it comes to this shit." I smirk, knowing they are going to be displeased with my knock on their intelligence. Fucking sue me, it's funny as shit giving them hell.

"Way ahead of you, G. I'm going to send a few of the plebs on some ridiculous food runs. Chinese, Italian, and tacos sound good?" D asks, a wicked glint in his eyes and an equally devilish smile plastered on his face.

As I get up to head to my hub station, I shrug. "Don't give a shit. Have fun torturing the children. Just make one of them get food here quickly. The others, go wild with the fucked up tasks you two are thinking up." I sit down and start powering up all my shit. "Also, do *not* let them order our shit. Place the fucking orders on the goddamn apps so it's not fucked up. I'll murder someone if they fuck our food up like last time." I shiver. General Tso's chicken mixed into seafood soup is fucking *horrendous* and burns dirty ball sacks coming back up.

"We promised not to talk about that shit *ever again*."

"Yeah, yeah." I wave my hand around while throwing my headphones on. "Take your shit and get out. Text me when my food is here."

They say something, but I've already queued up the music to ignore them. I start my work to hack our school systems. The quicker I can get in, the sooner I can solve one mystery to the compounding list of curious shit that is starting to pile up around Bethani.

"FUCK!" I shout as I'm chucking my Bose A20 Aviation headset toward my door just as the guys open the door to my room. They barely duck as the headset hits the marble flooring and shatters along the hallway. *Third set this month alone, you dumb ass,* I think to myself as I scrub my hands along my face. I'm frustrated and getting more and more irritated by the second as I sit here. "If you guys are coming here for a damn update, I don't fucking have one. And no, I obviously don't know why either." I groan. "Where in the bullshit system this crap is hidden is beyond me."

"And the great computer hacker Giovanni Martinelli comments on us being useless with computers. Right." Sinclair snickers, causing me to stand and get straight up in his face, completely ready to use his face as my personal punching bag.

"Motherfucker. You sit your ass here for the next three hours and see if you come up with anything!" He squares up against me, not ready to back down. Well, me neither, fuck face. Bring it. "I've searched our school's database four damn times already trying to find anything to figure out what her scholarship is and how she goes here. I've cross-referenced her info across multiple databases in California and Washington State. I'm also trying to find shit on the prick who assaulted her last night, if you haven't fucking forgotten that minor detail. I am a one-man motherfucking show here. So unless you want to get your lazy ass in here and do this work, I suggest you back the fuck off before I knock your ass out," I grit out through clenched teeth.

As we both stand there, toe to toe, eye to eye, fists ready to fly, Declan finally steps up and shoves us both back, putting the much needed space between each other. "Dammit, Sinclair, knock it the fuck off. You know neither of us gives a fuck about this shit like he does, or are good enough to hack it like him. Give him a fucking break." Then he turns my way. "And you know princess here"—he points a finger toward Sin—"who is an impatient brat that just wants answers. *We all* want answers. But being arrogant cock-munchers isn't going to accomplish anything."

"Cock-muncher." I snicker, then proceed to a full-out laughing fit, like a dumbass sixteen-year-old chick, which causes the other idiots to do the same.

"Sorry, man," Sin says through his laughter. "I know this shit can't be easy, and I sure as fuck have no patience for it. So it's all you, bud."

"Yeah, yeah. All good."

"Juveniles."

"Fuck off, Deck. You are the biggest juvenile of us three, and you fucking know it, asshole."

He shrugs and smirks. "Well, *one* of us has to be insanely good-looking and funny, unlike you two sticks in the mud."

"Fuck off," we both say in unison.

With another grin from his big ass, he turns toward the door. "Throw some shoes on. We're going on a little mission."

Yet again in unison, Sinclair and I ask, "Where?"

"Well, *one* of us isn't a total fruitcake when it comes to computers. I hacked your tracking app. Bethani's phone still hasn't moved from the storage building. So, throw on some dark sweats and let's check out why her phone hasn't moved for"—he looks at his phone —"four hours and twenty-two minutes." Then he is gone, the door to his room opening and shutting, leaving Sinclair and myself stunned.

"When the fuck do you pay attention to shit, asshole?" Sinclair yells at Declan, which is quickly followed by my own booming voice. "Wait...*You* hacked *my* program from your phone? The fuck?!"

Declan's laughter from afar is the only response to our questions.

"Son of a bitch," Sin mutters before heading toward his room to change, leaving me to do the same.

After finding my black Nike sweats and shoes, I look through my drawer for a Blackwell cutoff. I throw it on, grab my phone, wallet, and keys, then head toward the elevator where the other two are waiting. As we all step in to head to ground level, our phones all ding simultaneously, causing glares and groans from us all.

Pulling out my phone to open the message, I already know what's coming.

Unknown: You have until the clock striking midnight to be where we converge.

"Jesus Christ. It's like every damn time we have shit to do, they fucking summon us."

I sigh. "Yeah. But at least we have time to see her and figure out this shit before we have to get back."

"How much do you want to bet this has something to do with our arranged marriages those bastards are trying to force on us?" Sin bites out, then slams his head against the elevator wall.

Deck mutters, "Probably everything."

"Doesn't matter. We still got seven hours to figure this shit out, get back, and get dressed for our arrival to the gates of hell and the three-demon spawns," I stress. "So let's just get to the storage building, then deal with dumb fucks after that."

They nod in agreement, and we remain quiet as the elevator finishes its descent from our penthouse dorm to the main floor. We then sneak around the campus toward the storage building. Most students don't fuck with us out of fear due to our given namesakes, our towering statures, and our constant 'mean mugs/resting bitch faces' as some like to call it. Others don't associate or acknowledge us due to the fact that they're fellow Trident members, though just underlings. We don't generally group together in public settings, unless they are sanctioned by the elders. A big group of us 'just hanging' out could cause suspicion.

If someone pisses us off by trying to be friendly, we just haze the shit out of them. Our reputation for being ruthless and sometimes sadistic bastards is pretty staunch but isn't far from the actual truth. Still, the occasional dope tries their hand at 'making nice' with us. So here we are, sneaking around like we're fourteen again and trying to get off our parents' gated properties to hang out with the more normal kids than we dealt with on a daily basis. Thankfully, we're already three quarters of the way there. Our hoodies are up and our sunglasses are covering our eyes, giving us the typical hung-over idiot on a Saturday afternoon look.

"There a way for us to even get into that building? I can't fucking remember," Sinclair semi whispers, trying to avoid anyone hearing our voices.

A stifled laugh comes from Declan. "I'm six-foot-six, idiot. I can reach windows if needed. But I also brought my lock pick kit just in case."

"Got my phone with me so that I can scan the locks if they are electronic," I answer as we hit a small set of trees, big enough to hide our asses and also give us coverage to see if anyone is around. "No cameras around here or in this building."

With an evil glint to his eye, Declan smirks and looks around one last time. Then he starts skipping his oafish self toward the building. "Come along, kids! We have shit to break into," he says, ending with a maniacal laugh.

"Jesus Christ," Sinclair mutters.

I snort at Sinclair's obvious distaste for Declan's lack of plan and jolly-go-fuck-it-all attitude. Always the methodical masochist.

"Not everyone needs seventy fucking plans for a simple break-in, unlike *someone* we all know," I say.

"Fuck off," he huffs out. "Come on, better go make sure he doesn't start breaking windows or setting something on fire."

As we make our way toward wherever Deck went, we hear him calling around the opposite side of the building. "Found it! Hurry the fuck up!"

Turning on our heels, we switch directions, heading toward the sound of his voice. As we turn the corner, we catch him moving around some overgrown hedges. As we get closer, the profanities spilling from Declan's mouth get more and more vulgar, as does the tone. It's edging closer to pissed off the closer we get.

"The hell are you doing?" I ask, finding him stomping down on bush branches, trying to make the clearing to the door bigger.

"This is where she went in. Her tiny-ass footprints went straight to the door, stopped, then stepped back as she was opening the door to go inside. Fuck!" he spews, along with other curses as we start helping make the way bigger.

Finally after about five minutes of nothing but stomping and swear words reverberating from all of us, we have enough pressed down to make the entrance more feasible.

"Good God, how the hell did she get to this door?" I wonder out loud.

Declan notes the tiny concrete path beside the building leading to the door. "There were enough branches cut or broken off for the average person to get through, just not people our size. Hence my attack on this bullshit fuckery of a devil plant." He turns back toward the door and gets his picking equipment out. "Now, on to the good stuff."

As he quickly picks the lock and opens the door, we all retch at the musty odor that assaults our nostrils.

"What in the ever-loving nursing home meets mothballs meets cheap grandma perfume is that smell?" I ask while trying to keep my stomach from tossing its shit in revolt to the stench. "How in the fuck is anyone down there?"

"Don't"—Deck makes a gagging noise—"fucking know..." Another gag noise comes from Declan as he attempts to compose himself.

Glancing over at Sinclair, he is faring better than either of us. Not by much, though. He finally gains the most resolve of us before he steels himself and barks out his usual orders. "Get your ass down the steps, Declan, before I shove your ass in there and barricade the door. You too, G. Get this shit over with so I can light my clothes on fire and bathe in bleach."

We all make our way, finally, into the building and down the stairs as quietly as possible. When we reach the bottom, the sight we come upon is an utter gut punch. There's a grungy hallway that we slowly walk down, with a damn carpet that has mold growing up the walls in little patches. Paint that's some nonsensical off-white-brown you can't even guess the color of stretches into the common area. Utter garbage mismatched 1970s fluorescent lighting is scattered about the ceilings.

Furniture from I'm not even sure what era sits around broken or half broken. Everything is covered in a layer of dust that looks like they haven't been touched in ten years. Along the walls, there are ten different doors with the letters A-J marked on them in a faded stamp, almost like someone was above putting real markers on the doors. The damn and musty grandma smell isn't as completely horrendous in here as it was in the hallway or staircase, but it isn't much better either. This place looks like a walking disease-filled cesspool that's itching to claim its next victim. Glancing for a light switch, I cover my hand with my hoodie sleeve.

"Turn the lights off, see if any of the doors have light coming through them," I order.

I flip the switch, plunging us into temporary darkness as I look to the ground, searching for light behind a door.

"Here," one of them says, and I flip the switch back on as the lights all groan in protest to function.

Sinclair moves over in front of the door marked J while Declan and myself all move up beside him.

"Well...Here goes fucking nothing." As he starts to pound on the door repeatedly.

Yeah. Here goes fucking something.

Chapter 9

Bethani

I must be dreaming as I hear that familiar pounding on the door. The one where one of my momma's friends came over and had to wake her up for their fun. I roll on the familiar small uncomfortable bed when the pounding keeps going.

"Momma. Someone's at the door. Get up," I groan.

The pain radiates through my body from when one of her buddies got mad that I interrupted. I was hungry and not quite big enough to make my own food. That got me thrown into a wall a couple times before he shoved me back into my broom closet of a room and barricaded my door closed from the outside.

"Momma...Get. The. Door. Please!" I yell out before the door damn near busts off its hinges, throwing myself out of whatever sleepy haze I was in.

I shoot up in bed, groaning at the pain racking my body. Dizziness hits me like a ton of bricks as I grasp my head to stop the spinning when voices start assaulting my senses.

"Kitten! Baby B, what's wrong?"

Their loud noises made my brain pound like my skull is being crushed between a set of vices.

"Too loud."

"Fucking idiots. I'm sorry, Tesoro." I assume Giovanni, just by the nickname I'm somehow remembering, apologizes.

Wait.

"How in the...? What in the...?" I stammer.

Taking a deep breath to gather my thoughts, I finally settled on the one coherent thought I can formulate. The desperate one that needed to be answered from these asshats. Releasing that breath, I say, "I'm only asking this once. If I don't like the answer, you all need to get the fuck out of here, regardless of your bullshit hero complex. K?" As I finally open my eyes just enough to get the point across, I'm reminded of how fucking handsome these three are. That slightly pisses me off, causing a glare to be pointed their way. When all three finally nod in understanding, I start to open my mouth, but Giovanni stands up next to Declan and Sinclair.

"I have a feeling I know what you are going to ask already. It is how we figured out where you live, right?" Giovanni correctly guesses.

Stunned slightly, I nod.

"Yeah..." he starts. "I'm gonna take the blame. Last night when Doc was taking care of you, I may or may not have taken the liberty to slip a GPS tracker between your phone and phone case. I wasn't quite sure how you'd take to waking up with us around, and I wanted to know you were safe," he confesses with a boyish half smile that highlights his beautiful features.

All three of them have their own distinct square angular jaws, but Giovanni is definitely the boyish one of them. His face is clean-shaven, if he really even grows a beard. His eyes are a bright cyan in color, the color of them popping against his tanned Italian skin tone and dark brown hair.

I remember how all of them are incredibly ripped like a weird mix of a boxer and football player. All three have broad shoulders, well tapered waistlines with those sexy V cuts. Even in my sore exhausted haze from earlier, I remember their narrow hips, thick thighs, washboard abs, and sexy dusting of hair that leads down into their tight sweatpants.

They are tall, well, all three of them are freakishly tall compared to me. They range from six-foot-two to probably six-foot-six, at least. But sitting here on my dorm room bed, studying them, deciding on a proper answer, I can see that I'm the one with the actual power. Their eyes are all giving away varying degrees of remorse over tracking me without my knowledge. The concept of these powerful guys showing remorse makes me snort comically, then wince as the pain reminds me of last night's events. They all flinch and attempt to move before I hold up a hand to stop them in their tracks.

"So let me try to get this straight. You put a GPS tracker on my phone and have been what, watching since I stormed out of your fortress of luxury earlier? Like I'm some sort of science experiment or whatever the hell else was running through your entitled minds? The fuck?"

With a snort, Sinclair's handsome face hardens as he pierces me with his emerald eyes. "No. You're not a fucking science experiment, kitten. You were assaulted last night by some fucked up ex-boyfriend who spiked your goddamn drink. He was going to do whatever the fuck it was he wanted to do while you had no way to fight back. So yeah, after saving you, Giovanni made sure we knew where the fuck you were in case that bastard tried to get to you again. Then, of all motherfucking places, we find you here. In some fucking shithole that isn't worth a fucking fuck, like you are a stain that the university needs to hide away. How fucking long have you lived here, Bethani? How. Fucking. Long?" he heaves out.

His chest is rising and falling, and waves of venom are dripping off him the longer I don't answer. Looking down at my knees, afraid of the coming reaction, I whisper, "August of last year, before freshman year started."

"FUCK!" he roars, making me flinch while storming out of my shoebox room.

The next thing I hear is the obvious breaking and flipping of furniture outside in the common area. He thankfully avoids my room as he takes out his rage at what exactly, I'm not sure of. I chance a glance toward Declan and Giovanni, wondering what is going to happen next. Declan's eyes are closed, and his fists are clenched so tight that his knuckles are ghostly white. He's taking deep breaths through his nose and exhaling through his mouth, almost like he is trying to avoid going out there with Sinclair and joining in on the utter destruction.

Giovanni is sitting in my desk chair, with elbows on his knees and his head hanging in his hands. It's almost like he is disgusted and ashamed by the scene. All of their reactions are equally confusing, and they are making me start to regret my actions earlier.

"A-are you guys going to clean that up out there? I really don't feel like, you know, cleaning up a giant mess just to be able to get into my room." Both of them open their eyes simultaneously and look at me like I just spoke to them in Russian. "What? I really don't feel like tripping and falling in that warzone out there."

"Your stay in this room is over, baby B," Declan finally speaks. His voice is void of emotion, while those turbulent gray eyes pierce my soul. The finality of his voice with that statement shocks me.

"Excuse me? My stay in this room is over? What does that even mean?!"

"It's a pretty self-explanatory statement. You. Are. Done. Staying. In. This. Room."

Over-reaction fills my body, as I propel up off the bed and storm over to him. My hands hit his strong chest as I try to push him back but fail miserably. So, I settle on just hitting him repeatedly.

"You can't throw me out of school for living here. It wasn't my choice! This isn't fair! Why am I being punished for this? What gives any of you any right to throw me off campus?" I start sobbing again, pissed that everything I've worked toward is being taken from me. When Declan's strong arms wrap around me, I collapse into his arms. The warmth of his body brings on a turbulent range of emotions from me, causing my sobs to grow even harder. "T-this i-isn't f-f-fair." Somehow the words stumble out of my mouth.

I'm not even sure how long I've been sobbing shamelessly into his hoodie when I feel Sinclair's and Giovanni's bodies step up behind me. It's almost like they are in a protective stance as I let loose on my emotions.

"Tesoro, why would you think we are expelling you from the college?" Giovanni asks to the left of me.

I shrug, not knowing how to answer. It's just something that would happen in my life with the way it's played out so far. Sinclair's hand comes up to cup my chin, and electricity pulses through my body, causing me to gasp as my eyes slam open from the feeling. He slowly tilts my face toward his, almost cradling my head like it's some precious jewel. I avert my eyes to his chest, looking at the Nike logo on his black hoodie, terrified of my future if I look into his eyes.

"Bethani, look at me." When I start to shake my head, his grip tightens slightly. It's just enough pressure to let me know I'm not in control right now, but not enough to physically hurt me. "Now, kitten," he demands, his voice taking a slight edge. Knowing my moments are numbered, I glance up into the churning storm of his emerald, green eyes. When he is obviously satisfied that I'm not going to look away, he speaks. His voice is firm, but not hateful or scolding. "You are not being kicked off campus. Do you understand that?" I nod, just enough for him to see I understand. "You are just not staying in this absolute shithole of a fucking place anymore. All of your belongings are going to be packed up, and you are going to move into our place with us. Tonight."

Looking into his eyes, my mouth hangs open momentarily before I find my voice. "No. I'm not."

"Yes. You. Are."

"And who do you think you are to decide where I fucking live? Surprisingly, this *isn't* the worst place I've ever lived. So *no*, I'm not leaving." I push out of Declan's arms to gain some traction, and his and Giovanni's hands both brush along my arms. More electrical currents pulse through my body from their touches, but I ignore them. Mustering up enough courage, I pop one of my hips slightly and settle my hands on each side of my waist. "You have no right to break in here, bust my door down, and then demand I leave like a Neanderthal. That's not how shit works in the real world, and I'm not going to just let you think you can make the fucking rules and expect me to follow them like some obedient little pet."

With a hand running through his thick black hair, shoveling it around into a sexy mess, Sinclair steps toward me. With a smirk, he quickly picks me up. His hands are on my ass as he tilts my hips just right to make my legs wrap around his trim waist tightly so I don't lose my balance and fall onto the disgusting carpet of my room. Turning just slightly, he backs me up into Declan's chest, whose hands replace Sinclair's and slightly squeeze. I can feel my pulse picking up and arousal flooding my veins at their caveman actions.

"Kitten, while on a normal day your fiery personality is nothing but a sexy little turn-on that makes me want to do nothing more than shove my cock in between your sweet sinful little lips to shut you up... right now it just makes me want to bend you over my knees and spank your pretty ass until my handprints are imprinted all over it."

He pushes slightly closer to my center, and I can feel his erection pushing up against me. Behind me, I can also feel Declan's hardening cock against my ass. The pressure from them both causes a breathy moan to fall from my lips unwillingly, which makes them all chuckle slightly at my rapidly turned on state.

"That's better, our sweet little Bethani. So let's get one thing straight. This isn't the real world, this is the campus of Blackwell University. *We* own this campus. *We* make the fucking rules here, sweetness. And there's a new rule that's been established. You are not living in this god-forsaken hell hole for another fucking night. I don't give a flying fuck if this is the Taj Mahal in comparison to what you are used to. Either come stay with us, or Declan here can light this place on fire. Which given the state of it, and the fact that our moronic fathers have obviously orchestrated this as appropriate for someone to live in, may happen anyway. What do you think, D?" His venomous eyes finally tip toward Declan's face, which has somehow settled on my head.

A dark chuckle falls from his lips, the reverberations sending me into a further tailspin. Their giant cocks create more friction from the laughing, when suddenly Sinclair's dick pressures just slightly against my clit. My eyes widen, and I bite my bottom lip to stifle the moan, but my expression tips off Giovanni.

"Think you hit her clit just now, Sin." Giovanni chuckles.

As he comes closer to this damn Bethani sex sandwich the other two oafs have me in, Giovanni leans in as the other two are still slowly rocking me up and down against them. I'm completely overwhelmed by them and their dominating presence. It's turning me on more than I'll ever care to admit, but my body betrays me as my hips join in undulating against them.

"Also, Tesoro, all three of us have our dicks pierced. And one of these days, you are going to be begging for each of us to push into you. You'll feel the indescribable sensations that come from them while screaming our names as we fuck you long, hard, and all fucking night long."

He flicks his tongue against my earlobe before nipping my ear while Declan and Sinclair grind their hips against me. Sinclair's shameless grinding against my clit sends an unsuspecting orgasm rocketing through my system. My back arches, pushing my stomach closer to Sinclair, and my head falls back on Declan's shoulders at the same time. The moans escaping my body sound nothing like myself as my vision blanks and blurs.

After what feels like an hour, but I know is maybe only a minute or so, my vision clears enough to look into the faces of the savage kings of campus. I don't say anything, as I try to regulate my breathing and heart rate back to a normal function after orgasming from barely any stimulation. Good God, a person could only imagine what these three beasts are like if given a proper chance to fuck a person. The thoughts that race through my mind make me shiver.

"Are you going to let us take care of you, baby B?"

I tilt my head to look up at Declan's face, and I can see the pleading look in his eyes. Why they don't want me staying here, I'm not exactly sure. But the thought of staying somewhere nicer than here, even if it's just temporary, is enough of a positive that I just close my eyes.

"Yes. I'll go. For now."

I find myself suddenly yawning as an after wave of orgasm wonder washes over me.

"Sleep, sunshine," one of them says as I'm shifted into Declan's arms. Then they all give my semi-conscious, sleepy, sated self a kiss on the cheek, and I float off to sleep. Unusually content for the first time in years.

Chapter 10

Declan

S taring down at Bethani as she falls asleep in my arms, my dick is still rock-hard. It's pulsing and begging to be let out, but a rare peacefulness settles over me, and honestly, my dick can just deal with it. I carefully turn to sit on her tiny junk-ass bed, posting myself up against the wall and using the few pillows she has to prop them under my arm where her head rests. Hopefully minimizing how quickly my arm falls asleep.

"So what's the damage out there? Anything left for us to destroy at a later date? Or did you fuck everything up beyond recognition?" I ask.

Sinclair is obviously still trying to will his cock to behave, same as Gio, because it takes him a few before he answers me. "Fuck no. Demolished everything, which didn't take much effort either. Pissed me off even more before the smart mouth there had to go be a bossy ass and turn me on with her attitude." Grumbling, he opens one of the doors in her room and finds a small bathroom that isn't much bigger than my shoe. "Thank fuck. Figure out what we are doing. I gotta fix this before I can goddamn think straight again." Then he slams the door to 'fix' his dick problem.

Snickering away, Giovanni and I laugh as we hear his grunts and groans that he is horrid at hiding, which earns us both a "fuck off", causing more laughter.

"So you got a plan, G?" I ask.

"Yeah. Sin goes to get the Tahoe, since it's the most normal looking vehicle we have, then drives it back. I'll go upstairs and try to empty out some extra boxes. You stay here with her. If you decide not to be a lazy fuck, start trying to pack her stuff up if she has any luggage here."

I mull over his words for a second, deciding which asshole comment is going to come out of my mouth.

"First of all, suck my cock," I say with a wink, which I know will rile him up. I know it does, by the obvious stifling of his groan. "Second, since you decided to be the dumb twat who insulted me, I'm going to keep my tall ass on this small, uncomfortable as fuck bed cuddling with Bethani until both of you are back."

Sinclair chooses to come out at that moment, finally not looking like a complete and utter asshole. However, he's still pissy assed that he had to get himself off.

"Third, get to moving, assholes," I order with a giant grin plastered on my face. They already know I'm not moving my big ass in the slightest. And they won't dare fuck with me either because that could hurt Bethani, and she is already in enough pain as is.

That thought alone has me scowling as I glance around this toaster waffle sized shithole. "How in the fuck is she staying here in this?"

Sinclair grumbles a response, "We will fucking find out, then torch the fucker after. That bathroom is the most unsanitary thing I've ever seen. It's unfathomable how she is living here at all."

"Worse than the hallway?" I tentatively ask, not quite sure how I'm going to react to the response. A resounding scowl from him gives me all the answer I need, but he proceeds to tell us anyway. Most likely to bestow the anger fueling him onto us. Fuck stick.

"Everything she owns is in Ziploc bags. There's mold all inside the vanity, mold on the ceiling, and it's starting to travel down to the walls. The exhaust fan doesn't work. I'm not even sure if I'd consider her water even passable as water. There's a strange tint to it and it gets lukewarm at best. Once we get home, I'm burning these fucking clothes, taking the hottest fucking shower of my life to scrub the shit off me, and paying to have everything she owns professionally cleaned. Or maybe just saying fuck it and buying everything new. Our vehicle is going to get a deep clean after this too. And we should possibly make her a fucking doctor's appointment for mold exposure."

"Jesus. How is she not sick as fuck?" I ask. "Just sitting in this place makes me want to throw up."

I glance down at her sleeping away in my arms, wondering how in the hell she has survived in this god-forsaken place. "Damn fucking warrior she is, and we don't even know the half of what she's gone through." I look up at the other two. "We aren't gonna like the rest either, if we ever get her to trust us enough to tell us. I already know our arsenal is gonna need to be stocked up before we go on that revenge mission, though."

They both nod, probably thinking up just as many different forms of torture or revenge as I am for those who have wronged her.

"Time?" I ask.

G looks at his phone. "Got three hours to get this shit packed and moved back to her place before we have to go to the sanctuary for counsel. Sin, go get the Tahoe real quick. Deck, give me your lock pick shit so I can break in up there."

As Sinclair steps out, he flips us a usual bird as his form of asshole endearment, so we flip them back. Then I try to dig my shit out of my pocket. When I finally have them, I hold them in my hand out to G but not before asking, "Your ass, my mouth, a little later for some stress relief?" I finish off the request with a deviant smirk.

"Dude...I just got my shit to go down, then you say something like that?"

He quickly snatches the stuff from my hands but throws me for a loop when he uses his free hand to wrap around the back of my neck and smashes his lips against mine for a punishing kiss. When his tongue darts out as a demand, I open my mouth and plunge my tongue directly into his mouth. I'm surprised when my tongue catches his tongue ring, bringing a groan from my lips. The snarky shit smirks as we continue to fucking destroy each other's mouths, so I reach my free hand down to his fully erect cock and wrap around it through his sweatpants. Slowly and firmly stroking it until I reach his apadravya piercing and flick it just right, like I know he loves, to elicit a throaty groan from deep in his chest.

When he suddenly pulls away, both of us are hard as steel and ready to tear each other apart. Our breathing is shallow and ragged, lips swollen, lustful hazes across our eyes.

"Yeah. I'm gonna take you up on that offer. Stress relief sounds fan-fucking-tastic right about now."

All I can do is laugh. It's a much needed laugh after the past thirty-six hours. But thinking about sinking my dick in his greedy ass right now has me groaning in frustration.

"Go find some fucking boxes, asshole. I'm gonna move her and attempt to get my dick to cooperate before Sinclair gets back with the Tahoe. You know his panties will be in a fucking twist if we don't have shit packed and ready like the bossy bastard he is."

G snorts a response, "Yeah, yeah. Be back shortly." And he's gone, dashing away and cursing through the mess Hurricane Sinclair made.

I slowly shift Bethani off my lap to keep her asleep while praying she doesn't spook and kick me in the dick because the moody fucker doesn't want to cooperate and behave. No, he is currently standing at his long and thick attention in my sweats over the promise of getting action. Between rubbing my dick between B's sinfully voluptuous ass cheeks and twat face's domineering kiss, my dick is swinging for the fences for release.

As I find a few black trash bags to put shit in, I'm thinking every dumb thing I can conjure up to get rid of my erection.

Business 405? Nope.

My Trident initiation? Nada.

State capitals? Ha.

Cleaning the bathroom after a rough night? Still standing bitch.

"Think of your dad having sex with your mom. It's what worked for me," Giovanni says as he comes into the room with some plastic totes.

Thinking of my fuck face dad having sex with my stick-up-her-high-society-ass mother? Gross. Nasty. Worst. Fucking. Thing. Ever. I need someone to pour bleach in my brain to rid myself of the horrific image that my twisted ass head comes up with. A violent shiver rips through my body at the whole thought process.

I look down at my cock to see the demon is completely flaccid and unhappy at how turned off I am now.

Ding ding ding. We have a winner.

Thank fuck.

"It worked. But fuck you, dude." I shiver at the thought again. I'm going to go slam my head against a brick wall and pray for temporary amnesia.

A sardonic chuckle comes from him as he starts placing books and shit in the totes while I'm tearing a hole in the bottom of a trash bag to slip over the hangers in the closet. Just one of the useless tricks

I've picked up over the years when traveling and forgetting shit everywhere.

It only takes us about ten minutes to pack everything up, which is unsettling. We pack more for a two-week vacation to Vegas than she owns altogether. If any of the shit she said was true about being a charity case, then what is in this roach motel dorm is really all she owns. It's infuriating that our school treats her like this when she is in the top 5 percent of her class. Of course, G had to look that up, regardless of the social standing differences.

"You really think she is gonna be okay with living in the guest room?"

G leans back against the joke of a desk and it gives a noise of protest in the process.

"Doubt it." I give a noncommittal shrug. "Not really gonna give her a choice either, though. This all here is a mental fuck-up of a psyche game if I've ever seen one. 'Hey, we are going to give you the opportunity of a lifetime but still treat you like a leper.' Fuck that."

The flare of anger in G's eyes is evident. None of us are enthused about this situation, but none of us mind it either. Bethani is a magnetic, fiery force field of wonder and awe that is drawing us all into its wake. There are zero fucks given as to the consequences, and we are all the dumbstruck bastards not looking when we cross the street both ways to reach the wondrous center.

Our phones go off, reminding us that our favorite sadist can't be left out of the conversation. Fucking drama king.

Sinclair: Be there in 5. Shit better be ready to go.

I roll my eyes and type out a reply.

Me: Of course master. Your wish is our command.

Sinclair: *middle finger emoji* Fuck off.

Me: You already did.

Giovanni: Shit's packed. Taking it up now. Chill out.

Sinclair: K

I glance up from my phone, pissed off at G for ruining my fun. "Fuck was that for?"

He starts grabbing boxes and heading out while completely ignoring my ass. I grab some shit and head out to follow him. As we are heading back down for the last of it, he finally responds, "Got enough shit going on. Don't need you fucking poking the damn dragon and setting him into one of his moods because you enjoy being an instigator and acting childish."

Scoffing, I bite back, "Do fucking not."

"Doing it right now, dickhead."

I go to counter back, then shut up as Sin pulls up and pops the trunk. "That everything?" he asks.

"Yeah. That's it," I reply.

"She still asleep?"

"Was a minute ago."

"Finish loading everything. I'll go get her. Gio, you drive back," he orders.

I bow to him like a smart-ass. "Yes, master. Anything else, master? Do we get cookies for being good boys, master?"

"Jesus Christ," G mutters while shaking his head.

Clearly I'm all about acting my age right now. *Not.*

Obviously even more unimpressed with my shit weasel antics, Sinclair just hits me with one of his looks, flips me off, then turns to go inside.

Hopefully Bethani can appreciate my unique and wonderful sense of humor because my friends have the sense of humor equivalent to a toad. Buzzkills.

Chapter 11

Sinclair

As I reach our dorm building, I head in through the front entrance and go over to the private elevator we have for our garage and penthouse. It only works by using a key, which keeps out people we don't want in. Which is pretty much every other motherfucker on this campus. It also gives us access to any other floor, including a custom armory we had installed into what was originally a bunker.

With over five point five million dollars' worth of vehicles in there, not to mention the vast amount of weapons and personal information we keep on people of our vested interest, the one of a kind keys we have are an expensive, but necessary, investment.

As I hit the button to go to the garage, my mind races over the events that have gone down in the past day and a half.

First, our manipulative fucking sperm donors thinking they can just pick and choose how our goddamn lives are going to go. All because they want to expand their already vast, lucrative, and mostly illegal empire by forcefully merging us with beneficial-to-them arranged marriages. No doubt to dipshit bimbos we have zero interest in. Fuck that and fuck them. I'll fake my own death or take an oath of celibacy before that shit happens.

Ehh, celibacy? I think I might prefer death over never having sex again.

Thank fuck Giovanni has a damn near perfect photographic memory and knows our Trident code of conduct and manual with all the rules that have been put in place since the school was established in the 1870s. The rules and regulations that have been upheld with the utmost respect. Well, until our fathers took power. Now it's just a shit show of even shadier shit than the normal.

The ding of the elevator brings me back to the current situation at hand: a five-and-a-half-foot spitfire from hell with aqua eyes, long brown to blond hair, and curves formed by the devil himself that I want to sink my teeth into and never let go of. The visceral reaction she pulls from me is unlike anything I've ever felt before, and I'm not sure how to handle the onslaught of emotions.

One minute I feel like I want to shield her from all the evil in the world, myself included. Then the next minute I pull shit like I did in her room as I rubbed my dick up and down her cunt until I hit her clit to make her come. All to demand her submission and get her stubborn little ass to agree with us.

Fuckity fuck she is going to be the death of me.

Maybe I need to rethink that celibacy thing? Nah.

I'll take my chances. Risk and reward and what not.

Hopping into our most basic vehicle, a blacked-out Tahoe with tinted bulletproof windows and a micro weaponry hideout within the vehicle, I turn the key over and head out the gate. As I'm turning out of the underground garage, my grandfather, Arthur Sr., calls.

Well perfect fucking timing for me.

Hitting accept on the Bluetooth feature, I keep driving a roundabout way to throw off potential threats as I talk with Pops.

"Hey, Pops, what's going on?"

"My favorite grandson! How are ya, my boy?"

"I'm your only grandson, Pops." I chuckle. "But good, just running a quick errand, then heading home for the night. Hats to make later." He knows that means Syndicate business. We wouldn't want to tip off a potential wiretap or screen calling somehow. Never fucking know who we really piss off nowadays. *Not surprising.*

"Ahh yes, been meaning to ask about those, my boy. Everything good with the hats?"

I snort. He knows I never sugarcoat shit with him. He hates my father just as much as I do. *Thank fuck.*

With a loaded sigh, I know exactly what he is going to ask. "And what might I ask did my *joyous* namesake do *this* time? I can only imagine what he could do that would actually surprise me anymore. His list of infractions is rather long."

"Forced arranged marriage. For Declan, Giovanni, and me. This coming summer."

Dead silence.

"Pops? You there, old man?"

"Old man? Sinclair, I can still kick your ass, and you know it. Don't fuck with me, boy. Is this some sick joke to send me to an unwanted grave?"

"I fucking wish, Pops. They sprang it on us last night. All in agreement and they have made their choices as to who each of us will marry. Something about stronger ties and bullshit like that. Thank fuck Giovanni saved our asses with Grandpa Carter, Nonno Martinelli, and you. Said that shit isn't possible without you three agreeing too."

"Goddamn right that boy Giovanni is. Gianluca! James! Get your useless ball sacks in here! We've got an issue."

Issue? That's putting it lightly. Then I hear muffled shouts from Deck's and G's grandfathers as they are all going to wherever Pops is located in whatever time zone they decided to enjoy for the week.

"Sinclair, setting the phone down real quick. Don't hang up."

I don't even bother responding, and I just keep driving as I text the guys that I'm about five minutes out. Of course, Declan has to be a smart-ass about it, further pissing me off until G answers and ends the feud. All the while I heard the heated and animated voices of our grandfathers, furthering suspicions that they have all been excluded from this decision and are now furious about it.

"Sinclair, you are on speaker."

"Hey, Nonno. Hey, Grandpa. Yes, Pops. I'm not lying. Get a hold of Deck and G to prove it. It ended with a drinking wager against Declan if that helps verify the truth for you. Also, disappointed in your skill set, old man. Can't fucking lie to any of you. Too much respect."

"Sweet mother, that boy," Grandpa Carter mumbles.

We all know when Deck is in a rager mood, he is furious. They have also lost way too many bets against us in the process.

"Not slipping ya little shit. Well, we will be in touch very soon. Gotta pick up that unannounced hat order. Love ya, boy."

"Love you fuckers too. Kiss the wonderful women too."

Nonno Martinelli finally chirps in, "You just want Nonna's cooking and sweets, you voracious gluttons."

"Damn straight." I laugh, then hang up as I pull up to the entrance. I find the shittiest excuse of belongings sitting with Deck and G standing nearby as I park, pop the trunk, and get out.

"That everything?"

"Yeah. That's it," Deck deadpans. Asshole.

"She still asleep?"

With a smart-ass shrug, he says, "Was a minute ago."

Fucking Christ. I can feel my blood pressure starting to spike with his juvenile attitude.

"Finish loading everything," I order. "I'll go get her. Gio, you drive back."

As I start to walk toward the door, Declan turns up the delinquency to a perfect ten. The shithead bows, then smirks while talking out his ass. "Yes, master. Anything else, master? Do we get cookies for being good boys, master?"

Almost instantly G mutters, "Jesus Christ." While I just deadpan him with a look that would have most shrinking back into their self-righteous shells. After a quick second, I just toss the keys to Gio and walk away before I knock Declan off his six-foot-six high horse.

As I walk down the stairs, my blood boils even more at the situation in general. I know this shit that both Bethani and God only knows how many more people have lived through is a direct result of my self-absorbed father. This is nothing more than a giant tax write-off, something to show at the events he parades himself at, or some sort of cover for an even more nefarious activity. I'm guessing the second is more of a likely outcome, with the first just being a bonus to the bullshit facade he promotes to the world. Humble philanthropist my fucking left nut.

Bethani is still passed out, which isn't surprising in the slightest. She is a hot-ass mess compared to the other night, but still one of the most gorgeous and infuriating creatures I've ever come in contact with. I quickly scoop her up into my arms, and as her head lulls into my shoulder, a wince of pain whimpers from her lips.

"Shit. Sorry," I whisper, knowing she won't hear me. But since I'm not a complete monstrous dick head every waking minute, a little chivalry goes a long way. And for some unknown reason, this curvy, mouthy little vixen has crawled her way under my skin—*our* skins. She's already bringing out sides of myself I wasn't even sure were possible within my frigid dead soul.

As I'm walking up the stairs, she starts mumbling in her sleep, making me chuckle until she utters words that stop me dead in my tracks.

"Ante...Mortem." Then there is a small snort of, "Infidelitatis," before she mumbles more nonsense and goes back into a deeper sleep. Her breathing evens back out while I'm standing there with my mouth agape, eyes wide as fucking saucers, and completely in unrequited shock.

How does she know our motto?

Our fucking motto.

The Trident Syndicate motto.

Not even the wives of members know that motto. Utterly oblivious to our...for lack of better terminology, cult like status.

"You look like someone hit your G-wagon, dude. What's going on?" Gio asks, violently throwing me out of the tailspin my mind is going through.

I quickly regain my usual asshole demeanor, steeling myself because this is a conversation *not* for anywhere but our penthouse.

"Tell you when we get back home," I mutter as I walk away to get into the back seat with Bethani still in my lap.

Gio shuts the door for me and I mutter a "thanks" out to him, which causes Declan to whip his head back at me, giving me an incredulous expression. "Someone hit your G-wagon dude? Did you die and get replaced with a Sinclair that has manners?"

"That's what I said," G adds, glancing back at me through the rearview mirror. His bright blue eyes pierce me with one of his studious gazes. He knows something has knocked me out of sorts.

Trust me. Your time is coming quickly, cocksuckers. You'll be equally stunned.

Glancing out the window as we head another long way back to our building, I remind them, "Not a conversation for anywhere but our place. Multiple things that need not be said in public, if you catch my drift." I turn back, catching the ominous looks on their faces as they nod in understanding.

The rest of the ride is silent as we get back to the garage. Once parked, Deck hops out and grabs one of the carts we use for heavier shit to load Bethani's belongings on. They both unload while I sit in the SUV, studying her and wondering how in the ever-loving fuck she knows our phrase. I barely register the back hatch closing as I auto-pilot my ass out of the vehicle, and we all walk to our private service elevator.

Once we reach our floor, we all make our way to one of the guest rooms in the same hallway. We choose the one closest to our rooms in the opposite hallway, but also closest to the main living space. I quickly set Bethani on the bed and get her covered up, then I go to grab her a glass of water and painkillers and set them on the end table. Once she's taken care of, I walk out to the bar area and pour myself a heavy dose of bourbon. I slam it back and start pouring a secondary glass for myself, then grab two others and fill them as the guys walk over.

"Gonna need these," I say as I hand each of them their rocks glass. I chug the second one, feeling the glorious burn as it ripples down my throat and settles into my stomach. That warming of liquid courage flows through my body.

"She knows the motto," I state, pulling off the Band-Aid.

They both look at me like I'm a blithering idiot, which I probably am in my current state of mind.

Declan speaks, "Uhh...tons of mottos, dude." He shoots his drink, then shoves it to me for a refill before continuing. "Why don't you like, I don't know, start at the beginning or something that actually makes some sort of fucking sense?"

I sigh heavily, not sure which part to even begin with. Apparently my incorrigible mouth decides word vomit is the better choice, furthering their affirmation that I am, indeed, a blithering idiot. Thank you, alcohol and shock. Fucking trifling bastards.

"Called Pops on the way back. God knows where he, Nonno, and Grandpa are with our grandmothers, but they sounded like they were having fun. He asked what was up. I told him about the shit show our fathers have orchestrated. Cue him going off his rocker, then calling Grandpa and Nonno into the conversation away from prying ears. He put me on speaker so they could hear the confirmation from me. Also, prepare for phone calls from them. And an ass chewing for you over us betting against your alcohol usage of the night in question, Declan." I stop to take a deep breath for the next part, while also noticing the glare from Declan. "They all made the decision to be here soon, very soon. Our dads won't know until they are walking into counsel to light the proverbial shit on fire. Now the other part..." I trail off, still not sure how this one will go. "As I was carrying Bethani up the stairs, she started mumbling in her sleep. That cute girly mumble bullshit. Then she said the motto."

Yet again. More confused glances mirror back at me, amping my frustration and agitation up even more. "The. Fucking. Motto."

They sit there another second before a damning realization crosses their faces. "You don't actually mean *that* motto, do you? Like, *our* motto?" Giovanni finally asks, disbelief coloring his features.

"Ante Mortem Infidelitais. Yes, *that* fucking motto. You asked me earlier why I looked like someone hit my vehicle. Well, there's your damn reason." I snarl at them like a caged lion, which would honestly be an accurate as fuck description of my thought process. Chaotic, messy, ready to be let the fuck out and unleash hellfire on the world. Yeah, my body tingles with sensations that only happen when that deep-seated thirst for blood comes into play.

Control keeps the urge at bay, but with everything going on, the monster is scratching the surface, ready to play. Ready to make someone bleed. Craving that infinite rush that comes from seeing a crimson pool on a floor is the most indescribable feeling ever.

I'm losing the battle with the urge, so I quickly chug my third glass and pour a fourth. Sometimes alcohol quiets the beast within me, other times fueling the passion. I'm hoping for the former, seeing as how we have counsel in a bit.

"Fuck, how much time do we have?" I ask.

Muttered curses flare from all of us as we look at our watches. We realize we have thirty minutes to be ready and in the catacombs. *Fuckkkkk.*

Each of us breaks off to find our suits and make ourselves half-assed presentable, which takes zero effort seeing as how our black Armani suits are fitted to perfection for us. I pair the suit that I only wear for Syndicate business with a black dress shirt, black tie, back dress shoes, and my Trident ring. I'm done in roughly seven minutes.

Walking out of my room, I see the guys standing in the living room in their matching suits. There is a customary curse that we all have to look identical for this. But rules are rules. We head to the hidden elevator in our penthouse that is used for this specific purpose alone: going to Syndicate business in the catacombs beneath the campus. One of the perks of being the future leaders of the Trident and the current kings of campus.

Private elevator. Expensive 8,000 sq. ft. penthouse on campus. Houses all over the world. Top-notch service anywhere we go. Women who flock to us in drones, down to do whatever we want, when we want, just to say they've been with us. Extensive vehicle collections. The list goes on and fucking on.

I'd give it up in a fucking heartbeat.

This lifestyle has turned me into a bloodthirsty motherfucker. I'd rather slit someone's throat and watch the life drain out of their eyes than negotiate or make amends to appease the masses. Working out for hours or fucking chicks into a damn near coma are the only ways to keep the beast at bay sometimes. Other times, I have to drink myself into goddamn oblivion while locked in my room and wishing the liquor would end my miserable fucking life.

Nights like tonight, the alcohol is only fueling the monster. It's raging inside me, eager to escape. As I'm riding the elevator down the roughly forty flights, it's only getting worse. I'm clenching and unclenching my fists, trying to contain myself. Declan and Giovanni don't even bother me. They already know the internal war I'm fighting.

As the elevator dings, we step out into the hallway only to be greeted in the lounge area with our drinks on a platter being held by one of the junior members. Then three other members walk up with our robes and masks and one bows to speak.

"Master Blackwell, Master Carter, Master Martinelli, if you will allow us, we have been tasked with the honors of dressing you in your ceremonial robes for the newest pledges. May we?" he asks with a slight gesture to my robe and mask.

I snatch up my drink, shoot it down, and then nod to the pathetic kid in a 'go ahead' motion.

New pledges?

Well, that was the notch in the right direction I needed.

Guess my blood lust will be satisfied after all.

Embrace it. Accept it. Relish it.

Unleash the inner fucking beast.

Chapter 12

Giovanni

G lancing at Declan as Sinclair nods to the junior members in allowing them to dress us, we share an all too fucking knowing look. Sinclair will be shedding blood tonight. There is no controlling him when he gets this way.

Just let it fucking happen.

The pledges better be prepared for what's to come. Other than the ridiculous process of even being considered as a member, let alone the even more insane process of being accepted into the folds. This, *this* is the *true* test.

Do you really have what it takes to become a part of this soul-sucking society? The constant secrecy, lies, manipulation, illegal acts and more?

Can you fucking kill someone who has crossed you wrongfully? Can you really stand there, slit their throat for their crime, and come out of it without killing yourself in the process?

If so, welcome to fucking hell. Welcome to The Trident. You signed your death wish the moment a person's blood starts spewing from their jugular. Yes, the connections and lifestyle are even better than you've ever experienced, regardless of your wealth status. But your soul is eternally damned for the rest of your days.

You also acknowledge that if you cannot go through with the process of cold-blooded murder, you *will* be looking over your shoulder for the rest of your damn life. Try and outsmart us, we dare you. Give us a reason to drag you back kicking, screaming, crying, and pissing your pants to our sacrificial room. We will make a mockery of you. We will torture you until you are begging for death.

That's the price you pay for speaking of us. For trying to bring us out of the shadows.

Most that don't pass the final test, eventually end up dead at our hands in one way or another. Declan, Sinclair, and I are all numb to it. As much as we are obstinate assholes who take no shit from anyone, we are also horrifically groomed to this. We had no choice. Either become numb to the shit or be six feet under because the leeches didn't raise pussies.

Fathers of the year? Yeah, not a chance.

More like cynical, borderline psychotic tyrants of the year.

As we stride into the induction room, a frigid chill settles over us. It's like the souls that have perished here never leave. Since their ominous souls cannot cross over into the afterlife, they run amuck in here.

We settle into our chairs on the podium, our weapons of choice sitting next to our chairs. The platform above us already has our fathers sitting there, waiting for their grand gesture bullshit speech to all. Five bodies in front of us are kneeling on the ground. There are black cases over their heads, while their wrists are shackled and attached to metal rings bolted into the stone flooring. The five pledges all stand behind them, all with facial expressions ranging from cool and collected to downright terrified. It's comical as fuck and takes everything in me to remain stoic, regardless of the mask.

I haven't even got my hands fully on Bethani yet, much less my dick inside her, so I'll take 'Staying professional and keeping my life for another day' for five hundred bucks.

And of course, thinking about sticking my dick inside Bethani has the bastard back to full attention. *Down, you pre-teen bastard, we do not have time for this.* Thank fuck for the robes, otherwise I'd be looking like a fifteen-year-old seeing tits for the first time.

My father starts speaking first, bringing my focus back to the present and knocking my dick back down to normal due to the realization that it's not getting any action right now.

"Welcome to your final test, gentlemen. This is your last chance to prove to us if you are committed and worthy to us. You have been vaguely briefed. Do you all acknowledge the consequences if you so happen to fail?" He stops while the pledges all nod and collectively say "Yes, Master" in unison. "Excellent. Gentlemen, I pass the torch to my fellow brother to explain the induction process." And with that I can hear him sit back down as Declan's dad stands to explain. Same shit different day.

"Your final test. You see in front of you a person kneeling in submission. Do you boys all remember the questionnaire where we asked who you hated with unrequited passion?" They all nod. "Well, who you have before you is that person."

Their eyes all go wide as saucers as understanding slowly crosses their features. Robert motions to someone, and they walk over with a covered serving platter. They open the lid to reveal five knives.

"Each of you will take a knife from the plate, announce your name, and then the person's name kneeling before you. After that, you will tell us why you despise the person so much, then you can either take the bag off to face the person or leave it on. It doesn't matter. Either way, you will end their lives. If you pass, you will be welcomed into the brotherhood. If not, let's just hope you don't have loose lips." He stops, obviously doing the same thing we are, gauging their reactions and wondering who is strong enough and who isn't. "Who would like to go first?"

The one kid I notice, the shortest of them all, closes his eyes, takes a deep breath, then opens his eyes. "I will, Master Carter."

"Name, boy," my father instantly demands from right behind me. He's probably irritated at the kid for showing initiative. Typical.

The kid steels himself a little, *good for you kid*, before answering. "Alfonso Berchelli, Master Martinelli."

Ahh, that makes sense. His family is a bunch of weasels in the 'cheese business'. Basically importing cheese from Italy, with a notorious history of drug smuggling in the process along with other illegal ventures. Sitting here watching the cowardice rolling off him in waves, I'm wondering what could rattle a person in his family.

"State the person you hate below you and the reasoning for said hate."

"The person I hate is none other than my uncle Roman Berchelli. The reason for said hate...he raped my sister. She killed herself last year at only fourteen. No one believed us over him." A tear rolls down his cheek, breaking through his attempt to be ruthless like the rest of us.

Glancing through the mask, I see Sinclair's and Declan's white knuckle approach the same as mine. This sick fuck raped his fourteen-year-old niece? If whatever-his-name doesn't kill him,

Sinclair is definitely in the mood to step up to the plate, along with Declan and me.

"Your reason is valid." With a snap of one of their fingers, another lower member walks over with a tray holding a knife for him. "Take the knife, uncover his face if you so wish, then dispose of him."

The kid shakily grabs the knife, pulls off the sack on his uncle's head, and then steps around to face him. Roman sneers at his nephew, then spits on his feet.

"Fuck you, you little traitor. I fucking told you your time was coming next. That little bitch sister of yours asked for every damn thing I did to her. Dirty little whore, just like her queer older brother." He laughs maniacally. "My brother raised the weakest little punks ever. Disgrace."

The kid stands there, taking the shit and not moving. He's almost petrified facing him. Finally, after a few moments, he strikes. A single deep slice across his face. It's enough to make the man swear in English and Italian, but he still throws insults in the process. As the kid stands there, shaking like a wilted leaf, Sinclair must have decided that this kid didn't have the gall to actually go through with it.

He quickly stands up, walks down the stone steps, snatches the knife from Alfonso, and then violently thrusts it into the man's dick, making him scream out in excruciating pain. Sinclair gets off on this shit. Fuck, to some degree we all do. After torturing and killing the bastard that aided in my mother's death, I got back to the penthouse and fucked Declan for three hours. The high is unbelievable when serving our own fucked up form of vigilante justice.

As Roman is still withering in pain, Sinclair steps around behind him, grabbing his hair and wrenching his head back at an odd angle to face him.

"Sick fuck. Your own motherfucking niece? I'll fucking show you just a taste of what you deserve." Then Sinclair shoves him back forward before leaning down and shoving the knife as hard as he can straight into Roman's asshole. Then he twists the knife around, shredding his anal cavity into dust as the screams pour from Roman. "You deserve much worse than this, you twisted, demented bastard." Through the strangled cries, Roman spits a "fuck you" at Sinclair. I just laugh.

Wrong thing to say, cunt bag.

Deep psychotic laughter comes from Sin as I feel our fathers inching closer to our chairs in front of them.

"Far enough, Sinclair. Finish him so we can move on." His father's demanding words silence him temporarily.

Slowly Sin takes his mask off, and his eyes are demonic-looking. They look almost pitch-black because of how blown they are from being under the mask. He grabs Roman's head again and easily tilts it back as the blood loss has finally immobilized him a bit.

"You want this pervert gone? Fine." And with that, he slashes the bastard's neck from ear to ear. It's deep enough that he almost decapitates him as the blood pours from his jugular, pooling all around him.

Sin's breathing is labored from the adrenaline and alcohol, which fuels his actions, but the tinge of exhaustion is there. Handing the knife back to Alfonso, he states, "You were never cut out for this shit. Get the fuck out and never speak of us again, or I'll fucking hunt you down myself and do worse than that to you."

Then Sin walks the fuck out, leaving a room of shell-shocked initiates all trying not to vomit or pass out. I stand up, Declan following suit, and we walk down the stairs.

As I pause at the body, I take my mask off and look at the other initiates. "If you can't do that." I point at Roman's body. "Walk your bitch asses out now. The same offer Sinclair offered Alfonso here stands for your prissy rich boy selves too. Don't fuck with the Trident. We will find you. We will end you. Choice is yours."

We walk out to the dismay of our fathers and can hear them cursing us from here to Mars and back as we walk out of a mandated event. I flip a one-fingered salute in retaliation, knowing that soon enough our grandfathers will be here to settle some scores and bring order back to the chaos our fathers created.

"Think he is gonna lock himself in his room after that?" Declan's voice spears through my thoughts.

I shrug as we walk toward the elevator. "Who fucking knows? He has no discernable pattern when he is that far gone and then gets to act on the urge." I pause as D presses the button, and I check the locator app. "Says he is in the gym showers right now. If he actually stays down there, I'll be highly surprised." The doors open as we step inside. I shove my phone back into my pocket, over tonight.

Groaning, I pinch the bridge of my nose in between my fingers. "Should we check on him or leave him alone?"

When Declan doesn't immediately answer, I open my eyes slightly to see a smug as shit grin on his face.

"What?"

He stays silent but flips the kill switch to stop the elevator. "On your knees, G. Don't worry about him. All you need to focus on right now is sucking my dick long enough to forget shit for a minute before I sink deep into that tight ass of yours and fuck you into oblivion."

My dick instantly stands to aching steel in my suit, threatening to bust the goddamn zipper apart. I like being in control during sex, but fuck if submitting to Declan on occasion isn't one of the biggest turn-ons ever. Slowly, I sink to my knees, then reach for my belt to release my cock, hoping to relieve some of the ache. He tuts, steps directly in front of me, and uses one of his feet to stop my movements before he kneels in front of me.

"Did I say you could do that?"

I gulp at that gravely, deep, authoritative tone in his voice, my libido ramping up even more.

"No, sir."

"That's what I thought." Standing back up, he quickly removes his tie. "Hands behind your back." I fight his demand for submission for a second but then give in. Declan can be a teasing cock munch when he wants to. Last time I disobeyed his order, the fucker teased and tortured me for three weeks. But holy shit if that orgasm wasn't perfection when it finally happened.

With a devilish smirk, Deck is pulling his nine-inch throbbing dick out of his boxers. It's already dripping with precum, and *that* has me salivating. I lick my lips, ready and willing for him to shove it deep down my throat.

"You gonna be a good boy and take this cock deep down that willing throat of yours? Are you going to be a good little fuck toy for me?"

Fuckkk...his filthy mouth makes my already strained cock pulse even more. Like I said, I relish being in control in the bedroom. But this deviant somehow flips the tables on me, turning me into his willing submissive like it's nothing.

"Of course. Now move closer so I can suck your already dripping cock, *sir*."

That has his nostrils flaring, both at my smart-ass remark *and* the fact that he knows I can deep throat his ass better than any of the sluts who have crossed his willing and eager path. I quickly open my mouth and stick out my tongue, the silver of my tongue ring flashing in the light of the elevator. Declan's eyes flash in remembrance of what that tongue ring does to him.

"Goddammit," he growls, then steps forward to grab my hair and shoves his dick down my throat.

I groan as the taste of him hits my tongue. It's almost an aphrodisiac in and of itself. The vibrations of my groan reverberate up his cock, making him shiver.

"Fucking hell, G."

I smile while his dick is lodged down my mouth, thrilled at the reactions I can pull from him. His grip on my hair tightens as he starts slowly thrusting back and forth, going deeper and deeper down until he is seated fully down my throat and my nose is pressed against his stomach. As he starts to pull back out, I suck as hard as I can while wiggling my tongue around the underside of his cock. Both the suction against him pulling out and the sensation of the barbell in my tongue have him slamming his free hand into the elevator wall behind me, slightly catching me off guard and making me lose some of the suction in the process.

When he pulls almost all the way out, I start swirling my tongue around his dick, moaning at the glorious feeling of his erection in my mouth. I slow the swirling of my tongue down just enough to catch my ring against his dick piercing, eliciting a throaty moan from Declan, followed by a series of expletives.

We repeat the process for a few more minutes before he unexpectedly pulls out of my mouth with a wet pop from my drenched lips. Both of us are breathing heavily, and I'm ready to fuck him up over stopping when he reaches into his pants pocket and pulls out a condom and travel lube container.

"Stand. Up. Now," Deck demands through his heavy breathing. He's either ready to snap or come. I'm not sure of which.

"Mind untying me so I don't fall on my face?"

He chuckles. "You already did. I'm not fucking stupid."

Shit...thought I was sneakier than that. Guess not. As I pull my hands from behind my back, I quickly stand up.

"True. Just thought you didn't notice for once."

"Nice try, G. You may know how to suck my dick like a damn Hoover and make my eyes roll back into my head, but I'm still paying attention. Now turn around. Hands on the wall."

I smirk. "Yes, sir." Then I turn around and put my hands on the wall like he asks.

I feel him slowly walking up behind me. His hot breath on the back of my neck sends shivers down my spine as his hand reaches around to undo my belt and zipper. He's a lot slower than I want, but I don't say shit. As my pants hit the ground, his right hand grazes along the top of my boxer briefs, just enough to turn me on and piss me off at the same time. I already know this is payback. For what? The list is continuous. Ever so slowly, his hand inches its way farther and farther in, and my dick pulses so damn hard it's leaking with anticipation. I damn near come on the fucking spot when Declan's giant-ass hand finally encases my cock and starts stroking it with the perfect amount of pressure.

"Shit, Declan. Fuck, that feels good."

"Oh, it's gonna feel a hell of a lot better in a second," he says as he releases my cock and quickly shoves my boxer briefs down. Yet again, I'm ready to stab his ass because my sanity is a tight rope ready to snap over the sexual frustration from today. When I hear the condom wrapper rip open, I'm damn near delirious. And when I hear the lube packet tear, I know it isn't long until this god-awful tension will melt away.

Just as quick as Declan releases my dick, one hand is back on it and the other is lining his cock up between my ass cheeks. The slightly cold lube catches me off guard.

"Fuck, man, warm that shit up better next time. Christ!"

As his dick lines up with my glory hole, all coherent thoughts fly out the window. The pressure of his dick against my ass, his hand wrapped around my cock, and the newest sensation of his hand around my neck—my mind is completely blank. Fuck, I'm struggling to remember I need oxygen in my lungs. Thank fuck Declan reminds me, but I'm already on sensory overload, and we haven't even got to the best part.

"Breathe, Gio. Can't have you passing out before the grand finale."

As I'm inhaling much needed oxygen into my lungs, Declan's hand tightens around my cock, and in one hard, deep thrust, he is fully seated inside me.

"Fuckkkkkk," I moan while clenching around his dick, causing grunting noises from him.

He's most likely trying to contain himself so he doesn't blow in two point five seconds. I'm already so far fucking gone between the dirty demanding talk, him down my throat, and the teasing, that I literally don't give a rat's ass how long this lasts. Through clenched teeth, I take back some of the control.

"Declan, so help me if you don't fuck me hard and fast. I'm going to..." My words die as he pulls almost all the way out and slams his dick back into me while taking his lubed hand and jerking me off.

My hands are clenched against the elevator, knuckles white as fuck as Declan continues with his punishing thrusts in and out of my ass all while simultaneously keeping pressure on my dick with the up and down motions. How the fuck he can multitask so fantastically during sex, but can't walk and talk other times is mind-blowing. Currently? Thank fuck he can do both like a champ because I'm damn near ready to explode.

"Declan..." I moan.

"Fucking come, Giovanni. NOW!" he demands, then bites down where my neck and shoulder meet and flicks my apadravya piercing on my dick at the same time.

The sensations rocket through my body and I'm...just... fucking...gone. My orgasm smashes into me like a fucking dump truck. My head falls back into Declan's shoulder as a guttural groan falls from my lips. My dick seizes up as ropes of cum hit the elevator walls and floor. My ass muscles clutch Declan's cock and he thrusts into me a final time before I feel his body tense up. His cock pulses into the condom as he moans into my neck, the pleasure terrorizing his body with as much force as my orgasm did to me.

After a few minutes, our bodies finally regain some control, and we are able to somewhat coherently pull ourselves away from each other. Our bodies are sweaty giant heaps of 'I just had cock-tastically phenomenal sex, so fuck off if you think I'm going to function correctly' and neither of us can wipe the stupid-ass grins off our faces as we half-assed put ourselves into order somewhat.

Both of us still have our shirts untucked and our suit jackets unbuttoned when Declan hits the switch to finish our ascent to the penthouse. While I have my pants at least zipped up and buttoned, my belt is still hanging there like my spent dick. Declan's lazy ass barely got his belt on, but still has his zipper and pants completely undone.

"Shit. That was much fucking deserved and well needed."

I'm still attempting to regulate my breathing as I answer, "Yeah. Not gonna disagree with you. Pretty sure you broke my dick."

"Ha! Give it five minutes and we could both go again. Don't even bullshit yourself."

I can't even conjure a semi worthy response, so I just flip him the bird as the elevator stops.

When the doors slide open, we are met with the unexpected sight of Sinclair standing there in sweats and a T-shirt, just showered hair, with arms crossed and if looks could fucking kill, well, let's just say our asses would be six fucking feet in the ground already.

"Took you fucks long enough. Had to desecrate the elevator, I see. Fucking idiots."

"Uhhh..." Declan mutters, obviously just as flabbergasted as I am. We've never said anything about our sexuality to Sinclair.

"Wait...you know?" I ask.

His piercing green eyes continue their demonic assault on us as he glances back and forth between us. "Suspected for a while now. But your thirty-two-minute elevator ride and the fresh fucked looks when the doors opened confirmed it."

Rubbing one hand on the back of my neck, I'm at a complete loss of how to handle this. On one hand, I feel terrible keeping this from him because we don't keep shit from each other. On the other, his enraged reaction is the exact reason why we decided to keep him out of the loop.

Declan's dumb ass just shrugs because what else can he do. "Dude...we weren't exactly trying to keep it from you. Just didn't know how you'd take your two best friends both being bisexual, so yeahhh..."

Not exactly an 'I'm sorry', Declan, but I guess that's as good as it's gonna get because I'm still trying to find ground myself.

"Morons. Both of you." His arms finally drop as he motions us out of the elevator before turning away to walk toward the kitchen. "Don't give a flying fuck. But I'm pissed the fuck off you idiots kept it from me. Go fucking shower and meet me in the theater. You assholes get to watch my favorite movie as punishment."

The sick and twisted realization hits us at the same time, causing us to both groan and start bitching and moaning over Sinclair's trash-ass secret favorite movie, *Forgetting Sarah Marshall*.

"No! I am not watching that bullshit again, Sinclair. You can go fuck yourself with a fork for all I care," Deck bitches while I try to compromise.

"Come on, man, anything but that. Be reasonable."

Yeah, Sinclair and the word reasonable go together like hair dryers and bathtubs full of water. He pins us both with one of his notorious glares before dropping the dagger down on our pathetic asses.

"Nope. You've got two choices. Either watch the movie, or I print out those oh so precious pictures of you both dressed as girls when you were younger and plaster them all over campus. Maybe even a billboard on the freeway."

Fuck a duck and screw a kangaroo. That bastard prick.

With a defeated sigh, I just walk toward my room to shower. "Be down in ten, ass face."

I hear Declan's grump-ass temper tantrum steps not far behind me. "Stupid bastard ruined my post-orgasm haze. Cocky old fuck is just mad he didn't get laid today." Then the door to his room slams, as his bitching and moaning continue.

I just walk into my room, hit the shower, put comfy clothes on, and head toward the theater room after. I'm ready for another lame-ass night watching the one movie that somehow calms the murderous beast within Sinclair.

Whatever. He will get his payback one of these damn days for that stupid-ass picture.

Chapter 13

Bethani

Sun filtering through blinds...wow that feels wonderful. Wait, sun? My room doesn't have blinds. I'm thrown from a deep sleep as I shoot up in what has to be the comfiest bed I've ever been in. My body is completely unhappy with the fast movements. "Son of a bitch," I mutter as I try to gather my bearings. *Where am I?*

I sit there for a few minutes, glancing around at the minimally decorated room. I'm lying in what must be a king-sized bed covered in dark gray sheets, comforter, and pillowcases. The headboard is a simple dark wood with black padding on it. The night table, dresser with mirror, desk, and chair are all of the same modern design, making everything cohesive. A metal lamp sits on the nightstand with a black lampshade. The walls are a light gray and the curtains are somewhere in the middle for color between the walls and bedding. I can see what looks like the entrance to an attached bath, and I'm guessing that it's probably similar in design to the room. I'm currently too damn confused to move and find out.

Glancing back toward the nightstand, I see my phone sitting there along with a bottle of water, Tylenol, and a...note? Huh. Curious. Maybe the note has the answer to my numerous questions that are rolling through my sleep-muddled brain.

I quickly snatch my phone up before opening the Tylenol, taking three and chugging down half of the water to satisfy my thirst and get them all down. Normally I don't take the crap, but I know I'm going to pay if I don't. Reaching for the note, I glance at the unfamiliar writing, still curious. But when I finally look at the bottom, everything of the past couple days clicks back into place, and I'm instantly awake.

Bethani,
Morning, kitten.
Tylenol and water for you.
Take it so you don't feel like shit.
Bathroom is attached to your room. The closet is located in the bathroom.
That's where your boxes are with all your things.
Grab a shower, then come to the kitchen.
Sinclair

Shit! How in the hell did I forget this information? Then realization dawns on me, making me glare at the note. The cocky fucker gave me an orgasm to get me to agree!

I crumple the note and jump out of the bed, easily ignoring the pain with my newly found pissed off attitude. Stomping toward the door, ready to chew him a new asshole, my body reminds me that I haven't been to the bathroom in who knows how long. Rolling my eyes at myself, even more irritated that my body can't just get with the program that we are pissed and basic needs do not need to be a top priority, I turn toward the bathroom. Flipping the light switch, I'm temporarily stunned at how gorgeous it is.

A dark wood double vanity is what first catches my eye. A dark onyx marble counter sits on top of it with two deep bowl sinks that rest on top. A giant-ass mirror that looks bigger than anything I've ever seen complements the setup along with gorgeous pendant lighting. A huge natural stone open shower that looks like it could fit eight people is what draws my attention next. The glass is so pristine that you almost don't notice it, save for the metallic brackets holding it up. Three giant rainfall showerheads come from the ceiling, along with various others attached to the wall. A toilet and deep-set Jacuzzi tub are what I see next as I'm glancing around. Holy shit, this fucking bathroom is bigger than my dorm room! Jesus, it must be fucking nice to rule the school and be some of the richest and most influential people in the area.

As my bladder reminds me that it needs my starstruck ass to relieve it, I walk past the mirror and catch a glimpse of myself, thoroughly stopping in my tracks to fully turn and face the mirror in horror over my appearance.

Wow. Just...wow. I legit look like I got hit by a dump truck. My hair is a complete clusterfuck. Bruises litter my body along with tiny scratches that are thankfully starting to heal but are also itchy. My neck looks the worst, with the big bruises around it from Peter's hand, causing my body to shiver violently over the drug-induced memory of him.

I try to shake off the memory, knowing it isn't going anywhere anytime soon, but I need to compartmentalize it for a later date. Otherwise, I'll break down and bawl my eyes out or send myself into a panic that causes me to pass out. Neither of those sound like appealing options currently, so I close my eyes and take a few cleansing breaths until I feel normal again. Well, as normal I can feel right now.

I finally use the bathroom to my bladder's demanding request before taking a minute to find a towel and head over to the humongous shower. Glancing in, I see my stuff sitting in the cubby. That makes me quirk a brow, curious about their somewhat 'thoughtful' actions with this whole insanely messed up situation. Yet again, another thing to think about and get answers on. But first, I might as well take advantage of this badass shower with actual hot water before I potentially get thrown out on my ass.

Holy shit balls of fire and brimstone, so *that's* how the rich and famous shower. After spending a good half hour in the shower deep conditioning my poor hair and scrubbing all the dirt, grime, and some of the aches out of my body, I *finally* feel somewhat normal, given the circumstances. Wrapping the giant fluffy towel around my body and the other one around my hair, I slowly step out onto the marble floor. I really don't need to fall and bust my ass and add to the already long list of what hurts.

It would be easier to list what doesn't hurt in all honesty.

Sliding the pocket door open to the giant closet, I see all my possessions in a handful of labeled totes in the middle of the room.

Well, that sorry excuse of everything I own just sours my somewhat uplifted mood. Fuck you too, world. Fuck you too.

I rummage through them and find some socks, black leggings, and a lime sports bra before quickly saying screw underwear and going commando. After throwing everything on, I search around for a hair tie and damn near lose my shit over how I can't find anything. Thankfully, I finally find one and toss my hair up into a messy bun.

I'll deal with the consequences later for not taking a few minutes to properly brush it.

Whatever. My life is a current train wreck, so let's add my damn hair to the mix. I'll deal with it like I do with everything else. Sass and not giving up.

As I reach the door to my little, albeit temporary slice of heaven, I'm suddenly overcome with fear. *Who am I going to see? What are they going to say? Am I losing my scholarship and getting sent back to LA? What if they dug up shit on my past?* I do *not* have the mental capacity to deal with that can of worms right now. "Come on, Bethani, you got this," I mutter to myself, giving my body the much needed pep talk to get over it. Standing here like a scared damsel isn't going to achieve anything or answer the many questions I have.

With one last deep breath, I finally open the door to the unknown, only to have the ever-loving hell scared outta me.

"Jesus fucking ducks!" I scream as I launch the water bottle at Declan in retaliation. "The flying monkey hell is wrong with you!"

He successfully dodges my water bottle kamikaze as it flies into the wall across from me. His eyes are wide from shock as the bottle hits the floor. He slowly turns back to face me, palms up in surrender as I clutch my heaving chest, trying to regain a sliver of composure.

"Sorry, sunshine. I heard the shower turn on a little bit ago and uhh...got a little antsy waiting for you to come out. I was actually getting ready to knock when you came out," he finishes with a gorgeous but sheepish smile.

All I can do is hold my hand up in an attempt to get him to stop talking while I catch my breath. Currently, I'm not sure if I'm having issues from him scaring the donkey balls out of me, or if it's his mesmerizing rock god looks.

Declan is standing in front of me in nothing but a pair of low-hanging dark gray sweatpants, showing off a sinfully sexy V cut that tapers down into the land of the unknown. Of course, since I'm a glutton for punishment, I happen a quick glance at the prominent bulge in his sweats, and I have to struggle to withhold a gasp. *Holy shit, he is huge.* Like I can tell from just his sweats, he is bigger than any other man I've ever been with. Wow. Swallowing thickly, I move my way back up toward his face. Declan is built like an enormous, tattooed Greek god. The full sleeves of tattoos covering his muscular arms flow flawlessly into his shoulders, chest, and stomach. Waves, swirls, and shapes of color melt flawlessly between the blacks and grays. As I make my way up the expansive wall of chest and tattoos, I stop abruptly at his nipple piercings. His. Nipples. Are. Pierced. What I wouldn't do to give those sexy things a lick.

Lick? What the hell is wrong with me? Jesus, this walking Adonis sex-on-an-expensive-stick damn near scares the piss out of me, and all I can think about is how it would feel to have him pressed up against me. Hard and soft. Tall and short. His gigantic-looking dick maybe giving me a decent orgasm for once.

I close my eyes quickly, trying to control the undeniable lust that I know is showing on my face and oozing off my body. Stupid sweaty palms. *That's what happens when you don't get laid in over two years, dumbass.* Thanks for the reminder of my poor life choices there, internal voice of reason. Not. Also, fuck you too.

I slowly open my eyes, keeping my face neutral, only to be damn near screaming again when he is right. In. Front. Of. Me. I open my mouth to yell again, maybe kick him, when he surprises me by quickly lifting me up into his rock-hard body and walking us back into my 'room' just far enough to shut the door with his foot and pin me between the wall and him.

"What the—"

I don't even have the opportunity to finish when his mouth descends on mine. I'm so taken aback by the whole thing, I don't even realize I'm kissing him back at first until his tongue is demanding entrance to mine. I gather enough courage to deny him, making him growl a bit at my defiance before he caresses my lips with his tongue. I feel his tongue ring against my lips, making me gasp. That was most *definitely* his goal, because he quickly shoves his tongue deep into my mouth, causing our mouths to fuse together. We are fighting against each other for purchase as the passion and attraction flow through us. My lungs are screaming at me, but I'm not giving in to the burn. We are both so into the kiss, that we aren't even moving. There's no fondling of each other's bodies, we are just thoroughly enjoying the kiss that our brains can't compute anything else.

A sharp bang on the door finally separates us.

"Declan, you rotten bastard. Get the fuck out of there!"

I'm not sure which one said it, but from the bossy tone I'm going to assume it was Sinclair. I can vaguely remember his dominating aura yesterday when he gave me the first orgasm not by my own hands in a long time.

Declan is breathing just as heavily as I am when he whispers, "Ignore him," before flashing me a gorgeous smile. As I stare back into his flawless slate gray eyes, I realize I'm completely enthralled by them. While I can almost read the lighthearted nature behind them, I can also see the hazy turmoil. It's a troubled look, one that says his life is no walk in the park either, but he is still him through it all.

I feel that more than anyone will ever know. It's a struggle some days to keep my head above water and not just succumb to the darkness that wants to drag a person to the depths of hell.

"Declan Grant Carter. Either put Bethani down and come out so we can all fucking talk, or I'm coming in and dragging your horn dog ass out by your cock ring, fuck face."

Yup. That's definitely Sinclair.

Declan's eyes shut, and he tilts his head back, almost like he is praying for patience. Then, he groans. "God damn you, Sinclair *Alfred* Blackwell! Shit was getting good, fucker!"

Alfred? Alfred. I can't stop the giant, carefree laugh that bubbles out of me at that. I can't stop laughing to the point I'm almost doubling over into Declan's body at the admission. I'm still a giggling mess when I feel a kiss on the top of my head, and Declan moves to go back toward the door with me still wrapped around his body. He opens the door to a furious-looking Sinclair, and I can't help but laugh even more.

For what a stunning specimen Sinclair is, albeit a complete asshole, his middle name just doesn't suit him. My idiotic brain can't stop the manic laughing long enough to be even remotely serious at how irritated he obviously is over Declan's spill of his middle name.

"You just fucking had to say that, didn't you?"

Another amazing smile comes from Declan's full, slightly swollen lips, which are also adorned with a hoop piercing on the right side of his bottom lip.

"Made sunshine laugh and pissed you off. So that's a double win in my book. But you also started it by using *my* middle name first, asshole."

"Yes, but Grant is nowhere near as pompous and proper sounding as Alfred." I somehow force out the comment before another fit of laughter hits me.

A deep laugh rumbles out of Declan, joining in with me. That earns us both a vicious scowl from Sinclair's swirling emerald eyes, and his utter lack of amusement at our banter against him.

Giovanni's voice filters down the hallway from behind us. "Food's ready if you are all done arguing. I'm not waiting, so hurry up or piss off!"

And of course, my stomach and brain realize it's been way too long without food. It sends out a deep grumble in protest as my nose inhales delectable scents of breakfast food.

"Come on, sunshine. Let's get you fed before stick-up-his-ass here gets his panties all in a twist over his lack of control," Declan says as he starts walking toward the kitchen with me still attached to his body.

"You do realize I can walk, right?" I ask him as I arch an eyebrow at him.

"Yup," he chimes, popping the P at the end for emphasis. "Still not putting you down. You feel way too good in my arms, and since asshole there had to interrupt us, I'm going to hog all of your attention," he finishes as he walks us into the kitchen.

When we arrive, Declan promptly grabs a chair at the massive island, sits down, and then easily picks me up and places me back on his lap before sliding two massive plates of food toward us.

"Eat up, sunshine. G is a decent cook, and you haven't eaten in a while."

He then proceeds to shovel his own food into his face while keeping his left arm around my waist.

I'm staring at a massive plate of waffles, bacon, sausage, and eggs. As I'm trying to decide where the hell to start, Giovanni's voice breaks through my thoughts.

"Coffee, juice, milk, or water, Tesoro?"

I glance up to see an equally charming and shirtless Adonis smiling at me. Jesus Christ, what water did their parents drink when creating them? Seriously.

All three of them are fucking drool-worthy walking sex on sticks. Giovanni has gorgeous ice blue eyes that are just as entrancing and soul-stopping as Sinclair's emerald eyes and Declan's grays. But while all three of them are some sort of God's gift to mankind with their looks, I can see the differences between them easily.

Giovanni is somewhere in between the other two. He looks like he can be just as serious and rude as Sinclair, but he also looks like he can be equally carefree and wild like Declan. Giovanni has the least amount of tattoos at first glance. The only ones I can see are ones that match Declan and Sinclair perfectly. Something you see men from the mafia or an MC don in the movies. They are peculiar tattoos: skulls with a trident stabbed through the skull. They all have matching Latin scripts on their shoulder blades also. *Ante Mortem Infidelitatis.* I wonder what that means.

All three men are way taller than me. Declan is the tallest, while Sinclair and Giovanni are about the same height yet are not much shorter than Declan. Sinclair has the darkest hair, an onyx black color. Giovanni has dark brown hair that is just as silky smooth looking but slightly longer. Declan's hair definitely fits his personality. It's a chocolate brown color that is shorter on the sides and wild on top. It falls in his eyes when down, but when styled it's more faux hawkish, but in a way that is unique to him.

All three have the deep sexy Vs that cut into their low-rise sweatpants, adorned with sexy as shit happy trails that lead to their well-hung dicks. I'm going to assume Giovanni is just as well-hung like the other two. Sinclair most certainly is, verified by my spontaneous orgasm yesterday, and I can feel the boner I'm sitting on from Captain Cuddles lap, which hasn't quite left since our make-out session. All I see is chiseled chests, sinful six-packs, bulging broad shoulders, and sculpted facial features. Lord have mercy on womankind because just being here in the same room as these Greek gods is enough to make a woman want to strip down and let these lick-worthy specimens enact their deepest and darkest fantasies. Because these men, yeah, they can back up their cocky swaggers, and they know it.

I can feel the blush creeping up my cheeks as the thoughts run through my head of these guys naked and having their way with me.

"Coffee, please," I choke out. My voice is all throaty and breathy, giving myself away at what I was thinking. My blush flames even more as I quickly pick up a fork and start devouring the waffles.

I can't help but moan when the waffles and fruit combo hit my mouth, because *holy shit* are these good. One of them dropping their fork causes me to glance up to see three sets of eyes on me. I quickly swallow, then take a sip of the coffee.

"Why are you all staring at me?"

"Tesoro, you can't moan like that unless you want us to strip you down and see what else makes you moan."

"Would you rather me say your food tastes like shit then?"

"I'd much rather that moan come from you deep throating my cock and enjoying it, Bethani."

My eyes bulge, and my mouth gapes from his bold statement. "You can't be serious."

Sinclair snickers, which has me narrowing my eyes and turning toward him. "Yes, Satan? What glorious opinion would you like to share with the class?"

His smirk is now gone, and that glint that was in his eyes yesterday is back. It's predatory and dominating, stopping any more sarcasm falling from my mouth.

"Oh, kitten. That smart mouth of yours is going to get you in trouble one of these days." He straightens in his chair. The air feels thinner suddenly with his authoritative presence. "And when that day comes, you will be begging for it. I can't fucking wait to tame that smart little mouth of yours with my cock sinking deep in that tight little pussy of yours."

I can't fucking breathe for a second. My thoughts are a complete jumble as Declan's grip around my waist tightens and the throbbing of his dick between my ass cheeks is another reminder of what is going on here. Which in all honesty, I have no fucking clue.

Steeling myself a bit, I'm finally able to reply, "Just what makes you think I'm going to submit to you? Or any of you for that matter? I don't even get what you guys could see in some shitty scholarship student who lives in a basement, which you guys destroyed, by the way. If I get thrown out over that, I'm chopping all your dicks off. Because this stupid-ass school is my one shot at a decent life, and I'll be damned if your asshole actions ruin that."

Damn it, I probably said too much. The tension skyrockets over my admission, and the reminder of where I live here on this pretentious campus has three sets of dagger eyes pointed my way. I quickly start eating more food and keep my face down toward the plate in an attempt to avoid questions I don't really feel like answering.

"Nothing will happen to your status here as a student, Bethani Larie. You also don't live in that hell hole anymore. You live here with us, and that isn't changing anytime soon, whether you agree with it or not."

Okay, now he is just pissing me off with his bossy attitude. My temper flares, and I dish it right back at him. "Oh, excuse me? I wasn't aware that my permanent living situation changed indefinitely. What exactly is keeping me here? There are other rooms down in the basement that I can just as easily occupy. My key works in every other door down there. I also don't have a giant controlling pain in my ass down there to deal with either. So you can just fuck right off."

"Wait a fucking minute. The hell did you just say?" Giovanni hisses, throwing me off with the venom dripping from his voice.

"Uhh...that Sinclair is a giant douche canoe who needs a mannerisms class?"

He smirks at that but clearly isn't deterred.

"While I will agree with you on that, Tesoro, nice try. You were all issued the exact same key? That's what you said, right?"

I glance down again. "Not exactly," I mumble. Damn my big mouth.

"And what exactly *did* you mean, sunshine?" Declan says into my ear, making me shiver.

"You guys won't give up until I tell you what you want to know, right?"

"Yup," they all say collectively.

Inhaling deeply, I contemplate my options here. I have a feeling they can all be very, very persuasive if they want to be, and I don't know if I'm even remotely ready for something like whatever they come up with.

"Fine. I'll answer your questions. Within reason, of course. But I'm not answering another question until after I'm done eating, so suck it the hell up and deal with it."

"Fair enough," Giovanni answers.

Declan kisses my cheek. "Works for me, sunshine."

I glance at Sinclair, who still has his scowl on his face, but then he nods and goes back to eating with the other two.

At least I bought myself a few minutes of peace before the personal purgatory of my life gets dredged up.

Yay. Freaking. Me.

Chapter 14

Bethani

After finishing breakfast in silence, we all move to the living room area. I sit on one end of the massive U-shaped couch when Declan decides he still isn't done being up my ass. He promptly moves me and settles me against his side, while Giovanni moves to my right side and adjusts me to where I'm leaning against Declan, with my legs in Giovanni's lap. Sinclair sits in the middle section of the couch but not far away from all of us.

Clingy asses. It doesn't even make sense, but I'm not going to complain seeing as how Giovanni starts rubbing my feet and Declan is massaging my back gently, careful of the scratches.

"So...what would you guys like to know?" I finally ask to break the uncomfortable silence.

"Everything," Sinclair demands, which causes me to roll my eyes. "Watch it with that eye roll, kitten, before I come over there."

"Christ, Sin, can you chill out for two seconds?" Giovanni asks before turning back to me. "How about telling us about your acceptance here to the school and what it's been like for you, Tesoro."

That makes me smile. "Thank you for being so sweet, Giovanni. At least one of you has manners."

He smiles back and continues to rub my feet, which feels heavenly.

"Kiss ass," Sinclair grumbles, but I ignore him.

"I honestly wasn't planning on coming here at all. I was saving up and filling out scholarship options for one of the community colleges down in LA. One of the ladies where I lived saw an ad somewhere for this school, and she told me about an essay contest they have for people in situations like mine. I was skeptical about it, but she bribed my ass with her famous tamales and threatened to never make them again for me if I didn't apply. So I grumbled about it for a few days and finally sent in the essay at the last minute."

I stop and take a sip of coffee before continuing, "Somehow it was accepted, and I was awarded a full scholarship for tuition, books, a room, and the basic meal plan they have here. Three months later, I showed up for orientation all excited but quickly realized it wasn't that great. The nine other winners and I were excluded from the main orientation. We were basically given our maps of campus, told to declare our major and schedule classes, but we were not guaranteed to get them since we were some of the last ones to submit our stuff. Then someone walked us to the building we were staying at and told us that our key opened the door to our dorm area, but our rooms only had an internal lock and they aren't responsible for our possessions. Basically if you forget to lock your door when you are in there, then sucks to fucking suck. Thankfully, I taught myself how to lock my door and reopen it with my student ID, so I've been lucky for the most part."

I have to stop before I go down the rabbit hole of the jackass who thought he was funny and tried to scare the shit out of me. The memory makes me shiver, and Giovanni stops with his massage to give me a questioning look.

"What happened, Tesoro?"

I wave my hand in the air dismissively. "Nothing I couldn't handle."

Declan wraps his arms around me bear hug style. "Tell us, sunshine."

"I...took care of it. Trust me." I'm fumbling my words. It's embarrassing, humiliating even.

"Didn't say we don't trust you, baby B. We just want to know who needs their ass kicked, that's all."

"I'll answer if you can tell me why I'm not 'allowed' to go back to my dorm."

"Simple, kitten. One, that place is a fucking shithole from hell that's going to become unusable soon enough. Two, living in mold? Fuck that. Three..." He pauses, mulling over his words. "I guess you could say that we have an...interest in you. One that we would like to see how it evolves. You being here makes that easier, and after the attack, none of us trust that conniving rat and the seedy way he acts. This is the safest place on campus, and you won't have to be looking over your shoulder constantly."

Unusable? What the hell does that even mean? "I'll let the unusable comment pass for now. Only because, yeah, I agree that the mold everywhere sucked. I've bleached the place a handful of times, and it doesn't do anything. Also, I can handle Peter. He is just another spoiled prick who is mad because I wouldn't sleep with him."

Declan's grip around me tightens at the mention of Peter's name. Giovanni's and Sinclair's eyes flash with anger, but they quickly school it before Sinclair replies, "G will explain in a bit as to why we disagree and think fuck face isn't who he says he is, but back to the question, Bethani. What happened in your dorm? B+ for trying to deflect on the original question. F for thinking it would work."

"Dammit," I mutter before finally speaking. "A guy snuck into my room and attempted to get handsy with me. I kneed him in the balls. He walked out of my room, but before I could lock my door, he came back in with some brass knuckles. Thankfully I had my Taser at that point, so I used it on him. He cracked a couple ribs. I hit him with one point seven million volts, then broke his nose. Like I said, I took care of it. He left school a week later when he tried to talk to me, and I threatened to post flyers everywhere that he is a sick freak."

All three of them are just staring at me, faces blank. I'm not sure if they are surprised that I'm not a damsel in distress or at what Alessandro tried. As someone who witnessed her mother's demise with drugs, as well as the things men forced on her so she could get her fixes, I refused to be like that. While I don't know much about self-defense, I taught myself the basics to give myself a fighting chance if it were to happen to me. It's happened twice so far. The first one, I obviously prevailed. This most recent one, not so much. But the bitch drugged me, so it wasn't exactly a fair fight.

Giovanni pulls his phone out. "What was his name, sweetheart?" he asks while doing something on his phone, not looking up.

"Why?"

"Just answer him, sunshine. Trust me," Declan whispers in my ear.

"Alessandro something. I honestly don't remember."

"This him?" Giovanni asks, then he shows me his phone so I can see the student ID.

It is indeed him, so I just nod. He goes back to doing something on his phone for a minute.

"Currently serving thirty-five years in a California prison for rape of a minor, burglary, assault with a deadly weapon, and three parole violations."

"How did you find all that out so quickly?"

He just glances at me, flashing me a smile in the process, but says nothing.

"Self-taught hacker and computer genius, kitten. That's how we found you yesterday."

Declan also chimes in behind me, "He doesn't broadcast his skills, sunshine. Most nerds keep their skillsets well hidden because they get all pissy if someone takes their idea and makes it better."

Giovanni just flips him the middle finger while continuing to search on his phone. "Just don't want everyone and their damn mother asking for my help, like you two useless shit bags. I'm busy enough trying to meet your demands as is."

I laugh at that, then realize something. "Hold up. What all do you already know about me, then?" I ask, getting slightly defensive.

He just gives me a sheepish look, like a child being told they can't have candy. "Not much, Tesoro. That's why we are asking you. I figured I'd ask you before I started hacking the Washington state databases."

I still at the mention of my home state. I have nothing against Seattle, but it's not filled with many happy memories. I'm usually great at suppressing the memories and just ignoring that whole chunk of my life. I'm already mentally preparing for the questions about to be asked, but then I say screw it and start talking before they can inquire about something I physically can't answer without losing my shit.

"Before you even ask, I'll give you a basic rundown, but I can't go into details. You are just going to have to accept what I give you for now and let the rest go." They all nod, choosing not to speak and respecting my limited truth.

"I've never met my father. At least I don't *think* I've met him. My mother was a drug addict, so it was moving from shithole to shithole, while there was a random string of men that flowed through our door. I was never able to get a straight answer from her. Hell, I doubt she even remembered the truth when I was old enough to ask. It was either he left before I was born, or I was super young and she left him because he was abusive, or he is dead. Maybe it was a combination of the three?"

I shrug but continue, "Anyways, I became a ward of the state at ten when she got busted one too many times with a needle in her arm and while I was sitting beside her, begging her to wake up, one of her 'flings' came in. He had been there before and finally got sick of it, so he kept calling and coming back until the state finally came in and took me away. I stayed a ward until I filed to be considered a legal adult at seventeen. The state obviously didn't care. They approved me, and I took what little cash I had and made it to LA. I lived in the homeless shelter until I came here. Made a few friends in LA, and I still keep in contact with my one friend here, Stella. Other than that, I keep to myself, minus my lack of brain cells that caused me to spend the last two months of the last school year with Peter. I stayed in the dorm over the summer since I didn't have anywhere else to stay. I also found a little coffee house down the street I could walk to, and I worked there until classes started back up. So yeah. That's my life."

And I still do not understand how I have even remotely crossed these guys' radar, because they are their own damn universe compared to me. But that's a thought I keep to myself.

They just stare at me, not speaking. But the inquisitive looks on their faces tell the same story. They want more. More questions. More answers. More gritty details of my life that I'm not sure if I'm willing to delve into.

Chapter 15

Declan

Jesus Christ.

My dick wants to spring to life with this strong-willed woman in my arms. How in the *ever-loving hell* has she gone through all this shit, including things we haven't heard yet, but will once we gain her trust, and is still fucking standing proud like it's just another day of the week? It's such a major fucking turn-on that my dick continues to throb, so I have to nonchalantly adjust her in my arms so she doesn't notice. I want—no, desire to sink my dick so deep in her that all her bad memories float away and all she can remember is good shit.

Her intoxicating personality and feisty attitude is quickly becoming a vice I don't ever want to be rid of. Her will and grit to thrive, regardless of her environment, is a testament to what most could only pray for. She just naturally has that tenacity that turns me on like no other and makes me envious.

My thoughts get derailed when Gio hand signals '1-0-0'. Ah, so he is already in contact with someone about the prick who threatened her last year. Perfect. I nod in agreement and glance over at Sinclair. His features are schooled, but his right hand is white-knuckled in an attempt to control his demon. Just last night he killed someone over a similar, albeit more horrific situation. But that's one situation that can easily tip the scales against his controlled way of living. Abuse of a woman is his absolute one rule, and he will have zero remorse over teaching someone a lesson about it or flat out ending their life.

We have all become intensely and insanely infatuated with Bethani so quickly, and any threat against her, past or present, will be eradicated by us.

Finally, Sinclair motions '1-5-0' quickly, upping the price to ensure the problem is solved. Gio just glances back at his phone to confirm the details and use our offshore and iron-clad secret account for payment. One giant perk of being in our positions is more money than we know what to do with. We also have many ways to ensure our situations get handled when we cannot do it ourselves.

"I'm surprised you guys haven't bombarded me with a bunch of questions."

"Plenty of questions, kitten. Figuring out which ones to ask is the real dilemma," Sin states.

"You can ask any question you want, Sinclair. It's irrelevant. Whether I decide to answer or not is the actual dilemma," she fires back. I can't help but chuckle. Watching her verbally spar with Sin is pure entertainment because he does not tolerate shit from anyone, save for G and myself. Even that's debatable at best most days.

His arms cross over his chest, and he's glaring at her with an intensity that I know is both rage at her continuous defiance and lust for the exact same reason. Giovanni and I sit back to enjoy the show unfolding in front of us, wondering who will win.

Sinclair adjusts, resting his arms on his thighs and steepling his hands together under his chin. His calm demeanor is a dead giveaway that he has a plan to best her. I'm curious about how it's going to go when he finally decides to speak.

"Why LA?" he asks.

Huh? Not what I would have asked. Where is he going with this?

Bethani shrugs in my arms. "Easy. Seattle is rainy. I wanted constant sunshine, and the ample opportunities there seemed like a good choice. Plus, I ran out of funds for the bus, and I wasn't cutting into my food money to go farther."

Sunshine, if I have my way that will never be an issue again.

"And the city was good to you?"

"I guess."

"Elaborate, kitten," he commands, and she huffs at it.

"Manners, *Sinclair*?"

He just rolls his eyes but uncharacteristically complies. "Please elaborate, kitten. Better?"

B ignores his antagonizing. "Like I said, I lived at the homeless shelter the whole time but made a few friends. I fell in love with the culture of the Latin district nearby, which is why I love Spanish food now. Had a part-time job, so I didn't have to rely on the shelter for everything. But it's expensive there, so I wasn't able to change my living situation. But it could have been worse. I also volunteered at the shelter as my payment for being there."

Yet again, I'm blown away by her response. Also extremely humbled by it. While we have never wanted for anything in the aspect of frivolous things, she has had to suffer and fight for everything that was essential to living. We asked, we received. No questions asked. She probably had to beg and scrounge just for bites of food. But she does seem to share the similar broken home lifestyle we do. Shit for dick parents that are pretty much useless and unloving as fuck. Which has me wondering.

"You went hungry a lot, didn't you?" I ask.

I feel her tense a bit at my question. That's all the answer I need, but she still replies.

"Yeah. I did. More than I feel comfortable letting any of you know. But that changed in LA."

Giovanni still hasn't said much since we sat down, but I can see by the concentration on his face that he is close to saying something. He is most likely holding back because he is hacking whatever database he needs for information.

"While I would love to keep answering these questions, guys, I really need to start working on some classwork. I've got an essay due Tuesday, and I need to hit the library. Plus, I still have to find all my stuff, since I have no idea where you put anything in the boxes."

"Hold on," Giovanni says, then he stands up and heads to his room quickly. He returns with a Mac box and iPhone box. "For you, sweetheart." He sets them on her lap before sitting back down.

B just looks down at the boxes in her lap momentarily before finally looking up. "Uhh...what are these for? I have a laptop and a phone already."

Sinclair just snorts and mumbles, "Yeah, junk ones." Which quickly pisses off Bethani.

"Well, excuse me, cocksucker. I'm sorry my pedigree and bank account aren't impressive enough for you. But I'm not fucking sorry that I can actually appreciate everything I have, unlike you, you arrogant spoiled bastard. Fuck this."

She quickly stands up, dropping the boxes on the couch to leave, but Sinclair is quicker. He snatches her up and throws her over his shoulder.

"I never once condemned your situation, kitten. I'm just saying your shit is outdated as fuck, and you are lucky it still works. So knock off the bitch attitude." Then smacks her ass, hard.

"Motherfucker! That hurt! Put me down!" she screams.

"You done being a bitch?"

"You done being a bossy asshole?" she mocks.

He smacks her ass again, but before he can react, Bethani grabs a hold of the waistband of his boxer briefs and yanks as hard, fast, and high as she can, giving him an atomic wedgie. Sinclair roars and drops to his knees, most likely from the pressure against his dick and balls, but also the chaffing Bethani has accomplished between his ass cheeks. She turns into a terrorist as soon as her feet hit the ground, and she pulls even harder, forcing Sinclair to his hands and knees completely. He's cursing up a storm at the pain before she releases the torn underwear. Then she shoves him on his side while he is retching from pain and trying not to puke.

"I will not put up with your shit, Sinclair. I've dealt with enough already, so knock it off, or the next time I'll pull so hard your piercing tears out."

That has G and myself groaning and cupping our dicks in defense, bringing her attention back to us.

"No shit from us, sunshine, promise. Just leave our piercings alone. Please," I beg.

She blushes deep as shit when she remembers we all have our dicks pierced.

"Oh, yeah...I forgot about that," she mumbles, furthering her blush.

It's cute as hell, but I'm staying leery of the tiny, curvy terror that is in front of us currently.

"Yeah, Tesoro. We *all* have our dicks pierced. But unlike Sin, we value our male anatomy. So why don't you go get ready, and Declan and I will escort you to the library. We have papers coming up too and need to study. Asshole there can lick his wounded pride in private."

"Wait...we do?" I ask quizzically. Fuck me. What did I forget now?

G just stares at me for a second before looking toward the ceiling. "*Gesù Cristo.* Yes, Declan. We both have a paper due in Business Ethics 403. This right here is why we have the exact same schedule.

Giuro che vivo con un bambino gigante." Then runs his hand through his hair in frustration.

"A. English, asshole. B. When is it due again?"

"Ten pages. Tuesday, dumbass."

Whoops...yeah, forgot about that one. Standing up, I step over Sinclair, who is still on the ground. "Come on, sunshine. Guess it's time to be studious or some boring shit like that."

That has her giggling and it's music to my freaking ears. Then I run over to the freezer and grab a bag of peas before I return to Sin and drop them in front of him.

"Here ya go, fuck face. Figured your dick needs these more than G's carba-whatever shit that tastes good as fuck. So you better replace them. It's your week for groceries."

"Fuck you, asshole. She broke my dick."

"Cristo...it's *carbonara*. How many times do I have to tell you that?"

"And I'll do it again, asshole!" Bethani yells from the hallway, which makes Sin groan in pain.

I just walk away toward my room, laughing at his pain, then shrug my shoulders at G. "Whatever it's called, I want that for dinner."

"Uhh...just go grab your shit, and if you can actually accomplish something at the library, then maybe I'll make it."

I contemplate for a second, then agree. "Fine. But when I prove your ass wrong and accomplish more than the bare minimum you have in mind, I'll have more requests."

"Deal."

And *that's* exactly what I do. After spending fifteen minutes in my room finding my shit, Gio, Bethani, and I spend four mind fucking numbing hours in the god-forsaken library working on our shit. But I both prove G wrong and have a fan-fucking-tastic time flirting with Bethani like a goddamn teenager with his first crush.

And when we get back, G makes a bomb-ass chicken and bacon carbonara, homemade breadsticks, and somehow tiramisu. I eat like a fucking king alongside my crew and B, all while we berate a pissed off Sinclair.

For the first night in, well, I have zero fucks clue as to how many, I go to sleep with a smile on my face and no itch to numb myself with alcohol, pills, or even weed.

I think I found my new favorite vice.

Chapter 16

Giovanni - Two weeks later - Mid October

"**S**o you actually passed that midterm? You're fucking kidding me."

Declan hits me with a cocky smirk as we ride up the elevator, done with classes for the day.

"Yup. B+, motherfucker. Sunshine has been helping me study a bit. *She* doesn't explain it all fucked up like you do."

Well, color me impressed as shit. Declan doesn't study, and he doesn't show up for class much. Usually he relies on me for most of the homework just so he can slide by in classes. Like any of us could actually fail if we wanted to. Our parents rule this university. If none of us showed up for a single day of class, we would all receive a C+/B- average. Yeah, it's sickening as fuck the treatment we get here, but there is nothing we can do about it. None of us ever had a choice. The moment we were declared 'boys' on an ultrasound machine, our lives were set in stone.

Sinclair will take over Blackwell Industries and eventually become the leader of the Trident. BI has its hands in so many things it's not even funny. Technology and security are the breadwinners of Blackwell, but they also have about sixty sister companies in addition to the main operation.

Declan's family owns Carter Pharmaceuticals, which he will take over along with being second-in-command to Sinclair in the Trident. Carter Pharm is the leading company in the world for multiple drugs. Cancer drugs, a vaccine for a nasty and super contagious flesh-eating virus, and a drug to help with diabetes are the company's biggest producers. Also, like Blackwell Industries, Carter Pharm has its hands in as many drug formulations as possible. It's constantly trying new things for different ailments, viruses, diseases, and whatever else this fucked up world can conjure up.

My role? Other than being third-in-command to Sinclair and Declan along the walls of the Trident, I'll eventually take over Martinelli Entertainment Industries. My family owns luxury resorts, spas, clubs, and restaurants all over the world. While all the names are different as they can be depending on location, if you see the MEI logo, you know you will be stepping into the highest quality and best service money can buy.

All this shit is daunting, and it's stressful as fuck to think it's something we will be taking over one day. While our grandfathers paved the way for a phenomenal legacy, our fathers have straight up turned all the businesses into the most diverse and excessive shit ever. Their thirst for power and money is the driving force for the way they run their business with complete iron fists. It's also the biggest reason for our stellar fucked up home life. Nothing any of us did was ever good enough, nor will it ever be. We have mostly just become immune to the degradation, but we also have our vices that keep us from completely jumping off the deep end.

"Wonder what we are gonna be walking into. I don't think Sin or Bethani had class this afternoon. Jesus, they fight like hell."

I chuckle at D's observation. "Yeah. These past two weeks have been interesting as fuck for sure with them two."

We've had Bethani living with us for two weeks already. Declan and I have had a blast hanging out with her and doing the simplest shit. We've been watching movies in the theater room or on the couch, working out in the gym, or just bullshitting while one of us cooks. The same, however, can't be said for her and Sinclair. They are like oil and fucking water. Bethani flips out at Sinclair's overprotective antics. He's constantly asking where she is in the group chat when she isn't at the penthouse, and she retaliates with a vengeance. Her attitude pisses him off to no end, which is also a giant turn-on for him. He wants to "punish her sassy ass" as he says, but he knows he can't until she consents to it. So until she says yes, he is sporting the same ridiculous blue balls Declan and I are.

Pretty sure I've jacked off more in the past two weeks than I ever have my fucking life. Just a little glance, smirk, or giggle from Bethani has my cock at full fucking painful mast. It's ridiculous how bad I want her on top of me while I watch her sink down on my throbbing cock.

"Fucking hell," I mutter while rubbing my hands over my face, attempting to diffuse some of the sexual tension roaring through my veins as blood steadily rushes to my dick.

Declan just laughs, clearly knowing where my thoughts went. "I feel you, man. This is the longest I've gone without sex since I first got laid." I just flip him off.

The elevator door opens to the penthouse, and as we step out, everything is oddly quiet. I share an equally confused look with D as we slowly make our way toward the living room and kitchen when a flying glass shatters in front of us, abruptly stopping us. Yeah, we are all crazy fucks, but even we know when not to walk into a shit storm, *mostly*.

"You arrogant pig-headed bastard! How fucking dare you!" Bethani screeches from the kitchen area. "Why in the ever-loving fuck would you do that?"

As we slowly make our way around the wall, prepared to avoid flying shit, we are both stunned by the state of the kitchen. There are knives thrown into a wall, broken glass everywhere, and what looks like a bag of flour exploded all over the fucking place. Sinclair is standing at one end of the kitchen island, completely covered in flour. Bethani is at the opposite end with more glasses in front of her as ammunition to hurl at Sin. Both look crazed as fuck, ready to either fuck each other senseless or murder the other. Right now, I honestly can't tell which way it would play out.

Declan finally breaks the stare down. "What the fuck is going on here? Christ, we were barely gone two fucking hours."

Both of them turn their venomous gazes our way, and if I were a lesser man, I'd probably be cowering in fear over the vicious blaze in their eyes.

"Just a misunderstanding, that's all," Sinclair declares before returning his gaze toward Bethani.

Her eyes rear back at his comment. "Misunderstanding? A fucking misunderstanding? That's what you are calling getting busted going through my shit when I realized there was an app on my phone that you could open up to see everything I do from your room!"

He just shrugs noncommittally in response. "We told you, your safety is top priority here with that prick still missing in action. Or did you forget already?"

I wince at his crass behavior. "Sinclair..." I start to say something to diffuse the situation, but Bethani fires off in another retaliation.

"Did I? Did I forget that a motherfucker *drugged* me, then took me to a fucking alleyway and tried to not only *force* himself on me, but physically *assault* me? Hmm...let me think. Nope! The nightmare is still there every damn night. My neck still hurts sometimes from his grip, and I still have cuts healing. So you tell me if I fucking forgot or not."

Sinclair, Declan, and I all cringe at her brazen reminder, but Sinclair finally starts to realize he is pushing too hard.

"Kitten, I'm—"

"No! You do not get to talk right now! *Ты бессердечный ублюдок. Иди на хрен!*" she seethes before storming off in an absolute rage toward her room.

I look at Deck. "I've got her. You deal with him and this mess," I say, then rush off toward her room.

I manage to catch the door with my foot before it slams in my face. I find her in the bathroom running water over her face.

"Tesoro, you all right?" I ask from the doorway, scaring the shit out of her.

"Jesus! You scared me, Giovanni. You know you are all stealthy for being giants."

Her wide aqua eyes stare at me in shock, her breasts heaving as she tries to calm her heart rate. I find myself entranced with her instantly, and I need to get this moving before I jump her sexy little ass in the bathroom. My dick is already starting to stand at attention at the thoughts of those plush lips wrapped around my cock.

"Giovanni? Did you need something?"

"Oh, yeah. Uhh...you want to go somewhere with me? To, you know, get away from Sinclair?"

Smooth, Giovanni, real fucking smooth, idiot.

She smiles at me and I have to stifle a groan. Fuck, she is perfection.

"Where did you have in mind?"

I shrug. "Just a spot I go to when I need a moment's peace. It's nothing fancy." Jesus, can I act any more pretentious? Fuck me.

"Sure. Is what I'm wearing all right? Or do I need to change?"

I slowly peruse her body. She is wearing a sexy as sin halter jumpsuit and flip-flops. While the jumpsuit looks simple, on her, it's fucking drool-worthy. The comfortable material hugs her curves perfectly. The cut is just low enough to give a tease of her cleavage, and the back is so damn low it shows the dimples above that voluptuous ass that I want to sink my teeth into. As my gaze returns to her face, I realize I must have been gawking way too long. Her cheeks are blushed crimson, and I want to do anything and everything to make her feel that special, always. Quickly clearing my throat, I answer, "You look perfect, Tesoro. I've got blankets and a spare hoodie in the Jeep if you get cold." Then I hold out my hand for her to take.

Bethani glances at it for a second before deciding my idea is better than staying here. When her hand catches mine, I have to hold back against the electric sizzle coursing through my body at the simplest touch from her. I've never felt like this with any of the chicks I've fucked before. Hell, I'm lucky to remember their names half the time. Not because I don't have a damn near photographic memory for shit. I just don't care to remember them.

This woman holding my hand currently, I already know I'm never going to forget her. Every little fucking thing she does just permeates into my system, latching on to my soul. It's intoxicating and scary. But I don't want to give it up either.

"Come on, Tesoro, let's go." I gently tug her behind me out the door to her room and toward the elevator. "Be back later!" I yell to Sin and Deck, trying to avoid being stopped.

Declan storms out of the kitchen, catching us as we hit the elevator. "Seriously? You are leaving me with him? The fuck did I do to you?"

Laughing, I just shrug. "Nothing. Just going for a drive. That's all."

He scowls before turning away and muttering obscenities at me. "Bullshit. Fucking bullshit. I get stuck with fuck face temper tantrum and he gets to go have fun with sunshine. Bastard."

I don't even respond to his childish acts. Instead, I quickly step into the elevator, still holding Bethani's hand as I hit the button for the garage. I look down to see her smiling.

"You could have invited him, you know?"

"Nah. He's a big boy. He'll live."

She just laughs, bringing the biggest shit-eating grin to my face as the elevator descends.

––––––

"So where exactly are we going?"

I glance over at Bethani riding shotgun in the Jeep. She looks fucking ethereal with her long hair cascading down her back, and the slowly setting sun makes her glow.

"Ever heard of the cliffs?"

She just shakes her head.

"It's a spot I found when I started driving. It's secluded, overlooks the ocean, and is my favorite place to go when shit gets to be too much. The guys don't even know where it is."

"Holy shit," she whispers, causing me to glance over at her shocked face.

"What? Is everything all right, Tesoro?"

My heart rate spikes as I think of anything and everything that could be going wrong. She just smirks at me.

"Nothing. Just surprised you actually have secrets between you three."

The breath I didn't realize I was holding comes whooshing out of me.

"Jesus, Tesoro. Don't do that to a man. Holy hell, I thought something was wrong."

Her continuous giggles at me as I park have me quickly throwing the Jeep into park, undoing my seat belt, and turning to tickle the shit outta her. Her laughing is continuous as I proceed to harass her when she finally asks me to stop.

"Okay! I'm sorry, Giovanni. It was just too good not to pass up!"

"You are a little devil. You realize that, right?"

She just gives me another one of those sultry smiles of hers, sending blood forcefully to my dick. It's pulsing at the thoughts assaulting my brain, forcing me to close my eyes and take deep breaths to will my dick to behave.

"What's on your mind, Giovanni?"

I open my eyes slowly to see her mimicked and equally hooded gaze. *Fuckkkk.*

"N-nothing, Tesoro."

"Liar. You want to kiss me."

Test of willpower, here I come.

"Maybe."

"Then why don't you?" she challenges.

And starting to fail the test commencing in three...two...one...

"Because, Tesoro. If I kiss you, I won't fucking stop at just kissing you. I'll ravish those fuck-me lips of yours until they are swollen and bruised. I'll take my time kissing and exploring that cock tease body of yours until I have every single spot memorized that turns you on. I will devour your pussy with my fingers, tongue, and lips until you are so close to the edge of an orgasm...then I'll stop just long enough to sink my dick deep inside you. I won't stop until we are both so wrung out with pleasure that neither of us can walk for a fucking week."

We are just staring at each other, both with jagged breathing at my admission. My cock is fucking steel in my jeans, straining and threatening to bust the zipper. Her lips are parted, and those flawless aqua eyes are almost black with desire. Fuck, mine probably are too. We continue to stare at each other, not sure where to turn from here, when the feeling of her hand grazing my thigh jolts me. Fucking hell, I didn't even notice her moving.

Fuck it.

I reach my hand behind the back of her neck, fisting my fingers in her thick locks, then I pull her into me and crash our lips together for an earth-shattering kiss.

The moment our lips touch, I swear everything else fades away. There is nothing but the two of us. As our lips mold together, I open my mouth just enough to nip her lower lip, causing her to gasp. Our tongues quickly tangle together, and I moan in pleasure. She tastes like the sweetest treat, and I'm instantaneously addicted to it. My lungs burn from lack of oxygen, but I refuse to stop devouring her mouth.

Needing to have her closer to me, I fumble with the toggle on the seat to give me as much room as possible. When I succeed, I quickly snatch Bethany out of the passenger seat and bring her over to straddle me. She squeals at the change, breaking our kiss for much needed air. I just stare at her for a moment, captivated by her beauty.

"You are gorgeous, Tesoro." She just blushes and reaches behind her toward the halter of her jumpsuit. I grab her wrists, stopping the movement. "You know I won't be able to stop if you do that."

All she gives me is a sultry little smile before bringing her bottom lip between her pearly whites. I swear on everything my dick swells more than I ever thought it was capable of.

Fucking helllllll.

"I'm aware of that, Giovanni. I never once asked you to stop, now did I?"

Chuckling, I release her wrists, move my arms behind my head, and give her the best cocky smile I can conjure up. "Fair enough, Tesoro. Proceed."

Slight hesitation crosses her face before she jumps in with both feet by untying the halter on her outfit. When she slowly, torturously, pulls it down to free her breasts, I realize she isn't wearing a bra under it.

"Holy shit," I mutter as I just stare at her flawless tits.

They are full, symmetrical, and perfectly tanned like the rest of her. Her rosebud nipples are already pebbled, begging to be touched. I can't fucking resist any longer.

I move my hands from behind my head to cup each breast in my palm, relishing the feel of them in my hands. It's *like they were fucking made for me.* I slowly start kneading them, loving how just the slightest pressure has Bethani's breath catching in the back of her throat before letting off the slightest moan of pleasure. It's tantalizing and erotic as hell. We've barely done anything, and it's the most sexual experience of my life. I have to taste them. Now. But before I release her tits from my hands, I pinch her nipples, hard, and pull them taut.

"Giovanni," she moans breathlessly.

I smirk at her reaction. "Baby, you better not come off of me teasing your beautiful tits. Otherwise, I'll have to punish your sweet ass."

Bethani's head jerks forward, her eyes wide at my dominating tone. "I...thought you were the sweet one."

I laugh. "Tesoro, I *am* the sweet one of the three of us. But when it comes to the bedroom, we *all* relish being the dominant one in some form. So you better believe that when I give you an instruction, you follow, sweetheart."

"Or?"

"I'll bend your pretty ass over and brand it with my hands until you come off of just the sensation of that alone."

The shiver that racks her body has her breasts swaying just enough to bring my focus back to them, and to let me know she is into it. But without her verbal consent, I won't continue.

"Tesoro, look at me."

She complies. Good girl.

"Are you okay with all of this? I promise I will not go too far with anything. Plus, being in the vehicle limits some of the *experiences* we can have. But if you aren't comfortable with it, we can stop right now."

"I'm...good with everything."

I quirk a brow, unconvinced. "Tesoro, don't lie to me."

She just blushes, embarrassed. "Well, you see. Other than Sinclair the other day, that was the first...orgasm I've had that hasn't been from myself in over two years," she mumbles the last part, but it was still clear as day.

"Cristo, Tesoro! Two years!"

I just get a nod in response. Quickly catching her falling chin with my finger, I tilt her head until she's looking back at me. Then I gently bring my lips to hers and give her a sweet kiss before breaking it and resting my forehead against hers.

"Tesoro, I promise to make this as memorable and enjoyable as fuck for you. Now can you do something for me?"

"Mhmm. What is it?"

"Forgive me."

"Forgive you? For what?'

"For this."

I quickly grab the seam of her jumpsuit by her pussy between my hands and demolish it, separating it into two halves. This gives me easy access to what I now see is a bare pussy.

"Fuckkkk, Bethani. No underwear either? You are going to kill me."

"You...just ruined my jumpsuit. What the..."

My left hand snakes up behind her neck again to bring her lips back to mine for a silencing kiss.

While devouring her mouth, my right hand makes its way to her inner thigh. Just the softest touch grazing her sends her jumping slightly at the sensation. I move my way up until my fingers are right fucking there. Just barely grazing over the lips of her pussy. She is fucking drenched. I swipe back again, gathering more of her arousal before moving up toward her swollen clit. With slightly more pressure, I lazily graze over it, each time pressing a little harder.

Bethani breaks the kiss to lean back, her head tilting back farther and farther as she lets loose a throaty moan from the pleasure before her hips start to move unknowingly.

"That's right, Tesoro. Ride my fingers, baby. Fuck, you are so goddamn sexy like this."

I move my hand just enough to keep my thumb on her clit and adjust my fingers so she can sink down on them. When she does, I start swearing in Italian at the eroticism of it. She is tight as fuck on two of my fingers, and the casual sway of her hips as she fucks my hand is amazing. Soon she is changing the angle of them and she constantly has her hips moving faster and faster to get off.

My dick is painfully throbbing and aching while leaking precum in my jeans. I can see the wet spot forming through the wetness of Bethani's constant dripping arousal. I can't fucking take it anymore. I let her ride my hand while I use my left one to free myself. As soon as my cock springs free, Bethani's movements stop.

Her eyes are blown looking with the desire rolling through her system. Breathing heavily, her eyes finally look into mine, and I swear I can almost sense what she is thinking.

"Like what you see, baby?"

Chapter 17

Bethani

How I stopped moving, I'll never know. But hearing Giovanni's zipper pulling down brought me out of my haze enough to see his giant cock spring free.

Holy tamales and guacamole.

He is fucking huge, long, and thick. His dick is a slightly darker tan than the rest of his pristine skin tone. His veins are protruding, and precum is leaking from the purple mushroom head with a piercing straight through it, top to bottom. I've never seen a more perfect dick.

I slowly glance back up at the arrogant smirk on Giovanni's face when he asks, "Like what you see, baby?"

Oh, honey, I'll show you what I like. I'm such a giant ball of lust and desire that I can't think straight. There are over two years of pent-up sexual frustration and aggravation roaring through me. It's ridiculous how I've gone so long without sex without murdering someone.

Now I know. Giovanni Martinelli and his perfect Adonis dick.

I slowly grab the wrist that still has fingers lodged up inside me and pull it away, groaning at the loss. With a quizzical expression, Giovanni looks at me.

"What are you doing, Tesoro?"

I'm so gone, I'm not even sure what I'm doing when I ask, "Are you clean?"

"Yes. Why?"

"For this."

I quickly grab a hold of his cock and line it up with my entrance before I slam down. I'm screaming at the intrusion as my eyes roll back in my head over the mountains of sensations caressing my body at once. Even though I was well lubricated, Giovanni is still massive. *Plus,* his piercing rippling through my walls, *and* after that long without sex, yeah.

Not my smartest idea, but I'm too far gone to care.

"Holy fucking shit, Tesoro!" Giovanni yells at the same time as I screamed.

I lean up, wrapping his body around mine. We both just sit there for a second, letting our bodies recalculate at my brazen move. When I finally can't wait any longer, I squeeze my Kegel muscles around Gio's dick, and a guttural moan rips out of his chest.

Leaning back just a bit so we can see each other's faces, he finally speaks, "Christ almighty, Tesoro. Are you trying to send me to an early grave? I've never gone bareback before, and I'm already about to explode. Holy shit."

I start to laugh because now I'm slightly embarrassed by my actions. But my laughter has me squeezing around his dick and moving slightly, causing my laughter to stop and dragging a moan from my lips.

"I'm sorry. I just got...caught up in it all, and I couldn't wait." My hips start to roll on their own damn devices. "Holy shit, Giovanni. You feel...amazing."

His hands grip my hips, stopping my slutty actions.

"Say it again."

"Say what again?"

"My name. Say my name again, Tesoro." He punctuates his nickname for me with a quick upward thrust of his hips, burying him even deeper inside of me than I thought possible.

"G-Giovanni...please don't stop."

"Not a chance in hell," he grits out.

He barely finishes his statement before unleashing sexual heaven against my body. His hands grip my hips tighter, lifting me up slightly before slamming me back down. His hips thrust upward, the motion stopping all my thoughts, except for the feeling of him inside me.

Somehow in the midst of his sexual onslaught, I'm able to bring my hands up to his shoulders for better leverage as I become more of an active participant. My hips gyrate and roll against his hands as he keeps the up and down motions at a brutal and steadfast pace.

Sweat is dripping down both of our bodies, and I'm itching to see more of his skin. I pull up violently on his shirt, and his arms rise just long enough for me to rip his shirt off the rest of the way to expose his delicious body. I take in his tan Italian skin tone and the dark sprinklings of hair along his chest. There's just enough to be sexy. A happy trail of his dark brown hair between perfectly sculpted V lines along his hips leads toward where our bodies are connected. My arousal is pooling along the bottom of his stomach, and I can't help but moan at how sexy this all is.

"Tesoro. Look. At. Me."

My eyes quickly snap to his piercing ocean blue eyes, which are currently almost swallowed by his pupils. It's sexier than sin, and I can't help myself. I lean forward to kiss his full lips just as he adjusts our bodies. His piercing is hitting my G-spot over and over in this slightly shifted position. My nails dig into Giovanni's chest, and I swear I can feel his cock growing and pulsing more than before.

"I'm about to blow in your sweet pussy, baby. Look at me."

His dark and commanding tone instantly brings me back to his intense stare. I've never been one to like being bossed around, but like this, I fucking get it. It's sexy, and I swear my pussy clenches at his commands.

"Eyes on me, Tesoro. I want to watch as your beautiful body comes undone."

I will myself to keep my eyes on him as I feel his thumb move toward my clit. He vigorously rubs as his thrusts pick up the pace, and I can feel myself lifting higher and higher in the process. The deep burn from my impending orgasm starts in my belly and is quickly rushing through my body. I'm so close to exploding when Giovanni's face starts to contort as his orgasm hits him.

The rubber band to ecstasy is so close I can taste it. Our violent thrusts, gyrations, and his pressure on my clit are a wicked ticking time bomb waiting to detonate when Giovanni does something I've never experienced before.

"Tesoro. Come. NOW!" And then he pinches my clit and I. Fucking. Shatter.

My orgasm tsunamis through my body so quickly, that stars explode behind my eyes at the sensation. My pussy constricts around Giovanni's swelling cock as he slams into home one more time. He lets out a feral roar as his orgasm swoops through his body just as violently.

Feeling him pulse and explode inside me sends my body into a second orgasm. I've never experienced this before either.

"Giovanniiiiiiii," I scream or moan. Hell, I'm not even sure it's my voice right now. I'm on cloud 7000 as the pleasure rolls through me.

After what feels like hours, but it's probably only seconds, I collapse into Giovanni's chest. I'm a boneless, extremely sated, and happy sack of nothing. *I've never experienced something so amazing,* I think to myself.

"Me neither, Tesoro. Me neither." Giovanni chuckles.

I try to rise up but can't. "I said that out loud?"

His strong arms wrap around my shivering body, encasing me in his warmth. "Yeah, Bethani, you said that out loud." He stops long enough to kiss my forehead before leaning back slightly, his dick still half hard inside me. "That was...fuck me. I don't even have words for how phenomenal that was. Christ."

Snuggling into his body some more, I can completely understand. "Yeah. I've never experienced anything like that either."

"Wait, you've never gone bareback either?"

"Nope," I simply answer. I've never felt the urge to with any of the idiots I've dated before. But for some reason, that fear wasn't there with Giovanni. I don't know if it would be there with Declan or Sinclair either. None of them seem like the type to be stupid or dangerous with sex.

I can feel the proud smile forming on his lips as he hugs me even tighter before nuzzling against my neck. "Thank you, baby, for sharing that experience with me." Gentle pecks work up my neck until we are locked into a delicious post-sex kiss. It's lazy but perfect. "We should probably get back to the campus, Tesoro. You have an early class tomorrow, right?"

I groan at the reminder of my horridly early English lecture. "Thanks for the reminder, asshole."

His melodious laugh is deep and rich and envelopes my whole self. I can't help the smile stretching across my face.

Slowly I get up and un-impale myself off his dick, whimpering at the loss.

"Shit. I forgot I destroyed your outfit but seeing my cum drip down your legs is the hottest fucking thing ever."

I blush at his crass words. As quickly as my body will allow, I dump myself back in the passenger seat as Giovanni steps out and goes to the back. He returns just as fast with clothing in his hands.

"Here, sweetheart, sweats and a long sleeve."

I reach out and grab the clothes before saying screw my usual modesty and sliding out of my ruined outfit.

"That *was* my favorite."

"I'll buy you a million more if that means I can destroy them again." His devilishly handsome smile has me laughing.

"Cocky much?"

"Nope. I'm just confident. Plus, I saw the way your body responded to my dick deep inside you as I hit your sweet spot over and over. You aren't a one and done type of person, baby."

Holy blushing. My face is on fire.

Giovanni quickly and gently grips my chin, turning my face toward him and planting a deep, sweet kiss on my lips that leaves me breathless when we separate. "Tesoro, did you hear me?"

"Huh?" I open my eyes to see his face back to its usual stoic and studious look I'm accustomed to. "I'm sorry. What did you say again?"

"I asked if you were on the pill or something like that, sweetheart. While I loved feeling your sweet pussy wrapped around my cock like the perfect little present, that can't happen again if you're not, or until you get on something."

"Shot. Just got one right before school started. I've got one every three months since I was fifteen."

His sigh of relief is evident on his face before he reaches over and envelopes me in a giant bear hug. "*Thank God.* Pretty sure I'd take you right now to get on it if not."

Laughing at his admission, I ask, "Why do you say that? It's just sex, Giovanni."

He breaks our embrace to cup my face between his giant hands that still smell like my arousal and pins me with his glacial blue-eyed stare.

"That was *not* 'just sex', Tesoro. Yes, it was unplanned, chaotic, slightly messy, and somewhat quick, but it was also mind-fucking-blowing. I've never barebacked before, but feeling how your dripping cunt fluttered around my dick...and when my piercing hit your sweet spot? Fucking hell, it was pure ecstasy for me. Watching your facial features, moans, and little whimpers in the throes of passion? Heaven. Plain and simple."

He stops long enough to plunder my mouth again with another delicious kiss before talking again. "Now, let's get back before I strip my clothes off you and fuck you ten ways from Sunday again and again. Because I almost bet you are dripping for me again."

I am. I'm soaked again. A mix of his arousal swirling around with mine down between my clenching thighs has Giovanni's grip tightening around my face just slightly while his eyes flare.

"Fuck it. Back seat now, Tesoro. I need to taste you this time."

An hour later, we are finally on our way back to campus. Our hands are interlocked, and I'm glancing out the window at the scenery. My body is sore as fuck from rounds two and three. After we got in the back seat, Giovanni ate me until I screamed his name, then flipped me over and took me from behind as I was leaning against the seat. The third time, I'm not even sure what acrobatic position that was, but it was phenomenal.

I've never come that many times before in my life in one single sex session. But Giovanni was correct, he could have kept going all night if he wanted to. He was insatiable, demanding, but still extremely sweet the whole time. I tried to give him head and he refused, saying this was all about my pleasure.

"What are you thinking about, Bethani?" he asks while squeezing our hands.

I blush again for the thousandth time. "Oh, nothing."

"You are a shit liar, love. You were reminiscing about our perfect little tryst back there, weren't you?"

"Maybe."

"It's okay, Tesoro. I'll be jerking off to our excursion at least one more time tonight. Probably as soon as I wake up in the morning, too." Another sexy smirk crosses his face.

"I don't even have words for that. But you do need a shower. We both reek of sex."

He just shrugs as he pulls into the underground parking area. "And?"

"What about the guys?"

A deep, throaty laugh erupts from his chest, confusing me. He must obviously see it on my face as he parks and starts to explain, "Tesoro, you live with three of the most sexual men on campus. I see those two naked almost as much as I see myself naked. Hell, I can't believe I'm telling you this, but Declan and I are both bisexual, love. We have only been with each other, and obviously practice safe sex when it comes to it. But we have also shared too."

I'm slack-jawed. "Shared?"

He just sighs and leans back against his seat. "Yes. Shared. As in we have all been in bed together before, sharing the same woman and pleasuring her at the same time. Does that bother you?" he asks with a quirk of his brow and an air of uncertainty crossing his face.

I think for a second before attempting to answer. "I honestly don't know. My sexual experiences were shit before you, Giovanni. But sharing? It's never a thought that has crossed my mind." I can't even articulate the thoughts in my head right now. It's all a jumbled mess as I try to process his words. I'm so in my thoughts that I don't even realize Giovanni has gotten out of the vehicle until my door opens, making me jump. Being the sweetheart he is, Giovanni extends his hand for me, and I accept it as I step out. He shuts the door, and we walk in silence to the elevator. Once we are in and it starts moving, he turns me into his arms and my head hits his comforting broad chest while my arms wrap around his lean waist. He just hugs me for a second before kissing the top of my head.

"Bethani, we don't live conventionally. Never have. Our lifestyle in general is....different. But Sinclair, Declan, and I have always been there for each other. So most of our sexual exploitations have been with each other. It's not something we do regularly, but it is something we enjoy on occasion. If it's something you want to try, then let us know. Your pleasure will *always* come first. While we may be a little, how do I put it, *less gentle* sometimes, none of us would ever intentionally violate your boundaries or force you into something you aren't interested in. We all stand by that and would probably murder each other if one of us crossed that line." His tone is firm, which has me tilting my head to see how absolutely serious he is.

I just give him a salacious smile. "You weren't exactly gentle with me, and I didn't mind that."

"Tesoro. I'm serious. Don't tempt me. I'll tie your pretty ass up if I have to."

I can't help but pout, which has him groaning.

"Death of me, woman."

"I promise, I'll *consider* it. Maybe you and Declan, but Sinclair? He can fuck right off."

The giant smile on his face warms my heart, and his infectious laugh has me laughing too. The elevator ding brings us apart, but Giovanni's protective instinct doesn't let up, and his hand grips mine before we step out. He stops us long enough to give me a final deep, mind-melting kiss before whispering in my ear, "Promise, Tesoro. While Sinclair may be a controlling grumpy bastard sometimes, any and *all of us* will make sure you are well taken care of. We won't let anything happen to you, *ever*. We just have different ways of showing it." With that, he stands back up to his full height and continues our joined walk back into the vipers' nest.

When we reach the living room, Declan and Sinclair are sitting on the couch, and it looks like the giant angry tirade mess I made earlier has been cleaned up.

Sinclair just pins us with a brooding glare, eyes on Giovanni's and my interlocked hands, saying nothing.

Declan finally catches what Sinclair is staring at before looking our way. He quickly looks at us, taking in my obvious outfit change and interlocked hands before speaking, "No. Fucking. Way. You guys boned, didn't you?"

I quickly burrow my face into Giovanni's because I cannot handle all this, especially after what we just talked about.

"You did! Holy shit, I'm jealous. So, how was it, G? Is our baby B a sex kitten?"

Kill. Me. Now. PLEASE!

Giovanni just lets go of my hand to put a protective arm around me to shield me from Declan and his ridiculous questions. "Just took care of our girl. That's all I'm going to say on that."

"Motherfucker, we always share stories! The hell?"

"No, *you* always share your sexual exploits, Declan. While I'll give you details on occasion, this is not one of those occasions."

Thank you, Giovanni.

"You fucking suck, man," Declan grumbles.

"I know why he isn't sharing any details." Sinclair finally opens his asshole mouth, and I still at his voice. Arrogant jerk.

"Do tell o' wise one." Giovanni challenges.

It's quiet for a second, so I finally gather the courage to turn and face the guys. Sinclair studies me before speaking, "They fucked without a condom. That's why G is being so fucking protective and tight-lipped."

Giovanni tenses behind me. My mouth is agape. Declan is shell-shocked, and Sinclair just remains his usual asshole-ish self.

"Cristo," Giovanni mumbles, knowing we are busted.

I guess he was right when he said they are all close and know damn near everything about each other. I really freaking wish that wasn't the case, though.

"I'm next!" Declan yells before launching himself off the couch toward us. "So, was it fucking amazing? You explain anything to her? You asshole, I'm jealous!"

"Fucking hell, Deck, calm down. Yes, I explained. She even knows about us. She is going to consider her options before making a decision. Until then, back off."

There is no 'backing off' when it comes to Declan Carter, I've realized. He is a giant full tilt, tattooed, pierced, goofball with enough energy for ten people. He swoops down and snatches me from Giovanni's arms. I yelp from surprise, but he quickly silences me by kissing the shit out of me.

It's shocking, and after being with Giovanni you'd think it wouldn't affect me, but I'm just as entranced and obsessed with Declan's lips as I am with Giovanni's.

Just as quick as he picked me up, he is setting me down dazed, breathless, and surprisingly horny again. *What the hell is going on here?*

Declan is happy as hell with a giant shit-eating grin while Giovanni just stands there with a hand over his face.

"Way to back off, asshole."

He just shrugs, but the joy radiating off him is getting to Giovanni as he drags his hand down his face, a smile slowly forming.

"What is going on here? I'm so...I don't even know. Confused?"

"You really don't follow what's going on here, sunshine?" Declan asks.

I shake my head because I honestly have zero clue as to what in the fresh hell is going on. My lovely post-coital haze is completely gone, and my body is buzzing again. I feel like I'm being pulled in ten different emotional directions, and I can't figure out what to feel.

"It's simple, sunshine," Declan says, pulling me out of my thoughts. "You are attracted to all of us, and we are all attracted to you. There is no shame in that. Progressive times and whatever shit like that."

"Smooth explanation, dude. Real smooth," Giovanni deadpans.

"Shut up. I'm not all good with words like you."

I hold my hand up to stop their argument. "Okay, maybe there is some truth to this, I'll give you that. But that one over there?" I point to Sinclair. "No way in hell."

"Oh really, kitten? No way in hell?"

He stands and makes his way toward me. I cross my arms and tilt my head in defiance.

"Yes, Sinclair. No. Way. In. Hell. Do you want me to list the reasons again? I can do it in Russian if you'd like?"

He closes in on me, but I refuse to back down. When he is close enough, he stops and just stares at me for a second before slowly reaching out and using a finger to graze lightly up and down my neck. It makes me shiver, and my breath catches in response.

"You see, kitten, *that* reaction right there says otherwise. Deny all you want, but one day, we *will* happen. And when it does?"

He lowers himself to my level before burrowing his head in the crook of my neck. He breathes deep, then nips my neck in exactly the same spot as Giovanni did earlier. A damn breathy moan involuntarily escapes my lips, causing my eyes to flick back open, and I step back from his advance.

Sinclair's emerald eyes flash. Lust and desire are heavy in them as he stands back up and adjusts himself. You'd think I'd be able to keep my eyes up with his? Nope, those traitorous jerks flick to his massive length bulging behind his sweats before his evil chuckle brings my gaze back to his.

"Like I said, kitten, when it happens, be prepared."

Then he just turns and walks toward his room. Leaving me a hot mess of body buzzing emotions in front of Giovanni and Declan.

"H-how does this not bother any of you?"

They both look at each other and shrug before Giovanni answers, "We told you, Tesoro. We are all extremely attracted to you. As it stands right now, you're *our* girl. If you so choose to keep it that way, none of us will fuck around on you. You'll be the only one any of us have sexual relations with. Including Declan and myself. If you don't like that we fuck around together, we won't. Simple as that. None of us have been with anyone since we met you that night."

A jab from Declan to Giovanni's ribcage has him doubling over for a second. "Ouch! Dick! Okay, we haven't been with any other women. Declan and I may have had a little elevator fun one night, but like I said, it was done *safely*. If it would make you happy, we will gladly all go get tested and show you our results, or any previous ones. But as I was saying before the jackass here had to elbow me, right now you are our girl, which means no one will fuck with you. We won't fuck around on you, ever. If you choose only one of us, then that's fine too. We are a handful, to say the least. Regardless, one of us or all three of us, we will always protect you and take care of you."

Jesus...information overload. My mind is spinning. Declan must catch that because he stops my mental overload from exploding.

"Sunshine, go take a shower and lie down. Don't think about it anymore tonight. Just take your time and consider your options." And with that he kisses my forehead and walks away too, leaving just Giovanni and me.

"Good night, Tesoro. Go take your shower and relax."

With a sweet kiss to my lips, he is gone just as quick as the others, leaving me to turn and do exactly as they asked.

Chapter 18

Bethani

My bedroom door opening and closing has me jumping awake. "It's just me, baby B. No need to freak out." Declan's throaty deep voice instantly calms me since I know it's not some intruder, but my heart is still racing in an unsteady flutter.

"W-what time is it, Declan?"

"Little after three a.m., why?" he asks like *I'm* the crazy one being awake at this ungodly hour.

"Why are you even awake, Declan? Don't you have class in the morning too?"

He rips the covers off me before jumping into bed beside me, pulling them back over us and bringing me into his hulking tattooed arms. The warmth of his massive chest and muscular arms blankets me in an unusual comforting feeling. It's nice and unlike any of the normal emotions I'm used to feeling.

"Ehh...it's just class. And I was sleeping, but I kept dreaming of you. I couldn't deal with being away from you any longer, so here I am."

I snuggle into him, sleepily enjoying the feeling of his arms around me. "Class is important."

"Not as important as you, B."

The dropping tone of his voice is laced with emotions, which has me instantly snapping my eyes back open and craning my neck to see him staring down at me in the darkness.

"I can't stop thinking about you, baby. It's driving me fucking insane. I have this insatiable desire to be close to you, always, and knowing G got you to himself earlier..." He stops and shakes his head. "Fuck. I'm not normally jealous. But I wanted to be the first one to taste you. The first one to sink his dick deep down inside you."

A shudder rocks through my body at his salacious words.

He flips us around, putting my back flat against the mattress. His bulging arms are surrounding my shoulders while his one hand slowly starts playing with my hair. His massive tree trunk legs are on either side of mine, just pressing into me enough that I can feel his massive erection grazing my thigh. He continues, "Do you know I saw a little of your leftover juices on G's face? I could *fucking* smell your sweet arousal on him, and it took *everything* in my power not to snatch your pretty ass up, take you to my room, and have my wicked way with you until it was *my* cum coating your pussy's walls. Until it was your sweet juices coating my face, and it was *my* name being screamed from those juicy lips of yours? Goddammit, B, I'm turning into a raging monster just waiting on the go-ahead from you."

He leans down and gently kisses my lips. Nothing forceful or demanding. Almost like asking for permission.

"So what do you say, sunshine? Will you let me have my wicked way with you? Let me hear my name fall from your lips as I bring you a few delicious orgasms? Let me sate this primal need to devour your body?"

I must be losing my damn mind because his words, his sweet and needy and raunchy words, have me absolutely soaked already. I want him like he wants me. It doesn't make any sense, my attraction to these men, but the choppy, lust-filled words are falling from my lips before I even realize it.

"Y-yes, Declan." My breathy words and voice don't even sound like me.

"Yes? Yes to what, sunshine. I need to hear your words."

"Y-yes t-to it all, Declan. Claim me as yours also. Fuck. I don't understand it, but I want you to claim me just as Giov—" My words get lost as Declan descends on my lips. Crushing his lips to mine, he tilts his head slightly and uses his tongue to demand entrance to my mouth. And I willingly open for him.

The hand that was in my hair moves to the back of my head and grips against me, manipulating it to better mold our mouths together as he obliterates me with his claiming kiss. It's passionate as sin, the same but different than Giovanni's. While their styles are different, the intensity is the same. They don't take this lightly.

My willingness to let them claim me as theirs ignites a different personality trait that has been locked deep down inside them. Their kisses show it. They are not fucking around when they say they want me as theirs, and they will do anything to keep me safe. To keep me as theirs.

I can feel it in waves rolling off Declan as he starts to roll his hips into mine. The delicious feel of his erection rubbing against me has me feeding my moans to Declan, spurring him on even further. Our clothes haven't even come off, and I'm ready to explode at this sensual foreplay.

Almost as if he is thinking the same as me, he breaks our kiss and inhales deeply before talking. "I think it's time to get rid of some layers. What do you think, baby?"

All I can do is nod. Formulating words is apparently a skill that flies out the window with these dominating men and their wicked dicks and words.

He stands up from the bed, quickly ridding himself of his shirt and tossing it to the floor. Then he whips off his basketball shorts and is standing completely nude in front of me as my eyes widen to his miraculous body.

Declan's body is a work of art with all of the tattoos covering his body. His lighter brown hair, shorter on the sides and about three to four inches on the top, resonates with a rock god. There's an eyebrow piercing over his right eye, diamond studs in each ear, double rings in his left nostril, piercing in both nipples, and from what I've learned from the riveting and somewhat weird conversations, a Prince Albert dick piercing.

Apparently Declan won a bet between them and this was the prize. Declan with a Prince Albert, Giovanni with an apadravya, and Sinclair with a frenum.

"Like what you see, sunshine?" Declan's cocky playful attitude comes out, but I don't take my eyes off his already leaking cock. The intense need to taste him has me quickly scrambling to the edge of the bed and standing in front of him. "What are you doing?"

"Well...someone was more focused on me earlier and wouldn't let me do this. So..."

I quickly drop to my knees, putting me eye level with his dick. His piercing glints from the moonlight shining through the windows. I quickly reach up and grab ahold of his cock, making it jump, and Declan's head quickly falls back as a moan escapes his lips.

"I thought you could be the first one I give head to with a piercing," I purr, then stick my tongue out just enough and bring his thick dick to my mouth.

I slowly lick the slit as a small burst of cum spits out. His taste is salty yet slightly sweet. I quickly open my mouth to take in his head, swirling my tongue around and playing with the piercing.

"Fuuuckkkkk," Delcan growls, sending waves of pleasure straight to my pussy.

All of this has me reaching down with my free hand to my drenched panties. But then a loud pop comes from my mouth as Declan pulls himself out, irritating me.

"What the...hey!" I call out.

He quickly has me up in his arms, my legs wrapping around his waist.

"If you want to taste me, fine. But you will *not* play with yourself when I can do that for you, B."

He sets me on the bed and slowly takes my shirt with him as he stands, leaving me in nothing but some lacy boy shorts. His hands move to my hips, and I lift up for him to discard my panties. We are both fully naked, taking in each other's bodies before he speaks, "Turn around and lie back down. Head dangling off the edge, sunshine."

I scurry to do what he asks, curious as to how this is going to work.

Like I said, I've led a bland sex life before meeting these fools. As I'm lying back, I'm stopped when his hands hit my shoulders.

"A-am I doing something wrong?"

"Nope. Just had to do something first." Then his hands start to sensually massage my shoulders, instantly relaxing some of the nervous tension running through my veins. My head lulls to the side as his hands work me into a wondrous state of calm.

"My God, Declan, your hands are freaking magic."

He is chuckling but doesn't stop his pampering. "Well, you are in for a wickedly good treat, sunshine, when you feel how well my hands work in other places."

My face flames at the thought, but little bolts of pleasure zing straight to my core. My thighs clench together to attempt to alleviate some of the building pressure, but it's freaking useless. Over two years without sex, and these guys have me in a constant state of arousal in just two weeks. Stupid walking talking epitomes of sex and sin all wrapped up in big-dicked boxes.

Declan's lips against my right shoulder blade have me gasping, as his hands have slowly made their way down my arms. Goose bumps trail everywhere he caresses. I could almost come off it alone. The intimacy of it is so erotic that I can't think straight.

His kisses flutter along my back, down then back up, until his lips are a whisper touch away from my ear.

"I'm sorry, sunshine." His voice is a soft tone I've never heard from him, and it has me shivering at the sincerity. I can't help but lean back into his strong body and tilt my head toward his.

"For what?"

His face hardens and his eyes flame with a vengeance I've never seen before. It's almost unnerving if I didn't know who I was talking to.

"For what that spineless asshole did to you. I fucking promise you, Bethani, that when I get my fucking hands on him, you will never have to worry about seeing him *again*. What we talked about earlier, we all meant it. You're fucking ours, sunshine." Then he crushes his lips to mine, and the questions I have instantly die as our kiss grows desperate and needy.

His hands roam my body as mine slink up and lock around his neck, holding on for dear life. His palms against my sensitive nipples have me breaking our kiss and gasping for breath with the shocks rolling through me. I can't help but moan his name as he tweaks, plucks, and rolls my breasts around his hands.

I feel my body slowly lying back on the bed but don't register it until my head is dangling upside down on the mattress. I open my eyes to see Declan's dripping cock right in front of my face.

"Go ahead, baby B, he's all yours."

My mouth waters and my pussy flutters at his permission. I quickly open my mouth and stick out my tongue while reaching for his hips. Gripping them, I bring him closer to me so I can finally taste him again. As soon as his precum hits my taste buds, I moan at the taste and quickly close my mouth around his mushroom head to suck him further into my mouth.

The vibrations from me and the suction of my mouth have Declan doubling over me. His forearms hit the mattress on either side of me as a groan tears from his throat.

"Fuckk, Bethaniiiii."

His hips start slowly thrusting into me as I suck and twirl my tongue around his pulsing erection. I keep one hand on his hip to help control the depth of his thrusts as my other hand roams. Gripping his ass, sinking my nails into his thigh, caressing his balls. The sounds coming from Declan are ridiculous and are fueling my ministrations to keep pleasuring him.

A deep, slow, deliberate lick from the top of my clit to the bottom of my pussy from Declan has my ass flying up off the bed into his face. The explosion of sensations has every one of my nerve synapses misfiring. My eyes snap open and roll back at how amazing his mouth against my sex feels. My deep moan vibrating Declan's cock has him thrusting deep, and I almost gag before he lifts his hips.

"Shit, baby. Keep that up and this round is going to be over fast."

This round?

Are they trying to kill me?

I pop his dick out long enough to respond, "Don't you dare stop, Declan Carter."

I instantly lift my head up to suck him back down.

"Fuck!" he growls, then his hands are wrapping around my thighs. He pulls them up to link around his head before he goes back to work.

His tongue is a goddamn master of pleasure. His licks are long and slow, flattening along my sex to cover as much of me as possible. His flicks against my clit are fast and furious, almost bringing me to climax multiple times before stopping just long enough for my climax to wane.

My hips have a mind of their own, grinding and thrusting against his face while I focus on his dick. Pulling him out to just the tip and toying with his piercing long enough to drive him insane. Then forcefully sucking the tip back into my mouth, making him struggle to maintain control just as much as I am.

We are pleasuring each other in perfect tandem, trying to drive each other insane.

Suddenly, Declan stands. One arm locks around my waist to hold me in place as he speaks. "Hope you are ready, sunshine. Let's see who loses control first."

His mouth goes back to my clit, furiously working it while he plunges two of his thick, long fingers deep into pussy, all the way to his knuckles, then twisting them around. I'm filled with an intense desire to let the dam break as my pussy flutters and tightens around his fingers, but my determination to not lose wins out, barely.

Using one arm to steady myself against his thigh, I pick up my assault against his cock. Sucking deep and hard, I swirl and twirl my tongue around in a lust-crazed intensity that mirrors his intensity against my sex.

I'm so freaking close to losing, when I remember something I've heard that some chicks at the campus cafeteria say about blow jobs.

"Oh, if you just press and rub a little bit between his asshole and ball sac, a guy will totally lose his mind. It's like, you know, some sort of crazy good pleasure spot for them. Got me out of sex that night."

As I will myself to not break, I reach my free hand down to his balls and squeeze them gently before taking my middle finger and doing exactly what that chick said.

As soon as I press against that spot, Declan tenses slightly, and I start to rub furious little circles. It's only seconds before his whole body seizes up, and the first of many spurts of his cum flood my mouth. His head lifts away from my clit, and a ferocious growl shakes our bodies.

"Fuck fuck fuck fuck. FUCKKKKKK!"

As I'm swallowing the last of his release, a victorious smirk crosses my lips before I'm quickly separating myself from his cock to scream his name.

"Declannnnn!!!!"

My intense and insane orgasm rips through me with a violent force. He turns his fingers to rub against my G-spot, and his mouth closes over my clit to suck, hard. Then his teeth nip my clit, setting me off with a force I wasn't even sure was possible.

With a shaky step, Declan sets me back on the bed before crashing next to me. Our breathing is labored as we come down from our highs.

When I feel like I have a semblance of control back in my body, I proclaim my victory.

"I win."
All he does is laugh.
Which has me smiling like crazy.
Pretty sure neither of us lost just now.

Chapter 19

Arthur - That Same Night - Blackwell Industries Corporate Office

"Did you find out the results?"

"Yes, sir, I did. Got them back before I came here."

"Well, what do the damn things say?"

"They are 99.99 percent. She is the heir they have been looking for, for almost seventeen years."

"Excellent. Do you have the target acquired?"

I notice his tell. He is either about to lie, or he knows I will not be thrilled with his answer.

"N-not exactly, sir."

"What do you mean by 'not exactly'? You knew where she was staying ever since we came in contact with her and verified the potential of who she was!"

Trifling idiot. If I knew it was a possibility, I would have done the job myself. But a man of my position does not get his hands dirty anymore.

"Y-yes. I went to her dorm to pick her up before coming here. When I got there, the door was cracked. As I got down to the open area, it was completely trashed."

"Trashed? How can you trash a shithole?" Robert inquires.

"I mean every piece of furniture was busted into tons of pieces. The TV was shattered. And when I finally got through the wreckage to her room, the door was open and all of her belongings were gone."

I give my colleagues and fellow brothers each a questioning look. They look as perplexed as I am. "Do you have any idea as to her whereabouts?"

"I have a theory, sir."

"Well. Out with it, boy. We don't have all day for this shit."

"I think she is staying with your sons now. From what I can gather, they have been flying fairly under the radar. Not partying since the night of her assault. Actually going to classes."

Peculiar.

"Can you verify this...theory of yours?"

"N-not yet, sir."

"You are utterly worthless. Just send him in."

The boy retreats as I sit back, pinching the bridge of my nose in frustration.

"If she is with them, this really affects our plans."

"Mhmm." Robert nods in agreement when Lorenzo stays silent. "Any thoughts yet, ol' chap?"

Our thoughts are disturbed when he walks through the door. His training has been going well, and my colleagues and myself sit up. Pride is dripping from us at this true version of how a gentleman should carry himself, unlike the stubborn insolents we call *children.*

"You threw a wrench in the plans, you realize that?"

He casually sits in the chair in front of us and takes his tumbler, swirling the liquid around before sipping it. A proper way to do so, unlike our gluttonous heirs, who just chug it. Disgusting.

His eyes finally reach ours when he speaks, "Maybe." He shrugs. "But maybe not."

"Did errand boy fill you in on her potential whereabouts?"

"He did."

"How do you think this won't screw anything up? *Everything* rides on her." My dear old friend Lorenzo finally speaks.

"Simple. If she is with them, then we simply change the plan. And thankfully I have one. It may take a little longer, but this will kill two birds with one stone."

"How so?" I ask.

I'm intrigued. His sights are aligned with ours, so I'm curious as to how a longer wait will make this work.

"It destroys her *and* them. If she actually is staying with those irrelevant fools, then we let them all get attached. When the time is right, we take her, effectively destroying them in the process. They won't care about anything other than some pitiful attempts to find her, and by the time they do, we will have everything in order. Then nothing can be done except our steadfast rise to the top." He maliciously grins, beaming with pride.

I ponder it momentarily. The chances of what he is saying fit the bills with our 'sons'. We have mostly paid their way through school their whole life. Their silly attachments to things is true, and if all works the way he says it will, then it will be easier to dispose of them. Or feed them a different narrative, thus making them willing servants to our cause for greatness. Maybe then they will actually be worthy of their born rights.

I look at Robert and Lorenzo, seeking their opinions on this. They simply nod in agreement. It seems that all of our visionary works are in perfect alignment again.

I nod in his direction. "Very well. Do what you must. Just keep us updated on the process. Do you have a time frame by chance?"

"Not currently. But we all know how invalids operate. No longer than the first of the year, tops, if it goes to plan. Plenty of time to cause irreparable damage. I also plan to start my fun tonight, so all will fall into place."

Hmm...

"While it's a little longer than we had planned, I guess we can go along with it. As long as what you said holds true, then I see no reason a few extra months are worth a worry."

"Oh, it will. And once it does?" He stands, bringing his tumbler in the air, and we follow suit. "Well, let's just say this is our preemptive cheers to a very lucrative and powerful business venture."

We all toast, take sips of our whiskeys, and then fall back into our chairs in a glorious laughter at how well our plan is coming together.

Chapter 20

Declan

Her soft snores beside me are adorable, but from what I dug up from G, she is exhausted. So while I lie beside her, my raging hard-on is demanding a round two, maybe three or four. *Christ.* I feel like a teenager who just discovered masturbation and porn.

She was a goddamn dream, and I haven't even sunk into her yet. My dick is itching to fill her with my cum over and over again until she is so full there is no more room.

Surprisingly enough, I haven't had much of an urge to drown my soul in alcohol or pills either. An odd sense of calm that has washed over me since we convinced Bethani, well, since *Sinclair* went on one of his usual asshole demanding tirades. I'm surprised by how much of the usual shit that fills the gaping holes in my soul have just...fallen to the wayside. My need for adrenaline-inducing thrills or pushing the toxic combinations of alcohol with oxy, ecstasy, or molly to the limits is just...nonexistent.

It's making me question many things. *Like how can one person just make the bad shit go away?* Her snarky remarks, the way she does the simplest shit, when I catch her all-encompassing aqua eyes staring my way...nothing else matters.

The way she makes my heart come alive, the tarnished, battered, and blackened bastard that it is, terrifies the fuck outta me. I know, without a doubt, that the moment I sink into her heat, *I'm going to be fucking gone.*

Maybe I need to pump the brakes like Gio said. Slow the fuck down before I get too attached like I always do.

As I slowly attempt to move out from under Bethani to make my way back to my room, her arm tightens around my torso and holds me in place.

"What's wrong, Declan?"

Her sleepy murmur catches me off guard.

Dammit. Forgot she startles easily.

"Nothing. I, uh, was just gonna go get something to drink. That's all."

Those aquamarine eyes snap open, shining in the moonlight that's peeping through the blinds, then narrow on me in instant anger.

"Liar. Now tell me, why were you getting up?"

I fall back into the pillow and rub a hand through my hair before running it down my face in frustration. How do you explain that 'I want you so goddamn bad it's not even funny, but I'm scared shitless of the impending emotions that are going to follow because I'm a secret bleeding heart even though I come off as one of the biggest don't-give-a-fuck who you are, just suck my dick and move along toxic fucks known to man'?

Simple.

You don't.

"It's nothing. Just figured I'd give you some space, that's all," I reply, settling on the simple but vague response.

When I finally turn my gaze back toward hers, I realize quickly why she and Sinclair are so good at their verbal spar sessions. She has me struck stupid with her wicked glare. The familiar venom dripping from her expression is eerily similar to Sin's when he is pissed and ready to wreak havoc on the world. And I'm currently the unlucky bastard on the receiving end of a pint-sized female version of that demonic rage.

Way to go, Declan. You really outdid yourself just now, didn't you?

Yes. Yes, I fucking did. And I'm not sure if I'm going to like the consequences either.

She just slowly releases me from her grip and turns away, not saying a damn word. *Fuck.*

"Bethani? You not gonna say anything?"

I'm gifted with more silence. Ouch.

"Come on, baby B, say something."

"Go," is the curt, venom-laced one-word response I get.

"Excuse me?"

One of her hands flies up in the air, waving around dismissively. "You want to be a dick and give me some bullshit response that was clearly a lie, so just fucking go away, Declan. Go back to your room so I can go back to sleep in peace."

My eyes widen on the back of her head momentarily, shocked at her shitty dismissal of me. Then they morph, narrowing to slits for the same reason. *Oh hell no, sunshine.* I may be one of those people who 'feels too much', but her current attitude has my dick rearing back to full attention, ready to fuck that sass right out of her. *Consequences be damned.*

I've got her ass turned and pinned under me and her hands above her head quicker than she can register it all. Those gorgeous almond-shaped eyes are wide-open as the shock registers on the rest of her face. Her eyes lock onto mine, and I pin her with just as fierce of a stare as she gave me.

"Want to say that again, sunshine, since we are face to face now?"

I'm rewarded with a challenging look on her face. The shock is gone as she gears up for battle. *Bring it, baby B.* My adrenaline starts pumping through my veins, excitement of what's to come fueling me in a way I've never thought possible before.

"Say it again, baby B. I *dare* you."

My smile is sinister at all the ideas rolling through my head of how I can turn this attitude of hers into an extremely pleasurable and expressive experience.

Her resolve falters for a second, almost long enough to make me wonder if I'm being too much of a dick before her mouth opens, unleashing her anger on me.

"I said, if you want to be a fucking dick and give me some bullshit response that was clearly a lie, then just fucking go away, Declan. Go back to your room so I can go back to sleep in peace. Happy?"

She smirks, knowing that dishing out those words was just as much of a green light as they were a 'fuck you'.

In all her focus to be a brat, she hasn't realized one thing that I'm about to shed some light on.

"Hmm...that's what I thought you'd say, sunshine. But in your little shit fit just now, you missed something."

She gulps, a quizzical look crossing her beautiful features. It's just as fucking sexy seeing her all fired up as it is seeing her second-guessing.

"Oh, really? What did I miss, Declan?"

I lean down to whisper in her ear, hearing her breath hitch as my words sink in.

"Oh, nothing. Just that as you were dishing out that sassy attitude of yours to me, I was able to position my cock right at your pussy's sweet entrance. I'm ready to plunge deep into you and fuck you like the brat you are." My tongue darts out, flicking her earlobe just once before resuming my spiel. "I can feel your arousal dripping out of you already, coating the tip of my dick. You're clenching ever so slightly, ready to suck me in and take the punishment you deserve. Tell me, sunshine, do you need my cock inside you so bad you have to act like a little shit to get it?"

I pull back enough to look her in the eyes but keep myself stabilized, ready to thrust into her and seal my fate like a goddamn junkie. Her features are flushed, and her breaths are heaving, making those beautiful tits of hers rise and fall dramatically. They're begging me to play with them.

Later, beauties. I'll give you some attention soon enough.

Cocking an eyebrow, I demand my answer, "Answer me, sunshine."

She seductively licks her plump lips slowly, and I have to fight the urge to hold my position. I'm not allowing her to win this battle of wills.

Her gaze is piercing as she breaks the last fucking barrier of my willpower, punctuating each word with a finality that instantly turns her into my favorite addiction. "*Fuck me like you mean it, Declan.*"

I don't reply. I just give her my answer with a deep, hard thrust, sinking all the way to the hilt of her cunt's suctioning depths of wonder. My eyes cross at the sensations of going bareback for the first time.

Mind. Fucking. Blown.

"Holy mother of fuck!" I curse, breathing deep so I don't blow my fucking load as her muscles constrict around my dick. I hold my position until I feel like I can function properly again and not embarrass myself. "You good, sunshine?"

Her eyes stay closed as she nods. Pretty sure she is lost in the feeling like I am, but I still need her words.

"Words, Bethani. Tell me you are good, baby."

"I'm good. Just move, please," she says as her hips start unconsciously squirming under mine. Thank God.

"Hold on tight, sunshine. It's about to get wild."

With that, words cease to exist as I pull out to just the tip and plunge back into her silky slick depths over and over and over again at a pace I'm not sure I've ever possessed. I'm slower on my withdrawal but powerful on the thrust back in. My piercing catches just right on her G-spot each time, sending electrical bolts straight up to my slowly but surely tingling balls that are preparing for release.

Our hips gyrate against each other as we get utterly lost in each other's bodies. I've never experienced such a powerful connection during sex before and I don't even realize my body is picking up the pace. I lose the purposeful rhythm as we start to chase our fast approaching orgasms.

The moans and groans escaping our bodies are a dead giveaway that we are both close, but the burning sensation in my hips and abs from the continuous thrusting is getting worse. I push it back long enough to make sure Bethani gets off first. I finally loosen my grip on her wrists and reach down to throw her right leg over my shoulder as my right hand moves to her engorged clit. As soon as my thumb grazes the swollen nub, her hips jerk violently and change the new angle even more. A deep groan falls from my lips at how fan-fucking-tastic it feels, and I know I won't last much longer like this.

My thumb goes back to work circling, swirling, and pressing down into her clit quicker and quicker to send her over the edge. As her eyes roll back into her head, they shut while a loud moan falls from her lips.

"Open them back up for me, sunshine. I need to see those eyes, baby," I grit out as she lazily opens them back up. They are completely filled with consuming desire.

I pick up my pace just enough for her breath to hitch as I feel her walls start to clench on my swelling dick.

"Let go, baby. Come for me," I say.

That's all it takes as she starts to scream my name, her orgasm taking hold of her body as her back arches off the bed. I'm caught up in the beauty of her orgasm when I'm utterly blindsided by mine tearing through me as her pussy turns into a vice grip on my dick.

"Fuuuuckkkk!" I shout.

My vision goes completely black, my body seizing up in a frenzy as I give one final brutal thrust into her, and my cock starts pouring into her slick, tight heat. My dick jumps each time another wave of cum falls out of me, and her pussy convulses more, sending me into mini orgasms over and over again. After what feels like an hour, I'm wrecked and spent, and I collapse on Bethani's heaving body. I'm somehow careful enough to move just to the side of her, yet I'm still partially covering her in a non-crushing way.

We stay like that for a few, catching our breaths but not talking. I don't even think I know how to talk, let alone fucking move ever again after that.

Regaining enough bodily control, I pull out of Bethani. I'm groaning at the feeling of the loss of her pussy but reveling at the sight of my cum and her release dripping out of her. It's almost enough to make me hard again. But...

"Jesus. I think you broke my dick just now." I laugh and so does she.

"I highly doubt that, Declan."

I turn my head to face her and give her a shit-eating grin. "Yeah. But right now? He is fucking spent and happy."

And because I'm a needy fucker, I grab her and snuggle her into me so her arm is around my waist and her head is lying on my chest. Then I tilt her chin up to give her a searing kiss.

"Go back to sleep, sunshine."

She just hums in agreement. There's a sleepy, content smile on her face as I kiss her forehead and lean back into the pillow. I'm quickly falling asleep myself as satisfaction and contentment like I've never known before wash over my body.

Yup. I'm a royally screwed, whipped puppy for this woman, and I give no fucks.

I'll burn the world to the ground for her, which reminds me.

I still need to set some shit on fire and find the motherfucker who needs to die for touching what's ours. For now, having my girl in my arms as we both drift off to sleep is where I need to be. Other shit can wait until later.

Yeah, I'm going to regret thinking that one eventually.

Chapter 21

Bethani

"And today in class we will be learning about depth perception, delving further into the topic of how to perceive what you are trying to capture in your image."

And with that, Professor Gilford begins to drone on and on about a topic I taught myself, and I lose focus as I try to stay awake.

Every little movement I make has me reeling at how unbelievably sore I am after yesterday with Giovanni, and *then* the early morning escapades with Declan. I didn't think it was possible to feel *this* sore after sex. But I guess that's what happens when two six-foot-four plus, dick pierced horndogs proceeded to ravish my body beyond belief. They have both stamina and tenacity I thought was only possible in porn or some crazy third dimension.

I still can't believe I slept with both of them, separately, in under twelve hours of each other. Who am I, and where did normal me even go? While I'm not complaining about any of the sex, or even some of the new positions I learned in the process, feeling them still dripping out of me is a foreign concept I'm starting to get used to.

Mutual attraction jumping straight into no condom sex. I'm seriously hoping and praying all those STD-free sexual test results they showed me weren't just fake documents they made to get into chicks' pants, otherwise they won't have dicks for much longer.

Though both of their reactions when we were 'involved' looked way too real to be faked, so maybe they aren't the conniving rich fuckers I initially thought. Although to some degree, I still think they are.

"*Miss* Reece!" Professor Gilford yells, dragging me out of my exhausted, sex-induced haze.

"Y-yes, Professor?" I tentatively ask, meeting his gaze.

He absolutely loathes me and is always looking for an excuse to fail me even though others have paid me for the exact same picture. Of course they get an A, and I barely pass. It's probably because I refuse to go on a date with the sleazeball too.

Another joy to this archaic hell hole.

Not impressed, he just sighs deeply. "Clearly, this class is unimportant to you today. Pack up and leave. You'll receive a zero for today's class. Maybe *next* time you can show a little more enthusiasm to your academic career."

"Yes, sir," I reply, but I roll my eyes at his classic douchebag act while putting my stuff in my bag.

I stand up and walk out, ignoring the snickers and pity looks directed my way. Professor Gilford proceeds to talk again, but I feel his eyes on my ass as I reach the door. I'm thankful for when it closes and I don't have to deal with him anymore.

Glancing at my phone and realizing I was only in the class for fifteen minutes of the hour and a half long lecture, I decide to head to the far side of campus where my P.O. Box is located. I need to check and see what upcoming bills I have.

The crisp fall air bites a little as I step out of the arts building, so I stop long enough to throw my Blackwell U hoodie on to tame the slight breeze from freezing me. We may live in the mid to somewhat 'bottom of Nor Cal', but it can still get cold here. Thankfully it's not Seattle cold and rain, but bad enough.

I'm three quarters of the way across campus to my mailbox, when a series of dings from my phone has me reaching to see which one of the three overprotective oafs is wondering where I am.

Declan: Aren't you supposed to be in class sunshine?

Giovanni: Yes, she is. Photography 2 from 10-11:30. Did class end early Tesoro?

Declan: Why are you walking all the way to the farthest side of campus by the sketch gas station anyways? The fuck is going on?

Declan: Ha! I knew I was right! Score 1 for me!

Giovanni: *eye roll emoji* Bravo D. You remembered something other than the last time you got laid. You get a gold sticker.

Declan: Just under 6 hours ago, thank you very much. Dick bag.

Sinclair: Jesus Christ. Pay attention. She is still walking away from campus assholes. What is going on kitten? If you don't answer in the

next 30 seconds we are heading your way.

Giovanni: Agreed.

Declan: I third that notion.

Oh hell. Can they be any more overbearing?

Me: CHILL you overprotective Nancys. My professor is a jerk and tossed me out of class. So I'm walking to the P.O. Box the school gave me when I came for orientation. No need to send a search party or anything.

Giovanni: ......

Sinclair: .....

Declan: ....

Oh Lord. Bombarding of questions in three...two...one...

Declan: Why did you get thrown out of class B? What's going on? Whose ass am I going to kick?

Giovanni: P.O. Box??? The fuck?

Sinclair: Gio, I want the name of the professor. NOW.

Giovanni: On it.

Me: Will you guys stop? It's no big deal.

Sinclair: Got anything G?

Giovanni: Professor Gilford. 44. Taught here for 8 years now in the arts building as the photography professor. Room 305

Sinclair: On my way there now.

Me: NO!!!! Do NOT do that unless you want to see my knee in your dick again!

Sinclair: You better have a damn good reason as to why one of us shouldn't go there kitten.

Sinclair: Deck? G? Update. 5 min out.

Me: Will you guys stop? This is ridiculous.

Declan: Then tell us sunshine and maybe we will stop.

Giovanni: Don't stop. He is done here. Get rid of him.

Sinclair: ....Why?

Lord help me!

Me: Fine! Because you guys are gonna do whatever you want, regardless of how I'll look in this situation to you know, everyone. He asked me on a date at the beginning of last year and I told him no. He has hated me ever since and I barely pass his classes because of it. Happy now?

Giovanni: ......

Declan: ......

Sinclair: .....
Sinclair: NOT in the slightest kitten. Don't worry. This problem is going to go away very fast. Also, do NOT leave that shithole area once you get your mail. One of us will be there soon to pick you up.
Me: *4 eye roll emojis* Whatever.
Sinclair: Kitten.....
Me: Byeeeeeee!

And with that, I shut my phone off and stuff it back into my bag as I walk into the little building where my P.O. Box is.

"Overbearing chauvinists. Stupid bossy jerks," I mutter to myself as I slide the key into my designated slot.

I hurry up and grab my mail out and quickly walk back outside to sit on the stairs and go through everything. While the area isn't 'terrible' like the guys seem to think—trust me, I've lived in worse—the building itself is weird and creepy. So I prefer to get in and out as quickly as possible.

Sitting down on the bottom step, I toss my bag beside me and start looking through everything. My phone bill, no surprise there. What's this, a letter from the school? Opening it and scanning through the document, I see that my scholarship has been lowered and my food and housing are no longer going to be covered. *What? Why?* Looking further down, it explains that because my photography grade is borderline failing—*I freaking wonder why*—they have decided my scholarship needs to be adjusted to motivate me to get a better grade and earn the rest back.

I sink my teeth into my lip hard in an effort to stop the tears that are flooding my eyes over this bullshit decision. They don't even know why I'm damn near failing, nor do they fucking care. It's bullshit.

Closing my eyes, I take a few cleansing breaths to steady myself. Whatever. They want a fight, they have one. Opening my eyes, my resolve is back as I crumple the stupid letter and toss it on the ground in a childish but satisfying 'fuck you' to the school. All I have to do is get a couple of the others in class that aren't complete jackasses to side with me, maybe that will help. Or I threaten to not sell them the photos I take that they buy off of me and pass as their work. They wouldn't be happy about having to do the work themselves. That would take away from their easy lifestyle and they can't have that.

As I flip through the other junk, an unusually smaller letter catches my eye. It's a heavier, custom card stock folded over and sealed with a weird wax that has a stamp in it that I can't quite make out. It's almost like the person who sent it was in a rush and messed it up. Glancing up and looking around me, a cold chill passes through me, almost like I'm being watched.

As I try to nonchalantly glance around to see if someone is actually watching me, I carefully open the letter to find a handwritten script. Slowly reading it, my jaw drops in horror at the words.

Bethani,

You can run but you can't hide.If you think those fools will protect you, you're wrong.They hide secrets, just as you do.While you think no one knows about your sordid little past.I do.I've been watching you, sweetheart.Soon enough, you'll be forever mine.Together, we shall rule.Me as the King.You as my docile little Queen.Don't get too comfortable in that little castle on campus.When you least expect it, a dark little secret will be revealed.By then...you'll be forever mine.And those silly little boys?Fucking gone.Enjoy your time with them because it does have an expiration date.

-T

My stomach is nauseous reading the words over and over again. I've been followed? How did anyone even know where I lived before the guys found me? I've *never* let anyone see where I went to sleep.

My heart starts to race even more as the feeling of being watched fills me with dread. My palms are clammy, and a dizzying feeling washes over me. It's been a long time since I've felt like this and let my heart arrhythmia take control.

I quickly shove the letter into my backpack so someone, like the guys if they show up, doesn't see it. I zip my bag up and rush over to the bushes at the side of the building to throw up the contents of my stomach. I attempt to not pass out, praying the action will help calm me down and stabilize me.

As I'm letting the violent waves of my churning stomach wash over me, retching and gagging as everything lets loose, I hear a vehicle in the distance slam to a stop. Multiple doors open and slam. There are footsteps pounding toward me and voices yelling at me. I'm too far gone to care or even respond as another wave almost knocks me to my knees. But before I can fall, a pair of strong arms come up behind me to keep me standing. My throwing up has hopefully stopped as I inhale the sexy, unique scent that I instantly recognize as Declan. It's invading my senses and helping me to calm down. I lean my head back into his chest and keep my eyes closed, because I know if I open them right now, the world will be a hot, spinning mess.

"Bethani, you okay, sunshine?"

"Tesoro, do we need to go to the hospital?"

"Fuck that. G, call the doctor and tell him he has ten minutes to meet us in the garage. I've got her stuff and some bullshit crumpled letter from the school we need to address later. Declan, pick her up carefully and get her in the vehicle. She needs to get back to the penthouse."

Normally Sinclair's insisting tone pisses me off, but right now, I'm thankful one of them has their head on straight. The longer I'm here, the more I want to throw up.

Declan's muscular arms pick me up, cradling me gently like he is afraid I'm going to break in two as he slowly walks to the vehicle. He gets in while still holding me.

"Take a drink, sunshine. It'll help."

I open up just enough as a bottle of water hits my lips. I take timid sips so I don't unleash the devil gates all over the vehicle.

"Thank you," I mumble when I've taken enough to mostly wash the atrocious taste from my mouth and start the process of rehydrating. Gatorade and Tylenol are going to be my best friends for the next couple days. The last time this happened was after I was in LA for a few months. It took almost a week for me to feel completely normal again.

"Kitten, what happened back there?"

"Nothing important. I'll be fine."

"Bullshit, kitten. Why were you throwing up like that?"

I debate for a second before deciding it isn't worth it to let them know about the creepy letter. These guys are wickedly overprotective of me for some ungodly reason, and if I ever want to be able to walk to class without one of these guys as a personal escort or have a moment of alone time, they don't need to know. Plus, it doesn't even make any sense. What secrets are they hiding?

"It's just the letter. Pissed me off. I let my anger get out of control and didn't realize my arrhythmia was out of whack before it was too late. No worries."

The tensing of Declan below me is a dead giveaway that I just fucked up. Royally. Only Ramona knows about it, my heart condition, because she took me to the free clinic down there for some tests to figure out what was happening. Granted, it's not bad most of the time. Even during the crazy sex-capades with Giovanni and Declan I was able to control it. Stress or getting something insane in the mail, like a crazy stalker letter, will set it off because I lose focus on it quicker.

Deciding to face the music, I slowly open my eyes to glance around at the furious glares set on me. Yeah, I already know what's coming, so I start talking quickly to hopefully diffuse the situation as best as I can.

"Listen, it's not a big deal. That's the first time it's happened in like two years or something like that." The narrowing of silver gray, ocean blue, and emerald green eyes says that they don't believe a word coming out of my mouth. "I'm serious. I've been to the doctor for it before. They weren't worried about it. The only thing that would be a concern would be if it caused a heart attack or something like that." Deepening scowls and clenched jaws make me realize that yet again, I'm having a word vomit moment by saying too much. I simply just lean back into Declan and cross my arms in defiance. "I'm just gonna stop talking," I mutter while glancing toward the floorboard of Sinclair's G-Wagon to avoid the grumpasaurus's slightly deranged glares.

The rest of the ride is eerily silent until we get back to their parking garage. I'm dreading the conversation that I know they will want to have, but they can all kick rocks. I just need to chug a Gatorade and take a couple Tylenol before I head to my next class. I'm crabby, dehydrated, and annoyed with the nonsense, so they can all piss up a rope if they think I'm just going to comply. Especially when my scholarships are already on thin ice. Missing more classes won't bode well in my favor.

I'm still in a pissy mood when the elevator reaches their penthouse, now because I'm still being cradled like a damn doll. Declan quickly walks to the living area and swiftly sets me down on the couch before heading to the kitchen and coming back with a bottle of water and a strawberry-kiwi Gatorade electrolyte pack to dump in. Sinclair comes from somewhere with aspirin, dropping the bottle in my lap.

"Uhh...thanks. But can I get some like Tylenol or something?"

"Nope."

"And why the hell not?"

"For someone with a heart condition, that they didn't inform us of, you'd think you realize that aspirin is the better option, because it doesn't overly thin or thicken your blood. Which can cause the arrhythmia to be worse."

Dang it. How did I not know that? I just ignore him and read the bottle to see how much to take. Then dump a couple in my hand before emptying the packet into the water, shaking it, popping the pills into my mouth, and chugging half of the water to start the process of rehydrating.

"Well, thanks for saving me, again. But I really can't afford to miss another class, so I gotta get going."

I also need to find a spot to hide that letter so I can study it later.

I'm met with all three towering sexy jerks just standing in front of me for a second before they all sit on the coffee table to stare at me with displeasure.

Hey, I never once said I couldn't be a giant bitch when I wanted to be. Especially when I'm up against the kings of campus. I gotta pick my battles, and for some reason picking battles with these three is a sexy thrill that usually ends up with me in the shower, tub, or my bed masturbating until I explode in rays of pleasure.

"Go ahead. Spit out whatever caveman crap you three are contemplating to try to convince me to stay here and skip class. Spoiler alert, it's probably not going to work. Especially with the bullshit from that school letter. I can't afford to miss any more classes unless I want to kiss what's left of my scholarship goodbye."

The elevator dings and I nearly jump out of my damn skin. The guys all give me a questioning look at my antics, but I just dismiss them. Seeing an older gentleman walk in with a medical bag has my temper flaring right back up.

"Oh, come on! This is crap!"

"Come on, Bethani, we're just worried about you. That's all," Declan says and pins me with a pleading look. I almost melt at his puppy dog eyes. *Almost.*

"Don't you puppy dog eye me, Declan. That shit won't work. I already told you I'm fine."

Declan just tilts his head toward a brooding Sinclair, then shrugs while glancing back at me. "Suit yourself, sunshine. You're up, asshole."

Declan stands alongside Giovanni and they walk to shake hands with the doctor and walk down the hall to a room. I'm gobsmacked at how easily they just left me with Satan's son. Fucking traitors.

I pin Sinclair with a fiery stare, not willing to back down to him. At least not yet. Watching his control falter when we argue is a turn-on, not that I'll ever let him know that.

"What's the devil's choice today in an attempt to get me to comply?" I challenge, feeling my heart rate pitter slightly, but not in a bad way.

His arms are crossed over his tight-fitted black T-shirt, his muscles bulging as the shirt can barely contain him. Sexy, torn-up, and dark fitted jeans cover his legs but still let the few leg tattoos he has peek through just enough that it's slightly distracting me. I can't help it. They all parade around in different states of undress constantly. Their favorite is walking around in just their boxer briefs in the morning. It's hard not to notice the things about them that make me want to cover their bodies in chocolate syrup and lick it up off them.

A deep chuckle from him brings me back to see a sinister glint in his eyes. He quickly gets up off the coffee table and is on top of me just as fast. There is plenty of space between us as he hovers over me, but I still feel the suffocating presence of his commanding personality.

"Oh, princess, that little glint you had in your eyes while you were checking me out told me all I needed to know for my 'devil's choice' as you so eloquently put it." His eyes shine in sin, lust, and challenge.

My throat becomes as dry as the Mojave Desert as I attempt a witty reply. "O-oh yeah? And what's that, Lucifer?" I'm finally able to croak out.

He snorts, then gifts me with a wicked smile as he speaks. "You have two choices here, kitten. Option one? You be a good girl and let me take you into the room and have the doctor take care of you." His eyes flare as he stops talking. He sinks his top teeth into his lip and slowly drags them over his lip in a tortuous motion that has a fire rising in my belly. "Option two? I drag your pretty ass back to my bedroom, strip you naked, tie you to my bed, and have my way with you. I'll shove a plug up your virgin ass, put a ball gag in that smart mouth of yours, and fuck you long and hard until you are a complete and utter whimpering mess under me. I'll rip the gag out of your mouth and demand your sweet submission to me. Then, and only then, when those pouty perfect lips are begging and pleading for me, will I allow you to come. Watching you shatter below me as I paint your pussy walls with my cum will be one of the greatest satisfactions ever."

He stops as his nostrils flare, and he dips his hips just enough to give me a sample of his rock-hard erection through our jeans. My breathing is haggard as his vivid description runs through my head.

I want that. *God, do I want that.* But I'm not ready to let him win, yet.

"O-option one. I choose option one."

"I'd expect nothing less than that answer, kitten. But I'm willing to wait. It'll make it all the sweeter when you finally agree."

"Excuse me? Say that again?" I question.

"I said, we took care of the issue with the professor, Tesoro." Giovanni sighs at my questioning.

After Sinclair's little show, I went back to the room and had the doctor check me out like they asked. The doctor reassured them I was fine, but they somehow convinced the doctor to agree to bi-weekly checkups at the penthouse for the next three months to verify that 'everything is fine'. Although I was a horny and unsatisfied mess, I somehow was able to make it through the two hours the doctor was there. He answered every question under the sun the guys asked. Some of them were actually decent, and I was able to learn a few things. Others were just so off the wall it wasn't even funny, and I'm surprised the doctor didn't laugh at them.

When I finally was released from the torture, under orders to rest and rehydrate the remainder of the day, I finally started quizzing the guys on what they meant when they said they took care of the issue.

"Do we really need to talk about it, sunshine?" Declan groans while shoveling food in his face like usual. How he isn't five hundred pounds is beyond me.

"Yes, yes, we freaking do! You controlling cavemen got your way with the doctor, so I'm getting my way now, dang it!"

They just glance at me before returning their attention back to the TV and resuming eating. Guess I need to be more dramatic. "Fine. I'll just go pack my shit, grab a taxi to the nearest bus station, and go back to LA if you want to be that way."

"Fine, you win," Sinclair grumbles, surprising me.

I can only assume that's because I blue balled his ass earlier, and he is switching his tactics to throw me off. I just smile.

"Well? Do share, please."

He rolls his eyes but talks. "We obviously have pull here in the campus, kitten. All we did was threaten him a little with some hidden photos he thought he destroyed that could ruin his marriage to his high-profile district attorney wife. Either he quit, but not before he fixed your grades, or we sent all the evidence to his wife. He chose the right option. He fixed your stuff, submitted to the school that he was being unfair grading you, then resigned stating the workload was too much."

"Well, what about this?" I ask, showing them my phone where the video of my old 'home' being set aflame plays. "Which one of you had a part in that?" A shit-eating grin from Declan is all the answer I need as to who the culprit is. "You do realize that's a felony, right?"

"Tesoro, nothing will happen to us. Promise."

"How can you even say that? Lighting buildings on fire and threatening professors, like what kind of pull can you have to not get into any trouble?"

They all visibly stiffen at my question but return to their normal selves so fast I almost miss the temporary change in their demeanor.

"Spill it. Now. What aren't you guys telling me?"

None of them can look me in the eye, almost like they are ashamed of their status. Slowly, Giovanni turns toward me a bit so I can see the fear and frustration in his eyes. "How do I explain this to you?"

I'm confused by his choice of words but go along with it anyways. "Easy. Just tell me what has you three all twisted in knots and spit it out. If you think I'm going to judge you, then you're all wrong. I'm not that type of person, and I'd hope you all realize that by now."

He nods, clearly conceding to my point. "Well, you've obviously heard of our status here on campus, right? You understand it's our families' names across the campus?" he asks and I nod.

"Yeah. Your families are major donors and whatnot, right?"

"Tesoro, our families aren't just 'donors' or whatever. We *are* this campus. Blackwell University was started by our fourth great-grandfathers during the California Gold Rush. Boris Blackwell, Lachlan Carter, and Giuseppe Martinelli were the founders of this campus. We are namesakes to this place. Every male born from them has attended here. We can do whatever the fuck we want here and nothing will ever happen to us, ever."

"Oh," is my only response to that. What else can I say? I figured it was a family thing of some sorts. But *legit* campus royalty? Holy shit balls of fire.

"Oh is right, sunshine, but it's more than that too," Declan adds as my gaze swings to him.

"Okay? Go ahead."

His hand floats through his messy hair, reminding me of how it looked last night after our mind-blowing sex. I shake my head to clear that thought.

Focus, hormones. It's not time for that shit.

"Well...have you ever heard of Blackwell Industries, Martinelli Entertainment Industries, or Carter Pharmaceuticals?"

I rack my brain but come up short. "Possibly? I'm not one hundred percent sure, though. Why?"

He just tilts his head back, looking toward the ceiling. "Our families own those too."

I shrug because the connection isn't catching in my head. "Okay. And? Your families own some businesses and this university? Big deal?"

"More than a big deal, kitten. Those businesses are the top in their fields. You live with the next three CEOs of those multibillion-dollar companies. When we brushed you off about what we did saying it was 'no big deal', that's because it's literally *and* figuratively no big deal to us. Our pockets are so fucking deep that damn near nothing on this earth can contend with us."

I have nothing to say to that. I mean, what can I really say to any of that? Did I suspect these guys were loaded? Absolutely. Did I think they were that loaded? Ha! Absolutely not in a million fucking years.

As I'm sitting here, mouth on the floor looking at them, their behavior changes from unsure to glaringly uncomfortable. It's obvious my lack of reaction to this isn't what they expected. Or it's exactly what they expected, hence their change in demeanor. When they all move to stand is when I finally find my voice again.

"Where are you guys going?"

"Anywhere but here," Sinclair mutters.

"Sit back down. *Now.*"

Their eyes widen at my tone, but they flop back down after a second.

"First, let me say I'm sorry for my reaction, or better, lack of reaction. Second, why were you going to walk away?"

Giovanni goes to say something, but Declan cuts him off. "We were going to walk away because we figured you'd be pissed that we didn't tell you all that information. But we also assumed you knew it all too. Not something any of us like talking about in the slightest."

"Well, I didn't. Or, at least, I assumed you guys had to have some sort of society status to belong here at this campus. I just didn't put it all together that you literally are the status precedence here at this place and apparently the dang world."

"Fuck. This is why I hate fucking talking about this bullshit," Sinclair starts to grumble, anger radiating off his hulking frame.

Declan is just stating off into space, completely checked out of the whole thing, and Giovanni has that tentative sweet side of his peeking through as he looks at me, giving me time to process.

"What's the big deal exactly with talking about it all? I get it. Trust me, I do. But mine is because it's the polar opposite situation. I'm ashamed of some of the twisted shit I've had to go through."

Memories of some of the things my mother let me go through hit me like a ton of bricks, and I have to do everything in my power to not let it get to me. A second freak-out on the same day would throw these three over the edge, and I can't let that happen.

"Just because our lives are completely different sides of the spectrum, doesn't mean we haven't had our own twisted shit to live through, sweetheart. Our scars run just as deep. We just have the world at our fingertips to hide all the pain and misery."

My eyes start to well as I glance over at Declan

It's true, everyone goes through shit in life. Some just have the power and access to hide it while others like myself have to fight tooth and nail to keep the facade from crumbling.

As I glance at their faces, the anguish and pain crossing their features tears me open in ways I never thought possible. My heart bleeds a little for these men. While the looks on their faces say I'll probably never know the full extent of their suffering, I'm oddly okay with that. I don't even know my whole past according to that stupid letter, but what I do know about it, I may never share myself.

Some secrets are too hard to let go of because of the crushing repercussions that can follow them. I've seen the fierce protective nature these three have naturally oozing from their pores. They all look like the types that could very easily burn down the world for someone they care about when threatened. Obviously they just did, for me of all people. Someone who is a self-proclaimed orphan.

Shaking the negativity from my head, I try changing topics in an attempt to lighten the mood. "Let's just not talk about all this sad depressing shit anymore. If you guys choose to talk about it, I'm here to lend an open mind and listening ear. If not, oh well. I've asked you to respect my choices to talk or not talk about my past, so I'm respecting your choice to open up or not to. Fair?"

The deep sighs of relief escape their lips. A weight is lifted off their shoulders that I'm not being a bitch and making them talk.

"Fair enough. Thanks, sunshine," Declan happily answers, flashing a chipper smile.

I yet again feel the impenetrable walls I've built around myself crumbling just a little bit. I flash them a smile of my own before using my earlier situation to tip the scales in my favor tonight.

"Now since I know you three jerks won't let me move unless I want to use the bathroom, how about you all commandeer some snacks, drinks, and popcorn while I sit right here and find a comedy for us to watch."

They nod, but the smiles on their faces could make even the biggest Scrooge McAsshat crack. They all stand up and go to the kitchen, stopping to kiss my forehead before they continue on their mission I gave them. I'm even nice and let Sinclair join in on that, the surly grouch reveling in my temporary truce.

Don't worry, Sinclair. Just because I'm being nice right now, doesn't mean I won't go straight back to dishing out shit to you tomorrow.

And that's exactly how we spend the rest of the night. A white flag flying high as we laugh and joke about the ridiculous rom-com I forced them to watch while snacking and just enjoying each other's company.

Chapter 22

Sinclair - Beginning of November

"Where the fuck is she?" I demand, storming out of my room toward the kitchen where I know the guys are sitting.

Rounding the corner, their eyes are wide and mouths are stuffed with THE jumbo subs our little mastermind made for us earlier.

"Well, where the fuck is the tiny fucking terror tornado?"

Declan holds a finger up while chewing and swallowing, giving me even more time to grow pissed. My patience is at an absolute zero right now, and I'm fucking ready to fight her, then fuck her ass senseless.

"What's up, dude?"

Seriously? That's the question he gives me?

"Where. Is. Bethani? She and I need to have a little fucking chat."

A shit-eating grin rocks his face as he leans back, crossing his arms over his chest. "This should be good. What happened now?"

Knowing my fucking friends won't tell me where she is unless I give them more details, traitorous assholes, I tell them what our little prankster did. "Oh nothing, the usual shit. She offered to wash my whites since she was 'already doing laundry' and decided to color my shit hot fucking pink somehow. Sure, I'll let that slide since I can just order more shit. Then the brat dumped my cologne bottles into the same bowl and refilled them with the toxic-ass combinations of them all, destroying more stuff. But what she did this time? I'm done, and she is being taught a lesson. Now."

"And what exactly did she do this time?" G snickers, and I level him with fire behind my eyes.

"Motherfucker. You *helped* her?" My voice rises a few octaves by the end of my question.

His devilish smirk has me ready to pounce and choke the fuck out of him.

"I mean, she informed me of an idea. I just had to keep you entertained long enough for her to do whatever it was she wanted to do."

"Oh shit. What did she do?" Declan asks, already laughing at me like the fool I am for not remembering to lock the door to my room.

Instead of telling them, I proceed to drop my sweats to the floor and stand back up for them to see the utter carnage our resourceful little hellcat has accomplished.

My fucking friends just stare at me with their jaws on the floor before they both double over laughing at my misery. Declan's dumb ass falls on the floor in the process of his enjoyment.

"It's not fucking funny, assholes," I grit out.

Through a fit of obnoxious laughter, Gio replies, "Ha! I knew she wanted to pull something, but this?" He stops to laugh more. "Fucking hilarious."

Looking down at myself, I can see where it would be hilarious to someone *other* than me. The lower half of my body is a fucking shimmery shade of purple, thanks to her putting a glitter dye in my body wash. Then the little terrorist somehow found my frenum bars and replaced them all with one single hot pink and fake diamond studded one as my sole form of genital 'jewelry'. How she accomplished that yesterday in the ten minutes Giovanni was asking me random questions in his room, not twenty feet away from mine, is beyond me. Today she snuck in to snatch the barbell I took out right before my shower to soak in its sterilized solution so my only option was this pink piece of crap. That is a feat I wasn't aware the powerhouse of hell was capable of accomplishing. Because I didn't hear or see her sneaky ass when she snuck in my room, which pisses me off even more.

I quickly pull my sweats up. I hadn't even bothered with boxer briefs, because if I have my way, my dick is gonna be buried so deep inside Bethani that underwear is a waste of time.

Now, if only I could get the cohorts of chaos to stop laughing long enough to give me the answer I need.

"Nooooo! Why did you pull your shit up! I didn't even get a picture!" Declan exclaims through snorts and chuckles.

"Don't worry," G says. "Got one when he looked down to examine his Barney-ass self."

My eyes cut to Gio as I move closer to the dickhead. I slam my hands on the counter, and the sound stops them long enough to see I'm over joking around. The sting in my palms is a welcomed pain to keep me grounded.

"Where the fuck is she? I'm not fucking asking again. Unless you want your rooms trashed?"

"Hey, guys! What's—" Bethani's words die as I turn my head toward her, happy that I don't have to go search our giant-ass place for her.

Her eyes widen at the scene in front of her, obviously realizing that her little prank succeeded.

"Oh shit," she whispers, then she instantly turns and takes off like the bat out of hell she is as I start after her.

"Get your ass back here!" I thunder as I'm following her toward the staircase. She halts at my voice. "Kitten, get your ass back here so we can talk, and maybe your punishment won't be so bad."

What does the little siren do? Just gives me the hottest panty-melting smile known to goddamn man. Then jumps her curvy little ass up onto the banister and slides down the fucker, jumping off right before she crashes into the end. She lands and turns to see my dumb ass struck stupid at her ingenuity before she takes off.

I don't know if I'm more impressed at how she slid down thirty-five feet of banister without falling, her graceful landing, or how she easily evaded me before coming to my senses. The fire in my veins flares with an intent desire to capture my little vixen and finally punish her into submission while finally making her mine too.

While she has been randomly shacking up with Declan and Giovanni for the past couple weeks, I've been lying in wait while my nut sack shrivels up from lack of use other than from my hand and lube. Today, though? That finally fucking ends, pink dick jewelry and shimmery fucking purple Barney legs be damned.

Descending the stairs quickly, I follow the way she went, which leads to the gym, showers, and sauna area. *Perfect.* There is only one door. *Nowhere to hide, my little kitty cat.* Stepping over to the hallway closet, I quickly find a couple things I'll need before I lock us in the gym area. Thank fuck I keep multiples of the basics located in different areas of the penthouse for this exact reason.

While I have the majority of my toys in my room, I prefer to keep extras of certain items strategically placed in specific locations. Call me a boy scout of sex toys or whatever you want. But in a perfect moment like this? My overthinking and over-prepared ass is thankful for thinking ahead.

My dick is rock-hard under my sweats as I step into the gym area and punch in the code to secure it. Setting everything down on the ground, I pull out my phone to send the guys a text.

Me: Gym secured. Don't fucking come down here.

Declan: Wouldn't dream of it, or would I?

Me: Declan...I'm warning you.

Declan: Yeah, yeah. We know the drill Mr. Masochist.

Me: Fuck off.

Giovanni: Don't forget consent asshole. I'm not having my privileges revoked because of you. I quite frankly enjoy my sex with her, and I'd like to keep having sex with her.

Declan: What he said. Now get your ass to my room G. Sinclair doesn't have to be the only one getting a happy ending. *winking emoji* *Eggplant emoji*

Giovanni: Yes sir!

Rolling my eyes, I toss my phone down and strip my shirt off and pocket one of my items. I'm going to need it when I find her pretty little ass that I can't wait to sink my teeth into. Setting the lights dimmer, but still at a bright enough setting to see, I take slow steps and survey the area.

I have one spot I could hide and wait it out until she gets brave, but I think my feisty little kitten prefers the chase of it all. Me, her dark and dominant predator. Her, my tasty little prey, who is all willing and needy for her capture and punishment.

"Oh, kitten, where are you?" I ponder out loud. Keeping my tone bored, I convey that I don't give a shit, just enough to bring her out. The sound of one of the shower curtains rustling catches my attention, and I decide to amuse her. Walking into the bathroom area, I find that it's bright, and I see no telling shadows that she is here. Which means she is waiting for me in the sauna.

Humoring her, I start a dramatic act of looking behind each shower curtain, and when I hear the door opening and closing, I give her a two-second head start before turning and racing out to catch her fumbling with the door. She is pissed and unfocused, so I'm easily able to sneak up on her.

"Gotcha, kitten," I whisper in her ear as she screams.

Trapping her in my arms so she can't hit me in the face or junk, I toss her up in the air high enough to throw her over my shoulder. I then turn back toward the gym to see which machine will work best for my venture.

Finally I notice the useless Smith machine. We thought that fucker was a good idea, but it only ended up with us in pain from the lack of form when we squatted. Now I'm thankful for it, as it'll be perfect.

Bethani keeps squirming around and swearing me up and down like a Russian soldier as I make my way over to the equipment. I give her a firm smack to one of those gorgeous ass cheeks, smiling at the thought of my mark finally caressing that golden skin of hers.

"Knock it off, kitten."

"You fucking knock it off!"

Sliding her down the front of my body so she can feel my erection, I capture her wrists in my hand and quickly pin them to the bar above her. Taking the rope out of my pocket, I realize it's one of the ones that is pre-tied in a loose knot for situations like this. Fuck yeah.

Quickly lacing it over her hands, I pull on it just enough to secure them together and make quick work of wrapping it around the bar a few times, suspending them upward.

"W-what are you doing?" Her voice is timid and lacks all the sass she had just a moment ago.

I tsk her before replying. "Where is that big bad attitude of yours now, kitten? Hmm?"

Finishing the knot, I stand back to admire the work. Not my best by a long shot, but at this point I'm too fucking far gone to care. My need to possess her, own her, and finally fucking make her mine—just like my friends have done—consumes me to the point I almost want to say fuck the rules. But I don't, because the guys are right.

If I fuck this up, I could destroy everything.

To calm the raging storm inside me, I start walking around her and begin my explanation, "Here is how this is going to play out, Bethani. We're going to play a little game. For every question you get right, I'll give you a little treat. For every question you get wrong, well, let's just say you may or may not enjoy it. Does that sound fair, kitten?"

As I turn to face her, I'm met with an evil little scowl from the terrorist of temptation. Ah, I see that fire has come back now that she is tied up. Perfect. Standing in front of her, arms crossed over my naked torso with only a pair of sweats on that do not contain my steel pipe erection, I'm witnessing the subtle changes that give away her enjoyment of being restrained.

Her eyes begin to dilate as she peruses my body with her eyes. Her chest rises and falls a little harder and heavier as her breathing rate increases, making those supple tits of hers heave up and down in her sports bra and tank top. I can see the perspiration begin to form on her skin as her arousal begins to elevate her core temperature. The whole act of watching my little fawn wriggle and worm around while I stand like the stoic lion waiting to pounce makes my dick jerk as my resolve tries to falter. The movement makes Bethani's breath hitch, bringing my attention back to her flushed face and parted lips.

Walking toward her, I raise my arms to capture the bar between my hands as I tower over Bethani's small but curvy frame. When she finally tilts her head up to meet my gaze, I'm momentarily floored by her eyes. Those flawless aqua eyes that hold and hide so many emotions and secrets are a swirling bottomless pool that I want to fall into without regard for a life jacket to keep me afloat.

"So, my little kitten, do you want to play a game?"

She just nods 'yes', but that won't work, especially with how I play.

"Give me those words, sweet girl," I croon while cupping her chin with one hand and using my thumb to slide it back and forth across her bottom lip, wishing it were my tongue. *Soon enough*.

"Y-yes."

"Yes what?" I ask, wanting *and* needing her clarification.

"Yes. I want to play a game." Her eyes bore into mine, and I see no indication that she isn't just saying yes to please me. She wants and needs this as much as I do.

"Good girl." I kiss her forehead before going into detail. "Now for a few ground rules."

"Rules. Why do we need rules?"

"Because." I inhale deeply, then exhale to relax myself. "I'm a dominant, Bethani. Do you understand what that is?"

She snorts and starts to giggle, catching me off guard. My expression must show my surprise when she composes herself.

"Sinclair, I may be extremely limited to sexual experience, excluding the insanity of the last few weeks, but I'm not stupid. I've also read a few slutty books before, so I have a baseline of knowledge."

"And what may this so-called knowledge be?"

Her eyes roll at my tone, and my hand itches to bust her ass, but I'm biding my time. Because once I start, my little kitten won't know what hit her.

"You love being in control. You want to tell me what to do and expect me to 'be a good girl and listen' for you," she quotes and rolls her eyes again. "Punish me for being bad, reward me for being good. That's about my baseline."

Not bad for going off of some shitty books, but she is definitely what I consider as someone with zero knowledge about it.

"Not the worst definition I've ever heard." I begin my stroll around her again. "But it's so much more than that, kitten."

"Oh? Well, then enlighten me, *sir*." Her condescending tone pisses me off instantly, but that little smart-ass sir makes my cock painfully hard, and I have to sink my teeth into my lip to avoid a groan escaping my lips.

Fuck. I haven't been called that in a while, and hearing it fall from her lips is the sexiest fucking thing ever.

When I'm behind her again, I slink up and stand close enough so that I'm not touching her, but she can feel my body heat radiating off me. Gripping the bars again, I lean down so my lips are a whisper away from her ear.

"Kitten, not only am I a dominant, but I'm also a masochist and a sadist. While I may *want* your willing submission, I know it won't be that easy with you. I wouldn't expect anything less, which makes the other two things all the more fun."

Stopping, I flick her earlobe with my tongue. She gasps, and her head falls back into my chest with a breathy moan. Quickly changing tactics, I sink my teeth into said earlobe. Not enough to damage, but enough to leave marks. Her slight yelp of pain has me gripping the bar above us so tight that I think my hands are going to break. Releasing her lobe from my teeth, I suck on it gently to soothe it, and she heaves a sigh of relief.

Letting it slip from my mouth, I continue, "You see, kitten, as a masochist, I enjoy your insults and degradation of my character. I even enjoy the pain you've inflicted on me. As a sadist, it's the opposite. I enjoy dishing out the pain, degradation, and self-denial just as much as I do receiving it. Makes a wicked combination in the bedroom."

I smirk as I feather a few kisses on her neck, and her instant tilt of her head to open up and give me more room in an unknowing act of submission fuels the desire that's gut punching me for release.

"W-what about the third?"

"You mean the dominant part?"

"Yes."

"It's its own set of rules that flow with the other two. If you agree to it all, I promise you worlds of pleasure unlike you've ever known before. There would be a contract involved where we set ground rules that only apply when it's you and me. Like when you are being a brat like you've been today, you'll get punished. If you are a good girl, you get rewards.

Needing to look her in the eyes again, I walk back around to face her.

"Does all this make sense to you, kitten?"

"Yes."

Quirking a brow at her, I ask, "Yes what, kitten?"

My little smart-ass shows her attitude with that eye roll but complies, "Yes, sir."

These little acts of submission have my blood boiling to the point that my cock is ready to erupt in my sweats, but I refuse to give in to the temptation.

"I'm going to ask you this question only once, so you better listen or this game is over. Understood?" I pin her with a look that tells her I'm not fucking around. Discussion time is over.

"Yes, sir."

"Good girl." Pausing, a flash of worry hits me. Will she agree to this? If she doesn't, *what the fuck am I going to do*? Most of the chicks I've fucked at the sex club are easy. They've already signed the shit and are ready to go. I pick who I want, go into the room, have my fun, and walk away. No drama. The others are quick fucks or getting my dick sucked up in our private suite at the bar. All of it completely meaningless and time passing. This? This is the first fucking time I've ever worked for it, and I'm suddenly a nervous fucking wreck about it.

Because she actually means something to you, asshole.

That glaring thought stops my process. Do I really care about her like that? How can someone like me—a heartless, elite member of society, murdering, fucked up son of even more fucked up parents—have genuine feelings for someone? Shaking my head, I make a mental note to review this later.

"Honesty is a one-way ticket to hell, kitten. At least it is in our world. So be honest with yourself. Are you going to join our little train to the dark side? Or would you rather lie your way to heaven?"

"And what might the perks be if I join?"

Stepping closer, my hand claps gently around her neck. At the slight pressure, I can feel the blood rushing through her veins while her pupils explode. I push back just enough so her eyes are in contact with mine.

"If you join our chaos, princess, you are *ours*. You are Giovanni's. You are Declan's. You are fucking *mine*. No one will ever touch you without our explicit permission. If they do, I'll slit their fucking throats while everyone watches in horror. You'll be our precious queen that we bow down to. We will protect you until our dying breath. You'll also be our precious little slut to fuck whenever we want. If we want you splayed out on the kitchen counter to take turns fucking that sass out of you, we will. When I have you by myself? You submit to me, and I'll bring your body to the throes of pure ecstasy while pushing your limits of pleasure and pain in the best way possible. You would be completely untouchable to anyone else in the world except us. Only us for as long as we choose to be. So what do you say, kitten? An honest one-way ticket to hell as our queen, or a liar's way to the gates of heaven?"

Staring deep into each other's eyes, the little terror gives me the silent treatment for long enough that I'm almost positive I've royally fucked up. I figure I may need to plan my funeral because G and Deck already threatened to murder me, when a wicked glint flares in those enchantress eyes and a devilish smirk crosses her face.

"You're not the only one with blood on their hands, Sinclair. I signed my one-way ticket to hell years ago. So to answer your question, yes, I'll be your queen. But I also will not willingly submit. That, you'll have to work for."

Then she licks those pillow-soft lips and winks, sealing her fate.

The deep breath I hadn't realized I was holding releases. The raging storm of doubt is gone, now fully replaced by the insatiable need to sink my dick in her so deep that she feels me for a week.

She is fucking ours. For however long that may be, I don't have a fucking clue. But right now?

I'm going to enjoy the fuck out of Bethani Reece, in more ways than one.

Chapter 23

Sinclair

Crushing my lips to hers, I'm finally able to claim her as mine. And claiming her is exactly what. I. Fucking. Do. I *possess* her as our mouths fuse together. My lips, tongue, and teeth destroy her perfect little mouth. I nip, suck, and twist our tongues together in a brutalizing act that lets her know exactly who fucking owns her. The taste of her sweet essence is a stark contrast to the hot lava that spews from her mouth at times, and I drown myself in the bliss of it.

Breaking away, my lungs burn from lack of oxygen in the best way possible. I feel more fucking alive right now than I ever have before. Taking my time, I pull her shirt above her head and settle it over the part where she is restrained, so she doesn't lose her grip and dislocate a shoulder. I walk away, head over to the cabinet we keep medical shit in for accidents, and rummage around until I find the scissors.

Walking back, she eyes me suspiciously until she sees where the scissors are going.

"What is with you assholes and destroying my shit?" she mutters as I make quick work of shredding that god-awful containment device. Her breasts fall free and I'm in awe at their perfection.

"I'll forgive that sass princess, *this time*. But only because I need to get acquainted with these." Kneeling down to be eye level with her breasts, I glance up at her. "Make no fucking mistake here, kitten. When I kneel for you like this, it's to worship you like the willing sacrifice you are. And for that, be grateful. While within the walls of our domain, I have zero shame kneeling to our queen. Outside is a whole other realm that we will discuss at a later time, understood?"

"Yes, sir," she answers behind lust-filled eyes.

"Good girl, kitten." As I'm saying that, my hands reach up to caress her full breasts. I methodically knead them in my palms, squeezing a little harder than she is probably used to, to test her limits of pain. Noticing her head is lulling back as she lets out breathy little moans that make my cock twitch in anticipation, I quickly pinch each nipple between my thumb and finger hard and release just as fast. Her body jolts at the extra stimulation, and if I tried hard enough, I know I could make her come without doing anything else.

Dipping my head to her belly button, I start peppering her toned stomach with kisses while working my way up to the undersides of her tits. Reaching her left breast first, my tongue darts out. In a slow drag, I taste her skin as I move up to suck her pointed perfect nipple into my mouth while her hips jerk into me. I use my free hand to work her hard-on inducing athletic pants down her curvy hips until I reach her shoes.

Growling, I release her breasts from my mouth and use my other hand to tear off her shoes. I toss the fuckers to the opposite side of the gym, which makes her burst into a fit of giggles.

"Issues?" She snickers.

Making a snap decision, I rid her of the rest of her clothes and get up to walk toward the door. There I grab the soft rubber nipple clamps and silver metal butt plug before I head back toward my naked prey.

Standing in front of her, I take in all the dips and curves of her bare to me body. Full D cup breasts, curvy hips, and perfectly trimmed pubic hair leading to what I know from Deck and G is a delicious tasting and tight pussy. I can't wait to feast on it first, then fill her to the brim with my cock until I'm flooding her with my seed.

I already know I'm gonna have to have her soaked before I even try to fit myself in her. After growing up with my friends and the rare occasion we shared a chick, we've seen each other naked way too many times. The conclusion from that is that I'm the most 'well-endowed'. Where the guys fall around nine inches, I'm closer to ten, and I'm thicker in girth too.

I don't know how many times we had to play sex roulette because a chick couldn't handle my size, so I've mostly stuck to the sex club or to a chick who's into anal to save face.

"Do you know what these little beauties are, kitten?" I ask while showing her what's in my hands.

"N-no, s-sir," Bethani stutters while her eyes go wide as saucers in slight horror.

Walking back up to her, I dangle the nipple clamps in front of her. "These are nipple clamps, princess. They help heighten the sensations you feel during sexual acts. Usually I use ones that are a little more abrasive, but since you are new to this, I had some custom ones made for you."

Slipping the butt plug into my pocket, I take each clamp in my hand and gently stimulate her nipples so they are firm little peaks before fastening the clamps securely on.

"Oh my Godddd," Bethani moans as her head falls back, and I quickly tug the chain a bit, making her head snap forward and a loud moan fall from her lips.

"Tsk tsk, kitten. I never gave you permission to drop our eye contact. Bad girl." Then I quickly reach around and give her ass a firm swat.

"Ouch! You can't punish me when we haven't exactly gone over the rules, Sinclair."

Her eyes narrow in retaliation, and if my purple sparkled dick has anything to say about her acts of terror, I better rush over them before he gets injured.

"Fair enough. This is simple since we haven't gone over a contract yet to establish firm rules. Today is simple. If you are enjoying what we are doing, the word is green. If you are getting slightly uncomfortable with something, tell me yellow and I'll back off. If it all becomes too much, say red and we stop completely. Doesn't matter how much I may be enjoying it. If you use that word, we stop, I'll untie you, and then I take you and pamper you until you are happy again."

"Seriously?" she asks while eyeing me skeptically.

I cup her face in my hands, so she is looking me in the eyes to understand. "I'm dead serious about this, kitten. Just because I want complete control in this relationship, doesn't mean your needs don't matter. While I may be a sick fucking bastard, and while some of the shit I enjoy sexually is appalling to others, I will *not* fucking disrespect your hard limits. I will also make sure you are extremely sated and happy. The aftercare of this is just as important as the sexual acts themselves. Does this make sense?"

She nods in agreement but then verbalizes, "I understand. Now mind telling me what you put in your pocket?"

Reaching in my pocket, I pull out the butt plug to show her. "This is a butt plug, kitten. Would this be a hard limit item? If so, I'll toss it and we can discuss it another time."

She looks at it for a second before returning her gaze toward me. "To be honest, I'm not sure. I've never tried one before."

"Would you be willing to try? I promise that after a little discomfort, you'll enjoy it."

Her eyes close as she inhales and exhales a few times, contemplating her decision. When they open back up, fierce determination flares in her eyes.

"Yes, I'm okay with it, Sinclair. I'll never know if I don't try at least once, right?"

Her smile that flashes makes my dead heart skip a beat, and I almost feel the urge to walk away and end this.

The guys said this would happen, and I didn't want to believe them. Now, I fucking do. Her willingness to entangle herself with us, with the secrets she can never know about us, yet still open up to us and trust us, causes a shift in my world that I know I'm not prepared for in the slightest. But I'm still going to go through with it because the masochist in me knows it will be worth it.

"Shall we continue with the fun then, kitten?"

"We shall."

"Good." I stop, switching to a lower, more dominating tone. "Now, enough talking, kitten. The only words you are allowed to use from here on out are 'yes, sir', 'no, sir', or the colors when I ask you how you are feeling. Understood?"

"Yes, sir."

"Also, eyes on me the whole time. I want you to watch as I bring your body pleasure. If that gorgeous head of yours falls back, I'm spanking that ass."

Her breathing starts to become labored as I give her the rules, but she still responds. "Yes, sir."

Tugging the nipple clamps to see how she performs, Bethani moans but keeps her eyes on me. Smiling, I praise her, "Good girl, kitten." Then I dip in for one final kiss before I make my way down to her pussy. As I kiss my way down, my eyes stay glued to hers. She struggles but keeps eye contact like I asked.

When I get situated, I grip just behind her knees to bring her legs over my shoulders, giving me a flawless view of her dripping pussy. "Fucking perfect, kitten," I say as I lean in to kiss her clit.

Her hips start to wiggle, begging for more contact as sweet little whimpers escape her lips. No longer able to wait, I dip my head and take a long, slow drag from the bottom of her pussy to her clit with my tongue.

Jesus fucking hell. She tastes like the sweetest fucking peach I've ever tasted in my life. A deep moan rumbles through me and vibrates her thighs as my grip tightens, pulling me in to devour her even more.

Picking up my pace, I start a vicious assault of thrusting and twisting my tongue deep in her. I'm relishing the feeling of her cunt as it spasms while her hips grind into my face for more pressure. I can feel her getting closer and closer to release, and when I move up to give her clit a hard suck, her scream echoes off the walls around us.

In a rush, I grab the butt plug and squeeze my hand around it tightly to warm it up so she isn't so shocked by how cold it is: When it finally feels like a comfortable temperature in my hand, I move it up and plunge it into her pussy so it's soaked with her juices. It must still be cold because her hips jerk and she damn near breaks my nose, but I move out of the way just in time.

"Kitten, I need words. What's your color?"

She doesn't respond, so I give her ass another firm smack. Just enough to bring a dull sting to her ass and remind her of our agreement.

"G-green. Fucking green. Please don't stop. I'm so close."

Instead of giving her a response, I grab hold of the plug and swirl it around a few more times before pulling it out with a suctioning pop. Her eyes never leave mine as I begin to trace a light path to her asshole. When I feel the plug dip into the spot that is her rear entrance, she tenses up.

"I'm not gonna hurt you, kitten. Do you trust me?"

Aqua eyes swallow me whole as she studies my face. "Yes, sir."

"Good girl."

I begin to put slight pressure on the plug as I work her pussy with my tongue again to loosen her up. It doesn't take long before her moans and whimpers let me know she is lost in pleasure again, and I'm able to insert the well lubricated plug fully into her ass with a firm thrust that sends her into an instantaneous orgasm from the stimulation.

I lap her juices as they flow out of her before standing up, dropping my sweats, and lining up to slowly start sinking my dripping cock into her before her orgasm even finishes.

"Sinclairrrr!" "Shit!" We are both yelling at the same time. Hers from all the sensations coursing through her. Mine is from how motherfucking phenomenal her cunt feels as it tries to suck the life from my cock. I barely get a few inches in her when I have to stop her movements so I don't fucking blow in the next five seconds.

My body feels like it's in another universe. I feel the pressure from the plug inserted in her ass. I can feel the way her drenched walls grip my cock in an attempt to suck me in further. For the first time, I can feel the extra stimulation of my frenum piercing as it ripples against her silky walls.

"Jesus Christ, Bethani," I grit out as my labored breathing struggles to regulate so I can focus. Her hips begin to wiggle and I have to hold her steady. "Kitten, stop."

"Then move!" she demands.

"Woman, do you want me to fucking come in two seconds flat? Fuck, I want to enjoy this too."

"Oh, you will."

She gives me a malicious smirk, and before I can ask what the hell she means, her heels dig into my ass. Using all her leg strength, she quickly shocks the fuck out of me as I'm pulled in until my dick is fully seated inside her pussy, and I can feel the head of my cock punching up against her womb.

"Fuck fuck fuuuuccckkkkk!" I roar as my eyes roll to the back of my head, and black spots cloud my vision.

Bethani's scream echoes mine, and I feel like we can be heard all over campus.

This fucking woman is gonna kill me.

We don't move for a good minute as we regain composure from her brazen act. When I feel like I can form a coherent sentence, I pin her with a pissed off look.

"You want to play fucking games here, kitten? Answer me this. What is your color?"

I'm met with a breathy response, "Green."

"Not for fucking long you won't be."

"What's that—"

I don't give her the chance to finish her question as my fingers dig into her hips. I bring my cock back out to the tip, then thrust back in with a force I wasn't planning on using just yet with her. Her head falls back, and she lets loose a guttural moan that sends me into a fucking frenzy.

I turn into a savage beast as I own her fucking cunt.

Using extreme precision, I bring her legs up to tangle around my neck while never breaking my pace. The change of her position gives me the opportunity to reach even farther into her gushing depths, and her screams of passion match my demonic grunts as our bodies slap against each other in a sweaty mess of lust, passion, and pent-up aggression toward each other.

I can feel the tingling sensation start to cover my body as the burning sensation in my gut tells me I'm so close to exploding it's not even funny. I quickly move my thumb so I'm able to flick her clit rapidly and bring her to release before me.

I start slamming into her like an unhinged animal, the telling sign of her orgasm is about to break free as my balls start to suck up into me. I command her to come, "Fucking come for me, princess!" And I give her one final firm flick of her clit to send us both over the edge.

She screams so fucking loud I'm sure my ears are bleeding, and her body starts to convulse in orgasmic pleasure. Her pussy clamps down on me, locking me into her as I give one final thrust and roar my release.

Black spots and stars cloud my vision as I fight to stay standing when my dick erupts like a fucking volcano inside her. My body completely seizes up as a pleasure I've never fucking experienced before in my life consumes me.

After a few intense minutes, I'm finally able to blink my eyes a few times as my vision returns. Looking down at my little hell raiser, I find that her head has completely fallen back as she struggles to catch her breath. Glancing up, I notice faint bruising on her wrists from the restraint and realize I need to get my ass in gear for aftercare.

I slowly reach behind her and pull the plug out of her now somewhat de-virginized ass. A little whimper escapes her lips when I pull it out.

"Almost out, princess. You did amazing."

When it's all the way out, I chuck it on the ground to deal with later. I dislodge myself from her slightly spasming pussy and groan at the aftershocks rolling through me from my ultra-sensitive and flaccid dick. Kicking my sweats off, I give myself more mobility to cradle Bethani in one arm as I untie the restraint. When she is released, I reposition my body to better carry her, and I move her arms to a normal position to help with the feeling.

Heading toward the showers, I curse when I remember there isn't a bathtub down here.

"What's wrong?" Bethani mumbles into my chest as she starts to doze off.

Giving her a kiss on the forehead, I head toward the door to unlock it and go to my room where all my shit is located. "Nothing, kitten. Just rest and let me take care of you."

Instead of a response, her breathing evens out and a tiny snore escaping her lips makes me chuckle. For an introduction into BDSM, she was flawless, minus her bratty attitude, but I wouldn't expect anything else from Bethani.

Reaching the door, I unlock it with the code when a flash from my phone alerts me to an incoming message. Carefully stooping down to pick it up, my blood burns when I see the demand clean and clear as I open the message.

Unknown: Discussions to be had. Catacombs at 7pm tomorrow.

Of fucking course. I have some of the most explosive and earth-shattering sex of my life, and you cocksuckers have to ruin it.

I stew as I walk naked through the house and up the stairs to the main area so that I can get to my room with a sleeping and naked Bethani in my arms. She's keeping me tethered on the normal side of sanity.

As I reach the kitchen, I see the guys sitting there demolishing more food with fresh fucked hair.

"Looks like you two had fun. Which one was the bitch today?" I snicker as they pale, unsure of how to take my out of character joke.

"Dude, did you just make a joke?" Declan asks, and it takes everything in me to not double over at his fucked up bird's nest hair.

Shrugging, I reply, "Guess so."

"Questioning us isn't what needs to be happening right now. The real question is, what did she say?" Gio asks, his expression a mask of confusion and worry.

"Bethani agreed. She is ours, so we need to work on our contracts this week after our meeting tomorrow. That is, if you two choose to do one. You know my stance in that area, so for her and me it's necessary and non-negotiable."

"I think we need to establish one for if we all choose to play together at the same time. There definitely needs to be definitive ground rules, especially with you. Ass face here is already bossy enough. I don't feel like dealing with both you fuckers at the same time."

Deck retaliates by chucking part of his sub at Gio. "Fuck you, man! I've never heard you complain!"

Rolling my eyes at their childish behavior, I ask them about the obvious part of my statement they missed. "When is the last time you two checked your phones?"

Talking through a mouth full of food like the overgrown barbarian he is, Deck answers me first, "Uhh...when we last talked almost an hour ago, why?"

An hour ago? Jesus, no wonder I'm fucking exhausted.

"Got a message before I left the gym. Tomorrow, seven p.m." I don't need to elaborate. We all know when they summon us we must obey or face an almost certain torturous death.

They grumble and groan, but the shared anger and hatred toward the Trident Syndicate is deathly apparent as it has destroyed all of our sex highs.

Turning, I head toward my room. "Gotta do aftercare. She is sleeping with me tonight, so clean up your shit."

Shutting the door to my room, I tune the world out for the rest of the night. I soak us both in my Jacuzzi tub, rub lotion all over her body, and give her a massage. Then I heat up some leftovers and feed her like the queen she is. When she gets tired again, I wrap her in my arms as we drift off to sleep in a comfortable and close new dynamic as we finally let go of some of the hate and anger toward each other.

For once I'm not bothered by the mess around my room or the empty food bowls on the nightstand. My compulsion to have everything in perfect order is thrown to the wayside as my arms stay protectively wrapped around the woman who I know can bring me to my knees, while she sleeps soundly in my arms.

Chapter 24

Declan

This. Sitting here in the council room of the catacombs listening to our fathers drone on about the ridiculous list of holiday parties, fundraisers, and other bullshit events we all need to attend is why I fucking drown my soul in the shit I do. It's been a few weeks since all the members, from high-ranking leaders like ourselves down to the newbies, have had to be in attendance, and I thoroughly fucking enjoyed it.

Having Bethani living with us and verbalizing her agreement to be with us in this unique 'relationship', has calmed my itch to utilize my escapes tremendously. But right now, my foot is tapping uncontrollably, and my fingers white knuckle the chair as the urges flare with a wicked vengeance. We listen to all our requirements and some new regulations that are being enforced to make sure we all maintain our image as the elites of society.

"And that concludes everything for this evening, gentlemen." Our fathers stand and raise their glasses in the air for us to follow suit, which of course we do like the trained monkeys we are.

"Ante Mortem Infidelitatis!" they shout.

"Ante Mortem Infidelitatis!" we all shout in unison, and while everyone else sips their drinks like 'respectable' men, Sinclair, Giovanni, and I drain ours while our fathers look at us with utter disdain.

Feeling's mutual, dickwads.

As we all go to stand, my father's horrid voice breaks through. "Will Masters Blackwell, Martinelli, and Carter please stay back for a private discussion?"

We just flop back into our chairs as the rest of the morons file out of the room to enjoy their glamorized version of life they think they are living by being a part of this 'elite society' nonsense.

We stay silent as the last member leaves and shuts the door behind him, knowing it's pointless to talk unless they speak first.

"So, boys, have you thought of our proposal any further?" Gio's dad asks us.

I just roll my eyes as my answer. *Over my dead body.*

Thankfully, Giovanni saves the day. "If you'll remember our last conversation, unless our grandfathers agree to your proposal, we are under no obligation to agree to your asinine arranged marriages. You can cut us off, revoke our Trident memberships, and have us removed from campus. We do not agree."

"Agreed," Sinclair voices, uniting our stand.

Propping my feet up on the table, knowing it will piss them off even more, I voice my reply, "Agreed. Fuck your proposal."

"Boys, the arrangements have already—" Arthur starts to speak but is cut off by our saviors, aka, our grandfathers.

"Then dissolve the arrangements and move on. You never discussed this with us, and we do not believe it is in the best interest of the boys or the organization as a whole," Sinclair's grandfather, Arthur Blackwell Sr., booms. His voice echoes through the room as he, Nonno Gianluca Martinelli, and my fucking hero, Grandpa James Carter, make their grand entrance from behind the curtain. They leisurely stroll to the Kings' seats above us on the stage area and take their seats like the gangsters they are.

As my grandpa unbuttons his suit jacket to sit, his authoritative voice starts in on our fathers. "Did you really think you were going to get away with this crock of shit and we wouldn't find out about it?" Glancing at our fathers, who look like whipped puppies, I can't stop the glorious smile that plasters itself on my face as Grandpa continues his questioning. "Well, do any of you have the sacks to answer us, or are we going to play the spoiled little brat card? Huh? What's it going to be, gentlemen? Because if we don't get some damn surefire reasoning behind your treasonous acts, I'm damn tempted to revoke your memberships and positions at the companies."

Sinclair's dad stands to address them. "Father, Mr. Carter, Mr. Martinelli, with all due respect, our intentions were not meant with ill will. We found wonderful women who will complement the boys' status perfectly, while also uniting fronts in all areas of business for expansions of great benefit to the syndicate and the external companies."

"Oh, horse shit, Arthur. Don't pull your boardroom bullshit with me. We have all talked to the boys individually to verify the story. We also went back and got the mandated recording of the meetings as verification also," Arthur Sr. rages. "If you think for a goddamn minute I'm going to fall for the lies that pour out of your mouth, then you really are dumber than I thought. Maybe we all should have tried for another son. Can't do any worse than the disgusting creatures we call heirs. Only good thing any of you have going for you is the stellar grandsons you helped create."

Hot damn, Grandpa Blackwell! Burn, baby burn! Fuck yeah!

My grandpa turns toward us to address us. "Boys, before we dismiss you to privately discuss your fathers' fates, do you have dates for the functions coming up? *We* are not requiring you to bring someone each time, just the major ones."

My brain short-circuits as I think of a response. Can we even convince Bethani to come? How in the fuck are we going to explain our 'relationship' to them?

I'm still silent as Sinclair speaks, "Yes, Grandpa Carter. We have a date."

"Date, as in singular?" Nonno asks.

Damn you, old man, you don't miss shit.

"Yes, Nonno Martinelli. Singular. While I'd rather not discuss this in the presence of *them*," he spits venomously at our fathers. "But since we respect you three too much to hide anything from you, I'll elaborate. If that's all right with you?"

"Of course. Please do, my boy." Nonno nods along with the other two while our fathers ignore us.

"Well, while this may be a little unusual to most, we are actually all dating the same woman, Nonno. She is the person we plan to bring with us to events, as long as she feels comfortable with it."

"Why the fuck wouldn't she be comfortable with it? What, did you idiots find some trailer trash nobody you had to pay for this ruse? Utter nonsense," Arthur Jr. retorts to Sinclair. His menacing tone has me out of my seat along with Giovanni as we all see red.

"No one, and I mean *fucking no one,* threatens or talks shit about *our* girl, you son of a bitch!" I bellow as my temper flares.

"SILENCE!" the grandfathers boom, and we all instantly sit down.

"Boys, get on out of here. We would love to meet this lovely lady soon, if that's all right with you? She must be a miraculous woman to agree to date you three fools." My grandfather chuckles, thoroughly enjoying himself.

"Of course, Grandpa. Talk later. Nonno, Pops, good to see you, old fuckers." I nod to them and head out as Sinclair and Giovanni send their regards to the men before exiting behind me.

"Well, at least that's done." I exhale while walking to the exit to grab my phone and keys.

"Yeah. Now we just have to convince Bethani to go along with us to these events," Sin says.

Groaning, I just shake my head. "Leave it to G. He is the 'sweetest', as she puts it, so maybe he can cook her favorite meal and dessert to convince her. I'm not even gonna bother, and if you don't want glitter dick again, I suggest you don't say shit either, Sin."

"Good point. G, job's on you, asshole, so don't fuck it up."

"Fine. I don't even care right now. I'm just ready to get back to the penthouse and see her."

A-fucking-men to that one.

Chapter 25

Giovanni - A Few Days Later

Somehow, someway I'll never be sure of, but Sinclair's broody, controlling self gave the final layer of acceptance and trust to our group. Bethani randomly paused the movie earlier and proceeded to open up to us about her life in more detail. While some of it was rather difficult to hear, I already have the names saved onto my phone to research later. I'll either destroy myself or pay one of our associates, but I'll be damned if any of them live to see another normal day soon.

Bethani held strong as she informed us of how many times she went through days without food, had clothes that never fit right, lived in apartments that rarely had heat or water, and slept on a floor that she sometimes shared with roaches and rats. Then she got to the man Jim, who went through a rough patch himself. Which is why he bought Bethani's mom drugs in exchange for sex once, but then fell in love with our girl. I personally need to thank that man, because if it wasn't for him going to check on her, there is a good chance she would be dead.

I shiver again at that story, trying to swallow the bile that keeps rising up and threatening to break free while Bethani is sound asleep with her head in my lap.

"You still thinking about that Jim guy?" Sinclair grimly asks, knowingly in the same ominous mood as Declan and me as we try to focus on the movie.

Running a hand over my face then pinching the bridge of my nose, I sigh. "Yeah. She said she keeps in contact with him still. I need to get his info and thank him for saving her. I'm not...I'm not even sure how the hell I feel about what all she told us. How she isn't on drugs herself to deal with the shit is beyond me. Fuck, our lives have been hell, but don't even feel like they ghost what she has dealt with."

"Yeah, because we are all spoiled pricks. Our hell has always been a fucking facade of luxury. Fucking disgusting. No wonder she wants to be an investigative journalist and photographer to bring to light all the shit that people of our world frown upon like it's some fucking disease," Declan spits in a menacing tone that lets me know his struggle with her story is worse than we thought. He looks like he could drive up to Seattle and burn the city to the ground in vengeance, then torch the state for fun.

"Man, calm down. I know it's hard. Trust me, I'm ready to use every resource we have in her name, but she isn't there anymore. She is here with us. We already agreed a while ago we wouldn't let shit happen to her anymore. And we're not. So try to control it, or go down to the gym and demolish a few punching bags."

"Go destroy a few lives sounds better," he grumbles, and I roll my eyes along with Sin at his temper tantrum.

I decide to change the subject as a way to refocus his attention. "So her birthday is in a few weeks, and we all know they haven't been the best. Do we have any ideas, or are we just gonna chill here with her?"

"Restaurant," comes the boring response from Sinclair.

Declan looks at him in disgust. "Dude, that's such a typical boring-ass response. We need to do something different and meaningful for her."

"Well, what's your idea then, oh fucking wise one?"

"Easy. We take her to her favorite place."

"When did you find out her favorite place?" I ask. "She said she has never traveled, other than here and LA."

Declan just gives us an incredulous look like we are missing the point, which we clearly are. "You guys are idiots. Her favorite place is LA. It's simple, really. We book a long weekend at a nice hotel, show her how we do LA, but also let her show us *her* side of LA. We take in and appreciate the limited shit she had that made her life happy at that point. Then we write a fucking check to the shelter she lived at as a thank you to that Ramona lady for all the awesome shit she does." Deck takes a long pull of his beer, like what just fell out of his mouth wasn't one of the most grown-ass mature things he has ever said.

"Who are you, and what did you do with the dumbass Declan we are used to?" Sinclair asks astounded, giving Deck the same look of disbelief as I am.

He just gives us a sheepish grin. "While I may act like an idiot, I do pay attention on occasion. Especially when it comes to her." His gaze turns toward Bethani, and we all look down at the astounding woman who has us all wrapped around her pretty little fingers.

"Great idea, Declan. I'll start looking up hotels and get it all booked. Giovanni, make sure we can miss class and can pull it off without our fathers finding out. I think that is one of the few weekends we have off before all the events begin."

"Sure," I mumble as I catch a note of an oddly familiar tune Bethani is humming in her sleep. "Turn that shit off," I say, waving at the TV, and one of them does. I motion them closer to see if they hear the same thing I'm hearing, or if I've lost my fucking mind.

As we sit there and listen to her mumbling, our eyes go wide as familiar words we've sung so many times filter through her mouth while she sleeps

"With thine blood, We unite as one
With thine blood, Our enemies shall fall
Ante Mortem Infidelitatis."

"Holy. Fuck," we all whisper as she falls back into a deep sleep, and her mumbling ceases.

"How does she know that fucking song?" Sinclair demands as he moves back away from her, almost in shock and pure rage. "Is she some sort of fucking spy or something? What the fuck?"

"Hold on. Just slow down, Sinclair. We have fucking proof she is from Washington. We also have proof that she was in LA and has never come into contact with any known associates of ours," I counter in an attempt to calm his crazy ass down before all hell breaks loose.

His arms cross over his chest as he pins me with a quizzical, yet still pissed off look. "Oh really? We do? When were you going to enlighten us with that tidbit of information?"

Sighing, because I know they are both going to be pissed regardless, I choose the truth. "After she got better, I broke through her records at Washington State Children Services just to verify. I've known for a few weeks but didn't think it was anything worth bringing up because I only looked to make sure she was who she said she was. I didn't have it in me to open the forty plus different folders that had pictures and shit detailing what she told us tonight. Then I verified her whereabouts at the shelter in LA. The woman Ramona still works there. I just played it off that we were the school and were processing her for a room upgrade, but we had to make sure she wasn't lying. Bethani is who she says she is."

If looks could kill, I'd be fucking dead right now. I'm also thankful as fuck Bethani sleeps like a bear in hibernation because she'd be just as pissed as these two currently are with me.

"We will be discussing this later, Giovanni. But first, how the fuck does she know that song?"

All of us are silent. Because God's honest truth? We don't have a single fucking clue as to how she would know something that only 100 living men and maybe another 250 dead ones know.

Et Infidelitatis Conscius Natus, otherwise known as The Disloyalty Song, is the song the founding members made up as a joining force to our secrecy and loyalties of the Trident as a whole. The song is long and tedious as fuck to learn, but it is a shared requirement that every member must know and retain.

"Wait a minute. G, do we have any current or deceased members of the Syndicate located up there?" Declan asks with a look crossing his face that I can't quite decipher.

I ponder for a moment while stroking Bethani's hair to calm the nervous energy rolling through. Sinclair is pacing and Declan looks like a cracked-out child with whatever theory he has ready to burst out of him.

"Dude, chill the fuck out before you wake her up," I say.

He sits back down on the opposite side of the couch so he can keep up with his knee knocking. "Off the top of my head, no, I don't believe there are any living members up there currently. Deceased, possibly, but those records are located in the catacomb private sector that we do not have access to yet. The only ones with clearance for that are our fathers and grandfathers. All members would be in their private library in the original Trident book. It's that super old journal that came from Mother Russia with your fifth or sixth great-grandparents, Sinclair. To gain access to it, we'd have to break in or see if we can convince our fathers to let us have access. What is your theory with this, Declan?"

He jumps up quickly to start pacing, and rapid-fire whisper yells so he doesn't wake up Bethani. "Okay, so she doesn't know her dad, right? Well, what if her dad or a paternal male or whatever was a member and sang the song to her as a baby? Like we all know her mom is a piece of shit, but what if Bethani was part of the elite society like us? What if her mom couldn't handle the pressure and just dipped out and changed her name so he couldn't find them? But she obviously doesn't remember the shit because she was so little. It's just one of those things she does unconsciously or whatever."

"You mean subconsciously."

He turns and points at me. "Yeah! That! I mean it's a wild theory, but it could be one, right?"

Scratching my head, I look at Sinclair for advice on this. "What do you think, man? I mean, it sounds a little far-fetched to me. Why would someone want to leave a comfortable lifestyle for what she went through?"

Declan visibly deflates at my thoughts, but Sinclair saves it. "Deck, G isn't saying your theory is bad. It's just a little out there. The only way we can know for sure is by asking her if she wants to find out about her paternal heritage. Those tests take up to two months depending on how legit they are. That would give us time to figure out how to get the records of all members and at least do thorough backgrounds on them to see if there are any potential possibilities. It's a long shot, Deck, I will say that, but it's the only fucking theory I can even come up with that doesn't sound completely fucking stupid either. So good job, man." Sin gives Declan a reassuring slap on the back before turning back to me with a look that fills my stomach with utter dread and disgust. "G, I fucking hate this, but we need all those files and shit. You have them on the computer where we can look over it all?"

"Yeah, I copied everything just in case. I figured electronically breaking in twice was a bad idea, so I made sure to get it all."

His nod is solemn as he verbalizes the same thing I'm thinking, "We gotta go over it. Every sick and twisted detail of her life. I don't want to see the shit either because I know when it's all said and done, if any of those bastards that made her life hell are still alive,

I'll be making a trip to Seattle to personally end their worthless fucking lives myself."

"Hear, hear," Deck interrupts, agreeing that people will die.

"Hear, hear," I mutter in agreement.

"Let's take a day or two to prepare. We'll talk to her first about the DNA testing, then get everything planned before we start going over shit."

"What if she doesn't agree to the testing?" Declan asks, bringing up a solid point.

"What if we just wait until she agrees before we delve into the black abyss that is what we are about to do?" I pipe in. "I mean, it's all somewhat moot if she won't do it. And I'm not doing it without her consent. That could open up a whole can of shit we don't need to open with her, *especially* now that she trusts us. Plus, that gives us more time to come up with about ten different ideas and backup plans for how to get access to the records. I have zero issues with death, but I'd rather postpone it for as long as possible since we are basically talking about committing treason within the walls of our lives."

Sinclair and Declan both roll what I'm saying around in their heads for a few minutes before agreeing that the more conservative approach is the better option.

"Fair point, genius boy."

I chuckle. "Fuck you, Sin. For being the controlling fucker you are, you sure do enjoy going into a situation full fucking tilt. My non-apologies for preferring to have a multitude of options for us to have and be prepared for any and all possibilities."

"Boy Scout." Declan snickers, and I pick up the remote and toss it, hitting him in the shoulder.

"My Boy Scout ways have kept you happy and satisfied plenty of times, dick."

"Oh fucking hell. I'm out. Not listening to you fucks and your sword fighting stories," Sinclair mumbles while storming to his room, while Declan and I snicker at his slight aversion with our now blatant talk of our sexuality. By no means is he against us being bisexual, but you can tell he is still adjusting to us freely talking about it when we hid everything for so long. That's on us too for not saying shit, but at least now he knows and accepts it. So we can cut him a little slack.

Leaning further into the couch, I glance down at Bethani. "Tesoro, this would all be a lot fucking easier if you knew who your father was."

"Think her life will be in danger if my theory proves true?" Declan asks cautiously.

"Honestly, she has been attacked once. For all we know, she could already be in danger and none of us realize it. There could be someone ten fucking steps ahead of us and just waiting to strike. We won't know until we get what we need. All we can do right now is protect her the best we can and stay alert of any situation that has the potential for disaster."

"True. You got her, or do you want me to take her to her room?"

"Go to sleep, Deck. I got her."

He walks to his room, and I just sit there for a while, contemplating the shit storm heading our way. I adjust myself to fall asleep with Bethani on the couch when my eyes get too heavy to stay awake any longer.

Chapter 26

Bethani - Mid November - Birthday Weekend

"Where are we going, guys? Seriously, I hate surprises," I ask for the millionth time. I'm pouting. I've had a blindfold over my eyes for the past few hours as the guys drive us to wherever this surprise location is for my birthday. "I get you weirdos want to go all out or whatever but is this blindfold *really* necessary?"

"Yes," they all say in unison, clearly over my whiny antics.

I grumble, "Well, you assholes aren't the one who's blindfolded."

These guys all stormed into my room at 7:00 a.m. to wake me up and rush my ass to hurry up and get ready to go. I wasn't allowed to pack a bag since they 'had it taken care of' and they already had one of my warmer weather dresses ready for me as soon as I hopped out of the shower, sans underwear.

Bullshit. All of it, I think to myself when I'm suddenly ripped from my seat in the SUV and slammed against Sinclair's chest. He wraps a hand around my throat to bring me even closer.

"Say that again, kitten."

My body instantly erupts in goose bumps, and my sex clenches as Sinclair's scent fills my nostrils. I'm not sure which cologne he used today, but it's intoxicating. Honestly, anytime I'm super close to them and get a whiff of their colognes, I turn into a needy, horny mess.

In the few weeks since Sinclair finally broke through my last defenses and fucked me like 'his little slut', as he likes to so eloquently put it, things have been hectic.

We spent three damn hours one day ironing out a contract with details of things I would be okay with doing or using sexually, and others that were hard limits. I was pretty open to most of it since I haven't heard of any of the stuff. But I was given the addendum that if I didn't like it, it could easily become a hard limit, and he would respect that. We also discussed how if rules would be broken, for any party, there would be consequences. I've had my ass busted a few times and wrote stupid-ass lines a few times already for my smart mouth. But let's face it, I've never liked playing nice, so I usually deserve the punishment.

They also had a stipulation in the contract where I would agree to finally use the new laptop and phone they gave me. But I countered and said only if all of their sneaky hacker crap wasn't on there. We ended up in a compromise of only keeping the tracker app on my phone just for 'safety purposes'. I also won on keeping my two-day a week job at the coffee shop with the agreement that one of them could escort me to and from the place every shift.

It ended up being a major win across the board for me and one of the perks started a few days later.

They all took me to a private club that Sinclair is a member of, and we went into a private room where we watched others having sex so I could see some of the things I wasn't sure about. I was surprised at how much I enjoyed the whole scenario. I was hot and bothered and turned on like no other during the whole thing. Thankfully, the guys took pity on me and gave me the first experience of them all ravishing me at once. They didn't go full tilt like they wanted to but respected the fact that I wasn't ready for *that* just yet. So Sinclair, being the jerk he is, tied me down to one of the tables and proceeded to demolish my tits with his mouth while Declan fucked me hard, and Giovanni played with my asshole.

After I was a boneless, sated mess, Giovanni and Sinclair jerked themselves off all over my stomach and breasts. They dressed me, escorted me out of the club covered and dripping with their juices, and took me home to give me a bath and spoil me rotten.

They have all been sneaky and shifty when my birthday came up. Stella called demanding to know what I wanted to do. When I told her I wasn't sure, the guys all chirped in that they had it taken care of and would let her know. I'm not sure if they said anything, though. She still hasn't made it back into their good graces for not noticing that Peter spiked my drink that night. Even though I've explained to them that we both had indulged in a fair share of alcohol before we even got there.

I've met their grandfathers. It was awkward at first because I didn't know the older, more distinguished carbon copy versions of the guys were even at the penthouse when I got back from class. After a few minutes of conversation, though, we all quickly fell into loud conversations like we've known each other forever. Their grandfathers are loud, opinionated, boisterous older men who act nothing like I would have guessed old money society came from. They're polar opposites to everyone else you see on campus and a welcomed change of pace. They all saluted me, gave me giant hugs and kisses on the cheek, and thanked me for keeping their boys in line, which made the guys blush.

On top of all that, classes have been crazy. I've been trying to cram for finals and stuff before the holiday breaks begin, on top of being ravished constantly by some of the horniest men I've ever met.

Kitchen counter? Check. Elevator? Double check. All their beds? Triple check. I've lost count of how many places I've been randomly pushed against a wall for a quickie or stripped bare in the middle of doing something and bent over to be fucked hard.

I'm not complaining, though. I may be sore constantly, but they say it's my fault because I don't have to do anything except look at them and they are hard as steel.

I'm brought out of my thoughts when my dress is pulled up to expose my naked flesh to the air, and Sinclair sinks two thick fingers into my dripping sex.

"Always so wet and needy for us, princess. Now, would you rather come on my fingers or Giovanni's dick?"

I gasp when I feel the head of Giovanni's cock brush against my entrance. After Sinclair pulls his fingers out of me, I can hear him sucking off my essence.

"Fucking delicious."

"Come on, guys! This is bullshit! We are almost there and I'm fucking driving with a boner. Not cool," Declan whines from the front, but I'm too lost to care.

"Tesoro, you want my cock?" Giovanni asks as he pushes in just an inch to tease me.

My head falls back onto Sinclair's chest as I moan, "Yesss."

Sinclair's grip around my throat tightens as he manipulates the angle of my head. He brings his lips to mine as Giovanni thrusts deep into me. Sinclair swallows my moans of heightened pleasure as his hardened cock nestles between my ass cheeks while Giovanni fucks me senseless.

I feel the slight movement of the vehicle pulling over and being put in park as layers of clothes are tossed all over in a lust-filled frenzy.

"Next time we take a plane, dick face. Confined space bullshit is for the birds when we are all fucking giants." Giovanni grunts as his thrusts deepen.

This whole situation is hotter than sin, and I can't see a damn thing. A hand reaches down to stroke my clit as two others pinch my nipples, and I'm torpedoed with an unexpected orgasm. A scream rips through my throat as Giovanni starts swearing up a storm and my walls vice grip around him. I feel the heat of his cum flooding me.

"Goddammit! I wasn't ready to come!"

Giovanni pulls out of me, and I moan at the loss of him.

"Don't worry, kitten. Daddy's gonna fill your dripping cunt back up and fuck you silly while Declan deep dicks your pretty little throat."

Holy. Hot. Damn. Yes, please!

I'm lifted up by one of them just enough for Sinclair to position himself, and then I'm slowly set back down until he is fully seated in me. My body is still spasming from my prior orgasm, and Sinclair's size is almost enough to set me off again.

"Fuck, kitten!" His deep moan echoes around me as his hands grip my waist to control the movements. "Ready for my cock, sunshine?"

A smile plasters my face as I reach up and find Declan's dick, and I give him a firm squeeze and tug him toward me to stick my tongue out and lick the precum off the tip.

"Jesus Christ!" he moans, then curses when his head must hit the top of the SUV.

"Giovanni, where are you?" I ask, unsure of his location.

"Right beside you, Tesoro. Why?" he asks with labored breathing.

Instead of telling him my plan, I reach out with my right hand to find his chest and slowly work my hand down until I find his still semi-hard cock. With a feather touch, I put my hand around it and start working it back up to a full hard-on again as he groans.

Concentrating as hard as I can, which funny enough is easier with the blindfold on since it kills off one of my senses, I start to gyrate my hips over Sinclair. Then I pull Declan into my mouth to blow him while jerking off Giovanni.

The muttered moans and forced swear words fly through the vehicle from the guys as I focus on getting them off at the same time. I flick my hips and bounce on Sinclair while using my Kegels to keep the extra friction he loves. I'm sucking hard and deep for Declan while twirling my tongue on his piercing. Giovanni loves soft strokes with some added pressure at the tip, which is super easy to do with my juices coating him.

While this may not be the ideal location for us, I'm absolutely loving it for being my first experience getting them all off at the same time. It's unexpected and removes all the nervous pressure I was having about it.

After a few minutes of triple tandem on the guys, I can feel the tells that they are all about to come for me. Declan's hands fly to my hair to hold me in place as his thrusts become shallow and wild. Giovanni starts swearing in Italian, and his muscles start to tense up. Sinclair is a bit of a mystery still because he masks his emotions so well, but right now I can feel his cock throbbing and swelling inside me as he takes full control and moves my hips in a rhythmic motion on his lap.

Ready for us all to come, I reach down and pinch my clit hard, which sets off an orgasmic chain reaction. My pussy walls surge around Sinclair, setting him off. That makes me moan and suck harder on Declan, which has him thrust deep into me one final time before flooding my mouth with his cum. All of that has me giving Giovanni a final firm squeeze and tug. His hips jerk as he sets off into a second orgasm, and I can feel his release on my hands.

I'm so utterly lost in sensations and pleasures that I physically can't hear what the guys are saying. I feel like my soul has left my body, and what's left is just a sloppy mess. Declan pops himself out of my mouth, and I'm able to take a much needed deep breath, which burns as my deprived lungs fill with oxygen.

Another hand comes to mine and pries my fingers apart from Giovanni. He heaves a sigh of relief when I feel Sinclair lifting me up to pull himself out. I collapse back into him, feeling extremely disoriented.

"What happened?" I ask.

A bottle of water comes to my lips, and I greedily chug it for relief, not even noticing the electrolyte flavoring.

"I think we over-stimulated you, Tesoro. We need to be a little more careful."

Waving a hand dismissively, I say, "I feel fine. Don't even try that shit because I want to do it again and soon."

Sinclair's rumbling laugh comes from behind me. "Fucking hell, we created a monster."

All I can do is smile. I'm freaking delirious currently, so they can go to hell with the negative shit.

After a moment I'm moved, and I can hear the guys putting their clothes back on. There's zipping of zippers and belt buckles echoing around me.

"So can I take this damn blindfold off and know where we are going? I'm pretty sure I earned it just now," I ask cockily. I don't even care if it gets me punished later either. Bring it on.

A pair of hands come up behind me as lips brush against mine. The blindfold drops, and I put a hand over my eyes to help with the adjustment to the contrast. When everything starts to come into focus, tears flood my vision as a tidal wave of emotions hits me.

All of their deep sexy voices filter through me at the same time. "Welcome back to LA, baby."

Chapter 27

Declan

"Fuck, I'm still getting cold chills from earlier," Giovanni says while coming out on the balcony of the exclusive hotel we got for the weekend.

After letting Bethani know where we were, she broke down in happy sobs and thanked us over and over while taking turns devouring our mouths with passionate kisses. Once she let us go, we unloaded and headed to check-in.

Fuck the looks we got as we came in. Bethani was a smiling cheerful ball of energy, while we were all disheveled fucking messes. We sent her straight to the spa for gift number two, where she is gonna get God only knows what done down there. Meanwhile, we are all up relaxing for now, until we go to the area where she grew up later.

I snort at G. "You got off twice in under ten minutes. No fucking wonder."

"Yeah. Feels like I got my soul sucked out of me, and everything shifted off its axis." He groans as he moves to sit in one of the chairs.

I turn to look at him, arching a brow. "You good?"

Chugging his drink, Gio sets it down to rest his elbows on his knees and plants his face in his palms. "I'm not even sure anymore."

"Dude. I'm fucking lost here. Is this shit moving too fast between us all or what? Because personally I thought it wasn't moving fast enough."

"Yes. I mean no. I don't fucking know."

"Words, Giovanni. Use your goddamn words. We can't fucking read your mind," comes Sin's booming voice as he joins us with a bottle and glass of his own. He fills all our shit back up and sits down while G just glances at him with a scowl.

"Fuck off."

"Well, you are the one with your shit in a twist even though you just got laid, so what's up?" Sin asks.

I finally decide to sit down, realizing this shit may be more serious than my initial assessment.

It's quiet for a few until G mumbles something unintelligible.

"What?" I ask.

"Iminlovewithher."

"Yet again, Giovanni, we can't fucking understand you."

"I'm fucking in love with her! Are you happy now?" He stands up, running both hands through his hair and pacing around in circles. "I'm not fucking sure when it goddamn happened, but I almost slipped earlier and told her when she kissed me in the Tahoe after our group fun. The goddamn rush of fucking emotions hit me like a freight train, and now I don't know what the fuck to do. It's way too fucking early to be saying shit like that, right? Fuck, I don't know. Never been in love before. Not even sure how people go about this shit. Plus, there is the fact that you are both involved too. There are her feelings to consider. What if she loves one of you and doesn't reciprocate the same toward me? What about you two?" He stops and turns to face us. "How do you *both* feel about her?"

His declaration has my stomach twisting in knots. *Do I love Bethani?* "If I'm going to be honest here, I don't really know. I mean possibly? What I do know is I care about her. I want to keep her safe. But love? That I can't answer."

Sinclair studies us, sipping his drink before answering. "It's a dead giveaway that we *all* care about Bethani. She has been living with us for almost two months now. And given the potential connection to our family's extracurriculars, of course we are overprotective of her. Who wouldn't be? We live a dangerous life. Maybe not every day like the cartel or mafia, but there are always unknown threats hitting us left and right. Be it in the businesses or other ways."

"Always the fucking pragmatic, aren't you?" G sneers.

Sin just cuts him a look before continuing, "Anyways, while you may be in love with her, Giovanni. Hold off on saying it until you are one hundred percent certain. Don't just blow this shit to hell because you want to jump the gun on something that could have easily just been a double orgasm. We don't have the luxury of letting emotions plague us. So take the time, let this shit further develop between all of us, and see where the cards fall. Hell, for all we know something could change one day because we find out she would rather be our friend than a lover per se. Any of us jumping the gun could destroy either the best thing that ever happens to us, be it friend or more, or throw us all into turmoil if she loves one of us or none of us."

Mulling over his words, I glance at Gio. "Hate to say it, man, but he is right. We just hashed all this shit out between us, and she is on board. So let's just keep the happy bubble the way it is and discuss it again at a later date if things keep going well."

He isn't happy with us, but he finally agrees. "Yeah, sure. I'm going to shower and clear my head." Then he walks away, slamming the door behind him.

"Well, that was unexpected," I chirp while lighting up a blunt and letting the smoke fill my lungs as a sense of peace settles over my body.

I don't get a response from Sinclair, just a nod as he stands and heads back inside, leaving me to enjoy the sunny LA weather, my weed, and a strong drink in silence.

After smoking the last of my blunt and polishing off my drink, I lie back on the outdoor couch, deciding a nap is exactly what I need before we head out later.

Soft hands caressing my torso startle me awake. "The hell?"

A sweet laugh filters through my sleep-dazed state as I blink the sleep out of my eyes. "It's just me, Declan. They said you've been out here sleeping for over an hour, so I figured I'd wake you up."

As my eyes adjust to the setting sun, my focus falls on the flawless beauty in front of me with sparkling aqua eyes. "Damn, sunshine. You look...wow."

The smile radiating off her is infectious as she stands up. Her already perfect skin glows in the fading sunlight. Her long hair is slightly shorter and more shaped. And it looks like she is wearing a new outfit that hugs her curves like a perfect fit. My low-hanging destroyed jeans start getting snug as I stare at her, utterly entranced by the ethereal goddess standing in front of me.

"Declan, did you hear me?"

I shake my head to clear the wicked thoughts plaguing my mind right now. "Sorry, sunshine. Got lost in thought with all the dirty things I want to do with you right now." Then I wink and give her a salacious grin, which makes her blush.

"I asked if you were ready to go."

I look down at my pants, then back at her. "Right here? I'm ready whenever and wherever you want, B."

She gifts me with an adorable eye roll, then pops her hip and puts a hand there. "Nice try. Maybe later. Right now we are heading to the Latin district where I lived for some amazing food. Then we're hitting the dance club."

Pondering if I can convince her to let me have her for dinner, she stops my process. "Declan Grant Carter. I know what you are thinking. The answer is no. So get your sexy ass up and hurry up. I don't want to miss out on the food."

Damn you, sunshine.

I quickly stand up so I'm towering over her. "Fine. You get a pass for now, sunshine. But only because I know you are a grouch if you don't eat, and we don't want that. But if you don't want me to bend your ass over the railing and fuck you so hard all of LA will hear yours screams of pleasure, you better give me a kiss now to tide me over."

Her head falls back as she laughs, that wonderful sound that makes stupid tingly bullshit flutter through me that I refuse to process. "You drive a hard bargain there, Mr. Guttermouth. But I guess I can spare you a kiss for now, if you promise to dance with me later at the club."

Groaning, I trap her in my arms before leaning down to press my lips to hers. She falls into me as she opens up, giving me all the access to her mouth as my tongue tangles with hers. For a moment we are lost in each other when I feel her push back slightly, and I release my hold on her, unwillingly.

Her face is flushed, and she's breathing rapidly as she fans herself before turning to walk into the room.

"You three are terrible for my libido."

"More like you are good for ours, birthday girl." I laugh, then stop to adjust the raging erection in my pants that is currently pissed at me for not seeing any action. "Later, man. Let's just go make sunshine happy, and we will get lucky again before the night is over."

"Are you talking to your dick?"

Looking up, I see that Bethani is still near the door, and I shrug and give her a sheepish smile. "Can you blame me? He misses you already."

The flush on her face deepens as she shakes her head. "Animals. I live with filthy, vulgar animals."

Winking at her, I hurry up and follow her inside to get ready while everyone waits for me. As I'm looking for something to wear, I hear Bethani's voice filter into the room. "Keep the jeans on. I like the way your ass looks in them!"

I salute, even though she can't see me. "Yes, ma'am!"

And like the whipped pup I am that will do anything to make that woman happy, I keep my jeans on and toss on a fitted black tee, studded belt, and pair of Chucks before heading into the bathroom to piss.

As I'm attempting to fix my sleep fucked hair, Bethani's voice is in my head from a conversation the other day.

"Dammit," I mumble as I rush through my room looking for shit.

"What's wrong?"

I stop to see Bethani in the doorway, ready to go for class and waiting on me.

"Can't find the punch card for my barber. Got an appointment after class to get this mess fixed."

She saunters into where I'm standing and reaches up to run her hand through my longer-than-normal hair. "I like the length."

"Really?"

"Mhmm. Adds to that sexy rock star vibe you have going on." *Then she smiles and turns to head back out of my room. "It's in your bathroom. Top right drawer with the other half a dozen you keep forgetting about."*

Not believing her, I go to where she said, and when I open the drawer there are about a half dozen punched cards. I quickly snatch them up in disbelief and head back out, grabbing my bag. "How did you know where these were?" I ask as I stuff them into my front pocket.

"Helped you organize the other day. You must have smoked beforehand."

"Obviously. I haven't been able to find shit."

"So?" she asks.

"So what?"

"You gonna keep your hair like that?"

Punching the elevator button, I lean against the wall. "And what do I get if I keep it this way?"

She sends a sultry smile my way before walking past me into the elevator. "Guess you'll have to wait and see." Then she winks, sending the blood rushing from my body straight to my cock.

And what did I do after class? I went to the barber and only had the sides faded. I kept the length because she likes it. Then I went home to have her waiting in my room on my bed in some of the sexiest lingerie I've ever seen. The sex was wild as fuck that night as we went at it on every surface possible in my room.

My head snaps up as I look at myself in the mirror.

Shit. Maybe G was right. *Maybe I am in love with her?*

Chapter 28

Sinclair

"Yeah. We do *not* fit in here. Thank fuck I brought my brass knuckles and my belt that turns into a knife." Declan's words filter between G and me as we stand here like sentries in *La Mamacita*. It's a heavily influenced Spanish club in the Latin district of Los Angeles where our little kitten is having the time of her life on the dance floor.

We are up in the VIP section, no surprise there, looking like fish out of water. The hairs on the back of my neck have been standing up since we were at the restaurant.

First, Bethani about killed us with her 'proper LA driving'. Aka that pint-sized powerhouse can't drive worth a fuck. I almost dislocated a damn knuckle with the exertion I had on the 'oh shit' handle while she was cursing in English, Spanish, and Russian. She was swerving around vehicles and being a brake checking terror as she navigated the roads while we all watched on in horror.

I'm not afraid of much, but Bethani and driving? Fuck no. Never again. When we reached the shelter, because she wanted to see Ramona before the main doors closed for the night, I tore the keys out of the ignition while Declan and Giovanni both bolted out of the Tahoe and proceeded to puke up their guts in the nearest trash can they could find.

All our princess did was laugh and call us overgrown babies. Then she strolled into the shelter like she didn't just shave thirty years off of our lives. At the sounds of ear-piercing screams, we all trucked it into the front doors, damn near breaking them off the shitty hinges, to find her wrapped in an older woman's arms with the biggest smile on her face and tears running down her face.

We were introduced and given a tour of the place as Ramona told us embarrassing stories about Bethani. Oddly enough, that place felt more welcoming and family-oriented than any place I've ever lived. The culture shock was overwhelming as all of these people had absolutely fucking nothing, but they shared more joy and laughter than any of the pompous pricks I've ever dealt with. When we handed Ramona a check for ten thousand dollars to help out, she hugged us with a maternal love I've never felt before.

Shortly after I was born, my mother checked out. She had a business deal with my father. Stay with him until she gave him a son, then she fucked right off when I was three months old. While Declan's and G's mothers tried to share their love with me, they all had their own issues to deal with, so none of us really had a loving mother figure.

After we left, we went to some packed hole-in-the-wall restaurant called *Los Locos*. The food was fantastic, and everyone greeted our kitten with open arms and welcoming smiles. The problem? I'm almost 100 percent positive we were in cartel country, and we were spotted. That's the problem with being in a secret society like the Trident. Our hands are in every pocket imaginable depending on how they benefit us. Some fathers have sent their sons to our school in an attempt to forge an alliance. We let their son become a member, and they pledge their loyalty to us. But we also use their products and only their products.

If this territory we are currently in is the one I think we are in, which given the sneering death glares we have received all night, well, we just might be fucked.

"G. You fucking figure out which territory this is yet?" I ask from behind my glass so I'm not busted by someone who can read lips, which would surely give away who we are.

He just sends me a look that says all I need to know. Fuck!

Carina Cartel territory. We had a great relationship with them up until two years ago when one son that was our age got drunk at a public event and was bragging about his affiliations to anyone who would listen. Thankfully, everyone else was too drunk to care what a punk rich kid said. My father, on the other hand, not so much. His father signed a treaty when we inducted Felix into the Trident, saying if he mentioned us, he was signing his death warrant.

Felix Carina Sr. called my father's bluff, and when they turned to walk away, I pulled the trigger from a long-range rifle. That resulted in a bullet between Felix Jr.'s eyes, and our alliance was officially terminated.

As my eyes wander from Bethani for a moment, I notice in the far corner a group of people that are rapid-fire talking and pointing in our direction. "I don't fucking like this. We need to get out of here before shit hits the fan."

"Well, did you bring anything?" Declan asks again with that twinkle in his eyes.

He is psyching himself up for a potential fight. That's what he spends hours upon hours doing: training in different forms of Martial Arts. While he looks like a damn rock star, his body is a trained killer that doesn't need many weapons to take someone out.

"Of course," I tell him but don't go in further in case someone is watching.

I've got my custom black Dolce & Gabbana lace-up ankle boots with a knife slid down each ankle and a custom hidden knife hidden in each heel. I've also got my shoulder holsters with a Glock 19 on each side. They are hidden perfectly under my custom-fitted Armani leather jacket, which has compartments for four full extra clips.

"I'm good also. So is the SUV," Gio states.

That's why he was adamant about taking his Tahoe. Being our guru of knowledge, Giovanni is the wild card. He has taken the time to master skill sets in a wide range from weapons and boxing like myself, to Martial Arts like Declan. But he also has mastered the art of packing a few of our SUVs with an arsenal of shit including guns, knives, bugging devices, a few bombs, listening devices, and jammers. He probably knew there was a chance that coming here could potentially put us in the mix with either enemies or fellow associates of our fathers.

Glancing back and forth between the guys, I say, "We need to get her out of here and back to the hotel."

Unsure looks pass between them before Declan speaks again, "Yeah. But what do we tell her? I mean...wait, where did she go?"

Panic ices over my veins as I start scanning the crowd in front of us for Bethani. Flashing pink lights distort everything slightly, making it harder to identify her in her hot pink salsa style ensemble.

"Fuck. They know she is with us. The fucking pink lights are throwing me off. Giovanni?"

Frustration colors his face. "Her tracker isn't showing up."

I'm growling as I glare at Gio. "How in the fuck did you not think to check what fucking territory we were heading into before we agreed to this shit?"

"Error of judgment. Plain and simple. I screwed up."

Fuck.

How have we failed her so goddamned easily?

As my eyes dance around the crowd, struggling to spot her, a voice breaks me out of my frenzy. "Compadres! No need to worry. Chica is in good hands. But capo would prefer a word." His beady stare and lust-filled look as he talks about *our* woman have me reaching in my jacket before I'm even aware I'm actually doing it. "Tsk, tsk. I wouldn't do that if I were you."

"Where the fuck is she?"

"Capo doesn't like to be left waiting. Especially from members of *El Sindicato Tridente*." He spits the last part with a venomous tone that has my body stiffening. *Shit.*

We've been fucking made.

And if we want to live to see another day, or Bethani, we have no choice but to comply.

"Take us to Capo. Now." Fire fills Giovanni's tone as he spits venom right back at the cartel member.

Without even acknowledging us, he turns and walks away, knowing we will follow. Storming down the steps, we catch up within a few strides as the whole floor parts for us in an eerie act of respect. Realization dawns on their faces, some in mock horror and others in a calm understanding, as we stride by.

In these parts, it's easy for them to see it. We are another big player in the underworld, therefore we are treated with respect until given the orders otherwise. Us not starting a scene and willingly going to Capo? They won't touch us.

Reaching a guarded staircase, two bodyguards just nod at the man in front of us and move out of the way for us all to go up to a second level. Their faces give nothing away, the same as ours. We've played this game one too many times with our fathers in their attempts to tear us down.

Show no emotion. Do not react.

Seeing as how I can almost feel the blood pulsing through each vein as my mind pings between Bethani and this meeting, I'm not sure how well the second part is going to go.

Reaching the top, the errand boy slides a key card into the slot, and once the green light flashes, the door pops open to a smaller, but more extravagant room.

Ah, El Capo's office.

Stepping in, I can see the garish and ugly as fuck decorations that flash his wealth, but I'm not even paying attention. My eyes are on the man behind the desk.

Felix Carina Sr. The head of the Carina Cartel. El Capo.

Shit. Fuck. Cocksucking hell.

"Hola, gentlemen. Brave of you to venture onto our territory, is it not?"

His guards surround us, strategically placed around the room. *Smart.* We don't reply, willing him to speak first and get to the point. He must realize we won't cave because he slowly stands up and walks around his desk to lean against it while crossing his arms over his chest.

"I'm only going to ask this once. Why are you here? I've been hearing reports all night of you three and a woman waltzing around in my territory, then you show up to my club with her."

"Girlfriend's birthday. She lived in this area for a few years. Figured we'd bring her back as a surprise. Wasn't aware you were still in this territory."

"Hmm..." He nods, mulling over my answer. "You say this woman lived here? Where does she live now?"

"With us. Her dorm was shit, and when we found out about it, we moved her into our place. She is a scholarship student at the university," Giovanni answers in an attempt to keep the situation from elevating so we don't end up in a dumpster.

"Scholarship student?" he asks with a look of surprise on his face that I don't understand. Looking at who I'm assuming is his second-in-command, he says, "Don't we know someone who used to frequent here in a similar situation?"

The guy just nods. "Si. Gabriella made friends with her here one night."

Snapping his fingers like a light bulb went off from a memory, he turns back toward us. "Ahh, yes. My sweet *hija* made friends with a girl from here. No *familia*, but could dance like no other. Nice girl in a shit situation. We tried to recruit her before she left, but my Gabriella said no, she was too nice."

My eyebrow rises at his description. While part of that sounds like my little kitten, I can't be sure.

"Do you remember her name by chance?" I'm pushing my luck by talking out of line, but when it comes to Bethani, there isn't a line I won't cross right now.

"No. Only met her that one time. *¿Porqué?*"

"I have a feeling we are talking about the same person." I'm blunt and to the point. No reason to dick around. If he wanted us dead, we'd probably already be wrapped in plastic on our way to the desert to be dumped.

He eyes me suspiciously for a moment. "Hmm..."

Whatever he was going to say next halts as the door to his office slams open, and a loud voice has us all jumping and pointing weapons at the door. Suddenly a woman I would have once done anything to fuck comes barreling into the room, oblivious to everyone's weapons pointed at her.

"Pappaaaa! You won't believe who I found! Eek!"

Felix quickly waves us off to holster our weapons as he accepts his daughter's embrace. "Ay, Gabriella! What have I told you about knocking before? *Chica loca.*"

She stands back but looks around sheepishly like a kid caught with their hand in a cookie jar. "*Lo siento, papa.* But you won't believe who I found! Hold on!" She then proceeds to dart back out of the room only to come back just as fast, dragging Bethani behind her. I glance at Declan and Giovanni, who both look as dumbstruck as I do.

Holy shit, our kitten actually is friends with the daughter of the Carina Cartel. I'm not sure whether that is beneficial to us, or if it potentially puts a giant-ass target on her back that no amount of security can cover.

"Bethani is here for the weekend from that fancy college! I saw her when she went to the bathroom! Of course I had to talk to her and bring her up to say hello!" Gabriella is all smiles and talking hands while Bethani is just a timid thing standing there glancing around.

When her eyes finally land on us, they turn into the size of baseballs as mine narrow on her. She knew she was supposed to let us know if she needed to leave our sights.

"Guys? What are you doing up here?" Her voice sounds dry as the Sahara Desert as the shock settles in.

"Ay! Of course! I remember her now. Bethani, you know these fools?" Felix drags her attention away from us, and I add to the growing mental list of shit she needs to explain and that she will be punished for later. My cock stirs in my pants as I think of some ideal punishments. Shifting slightly, I avert my attention to the scene in front of me.

"Y-yes, Mr. Carina. I go to school with them. They brought me down for my birthday—"

She doesn't get to finish her sentence as Declan cuts her off, "We're her boyfriends. Figured we'd spoil our sunshine with some of her favorite memories." He ends his statement with his playboy smirk. It's a challenge to see if she refutes his statement. My own lips quirk as she flounders, unsure of our blatant declaration.

Felix's eyes rapidly flick between us all as he takes everything in before bursting out with a deep laugh. "Declan, you loco boy. All three of you fools are dating her? Ay, this is some funny shit." His laughter keeps up as his men join in, while Gabriella looks at Bethani in mock horror.

I quickly become fed up with the joke and feel the instantaneous need to stake our claim. "Kitten. Come here." I demand with a tap of my nose, which is one of our public signals we discussed when going through the contract together along with the guys. Most of them are universal between us with a few exceptions of ones that are catered to each of us.

She stands still until my eyes lock with hers. I give her a 'I'm not fucking around' stare, one more tap to my nose, and she quickly heads our way.

As soon as she is in arm's reach, I snatch her pretty little ass up and slam my lips against hers. Her mouth drops open quickly, submitting to my voracious demand, as I plunge my tongue into her mouth and tangle it with hers. As her hands go to slink up my arms, I break the kiss and spin her to Giovanni. Slapping her ass, she yelps as he claims her mouth in an equal fashion before sending her Declan's way.

Not to be outdone, the bastard quickly scoops her up to lock her legs around his waist as he palms her ass. My fingers itch to slide up that short little dress to see if she is wearing any panties and tease her until she is begging for us. But our little vixen will have to wait a while for that fun. She has watched others at the club we took her to, but we haven't let anyone see her while we fuck her senseless.

Call us selfish bastards, but no one except us gets to see our kitten's facial expressions when she is in the throes of ecstasy. Those are ours alone, and I'll slit a fucker's throat if they think they are privileged enough to see her like that.

A little moan escapes Bethani as Declan sets her down. I bring her back to me and wrap my arms protectively around her while glancing at the now dead silent room in front of me.

"Isn't that right, kitten? You're ours and we're yours."

The shining glint in her eyes and flawless smile as she stares at me is nearly enough to knock me off my ass. Instead of investigating the feeling, I simply tilt her chin my way and place a kiss on her nose. "Well?"

She just turns back toward the room and answers, "Yes. They're mine and I'm theirs. I fought it, but they are persistent jerks when they want to be."

Her devilish smirk at the end has me scowling at her. She is provoking the bear and she knows. Dipping down, I whisper in her ear, "You'll pay for that later, kitten."

I'm met with another gorgeous smile and small one-shoulder shrug as she gives me a provocative retort, "Bring it."

My nostrils flare, but before I can comment, someone clears their throat and we are brought out of our little bubble. Felix is still wide-eyed at our exchange, but he composes himself back into his stoic, crime lord boss self.

"Well then. Seems like all affairs are in order. If that's the case, let's head down to the booth so our gorgeous girls here can dance and have fun. How about that?"

I just nod along with the guys as we are motioned to follow one of the private guards that Felix keeps on his payroll.

As we walk out the door, my hand tightens around Bethani's small one. The need to keep her close as we enter this uncertain territory riles up every protective instinct in my gut.

"Sinclair?" she asks.

"Hmm? Sorry, kitten. Zoned out. What did you ask?"

"I asked how you know Mr. Carina."

I almost want to snort at her regard toward him. The blatant naive look on her face tells me she has no clue of his *business ventures* and that settles some of the uneasy guilt that has been there since we heard her mumbling our Syndicate hymn in her sleep. We still haven't figured out that connection, but we are waiting until this weekend is over to really dig into it.

Wrapping an arm around her waist as we reach the bottom of the stairs, I glance around to see if anything is amiss. "Just an old business associate of our fathers', kitten. Nothing to worry about." I pause as we reach the ropes to be escorted into Capo's private VIP area overlooking everything. "You just enjoy your time with your friend, and do *not* forget to let us know if you need to wander out of our sights." My voice drops, which sends shivers through her body. "Be a good girl, kitten, or daddy will tie you up again and whip your ass."

The girls are back on the dance floor as we sit in the rounded booth with Felix. Our eyes never stray far from the girls as the guards keep their heads on permanent swivel. The extra protection is calming, but I'm wary of how long it will last. Thankfully Felix doesn't make us wait long before broaching topics that need to be discussed.

"Gentlemen. The way you leave this club tonight all depends on how you answer. You are all obviously aware of our failed allegiance with your fathers." We just nod because there is no reason to answer. "While I may be upset with your fathers, I can hold no ill will against you. Especially you, Sinclair."

His gaze narrows on me, but I remain neutral while sipping my drink. Setting it back down, I glance toward Bethani before returning my gaze to his.

"I figured you already knew. Which is why I'm slightly surprised I'm still standing."

He just hmms in agreement. "Thought about it. Still am at the moment. But I realized also you boys are in a similar situation as *mi familia*. What is that American saying you all have? Loose lips sink ships? While I loved *mi hijo*, he was a stupid boy. Loved to flaunt too much for his own good. Thank God for his older brother, otherwise I'd be screwed. My sweet Gabriella is too good for this life."

He stops to take a sip of his drink as his gaze hits his daughter. A fatherly love shines through his eyes and the green monster of jealousy sinks its claws into me. I've never felt an ounce of love from my father. I always just feel how I'm worthless in his eyes. Seeing Felix's love and devotion for his daughter reminds me that many families aren't always as similar to the ones I've been surrounded with. My eyes flick back as Felix resumes talking.

"Any who. Can I ask what brought your attention to Miss Bethani? She doesn't seem like the type of woman to attract your tastes."

I ponder an answer, but Declan beats G and me to speaking. "She isn't. We usually don't give a fuck who they are or how much of daddy's money is lining their pockets. She caught our eye the night she was assaulted at our club."

My fists clench at the memory and I tamp down the rage that we still haven't found the piece of shit.

Declan continues, "We saved her from her dick ex. Had our doctor treat her. She was pissed when she woke up and called us all sorts of names, then stormed off. Giovanni ended up putting a tracker on her phone to make sure she was okay. Went to the dorm she was staying in." He gives a dark laugh before downing a shot. "Fucking shithole. Anyways, we convinced her to live with us and packed her up. She wasn't the biggest fan of ours at first, but you see how that ended up. We are all in a relationship with her."

"Shithole? I've seen your campus. How did she live in a shithole there?"

Now it's my turn to give a dark laugh. "Our *fathers* had her placed in a run-down basement of the storage building. She was under the guise it was a great opportunity, but she has been given shit for treatment since she set foot on that campus. Until we found her, of course."

"Your fathers can be some real *pendejos* sometimes."

We all snort at that. "Sometimes? Try all the time," I deadpan.

"I sense some hostility in the ranks?" His look is inquisitive, and it's a question I know we have to answer honestly. I glance at G to give the floor to him.

He just rolls his eyes but gives a more diplomatic response, "We've always known our fathers are bastards, Felix. But recent events have us questioning quite a bit more of their ruling."

That really piques his interest.

"Care to elaborate, Giovanni?"

Sighing, G just settles back into his chair. "While I know none of us feel comfortable just divulging this information, we are also aware that you will kill us if we don't. Correct?" Felix just nods in response. He is still pissed his son is dead and if it was anybody else, they would be dead. The only thing saving us currently is the iron-clad contract he signed to get his son into the Syndicate.

Sighing, Giovanni continues, "They tried to go behind our grandfathers' backs and set us up with arranged marriages. Also the stuff behind Bethani's acceptance to the school is questionable. Apparently they have this whole scheme that entices young men and women in similar situations to her to go there. None last long, though. For some reason she is the sole scholarship student who has ever lasted more than a month. They have a vested interest in her that we haven't figured out yet. But there are also all the records we don't have access to that would make our lives easier."

Felix contemplates the answer, studying our various expressions for any tell that it's a hoax. He must realize we are telling the truth before he speaks. "Well, your father had shady business deals before this. How do you think those flyers got hung up around here for your school?"

"Wait. *What?*" we all ask in unison. *What the fuck is going on here?*

Felix just nods. "Sí. That's how my boy was accepted into your folds. They were on a mission for some reason. Asked to hang up flyers to 'help diversify' the university. I didn't believe a word out of their mouths but played along. My counter was having my son accepted, and they easily agreed. After I signed that ridiculous contract of course. I never did get the chance to figure out their reasoning, though, which we all know why. Ever since our dissolved alliance, your fathers have tried to railroad me in some of my routes. Quite frankly, I'd assume to get rid of them, but they are so well protected it makes me look like a nobody." He chuckles at the last part, but I can't focus. My mind is swirling at this information.

"Well, what the fuck does this all have to do with our sunshine?" Is Declan's pissed off retort. I can feel the anger starting to radiate off him with hearing about this new evidence.

"Something isn't adding up," G mumbles before looking at Felix. "Felix, what are your thoughts about a secret alliance?"

My eyes flare at his question. *Where are you going with this, G?*

Apparently Felix is on the same wavelength as me. "I'm intrigued. Go on then."

Squaring his shoulders, G addresses us all. "It's all glaringly obvious of our distastes for them, right?" We all nod and wait for him to continue. "There is obviously a scheme here for some type of power play that they are hell-bent on. What it is, we don't know. But we can all guess Bethani is some sort of odd link to it all. I hacked Washington State CPS a while ago. Seeing what she went through..."

He stops to gather himself while Declan and I stay still. The barely there thread of control is ready to snap at the words he delivers next.

"She went through hell. No clue who her father is. Mom is a lifetime drug addict and prostitute. She was found multiple times scrounging trash for food and was lucky to have clothes that ever fit properly. Her mom constantly moved from one shithole to another. Places that were more likely to be infested with mold and roaches than have heat and water. Drugs, needles, and other paraphernalia was constantly scattered about. Tons of men constantly coming and going..." He trails off and the look of pain crossing his face tears my stomach apart. There is more to this than he is letting on, and now I see why he hid this from Declan and me.

Felix adjusts himself, settling his elbows on his knees and steepling his fingers below his chin. "Go on, Giovanni. I must know this. *Por favor.*"

Gio's gaze strays to Bethani and locks on to her as he delivers the final gut punch. "A few of those fucks sexually abused her when her mother couldn't afford the drugs. Her so-called excuse for a fucking mother never let them actually rape her, but she kept promising her to one of them for his trafficking ring if he hooked her up. Before that happened, a guy named James Williams, some big executive up there that hit a rough patch, slept with her mom. He ended up keeping tabs on them to make sure they were alive. The last time he went there, he broke down the door when he heard Bethani's screams. Her mom was passed out with a needle in her arm, and the dealer was trying to do more with Bethani. James called the cops and got her out and into the system, where she floated until she hit seventeen and filed to become a legal adult. Once the ink was dry, she took a bus, and that's how she ended up in your territory, Felix."

"¡Dios mio! Fucking scum!" Felix stands and starts to pace.

Declan is off in a world of his own while G's eyes are closed.

I'm barely able to choke out a deserved sentiment to him, "Thanks for sharing, man. Understand why you kept it from us now." He doesn't acknowledge me, but I know he heard me by the deep inhale and exhale. Turning, I speak to Felix, "Like Giovanni said, we have no idea what sick scheme our fathers have going on. But if it involves her, we will do whatever it takes to protect her from them. You want info, we will give it to you. If you want to lay low until we form a plan against them, that's fine. Just having your back in this would be enough for now. I can have G ship you a burner here to the club that we can keep in contact with. Otherwise we act like we still hate each other to keep shit kosher."

"You know, most people treat my daughter differently because of her wealth. You boys know it as well as I do how we are all treated differently. Your Bethani was one of the first people to give my daughter a dose of how a person is supposed to treat another, despite their financial differences. That's why my daughter felt so strongly about keeping her out of our world. Thought that she was too sweet to be corrupted by it. Apparently we were all wrong. Her poor soul has been corrupted by forces out of her control."

He stops and sits back down before giving us a formidable look and continuing, "Bethani has no clue about my position. She just thinks that I'm a businessman. I'd prefer we keep it that way, gentlemen." His tone is no-nonsense and leaves zero room for discussion. I nod in agreement.

"Understood, sir. She is still unaware of our positions also, so keeping with the theme seems best for now."

"Sí. I'll agree to this alliance. But the agreement is simple. We four are the only ones who know about it. Keep contact to a minimum unless it's through the burners. We give each other updates if we find anything. If we seek each other's services, then we shall figure out a form of payment. Keeping her safe is the current priority, so I'll reach out to a couple of my contacts to send silent security to help keep tabs around campus. No cost." I go to speak but am cut off. "I'm serious, Sinclair. My daughter considers Bethani familia because of how wonderful she treats her. Keeping her safe will make my daughter happy, so cost doesn't matter. Besides, I have a few pieces of blackmail to utilize anyways." His laugh has us all chuckling. We know the value of a good piece of blackmail against an enemy. "But before we can agree to anything"—his demeanor shifts to that familiar darkness we are all accustomed to—"heed my warning, though, gentlemen. If you even think of screwing me over, I won't think twice about gutting you and displaying you for all to see. I've been screwed once by your infamous last names. I refuse to go through that again. And when your sweet Bethani asks why, I will tell her the truth. So don't even think about fucking me over unless you want to die."

His words are cut, dry, and to the point. He will kill us and not think twice about it. While I have no active plan of screwing the guy over, the thought of Bethani seeing us dead leaves a sour taste in my mouth. I mull over his words along with the guys.

Finally, I stand and motion for the guys to follow suit. When we get near Felix he stands up.

"So, gentlemen, do we have an agreement?" he asks us.

After looking at the guys for approval, I stick my hand out to his, and with a wicked grin, we shake. "Goddamn right we have an agreement."

Chapter 29

Declan

Walking back into the hotel after a long-ass night at the club, I'm starting to feel the effects of all the tension that went down wear off finally. For a person like me who feels emotions tenfold to others, it makes for a wicked fucking hangover feeling that I don't enjoy in the slightest.

As we step into the elevator, I lean back against the wall and close my eyes to attempt to stave off the oncoming headache. *Fuck, I could really use a hit of something right now.* But of course, I didn't bring anything with me. Haven't really needed that shit much since sunshine came into our lives. But after hearing the amount of shit she has gone through, it's enough to make a person want to burn the world down. I get why Giovanni never elaborated about her file. It's fucking disgusting. But I can guarantee if there are names in that file, then Gio is already on a silent war path of destruction.

Small arms wrap around my waist as Bethani's chin lands on my sternum. "What's wrong, Declan?" A worried look crosses her gorgeous features.

Instead of opening my big mouth like I want to, I just pick her up until her legs wrap around my waist. I settle my forehead against hers and give her a reassuring smile.

"Nothing, sunshine. Just too much Latin music for my taste. How you danced to that shit all night is beyond me."

Her head tilts back as she laughs, a beautiful deep laugh that lights my soul on fire. When I go to kiss her, the elevator stops on our floor. Bethani wiggles to get down, and my firm grip around her full ass tightens.

"Nice try, sunshine."

"I can walk, Declan. Seriously."

Her full lips turn into a pout, but I stay strong in my resolve. Giving her a dirty smirk, I simply lay it out, "Not for long, sunshine. As soon as we get in this room, you'll be getting fucked so hard you won't know what hit you."

Bethani's mouth just drops, and my dick surges to life in my pants as I think about those full lips sucking my cock down her throat like a fucking Hoover. Groaning, I pick up my pace to get to the end of the hall quicker. Because my plans to get wicked and wild with our girl need to be acted out fast before the friction of my tight jeans and the pressure of her snug against me causes me to blow my fucking load prematurely.

As we hit the door, I quickly dig my key card out of my back pocket and swipe it to open the door. I have zero fucking clue how far behind G and Sin are, nor do I care. All I can think about right now is burying myself deep inside Bethani's perfect fucking pussy and hearing her screams of pleasure.

Walking in, I don't even bother closing the door. Looking around for the best surface, I quickly spot the dining room table and make my way there. As soon as her ass hits the table, my lips press to hers. I'm not in a talking mood right this second. I need a fucking Bethani fix, and that's what I'm going to get.

Swiping my tongue across her lips, I get a quick taste of her cherry lip gloss, and a guttural moan escapes my lips as I demand access to her mouth. She quickly grants me access, like she always does, and I waste no time tangling our tongues together as the flavors mesh together. The unusual fruity cocktails she chose tonight meshes perfectly with her usual sweetness, and it fuels my lust tenfold.

I'm quickly shrugging out of my jacket and breaking our kiss to tear my shirt over my head before glancing at her dress. "How many more of these dresses did you get, Sinclair?" I ask, feeling his and G's presence near me. They're most likely enjoying the show before they join in.

"Two in each color she liked, why?"

Smirking, I run my fingers against her cleavage, making her shiver. "Better order another in this color then." Then I quickly grab hold of the dress and tear it clean in half, only to discover our girl in just a flimsy black lace thong. "Fucking hell, sunshine. Could've warned a man." I hear the guys' groans of agreement behind me. I also hear their clothing getting tossed to the side, which makes me smile. "You ready for more of a party, Bethani? Once we start, baby, this is going on all night long."

Our sweet girl. While there is a bit of fear behind those lust-filled aqua orbs, she just smiles and reaches for my belt buckle to pull me back to her. Reaching up to clasp her hands around my neck, she brings my head down until her mouth meets my ear. Her whispered voice sends electrical volts through my body. "I thought you'd never ask, baby." Then she sucks my earlobe into her mouth and nips it, officially bringing out the feral beast inside me.

Quickly, I pull back and put a hand on her chest to direct her to lie back on the table. Using the torn dress, I slide her to the edge so her ass is just barely hanging off, and I stoop to my knees.

Perfect fucking level.

Her thong is torn to shreds just as fast as the dress, and I'm left with a wondrous view of her dripping pussy. Leaving no time to waste, I bury myself in her pussy and start devouring her as I throw her legs over my shoulder for better access. Her back quickly arches off the table as I take a deep lick from her opening to her clit, and a breathy moan escapes her lips, further driving me on. When I go to reach up and pin her back down, my hand is swatted away by one of the guys.

Opening my eyes to take stock of the situation, I see Sinclair and Giovanni are both naked and standing on each side of a thrashing Bethani. Sinclair, in all his bossy demeanor, focuses her with his Dom voice.

"Grab our cocks, kitten."

She moans even louder, which sends a glorious gush of her essence against my tongue that I greedily lap up, but she quickly does what he asks. As she is using their precum to lube up her hands, I get a wicked idea.

I slow my pace a bit to give her a little breathing room while she develops a perfect tandem dick stroking rhythm on the guys. They each reach down and grab one of her full breasts and slowly start to knead them as they tweak and pluck her flawless nipples into firm buds. Bethani's breathing becomes more ragged as we all simultaneously work her into a frenzy. Tiny yelps and deep moans flow from her body, which fuel us all on.

As I see the guy's eyes start to close with her ministrations on their dicks, I hurry up and stand, shoving my jeans down in the process. As quick as I stand up, I grip Bethani's hip with one hand and use the other to line up with her drenched entrance. As her wide, surprised eyes focus on mine, I simply smirk and slam my dick into her, setting her off into an intense orgasm.

As her head falls back, a scream of pleasure tears from her throat. Her pussy clamps and convulses around my cock as I pull out and thrust back in. I grit my teeth and grunt to keep from coming but never stop my firm thrusts in and out of her tight, spasming heat. The guys are wide-eyed in shock as Bethani's hands clamp down on their dicks in firm tugs, which set off their first orgasms of the night also.

"Fuck!" and "Goddammit, Declan!" are their deep voices, along with other strings of obscenities being thrown at me while I watch in fucking wonder as Bethani's tits are being coated in ropes of cum. The whole situation fuels the furnace to my need to reach an orgasm.

My grip on her hips tightens, and I start pounding into her like a deranged man. The fire in my belly turns into a raging inferno, demanding its release. Feeling that my balls are starting to suck up into my body, my pace turns utterly demonic and frantic as I grit out, "One. Of. You. Pinch. Her. Clit!" Each word emphasized with a brutal bottoming out thrust.

Just before my eyes start to roll back into my head, I see G reach down to rub her clit at a furious pace as Sinclair grabs her nipples. Our sweet sunshine is thrashing her head back and forth while Sinclair just coos at her.

"Come for us, kitten."

They pinch both her clit and nipples at the same time while Gio quickly pops a finger in his mouth to lube it up, then hurries and reaches around to my ass. I feel his finger probing around for a hot second before he is shoving it quickly into the Promised Land and crooking it perfectly to bump my prostate.

Feeling that quick nudge, my body seizes up as I make one finally thrust into Bethani, and my orgasm takes full control of my body.

"Shit, shit, FUCK!" Is all I hear fall from my mouth before everything turns into a white haze as my head falls back.

Bethani's pussy has such a tight grip on my swelling cock, I couldn't move even if I wanted to. The blinding pleasure is coursing through my body. Exploding deep inside her is a feeling that will never compare to anything else in this world.

I'm on another damn planet as electricity flows through my body while my cock keeps jerking inside her, sending tingling sensations all over me. It feels like an eternity passes before my body starts to come back to itself. Before my vision even totally clears, I slowly start to pull out of Bethani's dripping pussy. As a suctioning pop from my dick's head separating from her sends a final pulse through my super sensitive cock, my knees give out, and I crumple to the floor in a boneless heap.

My breathing is haywire as I rapidly blink in an attempt to gain my sight back. It takes a moment, but finally I'm able to see the complete extent of my sex-induced chaos.

Bethani is still sprawled out on the table with her legs dangling like they are completely useless. Giovanni is bent over the table, but I can make vague movements of him stroking her hair that cascades around her like a dark, sexy angel. When my gaze finally lands on Sinclair, I can't help but laugh. The grumpy bastard is sitting in a chair, scowling at me.

"What?" I barely croak out. *Jesus, I need water.*

His scowl doesn't leave as he proceeds to admonish me. "You fucking know what, asshole. The fuck was that?"

Leveling him with an equally terrifying glare of my own, I give him all the reasoning he needs to know. "You know *exactly* what that was."

Studying me, he just nods before returning his gaze to Bethani. He says something to her, but I've already tuned him out.

Closing my eyes again, I focus on regulating my heart rate and breathing. While I may have not said anything, he knew exactly why I did what I did.

After everything that happened earlier, I was close to spiraling into one of my deep depressions where I lose complete control of my life in a drug and alcohol-induced blur. Sometimes they have lasted only a day or two, just long enough to let shit go. Other times, they have lasted for a couple weeks, like when I found out my mom had cancer last year. She is still sitting at home 'fighting' it like the brave warrior she is. Which really means going on her constant retreats with her posse and rarely going to treatment. She says she is too beautiful for cancer and just ignores it. Yet every time I'm blessed with her witchy presence, I see how it is slowly eating her to nothing.

My mom never used to be that way either. My dad was the most faithful of the fathers until my mom slipped up on one of her getaways. After that, he turned into a flagrant fuck, and she slowly morphed into a mega bitch. The woman I could always count on when my father got too rough stopped caring little by little until I became nothing more than 'the fuck-up'.

I've always loved my mom, and I took her diagnosis hard. The guys found me down in a seedy section of Cabo snorting something off a stripper's tit. I was so blitzed out I didn't even know my name. Apparently I blacked out, vomited the whole jet ride home, and woke up in our medical room with a few IV drips to keep my dumb ass alive.

I haven't done that since, but tonight I was toeing the edge of self-destruction. After hearing Giovanni's confession about Bethani's life, I knew that if I didn't go full tilt like I did, I would have drunk the full bar in the room dry, then gone on a rager.

Yeah, so it was either an insane quickie to bring me back to earth or a ridiculous bender. I chose the former, and Sinclair can shove a dildo up his ass for all I care.

Finally feeling settled, I open my eyes back up to see my sunshine staring down at me. Her hair is a train wreck, and her makeup is smudged a little, but she is still the most beautiful goddamn creature I've ever laid eyes on.

"How ya feeling, sunshine?" I ask with a wide smile, hoping to gain a decent reaction from at *least* one of them.

When she flashes me a quick but sweet smile, I know I've won the battle. "You fucked me senseless, Declan."

I laugh, Giovanni snorts, and Sinclair just chuckles.

"Kitten, that was just the beginning. Let's call room service for fuel before round two."

Bethani's jaw drops and her eyes go round as she looks toward Sinclair. "R-round two?"

Standing up, I smirk at her reaction. "Told you, sunshine. We're going all fucking night long."

Chapter 30

Bethani

H orn dogs. I live with horn dogs.

Twenty minutes after Sinclair ordered half the damn menu, two men came in wheeling massive carts full of snacks, meals, and refreshments. While I just snacked on random things that sounded good, the guys each had massive steaks with an assortment of sides. How they pile all that food away like they do and *still* look like the fucking drool-worthy gods they are, I'll never know. If I were to eat like that, my ass would be twice the size it is now.

Now we are all just chilling on the massive bed watching a movie, but it doesn't take long before they start their teasing.

I'm lying on Sinclair's chest between his legs, and Giovanni is between mine with Declan lying facing the foot of the bed. But of course, he still has to have a form of contact with me by grazing his hand gently against my leg.

Sinclair's massive hands come up to my shoulders and slowly start massaging me. "That feels amazing. Please don't stop," I whisper breathlessly as his thumbs put just enough pressure between my shoulder blades to light my body on fire. He just chuckles and keeps going as my head starts to lull back and my eyes close.

I'm vaguely aware of Declan moving off the bed, but my eyes don't open back up until Giovanni shifts, flipping over to face me. Giving him a look, I say, "What are you doing, mister?" He just smiles sweetly and starts kissing my thighs. Moving up one side and down the other but never touching my pussy. When he gets down to the bottom of my left leg, he switches back over to my right. Just when I think he is going to kiss them again, he switches to gentle nips that have me shooting straight up. "Fucking tease." I moan, but Sinclair pulls me back into his chest to trap me.

His gravelly voice is in my ear. "Be a good kitten and stay still. Let G have a taste of that sweet pussy that's still dripping from Declan's cock filling you up earlier." His voice. *Fuck.* His voice and filthy words instantly turn me into a needy mess. Whimpering, I just nod. A nip and deep suck to my neck have me gasping. "Good girl, kitten. Always so ready to please us."

"Always, *daddy.*"

I smirk at the deep growl ripping from Sinclair's chest at my snarky remark. He loves when I call him that. Turns him into a beast in the best way possible, and I end up extra sated and sore the next day.

Giovanni's hand slaps my clit as he scolds me, "Don't tease, Tesoro."

The shock of his slap has my pussy tightening, and it takes everything in me not to grab his head and bury him between my thighs. "S-sorry," I grit out. Not necessarily to comply, but because I'm so damn turned on that if these guys don't start touching me, I'm going to lose my shit.

Declan tosses some things on the bed before climbing back up. I don't get the chance to see what he brought before he is back in front of me. He's naked and hard as fuck with his piercing already glistening with precum. Seeing that has me licking my lips, itching for a taste.

"See something you like, sunshine?" His cocky tone has me glancing up to slate gray eyes, and like usual, I'm entranced by the swirling shades and mystery behind them.

Realizing where this is all heading has my skin prickling with tiny currents, my breath hitching, and pussy dripping more and more. Every breath they breathe or feather touch has my body burning to the point of combustion.

"Please touch me. I need you. *All* of you."

They have barely touched me and I'm already begging. But I don't even give a shit for once. Usually I'm all for teasing them a little, but seeing the predatory glares in their eyes at how bad they all want to claim me at the same time has me throwing complete caution to the wind. I'm not even sure of schematics right now, nor do I care.

"What do you want from us, kitten?"

I go to answer but draw a complete blank when I feel Giovanni's fingers tracing around my opening before plunging in and swirling around. My head falls back against Sinclair again as my mind frazzles. I feel two fingers, then a third as he stretches me even further, and I can't control the jerk of my hips as they try to ride his hand.

"Kitten, answer me." His demanding tone brings me back to this planet just long enough to form a semi-coherent sentence.

"A-all of you. However you want me." I stop to gasp as I feel Giovanni working a fourth finger in me until he is knuckle deep. "Fuck me. Please."

Words cease to exist as my chin is tilted and Sinclair crushes his lips to mine. He growls, and I open up to his caveman demand. Our tongues tangle momentarily before he tears himself away from me. "Fuck, you taste like heaven."

My oversized T-shirt is ripped from my head as Declan works his way up my body. Starting with a kiss to my clit, just above where Giovanni is working my pussy like it's an Olympic sport. He slowly makes his way up before his mouth covers one breast, nipping and suckling it while the other hand works the other breast. He's massaging it in his giant grip before plucking my nipple quickly, which sends jolts to my pussy that clamps down on Giovanni's hand. "Fuck, you are so tight, Tesoro."

I snake my hands up around Sinclair's neck for purchase. My grip is tight against his neck as I pull him back down to kiss me. The slight pain has his massive cock jerking against my ass. I moan into his mouth, and he greedily swallows them down as I adjust my feet to grind on his dick and Giovanni's hands at the same time.

I'm temporarily displaced when I feel the loss of Giovanni's hands, but he quickly replaces them with his tongue, thrusting deep inside me. As he flicks his tongue, I feel his barbell thumping my G-spot.

I'm so overwhelmed by being ravaged by these sex god studs I call boyfriends, that I hardly notice Giovanni's hand that was just inside me probing my asshole. A slight pinching sensation has me jerking away, but Sinclair's hand settles on my stomach to keep me in place while Declan pops off my nipple to speak.

"Relax, sunshine. Let G in so he can loosen you up for his cock."

My eyes widen at that. Oh, holy shit, is he serious? He must register my shock because he gives me a sexy as fuck smile.

"Promise, sunshine. We won't hurt you. You trust us, right?"

Even though I'm still lip-locked with Sinclair, I'm able to nod that I do. He just smiles, reaches up to kiss my cheek, and dives back to my breasts like a starved man.

My attention is diverted by Giovanni's intrusion when they all start working in perfect tandem at a fast pace to bring my body to new heights of pleasure. Giovanni's tongue is delivering a punishing pace of swirls and twirls inside my pussy as a set of fingers find my clit and circle it over and over. Declan's hand and mouth are biting, sucking, pinching, and twisting my breasts into deliciously achy mounds. Sinclair's free hand has moved around to control my head as his hand is buried in my hair, gripping enough to cause a slight pain that has me feeding him all the babbling noise I can give him while his lips and tongue control my mouth.

The tension in my body is winding tighter and tighter, like a rubber band that is ready to snap into a trillion pieces. Fire is burning in my belly like a raging inferno.

I can feel two of Giovanni's well lubricated fingers probing at my back entrance again, but instead of fighting it, I welcome it. As two fingers begin the process of stretching me open, the dam breaks. I'm utterly blindsided by the freight train that is my orgasm as he shoves both fingers in...*deep*. My head jerks back from Sinclair's hold as I scream in pure ecstasy until my lungs burn from lack of oxygen.

The world goes black as my body twists and turns from the sensation overload. My body goes weightless, and I swear I feel my soul leaving to just float around on a delirious cloud of the unknown.

I'm not even sure how much time passes before I'm able to remotely understand my surroundings. Deep rumbles around me have me moaning from how overly sensitive I feel. Like every little motion sets off a live wire of tingling that feels amazing and weird all at once.

One of their voices has me blinking in disbelief until I can regain focus. "Holy fucking shit. You drenched his face!"

As I tilt my head up enough, I can see whoever said that is correct. Giovanni's lower half of his face is dripping from my explosive orgasm. My jaw drops at the sight.

"Holy shit," I mutter.

Giovanni just smiles. "Didn't realize you were a squirter, Tesoro." He pauses to drag a finger along his face before shoving his finger in his mouth to suck it clean. "Mmmm...fucking delicious."

I blush, *somehow,* at his crude words and actions. "Fucking cavemen," I mumble as my eyes close to soak in more of the wondrous haze of ecstasy coursing through me.

"Maybe. But we're *your* cavemen, sunshine."

I snort at Declan's remark but flip my limp hand dismissively at them.

"Yeah, yeah."

Strong hands grip ahold of me to lift and turn me until I'm wide-eyed straddling Sinclair. "Nice try, kitten. The fun isn't over yet." He smirks as his hands move to my waist to settle me against his erection. He slides me up and down against his massive dick before making the slightest adjustment, and I feel the head of his pierced cock against my entrance.

After that last orgasm, I didn't think it was possible to be instantly ready for more. But as I feel the slight rocking of his hips with just enough motion to teasingly probe me, my body flares back to life, ready for more.

Slowly pushing back, I carefully sink down until his cock is fully sheathed by me, and his head is adding a slightly painful but welcome discomfort at my womb. His head falls back as I use my Kegel muscles to grip him as tight as possible.

"Fuck, kitten, how do you always feel *so* goddamn tight?"

Not even bothering to respond, my hands move to rest on his shoulders for guidance as I slowly gyrate my hips in a figure eight motion. His grip tightens as he moves me, so we are almost perfectly chest to chest.

Sinclair rhythmically bucks himself up into me when I'm sliding back down, causing me to spasm around him. In our own little bubble, my eyes are locked onto his commanding emerald eyes. Sinclair has this unique way to make me feel like the rest of the world doesn't matter. Everything falls to the wayside until he is ready to allow it in.

While most of the time that sliver of hate lingers toward him and his demanding, controlling, OCD way of ruling with an iron fist, in times like these, I absolutely love it. My horrific past doesn't threaten to break me. The nasty comments I've heard don't blast through my head, threatening to shred my hard-earned self-confidence apart. My mind becomes blank in the most glorious way possible.

A second pair of hands comes up behind me, massaging my ass cheeks. A third pair comes and tilts my focus until I realize it's Declan and his sexy tattooed and pierced body demanding my attention. "You're fucking perfect, sunshine. But you are about to look even better in a second."

My rhythm falters slightly at the sound of a bottle opening behind me. I go to look, but Declan won't let me. "Focus on me, sunshine. It's going to hurt for a second, but soon enough all you will feel is pleasure."

Giovanni's lips hit that sweet spot where my shoulder and neck meet before I feel the slippery head of his cock sliding between my ass cheeks.

"Pull her down a bit and spread her ass for me." Giovanni grunts.

Declan adjusts so he is leaning on his side next to Sinclair, and he brings me down with him until I'm flush against his chest. Sinclair's hands move and spread my cheeks as two of Giovanni's fingers begin sliding in and out over and over until a third gets added to the mix. A slight stretching has me wincing slightly, but Declan moves to kiss me until I don't even notice the uncomfortable feeling anymore.

His tongue melts with mine, and I'm lost by the whiskey and *him* taste. It's exquisite and draws my focus completely into him. It's not long before my body takes control as I start riding both Sinclair's cock and Giovanni's fingers. Waves of pleasure roll through me as the added pressure from Giovanni's fingers create a new friction inside me.

"I think she is ready, Gio. Give our greedy girl your cock," comes Sinclair's booming voice.

I whine into Declan's mouth at the loss of Giovanni's fingers, but the emptiness is quickly replaced by a burning sensation as his lubed dick slowly starts to replace his fingers. My eyes go wide at the intense pressure and my body clamps down at the foreign intrusion.

"Fuck, Tesoro. Let me in, baby."

Tears fill my eyes when he moves and slides in a little further. "It hurts, Giovanni." My voice breaks just slightly at the end. I want to be able to let him in, but these guys are all so thick and long I don't see how it's going to happen.

"Kitten." Sinclair's stern voice fills my ears and my eyes fall to his. His hypnotic stare entrances me while he speaks. "You will take Giovanni's cock like the good girl you are. You're gonna let us fill every greedy hole, and we are going to fuck that vixen body of yours until it's dripping our cum for a week."

Filthy words have me falling back slightly into Giovanni's chest as the movement sucks him into me even more. My breathing is labored, and I feel the dramatic rise and fall of my breasts as a hand skims its way down my stomach to my clit. I'm fluttering around Sinclair and Giovanni, and their wicked growls of pleasure add to the thick layer of arousal floating around us heavily.

The moan that tears through me as Giovanni carefully pushes the rest of the way into me as his hips fall flush with my ass causes all the guys to groan.

"So fucking tight, Tesoro," is Giovanni's harsh whisper in my ear. It's erotic and forbidden and I'm overloaded by the realization of everything; how much they care, how they are doing everything in their power to keep me safe, And how they surprised me with this epic weekend ending in an intentional claim over me. Mind, body, and soul, these brazen, egotistical, ruthless men own me. Irrevocably and with a finesse I never saw coming. They steamrolled their way into my life, flipping it completely upside down, just to rewrite it with their names in a blood oath, never to be reversed.

I don't even realize I've started crying until Declan's tongue caresses my cheek, lapping up the salty tear that has cascaded down.

"Is everything all right, sunshine?" His voice is laced with concern as he continues. "We can stop if it's too much for you."

Shaking my head rapidly, I remove the thoughts from my head as I open my eyes to the men who have undoubtedly stolen my heart. Torn into three perfect pieces, each has their slice that I never want to give back.

"No. *God no*. Please don't stop." I pause, inhaling and exhaling deeply for the next part. Opening my eyes back up with steel in my spine, the words fall from my lips, "Fuck me like you *own me*. Fuck me like you are going to *destroy me*. I don't want *any* of you holding back. Give me your best. Give me your worst. I want it *all*."

I finalize the determination in my statement by bearing down against Giovanni and Sinclair, while taking Declan's cock in my hand and giving him a firm tug. The sounds they make are like music to my ears, but I have one more request to make.

"One more thing..." I trail off, unsure now that I opened my mouth.

Giovanni's arms wrap around me to fondle my breasts while moving, pulling back gently, and thrusting. The movement reminds me of the complete fullness I feel, and I moan at how just a minute ago pain was exploding through me. But now? Holy shit, this feels so damn good. Way better than the plugs Sinclair loves to use, especially if I've been bad.

"What's up, Tesoro?" Giovanni's chocolatey smooth voice glides through me, bringing me back to my request. His slow, languid thrusts haven't stopped, which makes concentrating hard.

"I-I...want to suck on Declan's cock for a few, then I want Declan to fuck you from behind at the same time you are fucking me from behind, Giovanni." His movements halt to a stop as Declan's dick twitches in my hand. I can feel Sinclair jerk below me, which causes his piercing to flick my womb, and I bite my lip to stifle the sound.

"Are you sure about that, kitten?" His voice is laced with concern.

Glancing down at the pools of green, I nod. "I'm sure. It's about my pleasure as much as it is all of yours. And I'm not about to deny the fact that they are bisexual. It's not fair to them. End of story. That's my rule to us all being together like this."

He just stares but nods. "Fair enough, kitten. Now enough fucking talking. I'm ready to fucking die if I can't fuck you."

I laugh until his hips thrust up into mine and my laughter dies, instantly replaced by a breathless moan.

Sinclair and Giovanni both start to thrust in and out of me at a torturously precise pace. As Giovanni slams home, burying himself deep inside my ass, Sinclair pulls out to the tip and then does the same thing with a brutal force that shakes me to the core. I can feel the intense fullness as their cocks hit a sweet spot in me while passing each other inside me. I become a screaming mess in a matter of minutes, absolutely in love with the insane current that courses through my body from these dominant men and their pursuit to bring my body to heights of pleasure I've never thought were humanely possible.

Feeling a shift on the bed clears some of the lust coursing through me. How the fuck did I forget about Declan? As Sinclair's and Giovanni's punishing thrusts continue, the light bulb dings in my head. These two are how I forgot.

"The fuck, Deck?" Sinclair demands as his grip on my hips tightens.

I'm going to have bruises tomorrow, but I don't even care. They love seeing their marks on me, and to be honest, I love it too. Seeing how their eyes flare with a protective lust fuels me, so I've left my fair share on each of them.

"Fuck off, Sin. Only for a few minutes."

Declan's voice above me has me opening my eyes to see where he is. Only instead of his face, I'm greeted by his delicious dripping dick right in front of me, and my mouth instantly waters. Slowly licking my lips, I let my gaze travel up his heavily tattooed body; past those sexy nipple piercings I love toying with to instantly turn him into a horny mess for me, past those full lips with the lower right lip pierced, and up to his swirling granite gaze. When our eyes meet, his lips twist into that signature sexy smirk of his, flashing the slightest amount of his dazzling white teeth.

"Better get to sucking, sunshine, before the asshole rips my dick off for straddling him like this." I glance down long enough to see Sinclair's trademark glare, clearly pissed Declan is standing straddling him and he has the pleasure of a ball sack hanging in his face.

Smirking because I know it will piss him off more that I find his displeasure hilarious, I revel in what falls out of his mouth as his pace picks up. "Gonna pay for that, kitten. Just fucking wait."

I smile, egging him on. His punishments are fun, so I'm not worried. I just turn my glance back to the wonderful thick veiny cock in front of me.

Reaching up, I adjust my left hand on Sinclair's chest for better balance as these cavemen destroy my body in the best way possible with their dicks. Using my right hand, I wrap it around Declan's base and hold it still as a bead of cum starts to drip down. I quickly stick my tongue out, running it on the underside until I'm lapping up the salty cum on his engorged mushroom head. Passing over his piercing, I run my tongue along his slit to gather as much of his essence before sucking his head deep into my mouth.

Glancing up, I watch in wonder as Declan's head falls back into the wall with a thud. "Goddamn, Bethani. So fucking good. Keep sucking my dick like that and I'm gonna blow."

Smiling around a mouth full of cock, I keep up my pace as I stroke him while sucking, licking, and toying with his piercing.

A quick slap to my ass has me yelping, then moaning because the sting is just adding another amazing layer to everything happening currently.

Sinclair rocks into me and my eyes flit to his as he speaks. "Fuck, kitten. Never thought I'd enjoy seeing Declan like this, but fuck me this is hotter than hell. Seeing you taking almost thirty inches of dick like the goddamn fantasy you are. Fucking made for three cocks."

They're vulgar words that have me on the brink of orgasm. I shudder around them all, vibrations from my body eliciting sexy rumbles from theirs.

"Damn, Tesoro, never thought I'd find someone that enjoys sucking his dick as much as I do. *Bellisimo amore mio.*" His sweet words are accentuated with sinful kisses along my neck that light my body on fire.

Declan pops himself out of my mouth. The sight of his glistening head makes me want to pull him right back into me. He steps to one side and crouches down to his knees before bringing me in for a quick but heated kiss. It's short but full of emotion that none of us are ready to delve into.

Just as fast, he has Giovanni pulled into him for a passionate kiss, and I'm entranced by the sight of them. I've never seen them kiss and my body has a visceral response to it. It's sexy as fuck, and my body is so close to exploding from it as I feel spasms fluttering through my pussy. Sinclair's deep growl brings me back to him. I bend down as best as possible for being impaled with two cocks to give him a passionate kiss of his own.

The sound of a condom wrapper being torn open along with the lube lets me know this is about to get interesting and quick. Breaking the kiss with Sinclair, I twist my head until I can see Giovanni leaning forward more.

"Gotta give the big boy room." He winks, making me want to giggle, but Declan's hand comes down in a harsh slap against

Giovanni's ass. The punishment has him lurching forward, and my hips scream at the angle change.

The rest of me damn near explodes as my clit grinds on Sinclair's abdomen, making my eyes cross at how close I am. "Jesus, Declan," I moan as I attempt to curve the orgasm so we can all come together. "Hurry," I pant, pleading. "I'm so close."

I can feel the bed move, and then feel it as Giovanni is pushed further into me, firmly sandwiching me between him and Sinclair. We are all breathing heavily as we all struggle to not blow up. Literally. Figuratively. Whatever.

Giovanni's teeth sink into my shoulder as Declan grunts behind him. "Shit, you're fucking tight. So fucking turned on by being deep dicked while fucking our girl?"

Another slap rings in the air as Declan swears like a sailor, and Giovanni's hips jerk, sending my head in a wild spin.

"Sunshine. Put your hands on the headboard, baby. Sinclair, hold her hips so she doesn't pop off you because this is about to get crazy." I can hear the sardonic pleasure in his tone. He is thoroughly enjoying bossing us all around, but it's even more of a turn-on when we all listen to him.

My hands are barely settled on the headboard when my body is slammed forward from the exertion Declan is using to bring us all to a unified climax in grand fashion.

The room is quickly filled with loud moans, groans, and babbles of nonsense as our bodies all slap together in a sweaty mess. Sinclair uses his ridiculous strength to fuck me so damn deep my eyes slam shut as I use the headboard for stability to push back onto Giovanni. His and Sinclair's thrusts are in perfect sync, filling my body to the brim, while Declan's wild gyrations have us all unstable enough for it to be a complete chaotic perfection.

After a few more body splitting thrusts, my back arches as an earth-shattering orgasm splits me open. A strangled scream tears through me as my pussy and ass muscles seize up on both guys at the same time, triggering their orgasms.

"Fuuuckkkkk!" "Holy shit!" "Jesussss!"

Their voices echo loudly through the room as all of their bodies tense around me. Heat floods me as Sinclair and Giovanni spill deep inside me, and I swear I'm coming a second time from it. Manic groans come from them as my body clenches again around their sensitive cocks, and I hear a breathless gasp from one of them.

We all lie on top of each other in a blissed out heap until Sinclair shifts below me. "Someone has to fucking move before I get crushed."

And that's our cue to separate.

Both Declan and Giovanni groan. "Fuck me, Gio. Christ," Declan says, then falls to the bed beside me looking like a train ran over him.

A whimper escapes me as Giovanni goes to pull out of me.

"Sorry, Tesoro," he grunts when he finally pulls out all of the way, then kisses between my shoulder blades. "And fuck off, Deck. That was fucking perfect and you know it," he finishes as he topples to the other side.

When I go to see if I'm even capable of moving, Sinclair's arms wrap around me to bring me back down to his chest. "Stay, princess. Your body isn't ready to move yet." I'm currently too tired to care as a deep yawn escapes me.

Snuggling into his chest, I reach out each arm until I find both Declan and Giovanni's hands, entwining theirs with mine as my eyes grow heavy.

Sinclair speaks with a sleep-heavy voice. "Never fucking letting her go."

"Fuck no," Giovanni replies.

And not to be outdone, Declan declares, "Over our dead bodies."

I smile internally as sleep finally overtakes me.

I'm never letting go of any of you either.

Chapter 31

Bethani

Pulling back into the guys' underground parking, a wave of sadness washes over me. This weekend was perfect. I didn't want it to end. From the bossy butts forcing me to shop at a bunch of stores I never thought of stepping into and spending insane amounts of money on me like it was nothing, to spending their time with me in the Latin district. It was amazing.

"What's wrong, sunshine?" comes from Declan beside me.

Sighing, I lean my head on his shoulder. "Just wish this weekend didn't have to end."

His arm wraps around me as he leans down to kiss my forehead. "Yeah. It was pretty awesome, huh? Especially you taking our cocks like a fucking champ."

Snorting, I say, "Stay away from me right now. I'm so sore it's not even funny." I emphasize it with a wince as I move. "My body needs a full-body massage and about a week's worth of rest after the way you guys destroyed me."

My eyes float to the rearview mirror as a snicker from the front seat grabs my attention. "Anything to say, asshole?" is my scowling response to Sinclair, as usual.

His eyes flicker with dominance. "Watch it, kitten. I'll play nice and give you a few days since you were a perfect fucking siren in the bedroom this weekend. But there are still a few things you *will* be punished for. Soon."

His tone sends a shiver down my spine, and I feel my body quiver in response to his domineering attitude. How am I turned on again already?

"Yes, sir," I grumble, knowing that if I push my luck, that punishment will come sooner. No, thank you.

He pulls the Tahoe into its spot and turns the vehicle off as we all slowly make our way out to gather the crazy amount of things we packed. I'm groaning when the back hatch opens. "This is gonna take forever to organize."

Giovanni just comes up behind me to wrap his arms around me and settle his chin on top of my head. "I'll help this week. Don't worry about it today."

Tilting my head up, I smile at him. "You are always the sweetest."

His smile flashes across his face as he leans down for a quick kiss. "Always for you, Tesoro."

After ten minutes of unloading everything onto the carts, we roll everything to the service elevator and make the slow ascent to the penthouse. Another twenty minutes later, everything is disbursed between our rooms, and I quickly head to the kitchen for some snacks and bottled water.

"I'm gonna shower and work on that paper due Tuesday. Do you guys want anything from the fridge?"

"Water." "Gatorade." "Both, sunshine!"

Rolling my eyes, I set my stuff down to grab their drinks and make my way to the living room where they are all lounged out like they aren't moving anytime soon. Passing their drinks to them, I lean down to give them each a kiss before going to get my stuff. As I head toward my room, I stop to turn around.

"Thank you, guys, again. I mean it. This was the best weekend of my life." My eyes become slightly blurry, but I blink the bastard tears away.

When my vision refocuses, I'm met with three pairs of shining eyes with the matching megawatt smiles that I am so crazy in love with. The sight of pride shines brightly through each of them at my words.

"Welcome, kitten. You deserve it."

"Anything for you, Tesoro."

"That smile on your face makes it worth it, sunshine."

I nod and quickly turn away before my emotions get the better of me.

Stepping back into my room and closing the door, I quickly dump my stuff on the desk when the flashing of an email catches my attention. Sitting down, I'm knocked off my ass when I read it.

From: Server Unknown To: Reece.Bethani@BlackwellU.edu
Subject: Dirty Whore
Fucking three men at the same time? What a dirty little slut.
Don't worry. Soon enough you will atone for your sins. What sweet
revenge it shall be to see you put in your proper place like the crack
whore slut you are. You think life with your mommy was terrible?
This shall be worse, and I cannot wait to see you break.

Quickly standing up, my chair falls back and I jump at the noise.

"You all right, kitten?"

"Yeah!" I yell with a little more gusto than normal. "Just stretching and knocked my chair over!"

It's silent for a moment, and I rush to close the email before they walk in at the shaky sound in my voice.

"All right. If you need anything let us know."

The breath I was holding comes rushing out of me as I close the laptop. "Yup!"

Retreating to the bathroom, I quickly strip down and step into the shower to wash away the sudden grime that feels plastered over my body.

Who keeps sending me crazy shit like this?

My nerves are completely frazzled as I sink down to the shower floor to steady my breathing before a panic attack hits me like a freight train. Using the techniques I've learned over the years, I'm thankfully able to prevent another fainting attack.

I let the water rush over me as I clear my head. Is Peter really that butt hurt over my rejection that he feels the need to act like a petulant child and harass me with threats? My eyes open as the emotions settle over me. He can fuck right off if he thinks I'm just going to go running back to him because he wants to be a little shit. For the first time in my life, I'm so unbelievably happy. Like true happiness that only some people are lucky to experience. I've got three amazing men who I know would do anything for me, and I'd do anything for them.

While I may not be considered a standard pick in the elite world they live in, I'll be damned if I won't hold my head up high in the process. I will not back down against some idiot who thinks they can bully me because of my upbringing.

While I may not be saying shit to the overprotective cavemen in the living room, I'm also not backing down either.

Stepping out and quickly drying off, I go back out and open the laptop to see if I can reply. I do a quick happy dance when it actually lets me before I sit down with a fire in my eyes as I type out my scathing response.

From: Reece.Bethani@BlackwellU.edu To: Server Unknown

Subject: Ha!

Seriously Peter? Resorting to bullshit keyboard threats. Go fuck yourself and stay the hell out of my life. I know it's you. Just because a person doesn't want to be with you doesn't mean you have the right to threaten them.

And searching my personal history? Wow. Good for you. Do it again and I'll file a lawsuit against you. My shit is sealed for a reason. I earned my freedom and independence while you are nothing but a mommy/daddy tit sucking bitch.

Do NOT contact me anymore. Grow up and find someone else to put up with your antics.

Seriously

Fuck. You.

As I click send, I sit back and smirk at my laptop. He thinks he is something because he has family money.

Deciding my homework can wait after that little blip of drama, I change and hop into bed for a well-deserved nap.

Chapter 32

Giovanni - First week of December

"**B**ethani! Are you almost ready? We're gonna be late!" I ask as I'm standing in front of her closed door.

It took a solid week of begging from us, but we finally convinced her this morning to join us at the annual Blackwell University Christmas Gala that's hosted for the top donors and the rest of the mega rich. It's a stuffy bullshit event we are forced to attend along with every other Syndicate member.

To most, it looks like a gracious thank you for supporting their alma mater or just their love of the school. But really, it's a secret networking event where us Trident members cozy up to the pretentious fucks and preen their feathers. Some gather intel. Others seek possible options for future members depending on how a person's family can benefit the Syndicate.

The main role of Sinclair, Declan, and I is acting like the picture-perfect sons to be flaunted around like marionette puppets. Only speak when spoken to. Speak highly of the university. Do *not* under any circumstances embarrass them.

Well, this year we have a plan to shake up the boredom a bit, if only our cranky ass girlfriend would hurry the fuck up.

Raising my hand to knock again, I don't even get the chance when the door swings open and my jaw hits the fucking floor.

"Holy mother of God," I whisper as my throat closes, a giant lump forming as I struggle to find a proper string of words that could correctly describe the total goddess standing in front of me.

Wearing a strappy pair of simple silver shoes that sets her about four inches taller than her usual five-foot-six, Bethani stands there looking like pure perfection. She is wearing a long, figure-hugging navy dress with elegant silvery beadwork throughout. A sweetheart neckline accentuates her ample breasts, pushing them up just enough to almost cross a dangerous territory. A long slit flows up to her mid right thigh, giving away just enough of her shapely, athletic, tanned thigh to tease the most saintly of men. Her long hair flows in loose waves around her. Elegant without trying too hard. Smokey eyes and long lashes frame her gorgeous aqua eyes, making them steal the show. A simple pink gloss paints her beautiful full lips while she has the whole ensemble polished with platinum dangling wind chime style earrings and a matching necklace.

She is the perfect cross of elegance and sexy. A truly unique and beautiful individual.

"What the hell is taking—"

Steps behind me halt in their tracks as we are all enamored by the beauty in front of us.

Bethani blushes deep as we all stand stock-still in front of her like gaping idiots.

"Do I look all right? I can change if this is inappropriate or anything." Her bashful tone brings me out of my trance and my words come out harsher than they should.

"Do not fucking change out of that." Her eyes go wide at my tone and I shake my head. Clearing my throat, I clarify, "Sorry, Tesoro. That came out a little rougher than I meant. You look perfect."

Her eyes shimmer, and I'm suddenly confused by her reaction. "Sorry. I'm just nervous about this. I've been stress eating all week. This is the only one that fits right and I don't look like I'm about to bust out of." She huffs in frustration.

She has been eating more in the past couple weeks, but we all have honestly. Keeping up with three men who are hopeless in love with you means a fuck ton of sex. Be it all of us as a group or something random. Like the other day when she laughed at something I said, and we ended up in an empty lecture hall with me balls deep in her as I bent her over the chair until she milked my dick, screaming my name.

Plus the stress of finals. We have all been up with boxes of pizza studying until our eyes were crossed, only to fall asleep reading and waking up an hour later to do it all over again. Classes ended yesterday, and we are all officially on winter break until after the New Year. Thank fuck.

"Sunshine. I don't know how I'm gonna make it through this fucking party without finding a spot to have you ride my cock. Fuck. Now I'm hard," Declan groans, and I'm now *well* aware of the erection straining in my suit pants.

I adjust in an attempt to will my dick to behave, then groan, cursing Declan. "Dammit, dude. Why do you have to say shit like that? Christ, do we have to go?"

All I want to do is slide her floor-length dress straight up her tanned thighs and pin her against the wall while my dick is buried deep inside her perfect heat.

A grunt comes from behind me as I'm entranced by Bethani. "We need to get going," Sinclair demands.

Sighing because he is probably the only one thinking without his dick the whole way, I reach out for Bethani's hand. "Come on, Tesoro. We have an event to attend, and I'm not going to miss the chance to show off our gorgeous girlfriend."

She blushes again as she reaches out for me, and I give her a devious smile while taking her hand. Spinning her around for a twirl, deep growls ripple from all of us when we realize her whole dress is backless with a wicked plunge that gives a teasing glance to the dimples above her ass.

"How the fuck do you even have this demonic torture device secured, Tesoro? *Cristo!*"

A sinister smile crosses her lips. "Body tape. Lots of body tape to secure myself in this. So no ruining it, boys, or I'll be flashing a bunch of pervert old men."

My blood runs cold thinking of *any* man, especially our fathers, seeing her naked other than us. Scowling at the thought, I go to speak but our resident grouch beats me to it. "If any of those dusty motherfuckers even think of touching you, kitten, I'll rip their fucking limbs off and shove them so far up their asses they come out their throats." He stops and methodically steps forward until he has her back against the wall. Her eyes flare with fear and lust, and I watch in awe as the blood rushes all back to my cock again.

Tipping her chin up with two fingers, Sin says, "You are fucking ours, kitten. Ours to fuck. Ours to touch. Ours to punish. No one else's. If any of those destitute fucks go to make a move on you, tell us and they *will* be taken care of. Do you understand?"

She stands there in shock, and I watch as her throat dips as she swallows. It makes me wish she were swallowing down my dick as it floods her with my cum. "Y-yes, daddy," she whispers.

Sinclair's eyes shut as he hisses. His eyes flash open with heat behind them. "Fucking hell, kitten." Then slams his lips against hers as he claims her.

It's all of thirty seconds before he has her quickly wrapped around his hips as he is slamming his dick deep inside her for one of the quickest fucks ever. She knows calling him daddy spirals him into wild sex. Maybe that was her play.

Soon enough he is roaring his release as she screams hers. Somehow Sinclair was able to keep them both looking like perfection as he slides her down to the floor.

"Be a good girl, kitten."

Then he pecks her lips before righting himself and strolling toward the elevator.

She is sexy and dazed as she glances toward Declan and myself. "Either of you going to assert your dominance next?"

I chuckle as a belly laugh falls from Declan.

"Nah, sunshine. I've got a couple places I can take you at the gala for a quick romp. I'll wait for now." He leans down to give her a kiss before heading off.

Making my way over to her, I place my hand on her lower back to guide her toward the elevator.

"What about you, mister?"

All I can do is smile as I think of *exactly* where I'm having my way with her.

"Giovannniiiii!" Her voice echoes through Sinclair's G-Wagon as her head falls back. Her pussy walls encircle around my dick like a perfect glove, and I'm railroaded by my orgasm.

"*Cristo,*" I grit through clenched teeth as our mixed juices settle on my legs and drip all over the seats. "You are a fucking dream, Tesoro," I whisper before kissing her. Her tongue tangles with mine and yet again, I'm flooded with the emotion to tell her I love her.

"We're fucking here, asshole."

Laughing, I snatch one of the spare shirts from the back to wipe Bethani down before righting her dress for her, then move to fix myself. The back door opens and Sinclair reaches out to help

Bethani before grumbling at me, "You are paying for this to be cleaned, motherfucker."

I don't even have a response. I'm just a happy fool currently and will gladly take his wrath.

This is the first year any of us have willingly brought a date. It has mostly been a forced pairing where someone has been 'recommended' to us, and we are forced to accept. Thankfully our grandfathers have been of great assistance to us lately in our quest to figure out what exactly our fathers have planned.

We have filled them in on certain situations, like a simple once-over of what Bethani has been through and her unusual acceptance to our university. We have made it abundantly clear that we are thrilled that she is here and do not wish her to stop attending. They have agreed, stating they have never seen any of us happier in our lives and do not wish to destroy that happiness.

They even brought our grandmothers to the penthouse last weekend. My nonna fell in love with Bethani instantly, enamored with her tenacity like Nonno and the others. Our kitchen was turned into a disaster as the women cooked up a feast fit for kings while us men went to the study to talk shop as best as possible. We explained some of Bethani's childhood events without going into too much detail. We also explained our little truce with the Carina Cartel. They were not exactly thrilled with that notion, but when we explained further about how their sons were involved, they relented and agreed. There is also more security floating around campus than what covers a president, all in a silent attempt to keep tabs on Bethani.

A shrill thought crosses my mind knowing our fathers are going to meet her tonight. Then my thoughts turn dark knowing they will be so close to her, and I'm ready to smash their skulls in. I prefer to use my technological skills to destroy a person, but times like these make me eager to use my hands.

"We have her, G. I know what you're thinking. We won't let anyone hurt her."

As usual, Declan reads my thoughts as he smacks a hand to my shoulder, nudging me along to follow.

i grumble, "I don't like how close she is going to be to them."

"Me neither, dude. But it was either we brought her, or she would have to chance seeing us with women forcefully wrapping themselves to us like leeches. At least here we know she is safe, and we don't have to face her fiery rage."

Chuckling, I nod in agreement as the thoughts of our girlfriend threatening murder flash through my brain. "Yeah. Our dicks wouldn't be safe if she was pissed over something like that."

We make our way to catch up just as we hit the obnoxious red carpet that is lined with photographers due to the high-profile nature of this event.

"Nope. No fucking way," Bethani says in a firm tone.

"Kitten. We don't have a choice. Let's just pose for a few photos, then get the fuck inside. Trust me, we are not thrilled about this either."

She pouts and looks back at us for some sort of reprieve, but sadly we have nothing for her.

"Sorry, sunshine."

I just give her a look. "Sorry, Tesoro. No other option. Let's just get through it and go inside. I promise we won't stay here forever," I placate, hoping to garner some points.

Her eyes are laced with venom as she stares us all down. "Fine," she says through gritted teeth. "We get through this bullshit, make nice for a bit, then we get the fuck out of here. You are lucky your grandparents will all be here to keep me from kicking all your asses on the spot."

Excuse me?

"Our grandparents are all here, sunshine? Since when? They haven't been to one of these in years."

Our little hellfire just winks. "Oh, I just had a conversation with them last week. Who else gave me the idea to 'cave' last-minute to coming here, making you boys think you won a battle? They agreed to come when I gave them my number, and they video chatted me a few of the times you guys tried to 'convince' me. They loved watching you all grouch and grovel."

I'm in pure stunned silence at how wicked our girlfriend can be. I'm also shocked our grandparents are here and Nonna, Grandma, and Momo all gave our girlfriend the idea to be a little shit.

"You are fucking ruthless, kitten. You know that? Fucking hell, we are never leaving you alone with those hecklers again."

Her deep, throaty laugh fills the air as we bump into line to finally step on the carpet of hell. She is thoroughly enjoying our pain, and I can't even fathom an ounce of anger. Her love for our grandparents and their love for her are apparent.

We slowly make our way down the carpet as camera flashes blind us. Questions are being thrown our way left and right asking about our mystery date and where the other two women are. Sinclair obviously takes the provoking comments as long as he can before stepping forward to shut them up. "She is our fucking girlfriend. There are no other dumb, snot-nosed, spoiled whores nor will there ever be any. So shut the fuck up, take your stupid pictures, and leave us alone."

My eyes roll. I can feel the headache forming at his blatant exposure of our relationship with her, and I can already see the headlines I'm going to have to track and squash.

We finally make it through the gates of hell as we enter the opulent space. Bethani's eyes go wide at the showcase laid out in front of us. "Whoa."

"Yeah. It's pretty crazy." I chuckle as I glance around the space.

The massive ballroom here at the campus is decorated like a Christmas wonderland. Simple blues, whites, silvers, and shades of purple have transformed the usually bland space into a place of opulence. A twenty-five-foot tree is the star of the show. There are so many decorations and lights on it you can barely tell there is a tree underneath it all. As usual, the decorators have somehow still made it look tastefully done. This ballroom gives those Kardashians a run for their money with how it's adorned. Our fathers have most likely hired the same company they use, which would explain how everything flows together in a seamless perfection that screams extravagance in an understated way.

As we stroll through the room, a server comes up with drinks for us. We all take a champagne flute and thank the person while Declan throws a few bills on their tray.

"For dealing with the bullshit," he mumbles, chugging his glass and snatching another before the person walks away.

Finding our grandparents, we all exchange hugs as our grandmothers dote on Bethani.

"Ay, child! You look fabulous!" comes from Momo, Declan's grandmother.

Sinclair's grandmother just clucks at Momo. "Fabulous? Crazy woman. She is flawless. The belle of the ball. Have you seen how everyone's eyes are on her! Showstopper. Our boys did well. While maybe slightly unconventional, they all radiate joy with her around."

Taking extreme pride at Grandma's comment, I can't help but steal a glance around. What she said is true. All eyes are on Bethani. I can feel the heated stares being thrown our way as they take in the woman who has us under her thumb in the best way possible. It's almost silent through the room as they take in Grandma's loud words.

My collar suddenly feels tight at the whispered scrutiny we are encountering currently over our relationship. Just as I'm ready to bail, my nonna chides the room. "Oh, go back to your boring conversations and leave us be. Trust me, I can find something more damning on each and every one of you to talk about than the state of my grandchildren here and their amazing woman. So go fuck off." Then she simply turns to Bethani as if she didn't just school a room of almost 500. "Ignore them, *dolce*. You are happy, no?" Bethani nods slightly, embarrassment burning through her face. "Nothing to worry about then. You are happy and our boys are happy. That is all that matters at the end of the day. In the words of you younger ones, fuck'em!"

Champagne rockets out of my nose at my grandmother's brazen phrase. "Nonna! Cristo! *Stai cercando di uccidermi*?" I'm choking and sputtering in an attempt to gather my senses.

The heckler just laughs at me. "Nonsense, my love. Just keeping you on your toes."

I go to give her some smart-ass retort, but the air suddenly feels stifling as everyone around me stills. The deep churning in my belly roars back to life, and the urge to vomit has me wishing I could find the nearest bathroom.

I close my eyes to give myself a second of reprieve before opening them and spinning on my heel to shield Bethani from the onslaught that is coming to us.

"Father."

Chapter 33

Arthur

"Father" is the juvenile greeting that Giovanni gives his father while Declan and Sinclair just stand staring at us along with our parents. The boys form a line in front of their date as some pathetic shield.

We saw them as soon as they walked in and just lay in wait.

"Boys, is that any way to greet your fathers?" I give them a scolding look before turning toward my parents. "Mother. Father. I'm rather surprised to see you and the others here."

Knowing our parents, they are up to something with the insolents we call children. They must now be watched.

My father gives me one of his droll looks. "Arthur. We need no reason to show up. *We* are the ones who started this tradition as a gratitude to the donors. You are the one who has turned it into this showboat of wealth. It's rather disgusting to see how you thrive on constant need of archaic flaunting."

His words grind my gears, but I stay calm. I refuse to act like them. Waving his words off, I continue, "Where are your lovely dates, children? I'm sure we saw them around socializing somewhere."

Sinclair finally steps forward to address me. "And *we* told *you* that we were not going to show up with some stupid whores when we have a date already."

I chortle at the remark. "So you think all three of you showing up with the same woman is better? Please. You look like giant buffoons, and you make her look like a high-class prostitute."

I thoroughly enjoy watching all their faces morph into shock. But what they don't realize is that we know exactly *who* she is and her pedigree is going to prove invaluable to our takeover. That is, once we get her away from their overbearing clutches and have her properly trained.

Declan just scoffs in unfiltered rage at us. "Of all people to talk about high-class prostitutes, it would be you three." His face forms into a wicked sneer as he practically yells the next words, "Because we all know how faithful you were to your wives. You'd rather sink your dicks in cheap whores than be faithful to the women who put up with your tyrant asses. All of us right here"—he waves his hand around their group—"*we* are all fucking faithful. *None* of us have fucked around while their wife has cancer. *None* of us have driven their significant other to suicide. *None* of us have signed an agreement just to be a willing hole to fuck solely for the purpose of producing an heir. Then ridding themselves of said hole after they achieved what they wanted."

The room around us falls into shocked silence as Declan foams at the mouth. Sinclair and Giovanni are also showing signs of barely restrained rage. Our parents are all slack-jawed at the admissions. Lorenzo, Robert, and I are all in shock. How do they know all of this?

Sinclair just sends death glares at me while speaking, "Big bad Arthur is speechless. There's a fucking shocker. And you aren't the only ones with the power to find things out. Don't think I haven't known about my mother for years. Living the high life in Monaco, never to acknowledge her only child. And when that said child took a vacation to meet her, she treated him like nothing more than a stepped on piece of gum."

I'm still speechless, but he turns to the rest.

"Come on. Let's go back to the penthouse. At least there we are all in like-minded company, unlike this bullshit place." Then he dips behind to put a protective arm around our target, Bethani, before escorting her past us with everyone else in quick succession.

Though embarrassment floods me as all eyes are on us, instead of addressing them, I walk off to the back office we have here for privileged meetings.

As we step inside, I slam the door with pent-up anger flowing through my veins. Turning to an equally pissed Lorenzo and Robert, I order, "Call him. Change of plans. I want this moved up as quickly and efficiently as possible. No longer will we be shamed by those worthless abominations we call children. I want them destroyed as fast as they just pulverized our reputation out there." Slamming my hand against the desk, I let myself have a moment of outrage. "Fuck!"

"All will be well, Arthur. Soon enough all this drama will be worth it," Lorenzo says in a calming tone as he hands me a drink. Taking it, I nod and straighten myself. "Of course. My apologies, gentlemen, for the outburst." I laugh. "Acted like one of them for a moment."

Sly grins mar our faces as we toast. "To the new rule. May our wealth and power surpass that of anyone else in the world."

Chapter 34

Bethani - The Day Before Christmas

From: Sender Unknown
To: Reece.Bethani@BlackwellU.edu
Subject: Tramp
Nothing more than a worthless tramp taking all the dick to get ahead in life like your tramp mother. Disgusting. Slut. You deserve to rot in filth like your mother. You will never amount to anything more than a low-class hooker. Enjoy hell, harlot.

Sighing, I delete the email and glance at the other fifty plus that are of similar fashion, and just trash the rest of them. I'm so sick to my stomach from the number of harassing emails I've received from trolls and, who I assume is Peter, since the night of the gala.

It's mostly been jealous women who saw us in the tabloids who are pissed about my relationship with the guys. They're irate women who I know will never mean anything to them, but it still hurts all the same being harassed by random people. I finally gathered up the courage a few days after to leave the penthouse, only to be bombarded by news crews and violent crowds of people throwing drinks and food at me. The guys got an alert from the security guard at the gate to the garage as to where I was, and they found me in the back corner crying from it all. I haven't left the house since. I know I have my heart checkup the day after Christmas, but I'm dreading it. Hopefully Andre, the gate guy, can help me out.

A knock on the door has me shutting my laptop as more emails ping through to call me all sorts of names. I know I should ask

Giovanni how to make them go away, but I don't want him seeing the stuff from Peter. Or at least who I am assuming is Peter.

Swinging the door open, I'm greeted by none other than Giovanni himself. His arms wrap around me and tears flood my eyes. "Why do all of those random-ass people have to be so mean?"

My cries quickly turn to sobs, finally breaking down from everything. He doesn't respond, just comforts me. They have received some pretty harsh remarks themselves from the media surrounding the Christmas gala. It's been chaotic, and we have pretty much stayed to ourselves, minus the visits from his grandparents in an attempt to raise our spirits.

Nonno and Nonna Martinelli, Grandpa and Momo Carter, and Pops and Grandma Blackwell have been absolute saints. They canceled all their events until the day after Christmas and have been at our beck and call. Their unfiltered anger toward the news about their sons is palpable. They can't decide how they want to act or handle the indiscretions of their children.

Surprisingly enough, we haven't heard one word from them. I figured Robert, Lorenzo, and Arthur would be firing back at us for the outburst. It was eye-opening to see the destruction that has caused so much pain for them. Once we got back that night, the grandparents asked a million questions. All about what has really been going on with everything since they retired.

Reluctantly, the guys opened up about years of abuse and other horrific things; arranged marriages, constantly being threatened to be cut off, and the shit that happened at home with their mothers. It was disgusting to hear, and my heart broke for them. The whole thing was eye-opening, and if I wasn't already so over the moon in love with them, I definitely would have been after that night.

My perspective of them has changed completely. I thought they were nothing but silver-spooned stuck-up snobs originally. While my thoughts have obviously changed as walls were broken down, realizing the trauma they have gone through behind closed doors was pure chaos that no one deserves to endure. Their lives aren't that much different than mine, other than their social status. It completely makes sense why they act the way they do and are so closed off to the world except for each other.

"Come on, Tesoro, we have a surprise for you." Glancing up, Giovanni's gorgeous ocean eyes swirl with what I can now see as well guarded pain. We are all suffering from how the world is turning against us.

"A surprise?" I ask with wonder.

"Yes, Tesoro. A surprise. Now come on." He quickly spins me around to head toward the main living area but covers my eyes.

"Oh, come on."

He doesn't respond. He just walks with me in front of him as we hobble our way toward the living room. We stop, and he moves his hands from my eyes.

"Open up, kitten."

When my eyes open, I'm in shock. The whole living room looks like a festive winter wonderland complete with a ten-foot decorated tree.

"H-how did you guys do this?" I stutter, still surprised by it all.

They have giant smiles plastered on their faces as they all shrug. "Our grandparents came to help this morning. They will be here in about thirty minutes with food. Do you want to open up some presents, sunshine?"

I shake my head. "Presents? But I didn't get anything for you guys!" I'm frantic and feeling utterly terrible that with all the drama going on, I haven't been able to leave the penthouse to go shop for anything.

They are all surrounding me in an instant. "Kitten, it's not a big deal. We don't need anything, and if we do, we just go buy it ourselves."

Why I'm suddenly irate, I'll never know. "But that isn't fair! I had plans to go get you guys stuff, but of course, I can't leave the damn place without being bombarded!"

They step back at my sudden outburst.

"Wait, you were going to get us presents, Tesoro?"

"Of course I was. Why wouldn't I?" I'm being defensive.

As usual, Sinclair picks up on my attitude and has me thrown over his shoulder before I can protest. My sweatpants are pulled down just enough to expose my ass, and his hand quickly spanks my right ass cheek.

"Ow!"

He ignores me and repeats the process on my left cheek. Then he proceeds to do it a few more times. By the time he stops, the sting has turned into arousal, and I'm begging for more.

"You going to tell us why you are acting like a brat? Or do I need to continue with some more punishment?"

Dropping my head into his back in defeat, I admit why I'm so upset, "I've never had a real Christmas."

"What does that even mean, sunshine?"

"It means I've never celebrated it before. I've never had a reason to until I met you guys, and I wanted to get you guys at least something small in honor of that."

Sinclair pulls my sweats back up and carefully sets me down. Suddenly the floor looks very entertaining as I refuse to look at them. With a finger, Sinclair slowly tilts my head up until my eyes meet his.

"This is your first real Christmas?"

Reluctantly, I nod.

"Why didn't you say anything before, kitten?"

I shrug. "Wasn't really a point. It didn't seem necessary to make a giant fuss of it."

His eyes burn with fire at my nonchalance. "Kitten. We have told you before that if it's important to *you*, it's important to *us*. We would have found a way to get you to a damn store or even would have given you a card to order the shit."

I realize he is correct, but I'm not quite ready to budge. "What would have been the point, though? You would have followed me the whole time, so how would I have been able to purchase anything? And you track every purchase like a bloodhound. You also have every package scanned before it comes to the penthouse, so you would have seen what they were. Am I wrong?"

His look says I'm pushing a fine line, but I don't even care.

"Dude. She isn't wrong. No offense, but everything is reported to you in emails."

"Thank you, Declan." I smile at my little win.

"Kitten..."

Rolling my eyes, I spin and head toward my room. "Be ready in twenty."

I've finally calmed down a bit after taking a quick shower and getting ready, so I guess I need to hurry and find the guys to apologize for being a giant bitch. As I open the door, the guys are all standing there.

"Oh hey. I was just coming to find you all. To, you know, apologize for being an uber bitch."

"Tesoro, you don't need to apologize. We do."

I'm stunned. "Wait. What? Why would you guys need to do that? You and your grandparents went through all this trouble making everything amazing for me, and I acted like an ungrateful bitch. No. Absolutely not. I'm just irritated over all this drama and took it out on you guys. It wasn't right, and I'm sorry for being a bitch."

Not giving them a chance to respond, I step up and wrap my arms around Giovanni and pull him down for a heated kiss before moving along to Declan, then Sinclair. Putting a smile on my face, I say, "Come on. Let's start this Christmas shindig!"

Four hours later, I'm completely stuffed from an ungodly amount of food.

"Good Lord. If Nonna tried to feed me another bite of food... ugh."

We are all stretched out on the massive couch like stuffed pigs. None of us can move. The living room is wrecked with wrapping paper, and the kitchen looks like a food bomb went off with all the leftovers we have to put up. But currently, none of us are in a position to move.

With a groan, Giovanni adjusts his position. "Try growing up with the woman. We were constantly working out in high school to make up for the massive amounts of food she fed us. Our coaches constantly threatened to cut us from the team. Then one weekend, Nonna invited the whole team over. Coach stopped bitching at us after he realized what we dealt with."

"Ha. Between her feeding us, Momo teaching us how to curse, and Grandma teaching us how to drink, it's a fucking wonder we have accomplished anything in life," Declan says, and we all start laughing.

"Shit! We have one more surprise for you, kitten," Sinclair grumbles as he struggles to get off the couch.

Glaring at him, I say, "Does it involve moving?"

He just scoffs. "Of course. Now get your sweet ass up."

"Help, please!" I ask as I raise an arm in the air. Unwillingly, Sinclair comes over to help my sorry ass before leading me toward his room with the others following. "If it's something sex related, you can use your hand. I am not in any form for sex right now."

"None of us are after a Nonna meal, sunshine. Trust me."

Reaching his room, Sinclair opens the door and motions for me to go in. Hesitantly I enter.

"What exactly am I looking for?"

They all just brush past me and jump on what I am now realizing is a giant-ass bed.

"Holy shit, that thing is huge!"

"Custom made and delivered late last night for us, kitten."

"For us?" I ask, confused as all get-out.

Giving me a taste of my own medicine, Sinclair rolls his eyes in a dramatic fashion. Fucking diva. "Yes. For all of us. We are sick of you either falling asleep in your bed or one of ours. So we came up with a solution."

"And this solution would be one bed?"

"Yup," Declan responds. "I mean, it makes sense. Why would we all fuck like crazy only to have to go back to separate rooms? This makes perfect sense."

While I'll give them an A for reasoning, they are definitely in the C or D range for method of delivery.

"Can I ask why we haven't discussed this? And what if we are upset with each other? Does it really make sense to all sleep together if we are pissed and not in the mood to be near each other?"

They pause momentarily before looking at the usual voice of reason in all of our disagreements: Giovanni.

"We actually have talked about that, Tesoro, and it's simple. Sure, there are going to be nights when one of us wants space. That's why we will still keep most of our shit in our rooms. If for any reason you decide you want to sleep alone, we will all sleep in our own rooms. If Declan or I want to sleep alone, we go to our rooms, and everyone else can sleep here. If Sinclair gets one of his burrs up his ass, then we can all sleep in one of our rooms together."

My eyes turn to slits. "And the reason we haven't discussed this as a whole?" I'm losing footing with Giovanni's damn good explanation.

He looks at me with exasperation before continuing, "Well, Sinclair ordered the bed the week after your birthday. We didn't find out until last week. But he made good points and we don't disagree with them."

"Sunshine, we are dating. Most couples our age are already sleeping together on a consistent basis at this point. While our relationship may be a little unusual, it works for all of us. Besides—"

"We are all selfish bastards, Bethani. We want you with us every night. Be it a night of wild sex or all just binge-watching a show that took us two damn hours to decide on. Doesn't matter. You're ours and we're yours. Why the fuck wouldn't we want to sleep next to you every night?"

Damn. Double damn. Triple damn.

I'm completely out of excuses and I know it. Hell, by the sly looks on their faces, they know it too. Slowly making my way toward the bed, I say, "Sometimes it's not fair when your three boyfriends gang up on you. You do realize that?"

I'm met with three snarky smirks.

"Of course, sunshine. But you fucking love it when we gang up on you."

I swat Declan's arm as I climb up on the bed. "Smart-ass."

He traps me in his arms and I squeal.

"I'd much rather be a smart-ass than a dumbass. So thank you for the compliment."

We make our way to the top of the bed. I'm in between Sinclair and Declan with Giovanni on the other side of Declan but reaching over to touch me. Warmth envelops me as their body heat radiates off of them. A deep yawn falls from me as the minutes pass.

"All right, maybe this isn't so bad."

They all just chuckle and get comfortable. Just before I fall asleep, a thought crosses my mind. "I don't have to attend any of your family stuff tomorrow. Do I?"

The thought of seeing any of their fathers makes my stomach plummet to my feet. I could feel their ugly curiosity weeping off their pores when I caught their glances that night. The one that unsettled me the most was Sinclair's father, Arthur. As we were leaving, a sick glint flashed across his eyes, like I was a twisted prize for the taking. It was a look I was used to as a child from the pimps or whoever my mom had at our housing arrangements when they bribed her over and over to have me. It has left an eerie lingering dread in me that I haven't been able to shake since.

"No worries, sunshine. We won't subject you to the shit we have to deal with again. But it's not tomorrow. Our fathers have standing plans on Christmas, so we get to deal with them the day after," he mumbles into my neck.

I sigh in relief that I don't have to see them. But I say, "I'm sorry you guys have to see them."

"Us too, kitten. Us too."

Soon after, we all fall asleep on the bed, and for the first time since the gala, I sleep the whole night without waking up from a nightmare.

Surrounded by the men I love, I know we can get through anything the world throws at us.

If only we knew how quickly everything would be tried and tested.

Chapter 35

Declan

As Sin, G, and I walk in the doors of our building here on campus after an exhausting day dealing with our fathers for our 'Christmas' celebration, an unsettling thought runs through me.

"You guys heard from Bethani at all?"

Our fathers dragged today out like no other. We got to my family estate at 8:00 a.m. dressed in Armani suits ready for breakfast. Then we all sat at the formal dining table for three fucking hours talking about current events with our grandparents and fathers. My mother was on another of her 'wellness trips' but sent me her regards. Then we had a 'pre-lunch snack' before spending two hours in the 'family room' to open gifts. After that was lunch, again in the formal dining room, before we were all finally released from the fresh hell at 4:00 p.m.

The whole day was a bunch of fake cheeriness that has had me on edge since the moment we walked through the doors.

We never heard a negative remark about the gala. There were no glasses being thrown at us. No violent threats to our lives. Not. A. Fucking. Thing.

We hit the elevator as Gio pushes the 'up' button and looks at his phone.

"Haven't heard anything from her yet. Her phone is showing it's upstairs..." His voice drifts off, making my gut fucking churn with unease.

"What the fuck is going on, Giovanni?" Sinclair demands as we go inside, and I violently smash the 'penthouse' button like it's going to fucking change the fucking speed of this slow-ass elevator.

Giovanni looks up as we are about a third of the way up, face grim as shit. "Her phone hasn't moved from the end table by the bed since this morning. Not a fucking inch."

Ice runs through my veins as I lean back against the wall.

Sinclair's fist slams into the wall beside me. "Cameras, Gio. Check. The. Cameras. If this is a sick fucking joke she is playing, so fucking help me her ass is gonna be sore for the next week."

The elevator stops with a ding, and we all jump, clearly zoned the fuck out as we try to figure this shit out. All three of us grab our guns and have them ready to shoot as the doors open torturously slow. When we step out into the foyer area, nothing looks amiss as we make our way slowly down the small hall that opens up to the living room and kitchen area. As we step fully into it, my hands fall to the sides, and I almost drop my gun trying to process the chaos in front of me.

Our house is absolutely and utterly *obliterated*. All the throw pillows on the couch are demolished; feathers, stuffing, what-the-fuck-ever you want to call the shit, is strewn as far as I can see. The sectional has slashes throughout it and is covered in...paint? Fuck if I even know. The TV has a golf club hanging out of it. The gaming systems had a baseball bat taken to them along with the shelving units the games and DVDs were all on. Pieces of it are thrown everywhere amongst the wreckage. Coffee and end tables are torn to fucking hell.

As I turn to the kitchen, it looks even worse. Every single food item is opened and thrown all over. And I mean...Every. Single. Fucking. Item. It looks like a fucking horror movie the way shit is just thrown all over the cabinets, walls, ceiling, floor, and even the appliances. Some of the cabinet doors are ripped off. Fuck, someone dismantled the fridge, freezer, and stove and turned them into a junkyard's finest pieces of shit.

We spent all day yesterday cleaning this fucking place from top to bottom after one of the best nights of sleep. While it sucked cleaning up Christmas chaos, Bethani made it a blast. I've never laughed so much in my damn life. Then after everything was done, we finally made our way to bed and fucked our girl into a coma. Sinclair demanded we 'christen the bed', and we all happily obliged. Then we all took a shower, where Bethani took the time to suck us off individually. She deep-dicked us like a champ. Then we got her to the bed and ate her out like she was our final meal. After that, we all took turns fucking our girl in as many positions as we could before blowing our loads in her and filling her sweet pussy until she was literally dripping with our cum. It was some of the hottest shit I've ever seen.

I don't even want to think about the rest of the house. I literally can't fathom it. I'm ready to murder someone with my bare hands as the infuriation sets in. "What. The. Fuck!" I scream damn near at the top of my lungs as panic starts setting in. "Bethani, where the fuck are you!"

My outburst has finally brought the other two out of their daze over the fucking shit storm that is our house, and they start moving. Giovanni goes toward the one end of the house where our service elevator is, and Sinclair heads toward the bedrooms as they yell for Bethani also. Me? I'm just fucking stuck. I can't get my mind to get my body to process the concept of moving. It's on a fucking exotic fuck fest vacation while I stand here like a useless dumbass.

Giovanni comes back from the one hallway, sees me still stuck like a jolly dumb shit giant, walks up, and smacks me across the face. Hard. I shake my head for a second as the impact from his hand brings my shit back together.

"Thanks," I mumble.

He shrugs like a smart-ass. "Figured you were in shock. Come on. Let's go see why Sinclair hasn't said shit."

We reach the first bedroom, mine, and I cautiously open the door with Giovanni right behind me. My room is untouched. Not a damn thing out of place from a glance. I'm fucking puzzled. Looking back at G, he is equally stumped.

"Let's check your room, dude."

It's the same process when we reach his room, only the roles are reversed. His room is completely untouched also. Almost as if the vandalism started in the main area, but something interrupted the process. My eyes go wide, as do Gio's as we put two and two together.

Bethani.

Instead of words, we turn and run straight to the end of the hall where Sinclair's room, really it's all of ours now, is and we bust open the doors the rest of the way. Sinclair is just staring at the bed, unmoving, almost sentry-like while holding something in his hand.

"Sinclair? Where's Bethani?" I ask.

He turns toward us and his expression rocks me. His eyes are bloodshot, a cold dead lifeless look in them, and he has tears streaming down his face. His hair is completely fucked from his hand running through it. I'm so focused on his facial features and the distress they show, I almost miss the one word he utters just above a whisper, "Gone."

"What in the fresh hell are you talking about? Gone? Where? Why?" I'm rambling. Demanding. That one word scrambling any coherent thoughts.

He doesn't say anything, just holds out his hand with the letter toward us. Giovanni steps forward to grab it. Then he starts reading. Reading words that slice through every fiber of my being. Destroying me. Slicing my stomach open to gut myself would be more pleasurable than the broken words coming out of Giovanni's mouth.

"You think you have all the power? The mighty Saints of the Syndicate. Never to be broken. Never to be tarnished. Well...how do you feel now? Your precious little whore is gone. Find her? You will not. You took what was rightfully mine and I have reclaimed possession. You have tainted her and she must repent for her sins. Punished for her harlot ways. Broken until I decide to piece her back together. She will never remember you three. Ever. And if she does, I will end her. So I ask again...how do the powerful Princes of the Trident Syndicate feel now? Knowing you will never see the orphan tramp again?" He pauses, taking a shaking breath, and I don't even want to know what's going to be said next. *"But before I end this, I'll give you one last view of the dirty slut. Pull back the cover to know what's to come for her. I win. You lose. Ante Mortem Infidelitatis, gentlemen."*

I'm just standing there. That's the only thing we can do. Gone? Fucking gone? The fucking love of my goddamn life is gone?

What a shitty motherfucking time to come to that realization, brain and heart. Filthy fucking traitors.

I never told her I loved her.

Fuck. Fuck. Fuckkkkkk.

I slowly lift my head. My bullshit, un-feeling body has tears running freely down my face. The guys are in a similar state as me. We are all hitting the same sick and twisted thoughts together.

We are all in fucking mad, unfathomable, wreck-less, pure as sunshine and unicorn glitter bullshit love with our mouthy, sweet, personal superwoman, Bethani Larie Reece.

And she is *fucking gone.*

I slowly make my way to the bed. For the first time in my life, I'm terrified. Truly terrified of what I am going to find. Closing my eyes, I grab the cover. I take in a deep breath, and as I'm exhaling, I rip the cover from the bed while slowly opening my eyes.

One Polaroid picture sits in the middle in her spot. I can feel the guys beside me as we all steady ourselves for the potential horror we are going to endure.

As we look at it, we are all sharing equally unsure looks. She is walking out of a building, but what building? I haven't a motherfucking flying donkey cock of a guess. The haunted look in her eyes brings more bullshit tears to my eyes as Giovanni's phone dings and dings.

"Will you get that already?" Sinclair barks.

I'm still looking at the picture of our otherworldly, gorgeous girl when Giovanni starts cursing. "We've got a fucking problem, guys. A major fucking problem."

As our heads snap to him, he shows us his phone and we read the message from our PI guy.

"Oh fuck," I say.

"Oh fuck is right," Gio echoes.

Another ding comes from his phone as an app pops up with a reminder.

I go to tap it, bringing up the app full screen to read the notification when the sickest of all dreads known to man assaults me. A lead fucking weight drops into my stomach as I glance between the picture and Giovanni's phone.

Oh...shit.

I drop the photo and head to the bathroom as my body revolts against the fucking world, and I retch up the contents of my stomach.

When I finally finish exorcising the demons, I glance up to see them at the door as I flush the toilet. The same soul-crushing realization is wrecking them too. I steel myself for the words that need to come out. The words that are going to change everything from here on out.

"I don't fucking care. I repeat, I do *not* fucking care what we have to give up here. What we have to sacrifice. What alliances need to be made with whatever devils they are. We *will* get her fucking back. And we are going to motherfucking *destroy* anyone and everyone who gets in our fucking way in the process." I stand as my body shuts down, retreating to the vindictive, ruthless, death-dealing, dead-heart bastard I was before Bethani turned my universe around on its axis.

I crack my neck as I'm adjusting my suit back into position, welcoming the deathly venom of darkness that lurks in my veins back to life.

I smirk at the guys as we settle back into our old ways.

"Let's show them what kind of *Saints* we really are, boys. Ten minutes. Pack some bags. We know where we need to fucking go."

They both nod, then turn off into their respective directions as I stalk out toward my room.

It's showtime, motherfuckers.

They wanted the Saints of the Syndicate, the devils of Blackwell University on their knees?

Not. Fucking. Happening.

Continue reading in book 2 – Revenge of the Syndicate

Playlist

These songs have been played on repeat so many damn times that I could probably sing them in my sleep, so yeah. It's all a part of the insanity that hopefully makes this the start of a great fucking series for y'all to enjoy!

1. "Bury Me Low" - 8 Graves
2. "Astronaut In The Ocean" - Masked Wolf
3. "Bang!" - AJR
4. "I See Red" - Everybody Loves A Criminal
5. "Big Bra" - Dotti Lynn
5. "DAYWALKER!" - Machine Gun Kelly & CORPSE
6. "Damn!(With Chad Kroeger) [Remix]" - Jeris Johnson & Ricky Desktop
7. "Boombastic" - Shaggy
8. "DEVIL" - Shinedown
9. "Change (In the House of Flies)" - Deftones
10. "Whoopty" - CJ
11. "Gasolina" - Daddy Yankee
12. "Candy" - Doja Cat
13. "Lights Down Low (feat. Waka Flocka Flame)" - Bei Maejor
14. "Despacito" - Luis Fonsi & Daddy Yankee
15. "Kings & Queens" - Ava Max
16. "Take What You Want" - State of Mine
17. "Cold" - Static-X
18. "System" - Chester Bennington
19. "Or Nah (feat. The Weeknd, Wiz Kalifa & DJ Mustard)" - Ty Dolla $ign
20. "Arcade (feat. FLETCHER)" - Duncan Laurence

21. "Swing (feat. Soulja Boy Tell 'Em)" - Savage
22. "Cradles" - Sub Urban
23. "Venom" - Little Smiz
24. "One Thing Right" - Marshmello & Kane Brown
25. "Way Down We Go" - KALEO
26. "Lollipop" - Lil Wayne
27. "Unsteady" - X Ambassadors
28. "A*****e" - Hooligan Chase

Acknowledgments

So...let me just say first and foremost, to the haters that didn't believe I'd actually do this shit? Yeah...I fucking did it, and I'm gonna keep doing it. I had a blast in the process so *middle finger emoji* to you. :)

Now that that's out of the way, on to thanking people.

Scarlet Lantern Publishing - ya'll seriously rock! After reading a few crappy chapters from some other books (that'll eventually come out), you guys signed my disorganized and chaotic self. Seriously, if it wasn't for you guys...I'd probably still be writing crap that would never see the light of day. Also for the editing and book cover design, you brought everything right to where it needed to be.

To one of my best friends. Kayla, I fucking love you and I'm thankful as hell you believed in me. Seriously, you were a major catalyst to me reaching out to publishing companies.

To some of my other friends and family that have been supportive also (you know who you are), I'm not gonna say your names out of respect, but go ahead and call my ass out and I'll be sure to put you in book two. Again, I'm speechless with the support when I felt like I was losing my shit sometimes and some of you flat out have stood beside me anytime you have talked to me saying it's going to be amazing. So cheers to fucking beers, shaken not stirred.

To my kid. Yeah, when you are older you are gonna learn your mom is a raunchy taboo romance writer. Some may give you hell, but it's all good. Just brush the shit off. I love you more than life itself and I will always support you in anything you do. If it makes you happy, fuck what anyone else thinks. Because guess what, my love? That's exactly what your mom is doing. She is saying fuck the negativity and doing something she loves. Take that bullshit, wrap it up, toss it in the fire, and let it fuel your drive to prove them wrong. Be the best version of yourself. Do good things and keep being my wild, outspoken, intelligent, stubborn, and phenomenal kid that you are.

To the ARC crew, aka my Sinister 17 team, I'm writing this before I even send it to you. But I know I'll get honest reviews so regardless if you love it or hate it. Thank you for your honesty and hopefully you want to stick on for the rest of the trilogy.

Bang Energy - You fuckers and your Cotton Candy flavored nectar of the gods have got me through many late nights. I've still got more to write so we will be spending a lot more time together. I promise.

Well, that about sums up my rambling for this book. So to anyone reading this, hope y'all love the book. If you do...go leave an awesome review and tell others about it. If you don't like the book? Well, shit happens, but you're still rad.

Natalie Nicole

Also By Natalie Nicole

The Syndicate Series

- Dark, New Adult, College, Reverse Harem -

Saints of the Syndicate

Revenge of the Syndicate

Rebellion of the Syndicate

Made in the USA
Las Vegas, NV
19 March 2022

45951470R00163